FLAME

KATIE CROSS

KCW

*For Dad. A
dragon in his own right.*

Leaves whipped past Sanna Spence's face.

She hurtled through the forest, clinging to a thick vine. The bright, lush canopy of Letum Wood flew past her and pulled strands of strawberry-blonde hair from her braid. Flames flickered ahead of her near the forest floor.

Sanna grinned. Right where she expected them.

A childhood of swinging through the trees had given her an instinct for gauging how long she could hold on, and this vine's arc would end on a sprawling branch twice as thick as she was tall.

Again—just as expected.

Sanna unwound her foot from the vine, transferring all her weight to her hands, and braced herself. Seconds later, she landed on the mossy branch without falling off the other side—which had happened often enough in the past.

For a moment, she stood on the branch, gazing down at the intermittent bursts of fire below. Witches weren't supposed to cross the dragons' border without a trained Servant unless absolutely necessary. She'd promised Daid years ago to obey the rule after she'd nearly dropped onto old Helis, a grumpy gray dragon who blew fire in defiance of the rule.

Then again, she wasn't *exactly* on dragon territory. In it, sure. If she never set foot on the ground, she'd never break her promise.

Because they didn't own the *trees*.

A high-pitched shriek echoed from nearby, followed by another snort of flame.

"Don't fight over me," she called, looping the vine around a smaller branch to use later. She used natural handholds in the trunk to work her way farther down. This tree, like most trees in this part of Letum Wood, was wide enough to fit at least two houses inside the trunk with room to spare.

The bright spurts of fire calmed. Two young dragon heads popped around either side of a younger tree—its span as thick as only one house. Hints of color glimmered in the dragon hatchlings' ebony scales. Sanna stopped and crouched when she reached two tangled branches. The youngest hatchling, Rosy, spread her wings and bent all four legs, readying herself to fly toward Sanna.

Sanna threw out a hand. "No! Rosy, you know the rules."

Rosy paused, then relaxed her wings with a little huff. A flying dragon was a dead dragon. Rosy knew that but constantly tested the rules.

"Jump," Sanna said. "You can make it."

Rosy snorted smoke. At ten years old, hatchlings could only breathe about thirty seconds of fire in a day. Rosy always used hers up by mid-morning. She was the smaller of the two, but feisty, with rose-pink threads twisting through her black scales. Rosy hopped across the space between the trees, snapping her baby teeth, which spanned the length of a hand, at Sanna's bag. Sanna didn't have to dodge—Rosy never *actually* bit her.

Sanna held up a finger.

"Ah, ah. You have to ask nicely."

Rosy's older brother, Junis, sidled up next to his sister. At twelve years old, Junis was still considered a hatchling, though both of them already loomed over Sanna. Rosy roared, exhaling another flash of smoke, then nudged Sanna with the end of her snout.

"Good enough."

Sanna yanked a toad from her bag and tossed it to the right. Rosy flailed to the side to catch it, slipped on a pillow of moss, and slid off the branch. With a quick movement, Sanna grabbed Rosy's foreleg and yanked her back. The scales sizzled against Sanna's palm until she released her.

"Sorry." She shook her hand out. "That was my fault."

Junis purred, ears lowered as he gently pressed his nose into Sanna's leg. Slivers of charcoal gray wound through his ebony scales. She set a dead toad at his feet.

"Always so polite, Junis. Thank you."

Bones crunched as the dragons chewed, squelching blood through their teeth. A low, barking sound came from below. They peered over the branch. Cara, their mother, and Viridis, a lithe dragon with emerald in his black scales, circled each other. Viridis was the sneakiest dragon that Daid fed. She'd only glimpsed him a few times in the last two years.

"Ah," Sanna murmured. "Viridis wants a hatchling."

The timing made sense. Dragons never mated for life— just for a hatchling—and the end of summer rapidly approached. A tug on Sanna's shoulder drew her gaze away.

Rosy had Sanna's lion-skin bag in her teeth in a not-so-stealthy attempt to steal the final toad.

Sanna wrenched it back. "Hey! This toad's for your mam."

Rosy purred, lowered her head, and inched closer. Sanna grabbed another vine and slid down to the last branch before Rosy could take it.

When she landed, Cara's and Viridis's heads were level with her perch. Viridis loomed more than four times taller than Sanna, his body hot as hellfire. Hints of emerald cascaded down his regal neck like fog. Two thick horns stuck out from the top of his head—bigger than the horns of any other male in the brood. The air shimmered against the dragons' heat. Sanna pressed a hand to her heart and bowed her head.

"*Avay,* Viridis. Cara."

Cara released a warm breath. Viridis slipped away with a growl, his slitted eyes like yellow moons. A forked tongue flickered between his black lips just before he snapped in her direction and disappeared.

She relaxed. Only forest dragons could move with such strange stealth despite their massive bodies. And only forest dragons hated witches with such a passion.

Well ... some of them.

Sanna pulled out her final toad. "I'd never forget you, Cara."

Before Cara could take the treat, a shriek shattered the calm air. Both Sanna and Cara whipped around to find a mangy forest lion clinging to Junis's back. Junis whipped back and forth in an attempt to throw the lion off, but it had sunk its talons into his scales, drawing ribbons of blue blood. Rosy screamed.

Junis rolled off the tree branch, plummeting to the ground. At the last second, he spread his wings, slowing his fall. Rosy leapt down the tree, landing with a *thud* on the ground. A second lion dropped from the canopy, toppling her before she could reach Junis. It pinned her left wing and snarled.

"Hey!" Sanna cried, shucking her bag off. "Get away from them!"

Cara screamed as she raced toward Junis. A third lion sank its teeth into Rosy's right shoulder. She threw her head back and yelped. Three more lions waited in the branches above while two descended the tree trunks using their razor-sharp claws. Forest lions always hunted in packs—there could be as many as ten.

Sanna sprinted down the branch and launched herself off with a battle cry, landing on the back of one of the lions attacking Rosy. She tangled her fingers in its mane and jerked. The lion roared and sprang onto his hind feet. Sanna leaned back, and they both fell. Air rushed out of her lungs when the lion landed on top of her.

Pain spiraled through her ribs with a *crack*.

The lion scrambled free, scratching her leg. Sanna rolled onto her hands and knees. Black dots clouded her vision as she gasped, ribs paralyzed. Just as a tingling sensation swept over her body, her paralysis broke. She sucked in a deep breath, clearing her sight. To the left, Cara whipped her tail, knocking four lions away from Junis, who dodged beneath his mother. Rosy flopped into the bushes with a scream as a lion charged her.

Sanna scrambled back to her feet, cursing. She snatched the lion's coiling tail as it ran by and pulled. The beast spun away from Rosy, snapping its pearly fangs. Sanna ducked as she released it. The lion's teeth bit the air a breath shy of her arm. She clawed through the undergrowth, seeking a rock just as another lion dropped onto the ground next to her.

"*Mori!*" she cried and slammed a rock into the lion's jaw. It yelped and darted away. Then a lion feinted toward Rosy, and Sanna threw the rock at it. "Fire, Cara! Use your demmed fire."

Cara threw her head back and roared but issued no flames. The furious beasts swarmed her, biting at her wings and feet—and Junis. They yowled when they felt Cara's heat and jumped away from her roasting scales and swinging tail.

Sapphire blood bubbled from Rosy's shoulder as she cowered in the crevice of two roots, crying.

A lion barreled into Sanna. She wrapped her arm around it, bringing it to the ground with her. The lion smacked his head on a tree root. He stilled, draped across her like a hot blanket. Pain shot through her side again, zipping all the way into her toes. Her right arm was pinned. At least six lions swarmed Cara now, not to mention those attacking the hatchlings. There was no way to win. Sanna gritted her teeth. No hatchlings would die unless the lions killed her first. She scrambled for a dangling gorseberry bush with her left hand. Her fingers brushed it once, twice, a third time. If she could just grab it ...

"Oh come on!" she cried. "Just ... a little..."

A vine fell from the trees, smacking her in the face. Sanna blinked. Where had *that* come from? Setting her confusion aside, she grabbed the vine with her left hand, wriggled free, and threw herself between Rosy and three approaching lions. Sanna bared her teeth in a snarl. "You don't scare me."

She picked up a handful of dirt and threw it at the big cats. A cloud of yellow fumes formed, smelling like rotten eggs and salt. Sanna recoiled.

"What the…"

The lions yipped, circled behind the cloud, and hung back, hissing.

"It's all right," Sanna murmured to Rosy, reaching toward her. Blood pooled beneath her in a puddle of sapphire. Sanna cursed under her breath. Dragons didn't have healing properties in their blood until they reached adolescence at twenty years old. A lion crept forward, and she grabbed a rock and lobbed it. It struck the lion in the mouth, drawing blood. He snarled.

A roar shook the ground.

The lions silenced, heads craned back. One crouched and slid backward, its ears flat against its head.

A shadow passed by. A second roar answered. Another shadow. Flashes of gold and sapphire, not far away.

Sanna let out a relieved breath.

"Finally."

Two dragons barreled out of the trees. Talis, the brood sire, sprawled his leathery wings and lashed his teeth. A latticed, sapphire design shone on his cavernous chest. Thyris, his second-in-command, followed. Glinting gold reflected off Thyris's scales like rivers of sunlight against a pitch-black night. Sanna shrank back, dazzled.

Talis snatched the closest lion and snapped its spine with a single shake of his head. He pitched it to the side and crushed another beast with his foreleg. His tail whacked a third into a tree. When it slumped to the ground, Thyris snapped it in half. The pack scattered away from Cara, clawing up the trees. Thyris sliced at another lion, sending it flying through the air. Blood spurted in a crimson arc behind the lion as it fell.

For a second, silence overtook the forest.

Rosy let out a cry. Thyris whipped around, his pupils shrunk to pinpricks. He focused on Sanna, snarled, and lunged. Sanna held up two hands and dropped to her knees.

"No!"

He paused an arm's-length away, teeth bared, his heat rolling over her palms in scalding waves. She swallowed, heart pounding.

"I am daughter of Drago's Servant and servant to the dragons."

Cara made a sound in her throat. Thyris backed away— his bloodlust dissipated—snorted, and turned his back to Sanna. Sanna relaxed.

Talis stared at her with a queer gaze—no doubt because she was *here* of all places, breaking the agreement. Blood dripped from his mouth and hit the forest floor in steaming beads. He loomed taller than any of the twenty-six dragons in the brood—at least six times her height—cowing her with his terrible majesty. She diverted her gaze and stepped away from Rosy.

"Sh-she's hurt."

Talis advanced.

In a swift movement, he scored his foreleg with a claw. Thick cerulean blood rose from beneath his scales and dribbled down. He lifted it over Rosy, allowing the blood to run onto her wounded shoulder. Rosy cowered, trembling. The blood hit her scales and sizzled, smoking in great plumes. Bubbles frothed from her shoulder. Once they stilled, Talis stepped back. Rosy calmed. Then Talis moved to Junis, who trembled beneath Cara. A massive rent marred Junis's left wing, and scratches covered his forelegs and belly.

Talis used his blood to heal Junis, just as he had Rosy, and then he turned to Cara. Though they remained silent, the three seemed to converse as they regarded one another. Dragons understood witches when they spoke but couldn't speak back. At least, not audibly. Talis communicated with Daid through his mind. Daid had bonded with him years before, when he became Drago's Servant.

With Talis standing there, Sanna hardly dared to breathe. She'd never been alone with the brood sire, let alone the brood sire *and* his apprentice. Being near Talis felt like standing next to something too bright. Uncomfortable, though fascinating.

She kept her eyes down.

The moments passed in near-silence. A forest as ancient and expansive as Letum Wood was never quiet. As her body calmed, a sweeping agony overcame her. Her ribs ached. Every breath sent shooting pain through her core. Blood dribbled down her leg from the wound in her thigh. An easy price to pay for the hatchlings' safety.

Thyris and Talis ignored her as they gathered up the dead forest lions in their teeth and left with a flick of their tails. The leaves barely rustled in their wake. She hung her head in relief. Talis had been merciful. No doubt he'd ignored her presence because she'd helped save the hatchlings.

Cara leaned down, pressed her snout against Sanna, and blew a warm breath on her feet. The grasses stirred. Sanna reached out, touching Cara's scales briefly. She thought of the vine that had fallen at the perfect moment. The mustard yellow smoke that emerged from the dirt.

Magic. It had to be.

A cold shiver rushed through her. Magic was expressly forbidden—just like dragons were prohibited from flying or using fire. But it *had* been magic. There was no other explanation. Where had it come from? Had she somehow conjured it herself? Impossible. She hated magic.

Sanna pressed her hand to Cara's warm snout when she nuzzled back. "You're welcome," she murmured. "Let's just hope Daid doesn't find out."

Isadora Spence glared at her teacup.

Beams of dusty light streamed through the kitchen, illuminating the locks of golden hair that drifted all the way down her back. The smell of oil, toast, and peppermint tea filled the air. Wooden pots of oil paints, carved from chunks of wood, fanned around her—a gentle lavender for petals; olive to bring out the wispy background. Her paintbrush raced across the teacup with practiced ease, leaving a swirl of vermillion in its wake.

Until it smudged.

"Honestly," she muttered.

Tension thrummed through her head like a line of hot wire, remnants of a headache that had started the day before. Felt like nothing compared to last week's enduring headache—triggered by some unknown cause.

Just like all of them.

Isadora stared at the flower on the side of the new

teacup with a frown. Why didn't it look right? A quick glance at the original teacup confirmed that everything matched. Crimson flowers. Dark backdrop. Hints of yellow in the leaves. But *something* was off.

She set her paintbrush in a bowl of mineral potion for cleaning and quirked her lips to one side. Her gaze flickered around the room. No one present to witness what she was about to do. She held the cup in front of her eyes and whispered an incantation. The teacup levitated from her hand to hover in front of her. Paint swirled on the cup, directed by the magic. The elongated petals shrank. The mossy green leaves expanded, nearly filling the space. She sucked in a sharp breath.

Of course.

Too much red, not enough olive. She shook her head, then regretted it. Her headache pulsated as if it would fill her mind. She pressed a hand to the side of her head.

Oh, *why* wouldn't they go away already?

"Isa?"

She snatched the cup from the air and set it down.

"Yes, Mam?"

Mam's skirts twirled around her thin legs when she shuffled into the kitchen with an armful of wildflowers. Her strawberry-blonde hair sat in a bun at the base of her neck, accentuating her light hazel eyes—the color of late summer grasses. Delicate, soft pink hyacinas and petals-o'-blue flowers peeked out from the top of her bundle. The sunburnt head of a roaring belle bloom sprawled out like a sun flare at the bottom.

"Oh!" Mam cried. "Look at that cup. Perfection, Isa. As always."

"What? Oh! Yes ... thanks."

"Did you see what I found?" Mam's eyes twinkled. She nodded toward the roaring belle. "Isn't it perfect?"

Isadora fixed a smile on her face. "Yes. Lovely."

"Roaring belles are for harmony, you know. Every marriage needs harmony. How are you feeling? Is painting making the headache worse? Sometimes the fumes..."

"No. I'm fine."

Mam frowned. "You're still quite pale. We need to visit Lucey and see about a different potion, I think. This last batch isn't powerful enough anymore."

"I'll go see her tomorrow."

Mam shot her an appraising look. She set the flowers on a chair—the table was clogged with paints—and studied them with a tilted head. "Have you written in your prayer journal for the day yet?"

"Sort of."

"What's that mean?"

"It's in my head."

"That doesn't count. Have you memorized a line from the Chronicles?"

"The cessation of servant loyalty to the great beasts of the forest would end the ancient agreement, resulting in total destruction of witch and dragon."

"Very good."

Luckily, Mam didn't notice it was the same line she'd used yesterday. Isadora eyed the pile of flowers with a feeling of dread. She had to find a way out of the kitchen. She wouldn't be in here when Mam brought out the full courting bouquet.

She couldn't.

"I'm getting a bit dizzy in here, Mam. Perhaps I could finish the tea set tomorrow?"

The delicate ivory curves of the teacups yet to be

painted drew Isadora's attention. They sparkled in the sunshine—their strange opalescence from dragon-egg powder. Their only real luxury out here in the middle of the forest. Isadora painted them once Mam finished firing them in her kiln. All witches in Anguis had to contribute some kind of work; this was Isadora's. Her *only* work.

"Babs Chandler stopped by last night." Mam shuffled a few of the flowers, then stood on the chair next to them. Several hooks hung on strings from the ceiling, for drying flowers. For Isadora's gargantuan courting bouquet.

"Oh?" Isadora squeaked. "What could Babs possibly want?"

"She wanted to talk about our plans for midsummer this year. There are ideas afoot in the Chandler house!"

Babs Chandler, one of three Servant wives, was the mother of Jesse, Isadora's longtime betrothed. Her *midsummer* plans could only mean a handfasting ceremony.

Don't ask, Isadora wanted to plead. She gripped the back of the kitchen chair. *Please don't ask me what day I want to marry Jesse next summer.*

A quick rap at the back door grabbed Isadora's attention, cutting the conversation short. Relieved, Isadora ran over and threw the door open.

"Avay!"

Her heart nearly stopped.

Jesse stood just outside, hat in his hands and a nervous smile on his face. Jesse. Here. Now. With pieces of her courting bouquet tossed all over the kitchen, as if she'd known he'd be here and wanted to send him a silent message.

She assuredly did *not*.

"Oh." She forced a smile. "H-hi Jesse. Uh ... c-can I help you?"

"I came with a message for your mam."

"She's ... sick. Deathly so. Coughing. Plague, I hear. You better not—"

"Jesse!" Mam called brightly as she glided past the door with a grin. "Come inside! Don't mind me. I'm just grabbing Isadora's courting bouquet. We've been working on it for *years* now. Lots of blessings waiting to be realized from that one."

Her singsong voice sent Isadora's face into a hot blush of mortification. Mam disappeared, stepping into her bedroom where the wretched bouquet lived.

"Well?" Mam hissed from the other room. "Let him in!"

Isadora opened the door wider, gaze cast down. There would be no recovering from this. "Please," she whispered, swallowing. "Come in."

"Oh, no. Can't. Thanks. Mam sent me over to tell Roxy that she could trade tubers this week if needed. We broke a few plates and could use some extras in exchange."

Isadora perked up. "Of course. We'd be happy to help. I'll bring them over tomorrow?"

He managed a hesitant smile. "Sure."

Jesse had a swath of thick brown hair, broad shoulders, and big hands. Though he was built like a barrel, he only just met Isadora's height. What he lacked in height, however, he made up for in pure brawn. No one in Anguis was stronger than Jesse, even if he was only seventeen. Isadora's age. An age, she had long ago decided, far too young for marriage. Unfortunately, no one in their tiny forest village seemed to agree.

"Thanks. Ah ... so." She braided her fingers together. "How are you?"

"Good."

She nodded. Silence fell over them.

"Your family?" she asked, then regretted it. She'd seen his entire family two days ago, at the Anguis monthly dinner where all three families gathered at the shelter to eat.

"Fine. Are you excited about the Selectis? Coming up soon, isn't it?"

Her stomach clenched. In two weeks, the dragons would decide her inevitable fate by selecting her as an apprentice. Because, Drago forbid, what witch could choose well for *themselves*?

After the Selectis, she'd serve the dragons for as long as she could bear it. If she reached a month, she'd be impressed, although most served for two years. Then she'd prepare to handfast Jesse in the summer. That's what the women of Anguis did. Unless they were Sanna. Since she was taking over as the next family Servant, she wouldn't be pressured to marry young.

Sometimes, Isadora wished she liked the dragons.

"Yes," Isadora said, forcing a bright tone. The words seemed to stick in her teeth. "The Selectis is coming up fast."

He nodded and tapped his hat against his leg. With a discreet shift to the side, he attempted to peer around her into the house. He quickly slid back over with a bright blush of his own.

"Is, uh, Sanna home?"

"No. She's out somewhere in the trees, like usual."

"Well, I better go."

"Thanks."

He nodded, a few strands of hair falling into his eyes. He brushed them out with a flick of his hand. Another awkward moment passed between them.

"*Alay*, Isadora," he said, using the traditional Dragonian farewell.

"*Alay*, Jesse."

Isadora watched him go, attempting to conjure some spark of emotion deep in her chest. Finding nothing, she turned away. Mam stood off to the side, out of sight, her eyes wide.

"That was adorable!" she said. "The two of you will make a lovely couple."

Isadora returned to the table, setting lids back on her paint pots. "May I ask a question, Mam?"

"Of course."

"How long did you train as an apprentice before you handfasted Daid?"

"Six months."

"Six?" Isadora cried. "So long?"

"Yes."

Far longer than Isadora had expected Mam to have lasted. "Did you like it?"

Mam hesitated, one hand raised halfway to another flower. She'd married into Anguis as an outsider after meeting Daid during a fall supply visit. Mam was seventeen when she gave up all contact with her family—and the rest of the world—to live in the safety of their forest world. She'd never once returned to her childhood home.

"I enjoyed getting to know more about the dragons, of course. Remember, I was an outsider. I knew almost nothing, just like Adelina Parker. Only she came from the Eastern Network, so her challenges were twice as difficult."

"Did you like hunting for and feeding the dragons? I won't tell Daid what you say."

For a moment, a shadow passed over Mam's eyes. Isadora waited.

"No, I didn't. Don't misunderstand me—I care deeply for the dragons. They're majestic, wonderful creatures. But it was a relief to be done trapping and stalking. I don't enjoy being dirty." Mam's nose wrinkled. "The carcasses smelled horrible, like rot."

To Isadora, the dragons' sharp fangs and surly growls had always been more terrifying than *majestic*. They stalked through the forest in near silence, spurting smoke just because they could. The thought of traipsing through Letum Wood dragging heavy metal traps and handling dead creatures made Isadora want to gag.

Mam shrugged. "It gave me a chance to get used to Anguis as an outsider though, and the dragons honored me for it. They don't expect every witch to be a Servant. We can serve them many other ways too."

"Was it hard to leave the Network behind?"

"No. It's chaos there. Witches killing each other. Inflicting pain. Using magic to harm. Talis offers a much calmer, safer life without murder or magic. It's much better here, Isa. Trust me on that."

"Magic," Isadora murmured, feeling a thrill deep in her body. She cleared her throat, casting a sidelong glance at Mam. "I wish I could use it."

Mam frowned. "That's enough talk of that."

Isadora opened her mouth but shut it again. Mam tolerated no talk of anything so prohibited as magic. Aside from Mam, Adelina, and Lucey—who had left Anguis for five years to be formally trained as an Apothecary—no one in Anguis knew how to use spells or incantations. Neither Mam nor Adelina dared. Lucey never spoke of it but secretly taught Isadora small spells whenever she went to refill her headache potions.

"Mam ... I'm nervous," Isadora whispered.

"About having babies?"

Fire flared in her cheeks. "No! Mam. Egads. Where did that come from?"

"Sorry, sorry. Lost in my own thoughts. You're worried about the Selectis next week."

"Yes."

She patted Isadora's back. "Cara will probably choose you. She's very sweet. She was barely into adolescence when I was an apprentice, you know, and mild even then. Rarely threw fire. Her hatchlings are old enough Talis would allow it."

"What if ... what if I don't want to be an apprentice?"

Something slapped her mouth. Isadora gasped, rearing back. She parted her lips to speak but couldn't. The light prickle of magic wrapped around her throat. Mam glared daggers at her.

"Why would you say an ungrateful thing like that?" she whispered. "Someone could hear you. A *dragon* could hear you!"

A cold knot of fear tightened Isadora's stomach. Her lips tingled. Mam never spoke so sharply. The magic slipped away, freeing her to speak again.

"I'm sorry, Mam. I just ... I just asked a question."

Mam's neck relaxed. She dropped her arms to her side. "A stupid question, at that. I'm sorry. I shouldn't have used magic on you ... I reacted instinctively. Please don't tell your daid. The dragons are our life, Isadora. They're *your* legacy. It's just ... if the dragons were to hear you ... can you imagine?"

No. She couldn't.

"May I go to Lucey's now?" Isadora asked, her voice low. Throbbing pain flared at the base of her head. "I-I need my potions refilled."

Mam glanced at the scattered flowers on the table, her shoulders stiff. "Be back in time for your lessons."

Isadora grabbed her potion bottles from the cupboard, rushed out the door, and breathed a sigh of relief when she left the heavy perfume of her courting bouquet far behind her. Maybe today Lucey would teach her an invisibility incantation.

Maybe even one to make her future invisible.

CHAPTER

TWO

Halfway to Lucey's, the trail thinned into a gnome track. No one visited Lucey unless they were sick. Even then, Babs, Mam, or Adelina—the three Servant wives—normally attempted to care for the ill ones before going to Lucey. Ever since she'd chosen to leave Anguis—and not marry and make babies to be dragon Servants—everyone had regarded her as an oddity. Lucey didn't seem to mind. She spent time with her birds in happy solitude.

Isadora deeply envied her.

Isadora pulled her uneven hem higher on her legs to avoid mud stains as she walked. No use getting Mam more worked up. Bulbous violet potion bottles the size of her thumb clinked in her pocket. Lucey would fill them with her most powerful headache potion. Isadora would drink them. Nothing would change. Just like the whole last year.

She let go of her dress and pulled the bottles out of her pocket, studying them. Would the headaches ever go away?

A haughty, unfamiliar voice jolted Isadora from her thoughts.

"Finally."

Isadora gasped, leaping back. A male witch, slightly taller than she, stood on the trail. His mop of thick black hair shone in the blunted light. A single curl dropped onto his forehead, leading to cutting green eyes that pierced through her. The bottles crashed into glittering purple shards at her feet. Isadora backed against a tree.

"Who are you? What are you doing here?"

He wore finer material than her plain, homespun linen. The kerchief around his neck gleamed like the slick scarf Mam had tucked away, her only memory of her former life. His jacket fit impeccably over his shoulders, running to his wrists like it had been tailored for him. A gold chain drooped from a pocket over his right breast.

"I'm not here to eat you," he muttered. He said a quick spell, and the glass shards hovered above the ground. After a burst of light, all four vials swayed in the air between them, not a single crack to be found. "You dropped those."

"Egads. That must have been a complicated spell!"

One of his eyebrows rose higher than the other.

She snatched the dangling bottles and jammed them into her pockets. One bottle fell out through a hole in the bottom, shattering again. He rolled his eyes. Isadora ignored it. At least twenty paces lay between them. If he attacked, she could still dart away.

"Your eyes are two different colors," he said. "That's very odd."

"So are you."

"Odd," he murmured, eyes narrowed. "But defining. How interesting."

She crouched, fumbling in the grass until her hand found a branch. She tried to lift it with a grunt, but vines anchored it to the ground. With a guttural cry, she wrenched it free and waved it in front of her.

"Go away."

"Or what?" he asked imperiously.

"I'll call down a lion.

"Sure you will."

"I will!"

He yawned. "Go on, then. I'd love to see it."

Isadora hesitated. What kind of witch actually called a bluff like that? She could no more call down a lion than she could snuggle Talis. "Who are you?"

"Maximillion. Not Max. Not Max*well*. Maximillion. It's important you get that right."

"Why?"

His brow furrowed. "Because it's rude otherwise."

"What are you doing here?"

"Do you own this forest?"

"No."

"Then why does it matter?"

She gestured to the nearby wall, blackened piles of trees that Talis had long ago laid out to mark the boundary. They reached far over her head. "You shouldn't be *in* here."

He held up his hands as if to say, *Then why am I here?*

A wave of pain ripped through her head as if her skull were trying to split in half. She grabbed a tree, her eyes squeezed shut. The headache sprouted, returning her to a gray, blossoming miasma. Her sight of Maximillion blurred. She pressed her palm to her temple.

"Please leave," she said, her voice drawn.

"Not yet."

His declaration, so utterly devoid of caring, sent her reeling. What an arrogant, pompous witch! Despite his probing gaze—and her walloping headache—she couldn't take her eyes off him. How did he get his shirt so white? Why did he wear a gold chain? Mam had told her once that witches carried clocks in their pockets.

Absurd.

"G-go a—"

The scent of juniper overwhelmed her seconds before she detected him. Her eyes flew all the way open. He stood an arm's-length away, peering at her in cold assessment.

"You're in pain."

"Get away from me."

She lifted her arms to shove him, but he deflected the push with a stray flick of his wrist. His chilly glare sent a shiver down her spine.

"Calm down. I'm going to press my fingers to your head. Don't try to bite me, or I'll remove all the hair from your head with a spell."

The tips of two fingers pressed into her temple. He murmured an incantation. She strained to make out the words but couldn't hear them. Lucey occasionally used spells on Isadora's headaches when Mam wasn't around, but none had worked.

Her current headache coalesced into spinning, hot threads. As if drawn by his touch, the threads sought him out and disappeared, funneled into his hand by the spell. Her mind cleared. Not a remnant of discomfort remained.

"What did you do?" she asked, agape.

"Magic. Please tell me you've heard of it."

"Of course I've *heard* of it. But we aren't allowed—yes. I've heard of it."

"Mildly reassuring. You'll have a hard time of it later, should things move that direction with us."

"How did you know what to do? Can I do it? I-I know a little magic. Simple spells. But still ..."

"Don't ask stupid questions."

"No question is stupid!"

"I assure you, there *are* stupid questions."

She scowled and stepped back. "Why did you help me?"

He paused. "Because you're of more use to me when—and if—you're competent. Now, I've answered your question; you will answer mine."

A flash of gold from his wrist caught her gaze. "What is that?" She gestured to his wrist. Something circular was pinned to the material. He cast it a cursory glance.

"You are clearly a creature of advanced intelligence. It's a cufflink. Not steep fashion by any means, I assure you. Although, considering the state of your dress—"

"My dress is perfectly functional."

He glanced at the broken potion bottle at her feet. "Clearly."

"You must leave. Now."

"I must not."

"Then why are you here?"

"To get *you* out of my head."

"What?"

"This meeting has been inevitable for a while now. I'm glad to be rid of it. Answer my question, and I'll leave."

"What are you talking about?"

Maximillion's eyes grew distant, as if he looked beyond her. For a long stretch of time, he said nothing. She waved a hand in the air, but he didn't move. Just when she thought he'd died mid-thought, he blinked, pulling out of what appeared to be a trance.

"Cursed witch," he mumbled. "Just my luck. You're on *more* paths now than ever."

"You're insane, aren't you? You're a wanderer who's lost his mind and isn't fit for society."

"The good gods, you're dramatic. I control society, for that matter, and am more *fit* for it than half the witches in the Network. Yourself included. Who or what I am is not as important as who you are. What is your name?"

She tilted her chin back. "I don't have one."

"I'm not surprised."

"What's that supposed to mean?"

"You're a confirmed heathen."

"Heathen?" she sputtered. "By Drago, you—"

Her words died on her lips as a flash of horror jolted through her. *The outside world knows nothing of Drago and the remaining dragons,* Mam's voice whispered through her mind. *We must always keep it that way.*

"There's no possible way you could misconstrue what I just said," he snapped. "You probably share rooms with a sibling, too, don't you? I had hopes for someone of greater intelligence. Can't imagine why this had to happen."

"What are you *talking* about?"

"Tell me about yourself."

"Absolutely not."

"You're eleven?"

"Fifteen!"

"Your older brother is named Alfred, correct?"

"What? I don't have a brother."

"Your sister was Alice?"

"No!"

"Ah, a sister it is."

Isadora fumed. "You're not going to get any more information out of me with your sneaky game."

"Damn," he drawled. "You caught me. How often do you have headaches? How advanced are they? Do you see a gray cloud yet?"

Isadora jumped away from the tree and stumbled back.

How could he know that much about her? He, a total stranger. "If you aren't gone in two minutes, you'll never leave alive. I may not be able to call lions, but there are worse creatures to fight in Letum Wood that—"

"Call your dragons. I can't imagine they care much for a witch like you."

Her heart stumbled over itself, flopping like a mad fish. He couldn't possibly know about the dragons. Couldn't possibly know they hated her. Was this a joke Sanna was playing? No. Sanna would never pretend to compromise the safety of Anguis by allowing an outsider in. Other witches in Anguis had reported seeing strangers in the forest before. Vagabonds. Wanderers. Witches running from the Network or lost in a bad transportation spell. By Drago, though, she'd never heard of a trespasser with such elegant clothes.

Or stinging animosity.

"What are you?" she hissed. "A poacher?"

"Do you really think I'd admit it if I was?"

"Ah..."

"Do I look like the kind of witch who cares a whit about animals or blood? You couldn't get me near a giant lizard if you paid me. The dragons won't come here for you. Not today, anyway."

"How could you possibly know?"

His placid indifference wavered for a moment. He fell back into the strange half-presence, then returned. "That is something for us to discuss later. I've done my duty today by simply meeting you. The paths will dictate the rest. Perhaps you'll never see me again."

"Sounds lovely."

"I agree. What's your name?"

"I'm not telling."

"Grogda it is."

She recoiled, nose wrinkled. "Grogda?"

He lifted his brow in silent question.

She paused. Did she dare introduce herself fully to a stranger? His casual indifference, the careful calculation in his gaze, made it difficult to decide. She'd never interacted with any witch outside the families in Anguis and couldn't imagine Daid or Talis would be pleased if she did anything less than run away and sound an alarm. But everything about Maximillion was new. Cufflinks—for whatever purpose. Perfectly white shirts. A strange accent with oddly crisp intonation. Did other witches dress so nicely during the day? She'd never seen shoes without scuff marks on them or a coat without lion fur to keep the warmth in.

"Where are *you* from?" she asked.

"The outside."

"Can you teach me more magic?"

"Someone must."

"Get rid of my headaches?"

"Inevitably."

"Today?"

"No, not today, you impetuous thing. It's not time."

A different life, a traitorous part of her heart whispered. *He knows it all.*

"Isadora. My name is Isadora."

"I prefer Grogda," he muttered and disappeared.

A STREAM CUT THROUGH ANGUIS, dividing it in half. On the south side lived the witches, their houses tucked into the thick foliage of a gradual hill. On the other side lived the dragons. Both were fenced in by a burned border heaped with dead trees, animal carcasses, and scorched earth.

No other witches lived here, deep in the northwest of Letum Wood, at least two days' travel by foot from any small village. Sanna only knew the layout by the one map they had in the school. Like most Servant children, she'd never left Anguis. Only the Servants left on the annual supply run.

Sanna stopped at the stream to clean the blood off her leg and practice moving without showing pain. With any luck, Mam wouldn't notice that her ribs smarted with every breath. Word of the forest lion attack would spread soon enough; the dragons killing that many lions would cause a stir. Less hunting for Daid this week, at least.

Massive trees screened their home from sight at first. When Sanna came into view, she took in the steep pitch of the shingled roof. A warm glow of candles burned inside the house. Darkness fell early on Letum Wood thanks to the vast canopy soaring overhead, so far away the top wasn't visible. Little natural light fell down here. She sighed. *Home.*

When Sanna stepped inside, Daid sat hunched over a ledger, ink dripping off his quill and onto a blotting paper. He muttered under his breath, his brow furrowed. Scrolls rolled off the edge of the table in pearly piles. Mam stood at the stovetop, wooden spoon in hand, humming. The smell of simmering carrots filled the air.

"*Avay,* Daid," Sanna said. "*Avay,* Mam."

Daid grunted.

"*Avay,* Sanna," Mam said. She caught Sanna's gaze, motioned to Daid, and shook her head. Sanna nodded. Daid loathed the monthly ledgers, and they'd run short of tubers this week. For a witch that had lived deep in Letum Wood his whole life, he hated running short on anything. They'd have to trade with the Chandlers again.

Sanna stepped up to the water bowl and splashed her hands in it, washing away the grime.

"How was class today?" Mam asked.

"Ah ... fine."

"Learn anything new?"

Forest lions don't like the smell of rotten eggs, she thought. "Not really."

"I already know you left early, Sanna Spence."

Sanna froze. "Uh..."

"I am not pleased. Babs stopped by to check on you. Said you left sick this afternoon. You were sick enough to leave school but didn't come home?"

Mam frowned, her hair escaping the loose bun at the back of her neck. Her face was flushed and pale. Fresh tomato stains covered her lace-edged apron.

"How'd you know?"

Mam pointed to Sanna's hair. "The evidence is right there." Sanna reached up, pulling a leaf away from her fraying braid.

"Fine. One of my paths was falling apart in the high canopy, and I needed to fix it, so I left school early. Good news: I can now get to school faster."

"It's *faster* to walk on the ground like everyone else."

"Where's the fun in that?"

"It's not proper to scamper through the trees. One of these days, you're going to fall and break something, and you're the only one this family can rely on to help feed the dragons. Besides, there are lions up there."

"So I hear."

Mam's lips twitched. She tugged affectionately at Sanna's braid. "You strange child. How are you mine? You don't like tea. You don't like other witches. You prefer to spend all your time in the trees instead of helping me paint my teacups. You're dirty enough to be a burrowing gnome."

Sanna grinned.

A reverberating *crack* rippled through the kitchen. Mam gasped. Sanna lurched in front of her, pushing her back. But it was just the ledger book slamming closed. Daid drove a hand through his beard and rubbed the grit from his jaw. He shoved the chair back, stood at the door, and stared outside.

"Another riveting day with the ledgers, Daid?" Sanna asked.

Mam shot her a quelling look. "Dinner is ready. Take a chair, Sanna. It's time to eat. You too, Rian. Isadora is upstairs with another headache. She'll eat later."

Daid obeyed. His pursed lips and taut jaw made him look like an old man, not Drago's Servant, the emissary between dragons and witches. Once they all sat down, Mam passed a dish heaped with potatoes across the table.

"No meat tonight," she said. "Save some potatoes for Isa, please."

"Why not?" Sanna asked.

"The chickens are gone."

"Gone? But we had twenty last night."

"The dragons ate them." Daid sliced into a potato.

Sanna sucked in a sharp breath. The dragons crossed the stream *and* killed their food? "*All* the chickens?" she asked. "What about the chicks?"

Mam cast Daid a sidelong glance. "They're safe for now."

A subdued *peep peep* drifted into the room from the cellar door. Sanna glanced at it, feeling sick to her stomach. The chicks were safe for now but couldn't stay in the house forever. If the dragons ate these chickens as well, the family might not survive the winter. Meat from trapping and hunting was scarce in the winter, and the summer had been uncharacteristically lean. They'd barely kept the dragons satisfied.

"Talis will take care of it," Daid said.

They'd lost their only meat source. This sounded like something Macnaris, a wily, adolescent dragon, would do. "Will Talis replace the chickens?" Sanna asked.

"Of course not."

"The next supply visit isn't for three months. If we don't have eggs through the winter—"

"I'm aware," Daid snapped.

Mam aimed a swift kick at Sanna's shin. Sanna stifled a grunt of pain and ducked her head. Dinner proceeded with strained silence until Daid set down his knife and fork. His robin's-egg blue eyes met hers.

"The Selectis is next week. Ready?"

"Born for it."

"Elliot predicts five dragons will choose you."

Mam's eyes sparkled. "I say six."

Every child from the Dragonian families underwent the Selectis near their seventeenth birthday, the day that marked the start of their apprenticeship. For up to two years, one dragon would take the witch into their life, showing them how the dragons live and how to care for them. Each apprentice had to learn how to make salves, treat wounds, hunt, trap, fish, and otherwise feed the dragon horde. For the Selectis, the three families gathered at the meadow, a strip of grassy land that paralleled the stream for five hundred paces. A handful of the twenty-six brood dragons would step into the meadow as volunteers to take the apprentice. To be selected by six dragons would be an honor. Her great-grandfather had set the record at seven.

"It's Isadora that I worry about," Mam said, frowning. "Not Sanna."

"Drago will provide," Sanna murmured.

Mam touched her forehead with two fingers in a symbol of repentance. "Yes. Of course. Drago will provide."

Daid swirled his cup with a heavy frown. Twilight coated the kitchen in a layer of darkness now, the faint light of the candles casting shadows on Sanna's food. Daid pushed his empty plate away and leaned on his arms. She thought of the strange yellow cloud that had repelled the lions and the vine that had appeared right when she'd needed it. She cleared her throat.

"Uh, Daid?"

He looked at her. She set her fork down.

"I ... uh ... thought you should know that I crossed the stream."

His eyes tapered into slashes. "What?"

"I kept to our agreement, I promise! I stayed in the trees. That is ... until a forest lion attacked Junis, and then an entire pack descended on both hatchlings and Cara. Cara and I fought them off until Talis arrived with Thyris and killed the rest."

Daid's bunched shoulders relaxed, but his intense eyes remained trained on her. "Were the hatchlings injured?"

"Yes, but Talis took care of it."

"And Talis?"

She thought of his queer gaze. The unexplained magical events. Had Talis done it? Talis used magic to communicate with Daid on rare occasions, but she doubted he could do any more magic than that. Besides, he hadn't been there when the magic intervened.

So, what caused it?

"He didn't get angry with me for being there. He just ignored me."

"You were lucky," he said, the sharp edge fading from his voice. "Don't take such risks anymore, Sanna. I mean it. Not now."

"What's so different about right now?"

"If the forest lions are moving into Anguis, they're desperate for food. To take on a dragon? I've never heard of that before."

Technically, they took on *three* dragons, but Sanna didn't point it out. Daid ran a hand through his hair.

"I need to check the village boundary." He pushed away from the table. "Talis said there are signs of something trying to get in."

Mam paled. "What? Not poachers, surely?"

"No. Something bigger. Mostly sniffing around, I suspect. Talis says it's a new scent but vaguely familiar. He's not sure what it is, or if it's been here before. I told him I'd do some checks tonight."

"A creature?"

"Maybe." He paused, opened his mouth, and shook his head. "I'll be back in a few hours. Don't wait up for me."

Sanna stuffed the last chunk of potato into her cheek and leapt to her feet. "Coming!"

"No."

"But—"

"I said no."

"Daid, I just—"

He rounded on her, eyes flashing. "I said *no!*"

Sanna opened her mouth to protest, but a hand around her elbow stopped her.

"Not now," Mam murmured.

Daid disappeared out the back door, fading into the forest like a shadow. The door slammed shut behind him.

"This isn't about the border or whatever creature is out there, Sanna. He just ... needs some time alone."

"Why?"

Mam glanced at the empty plates. Her gaze trailed to the northeast corner of their property, where the chickens used to live.

"We're all a bit hungry. More empty traps this year than usual. It's not easy trapping and hunting enough to feed twenty-six dragons, not to mention a family. It's nothing your father and Talis can't work out with Drago's help, however. That's all. Help me clear the table, then pull out your prayer book. We're offering the books on the pyre for Drago next week, before the Selectis. You and Isadora need all the blessings you can get."

FIVE DAYS LATER, Isadora's heart flopped between her ribs and spine like it wanted to escape.

Talis stood just inside the long, thin meadow near the shelter, where the three official Servants and Jesse kept the hunting and trapping supplies. Not far from Talis burbled the stream, which bordered the south side of the meadow. Heat radiated off Talis's giant body in curls of steam. He disappeared, then slipped back into sight farther down, capturing her gaze.

She turned away.

Isadora tilted her head back and drew in a deep breath. All the witches of Anguis—and a few other family members that hadn't become Servants but lived close by in Letum Wood—had gathered. Everyone sat on the ground near the shelter, chattering quietly. She tried not to hear them. Tried not to see Jesse lounge against a tree trying to talk to Sanna.

"I can do this," she murmured. "I can do this."

Daid strode into the meadow and held up two arms. The families fell silent. "With Talis and Drago's blessing, the Selectis will begin," he called.

A cheer rippled through the witches. Isadora's stomach churned, and she was grateful she stood apart. Sanna jogged over, her skirt flapping around her knees. She clasped Isadora's cold hand. "You ready, *amo*?" Sanna asked.

"No."

"It'll be fine, Isa. Cara will choose you."

Isadora grimaced, pressing a hand to her forehead. That was precisely what worried her. Once chosen, no witch could back away. Not without dishonor and possible banishment. Smoke filled her mind, swirling in a storm. Her headache was a driving *thud*, steady as a heartbeat.

On the other side of the meadow, Talis appeared again. Daid headed toward him. Once there, Daid fell to his knees and stretched out an arm. Talis pressed his nose into Daid's palm. They remained that way for several moments, communicating in the strange mental dance given only to Drago's Servant. What felt like an eternity later—but had likely been less than a minute—Daid pulled away.

"Permission given," he said. "The Selectis will now begin. Talis has commanded that Isadora step forward first."

"Sanna, I'm going to be sick," Isadora whispered.

"Everything will be fine. I'll be here the entire time."

"You can stand up there with me?"

"Well ... nooo. But I'll be right here."

Isadora's legs froze.

Move. She willed the command all the way into her toes. Her body remained still. Mam would never forgive her if she didn't try to learn more about the dragons. *Drago,* she prayed, *god of dragons and forest. Bless my efforts. Make my body move.*

Still, her legs remained fixed.

Move!

Sanna nudged her. "Isa, go!"

"I can't!"

"You can. Just take one step at a time."

Talis snorted at her, lifting his head. Isadora squeaked in fear.

"Move!" Sanna hissed.

With a gentle kick from Sanna, Isadora's knee bent a minuscule amount, but it was enough. She stumbled into the meadow. She stopped a few paces away from Sanna, barely out of the treeline, closed her eyes, and drew in a deep breath.

I can do this.

I can do this.

Certain enough time had passed for Cara to emerge, she opened her eyes. The meadow lay empty. Twigs cracked in the distance, but no dragon slithered into sight. Isadora's throat tightened. They must be farther back than she'd thought. Where was Cara?

The dark band of forest on the other side of the meadow waited in utter silence. Isadora's headache spun another pewter cloud.

One minute stretched into five.

Eight.

The gathered families murmured.

"Move farther in, Isa," Sanna said. "Maybe the dragons can't see you."

Isadora advanced four more steps, twisting her dress in her sweaty hands. *I want this. I want this.* But repeating it didn't make her believe it. She decidedly wanted nothing *less* than to be an apprentice. She thought of Maximillion, then banished it.

Another silence descended. Two interminable minutes passed. Tears filled her eyes. Never had a dragon failed to volunteer. Never had a witch, in all the *Chronicles*, met with such horrific failure.

Would none come?

Just when she thought her heart would burst with shame, she saw moving shadows. A dragon emerged. Isadora's breath caught.

Thyris.

The elegant dragon advanced into the meadow, scallops of gold swirling across his belly in wild tendrils. He snorted gauzy smoke in her direction. His eyes tapered. Clearly, *he* wasn't any happier about this than she was.

Behind her, Sanna swore under her breath.

Isadora wanted to laugh until the maniacal edge of hysteria faded.

Of *course*, Thyris stepped forward. Talis probably forced him to. When no one else would tutor the poor girl, *someone* had to. Why not the apprentice to the brood leader?

She pressed a hand to her forehead. Thyris would demand more than Isadora could give. Thyris, a talented, powerful dragon in his own right, deserved better than a witch who didn't care. Worse still—if she accepted Thyris, Sanna wouldn't get him. Sanna who adored the dragons.

Sanna who had looked forward to working with Thyris all her life. Who would train Sanna? It would have been better for everyone if Thyris had left Isadora standing there alone.

Sanna stood next to her now, her two reddish braids glinting in the sunlight. The astonished voices of the families weren't far enough away. The sound swelled into a chorus of disbelief. Tears clogged Isadora's throat.

"I can't do this, Sanna."

Sanna swallowed. Her voice wavered only slightly. "Don't be mad at Thyris, Isa. This is the highest compliment you could have asked for. Thyris is ... he's the best."

"He feels sorry for me. Talis made him."

"Maybe it was a mistake none of the others stepped forward. Cara could be busy with the hatchlings. Maybe Talis started too soon or—"

"Talis never makes mistakes."

"You must bow to Thyris and accept." Sanna nudged her with an elbow. "Working with Thyris is the highest honor an apprentice could hope for. You'll be ... you'll be the envy of everyone in Anguis. Go. Accept his offer."

"What about you?"

"This isn't about me."

"But..."

"Drago will provide, Isa. You *know* you must do this."

Isadora's heart sank like a heavy stone. With a flash, she recalled a pair of bright, judgmental green eyes. Magic on her lips. Perfectly shaped potion bottles in her hand. Felt Sanna standing next to her, tall, proud, and strong.

Maximillion had hinted he could teach her magic. That path offered her more at a great cost. What seemed too great a cost. But was it? Compared to resigning her life to a path she loathed? That, so far, she'd only ever failed at?

Thyris's sacrifice left her with one choice.

Isadora squared her shoulders and stepped forward. Resolve filled her chest. She could do this. No—she *had* to do this. She met Thyris's intense glare. With her hands balled into fists at her side, she drew in a deep breath.

Then she shook her head.

"No."

An unnerving silence settled on the meadow. For several moments, not a sound stirred. Thyris stomped forward, snorting once.

"No," she called. "While I am grateful for the honor, I choose not to be an apprentice to the dragons."

"You can't say no!" Sanna cried.

Thyris reared back with a shriek. Isadora backed away, fingers clasped. Fear coursed through her, but she forced herself to remain steady. There was no time to question her decision now. She had to run before Talis reacted. She spun and hurried past Sanna, who stood with her mouth half-open. Once she passed the tree line, Mam bellowed after her.

"Isadora Spence!"

Isadora broke into a run, her heart pounding a heavy staccato.

Freedom. Freedom. Freedom.

CHAPTER

THREE

Deep fear gripped Sanna as Isadora walked away.

Refused a dragon. No witch had done that in the history of … ever. "Isa," she murmured, "what have you done?"

The gossip of the families exploded into a cacophony of confused cries.

"Did she leave?"

"Refused a dragon!"

"Never heard of that."

Mam chased after Isadora, halted a few paces away, and turned to Sanna, her eyes wide in wordless question. Sanna lifted her hands in an expression of *I have no idea what to do now.* Mam's shoulders slumped. She stared at the spot where Isadora had disappeared.

Talis advanced into the meadow, steam billowing from his wide nostrils. Daid raced across the field, threw himself to his knees, and thrust his hand up. Talis shoved his snout into Daid's hand. Thyris slunk back into the trees, shooting lines of fire that singed the grass. Daid remained bowed for another full minute. When he withdrew, his face was pale, eyes drawn.

"Sanna," he called, his voice weak. "Talis requests you step forward."

Sanna swallowed. The buzz calmed.

Mam retreated back to the group, arms held around her sides, looking a breath away from fainting. Babs Chandler, a rotund woman with apple cheeks, put an arm around her just in time. Mam collapsed into Babs's sturdy grip.

Sanna stepped into the meadow. By the time she'd made it halfway, a dragon screamed. Her stomach jerked as if pulled by a barb. Answering dragons bellowed in return, screeching from everywhere at once. Color boiled out of the trees, racing for the meadow.

She skidded to a stop.

A flash of crimson appeared first. Rubeis. Behind him, a burgundy dragon with steaming nostrils. Meris. Salibis, a young, adolescent male marbled with mauve came next. Then Elis and Voltaris and Frida.

The dragons plowed into the meadow, trampling saplings, shoving like ornery teenagers. Tails whipped through the air. Two of the males butted each other with their bony horns, fighting for a spot. A teeming crowd of shimmering heat and black scales gathered before her.

Seven.

Nine.

Twelve.

The ground shook. Something crashed in the distance. A little girl cried out. The dragons' massive forms encircled Sanna. She pivoted, her blood catching fire.

Sixteen.

Well over half the brood chose her, a mix of male and female—but more males. Sanna's gaze trailed over each beast. Flavis, with his wild, curling umber pattern, like scattered earth. He was proud. Middle-aged at seventy years old and powerful. A worthy dragon—but not meant for her. Magentis, an elegant male. Eighty-four. Hated it when Daid only had wild hog available to eat.

Her throat caught. All of them honored her by stepping forward. But where was—

Thyris.

He slipped into the meadow again, head back, nose high. She met his gaze in disbelief. *Thyris* had volunteered. Thyris! He'd never volunteered, not once in the ninety years he'd been alive. Sanna reigned her thoughts in, bowing to each dragon surrounding her. She couldn't get so caught up in her shock that she offended them.

"Drago," she murmured. Who wouldn't accept Thyris? Isadora aside, of course.

A shadow passed over the meadow just as Sanna, with a giddy scream locked in her throat, turned to bow and accept Thyris's offer. She paused and tilted her head back.

The heavy *whomp whomp whomp* of wings followed the shadow. A deep call rang out. The dappled sunlight dimmed as the silhouette of a dragon dropped through the canopy.

"Sanna!" Daid yelled. "Watch out!"

The ring of dragons reared back, scattering. Thyris charged farther into the meadow. Sanna threw herself to the ground just as a burst of orange streaked overhead, barely missing her. A wave of heat slammed into the back of her neck. She popped back up. A lithe male dragon landed a few paces away. Burnt-orange scales glittered across his chest and legs in a lattice design. He crouched on all fours, eyes tapered, nostrils steaming. His abundant heat and the dried blood on his lips made it glaringly obvious just *what* he was.

A wild dragon.

Legends always ran rampant through Anguis about things like wild dragons, but no one really believed them. Dragons were brood creatures. They didn't know how to live alone. Besides, Talis knew all the eggs, the mams, and the hatchlings. It would have been impossible for one to sneak away.

Or maybe not. Sanna knew all the dragons, and she'd never seen this one.

She climbed to her feet again. The wild dragon feinted toward her, but she stood her ground. He snapped, but she didn't flinch.

"Who are *you*?" she murmured.

"Run!" Daid called. "Get—"

His words died under a thunderous noise. Talis sprinted across the meadow. The wild dragon stepped between Sanna and Talis, screaming with long curls of flame. Sanna recoiled, stumbling away from his heat. So rarely did dragons throw fire. Talis didn't break stride and closed the distance in only a few more seconds.

Daid rushed up to her side, grabbing her arm.

"Get back!"

Talis slammed into the wild dragon with his right shoulder. The wild dragon flew back and hit a tree with a *thud*. Sanna fell to her knees. Daid wobbled. The vague shouts of scattering witches filtered through the dragons' screams as the tree crashed into the meadow.

"Get back to the shelter," Daid yelled. "Now!"

He darted back into the forest. Sanna started to crawl away but hesitated. The wild dragon recovered, leapt back to all fours, and slammed his tail into Talis. Talis scored the damp earth with his talons as he slid back, then rammed into the wild dragon again with his broad shoulder. They whirled in a dance of dark scales, fire, and gnashing teeth.

The wild dragon broke free and climbed into the sky, circling the meadow with dizzying speed. Thyris attempted to follow, but dropped, his never-flown wings unable to bear his weight. Rubeis appeared from the tree line, eyes glittering. Sanna stared at the wild dragon while it circled. She'd never seen a dragon fly. How was it still alive? A flying dragon was a dead dragon. The Great Massacre a hundred and fifty years ago had proven that.

Sunlight glinted off Talis's gnashing teeth as the wild dragon dove back down. Talis snapped at its wing, but the dragon twisted away. He hissed, descending as gracefully as a robin on the far side of the meadow. The wild dragon locked his gaze on Sanna, catching her by surprise. Something visceral moved within his liquid yellow irises. Something livid.

Something ... desperate.

A feeling stirred in her chest, as if he roused her heart with his warm breath. Her entire body tingled. She held her breath, momentarily suspended in time. Something lingered in the air. A whisper. A stirring of breath she couldn't *quite* hear.

Sanna strained, listening.

Yours...

Magic. Again.

A shout from Daid on her right broke the moment.

"On the right, Elliot! Finn, from behind! Jesse, secure it."

A thick rope cut through the air, vaulting over the wild dragon's back. A second rope followed from the other side. Then a third. A fourth.

Daid darted close to the wild dragon, looping a rope

around its foreleg. Then Jesse showed up, securing the rope to a tree. The dragon threw fire so hot it crackled. He tried to unfurl his wings, but they couldn't open. The ropes—reinforced with flexible bands of steel—held strong when he snapped at them with his teeth. They were taking it prisoner.

Sanna pushed to her feet.

"No! Wait!"

Daid, Elliot, and Finn—the only official dragon Servants—sprinted in and out of the thick undergrowth, avoiding the sweep of the wild dragon's fire by ducking behind trees. What seemed like only seconds later, ten ropes fastened the writhing beast to the trees. The dragon strained against them, teeth bared. Why didn't he break them with his teeth? Sanna doubted such thin pieces of steel could stop a dragon that ferocious.

Talis crossed the meadow with languorous steps. The two stared eye to eye, growling and then falling silent and then growling again. She longed for a glimpse into their minds. Daid retreated to Talis's side and dropped to his knees, raising a hand.

What felt like an eternity later, the bushes surrounding the wild dragon swam with light. An invisible ring grew from the earth, rippling toward the treetops. It curved, creating a transparent dome around the wild dragon that occupied the full width of the meadow's end. The guttural sounds of his protest fell silent. The ropes dropped away, releasing him into the magical prison without restraint. He slammed his body into the glimmering wall. It held.

He clawed at the impenetrable, sheer surface, but no marks showed. Nothing but a sheer, rippling barrier.

Magic.

Everyone in Anguis knew that Drago's Servant could do

magic when approved by Talis, but Sanna had never seen it done. She doubted *anyone* here had. Daid stumbled away from Talis. He stood but wobbled and fell back to his knees.

"Daid!"

She started for him, but he held up a hand. Five seconds passed. Then ten. Finally, he struggled to stand. His nostrils flared as he straightened, legs shaking. He leaned over, bracing his hands on his knees.

"Talis orders all of you to ignore this wild beast," he said, panting. "The Selectis must continue. Sanna, choose your dragon. Quickly."

Her burning questions died away.

Sanna turned around to face the rest of the meadow, then stopped. Thyris stood five paces away, his golden scales casting slivers of light onto her skin. She gazed right into his luminous eyes. Every breath moved his supple, thick body. His wings relaxed. When he straightened to his full height, he loomed above her in glinting ebony majesty. She couldn't decide which was more terrifying—Thyris's newfound attention or the wild dragon at the end of the meadow. This day could not get any stranger.

"*Avay,*" she whispered.

He closed his eyes and lowered his head. A sign of respect. Something he'd never given, unless to Talis. Not even to Daid. Sanna forced her thoughts to slow.

Thyris's warm breath surrounded her like an embrace. She thought of the wild dragon. The voice in her head. The sixteen dragons behind Thyris that all stood for her—she knew she wouldn't choose any of them.

Sanna took a step back.

Daid straightened.

"Sanna?"

Sanna swallowed, rubbing her fingers together.

Courage, she thought. *Like Isa. Courage that will make Daid proud. Courage that will prove I can be better than the rest of the Servants.* She drew in a deep breath, then spun. The wild dragon peered at her from his new prison.

"*Sanna!*" Daid yelled.

She fell to her knees before the wild dragon, covering her heart with a trembling hand.

"My allegiance I give to you."

Later that night, Isadora lay on her bed in the attic, one arm thrown over her eyes. In the quiet, cool darkness, the Selectis replayed in her mind. She thought about refusing Thyris and tried not to vomit.

What had she done?

Mam bustled in the kitchen below, prattling at high speed. Dishes rattled. Daid murmured every now and then, his voice low and resonant. Isadora crawled to the door and pressed her ear to the crack.

"She's lost her mind, Rian. Lost it! Never ... never has anyone ever ... and that wild orange dragon? Did you know there were wild dragons? Our daughters are mad!" Her voice turned shrill. "Mad!"

Mam kept going without giving Daid a chance to respond.

"And Isadora!"

Isadora slipped back to bed.

She felt as wrung out as a dirty rag. Rejected a *dragon.* Not even Minerva the Suspicious had done something that drastic. Isadora's name would be as infamous among Servant legends as Sorcha the Belligerent and Dwayne the Sour. Her ugly, invisible scar would separate her from the rest now. Despite how greatly her life had changed, she felt strangely calm, except for the undying question that whirled in her mind.

Why didn't the dragons come?

No other witch from Anguis had failed in such a way.

The sound of grating wood and a low curse brought Isadora out of her thoughts. Sanna's silhouette dropped into the room from the window. She ripped her dress off, tossed it to the floor, and collapsed to her bed wearing only knickers and an undershirt. One leg, lithe and strong, draped over the side of the bed. Mud flecked the bottom of her foot, but Sanna never cared about things like that. She reached underneath her pillow, pulled out a small, leather-bound journal, and scribbled on the damp paper with a stubby pencil.

Isadora sat back, pushing aside a pang of guilt. She hadn't written in her prayer book to Drago in days now. Maybe weeks. Her throat filled with words. There was so much she wanted to tell Sanna. If she told her about Maximillion, Sanna would immediately think of the safety of the dragons. She might even tell Daid, and Isadora would *really* be in trouble for conversing with—and not reporting —a stranger.

"Where have you been?" Isadora asked. "Mam and Daid were home an hour ago."

"Out."

Sanna closed the journal around the pencil, shoved it under her pillow, and stood up. She crossed to the water bowl to wet a rag.

"You disgraced us just as much as I did, I hear," Isadora said.

"Worse."

"Not possible."

Sanna tilted her head to the side, as if considering. "You may be right. But I didn't help things, either."

Isadora watched Sanna wipe down her face, neck, and calves. "You're not hurt that I was gone for yours, are you?" Isadora asked.

"No."

"Are you mad at me?"

Sanna's brow furrowed. She pitched the rag back into the bowl and sprawled onto her bed, head resting on her folded arm. "No … I just don't understand."

"Me either."

Sanna propped herself up on an elbow, a waterfall of strawberry-blonde hair spilling over her shoulders. Heavy shadows stretched across her face, obscuring her freckles and porcelain skin. "You refused Thyris for me, didn't you?" she asked.

"Partially."

Sanna snorted. "How ironic."

"He terrifies me, for one. And I couldn't let you lose the chance because of me. But I didn't, I mean … I just … it doesn't feel right. It's not enough."

"What isn't enough?"

Isadora spread her hands. "This. Don't you ever want to do magic? To leave? To see something besides trees and dragons and … Finn? Don't you ever just … just want to see what's out there?"

Sanna hesitated, then shook her head. "Magic is dangerous. It nearly destroyed all the dragons in the massacre."

"I want it."

"That's not what we're meant to be."

No, Isadora thought. *It's not what you are meant to be.*

"Some of us aren't as talented as you, Sanna. The only thing I can do is paint. I'm terrible at laundry. I can't sew a straight line. Everything I plant ends up dying. And the dragons hate me. How can I contribute to Anguis by painting?"

"You can have children."

Isadora gritted her teeth. "What if I don't want to? There has to be more than just getting handfasted and having children. More than just being … a slave to the dragons."

Sanna stiffened. "A slave? We aren't slaves."

"We aren't free."

"That's a lie!"

"Why are we surrounded by walls that keep us inside? Why can't we do magic? Why can't we *leave*?"

Sanna opened her mouth, then snapped it shut with a growl. She dropped back to the bed and threw an arm over her eyes. The ropes beneath the mattress creaked beneath her weight.

"We're *not* slaves," she muttered. "We're protecting the dragons."

Isadora wrapped her arms around her knees. So many words sat on the tip of her tongue that she didn't dare speak. *I met a stranger. He said he could teach me magic. He's from the outside.*

"Sanna, please don't hate me. Mam and Daid may never talk to me again. I don't want to be all alone."

She braced herself for one of Sanna's usual gritty replies. Sanna swallowed, shifting on the bed to peer at Isadora from underneath her arm.

"I don't hate you, Isa."

"Promise?"

"I promise."

Sanna padded across the floor, moving with her customary sharp intensity. Isadora lay back down, and Sanna crawled underneath the covers. Pressing their shoulders together, they stared into the shadows dancing across the ceiling. Nothing but the occasional screech of a screaming gnome interrupted the dark night. Sanna's body was warm and powerful. She always ran like an overheated oven.

"What now, Isa?" Sanna asked. "What's going to happen?"

"I don't know."

"You're not angry because so many dragons chose me, are you?"

Isadora reached out, pressing two fingertips to Sanna's cheek in the Dragonian expression of love. "I'm proud of you, Sanna. You're meant for this."

Sanna snuggled deeper into Isadora's pillow. "The dragons won't love me now that I chose a wild dragon."

"But I will."

"No matter what?"

Isadora held out a hand. Sanna slid hers into it, interlocking their fingers.

"No matter what."

A yawn split Sanna's lips in half. Her coppery eyelashes fluttered closed against her pale cheeks. "Tomorrow," she murmured. "We face whatever comes next."

"Yes. Tomorrow."

"Night, Isa," she murmured, breathing out the word for *love* with the last of a yawn. "*Amo.*"

"*Amo,* sister."

Once Sanna's breathing evened out, Isadora reached deep into her mind. Nothing remained of her earlier thoughts but a smoky blur. She thought she saw flickers of something. A face. An old house. But they flittered away, leaving only echoes. She slipped into the unassailable safety of dreams, Sanna hot at her side.

Isadora stood at the top of the stairs, fists clenched.

Despite the morning hour, the late summer heat lay as thick as a blanket on the attic. The back of her neck tightened like someone had plucked it with their fingers.

Stupid headaches.

How could you betray us? she imagined Mam asking, tears brimming in her reddened eyes. *How could you fail in this one task?* Thinking about the inevitable confrontation sent a chill through Isadora's spine.

"I will stand my ground," she whispered. "I will *not* work with the dragons. I made my choice. It was the right choice. Mam can't force me."

She descended the stairs, chin held high even though her knees quivered.

"Good morning!" Mam called. A bright smile wreathed her face. The smell of fresh-baked bread lingered in the room alongside the tang of tea. Isadora stopped dead at the bottom of the stairs.

"Mam?"

"Glad you're up. We have lots to do today! Abigail needs a tea set for their handfasting this spring, and we need to replace the plates we traded with the Chandlers for tubers. Now that Voltaris's egg hatched, we'll be able to grind some powder. Oh, I added a few dried figs to the bread this morning."

Isadora blinked, dumbfounded. Had she dreamed about the Selectis? Had it all been a terrible nightmare after all?

"Figs?" she murmured.

"Your father's favorite."

No. She hadn't dreamed it. She would never have dreamed she could be bold enough to refuse Thyris. Only reality could be so terrifying.

"Mam, are you all right?"

"How did you sleep?"

"Fine. Aren't you ... ah..."

"Angry?"

"Yes."

Mam's eyes didn't meet hers as she pulled a loaf of bread from the oven. "No, I'm not angry with you, Isadora."

"Are you disappointed?"

"Should I be?"

No nuance or tension colored her tone. A trap, surely. Could Mam have possibly come to terms with this overnight?

"Ah..."

Mam motioned to the table. "Have a seat. Let's eat together and ... *chat*."

Isadora obeyed. *Chatting* sounded as benign as a pack of hungry forest lions. Two minutes passed in a strained silence, interrupted by the *clink* of spoon against teacup, plates against table. Isadora used a spoon to press the flavor out of her tea leaves. A murky cloud billowed in the hot water. She forced herself to take a bite of bread, chew, and swallow. It tasted like stone.

"So," Mam asked. "What are your plans today?"

Isadora opened her mouth, then shut it again. What *were* her plans? Abigail Parker would be banned from speaking to her—Abigail's father Finn, one of the three Servants, already hated them because he envied Daid's position as Drago's Servant. Abigail spent most of her time with her betrothed—James, from the outside—anyway. No one else would befriend Isadora now. She fidgeted with the edge of her sleeves. She hadn't thought this far ahead yet.

"No plans?" Mam asked.

The unfortunate truth hit Isadora like a cold slap. Without the dragons to order her life around, she *had* nothing to do, except paint teacups, perhaps. She'd effectively isolated herself to her family.

No, to Mam.

"I don't ... that is..."

"Nothing to do? That's surprising. Nowhere to go? Unfortunate."

Isadora's skin crawled. Panic filled her, hot and fast.

"Ah..."

Mam pursed her lips, making a low sound in her throat. "Your eyes are drawn. You look pale, poor thing. Are you having a headache?"

"Y-yes, Mam."

Mam hummed, lifting her tea to her lips without taking a sip. "I hope you recover quickly."

"What for?"

"Babs has invited us over for tea this morning. You will go with me," Mam said, her jaw tight. "You will sit. You will listen. You will apologize for your mistake and reassure Babs that you will be the best wife that Anguis has ever seen."

"But..."

"There is no alternative."

Isadora's throat nearly closed. It all pieced together now. She'd jumped right into the fire. Instead of freeing herself, she'd planted herself into an infinitely more tenacious trap: Mam's determination to satisfy Talis, no matter what. No apprenticeship didn't mean more magic.

It meant more *nothing*.

"I-I don't understand."

"There's little doubt in my mind that Babs has invited us over to cancel the betrothal. Who wants their son to marry the girl that refused the dragons?"

Despite a lifetime of planning, Jesse would no longer court her. He'd forget her, handfast someone else. Like Sanna. Her nose wrinkled. No, that would never happen. Jesse would find a stranger outside Anguis who was seeking a different life, like Daid had found Mam and Finn had found Abigail.

The feeling of a pinched sensation, like someone drawing a string through her heart, robbed Isadora's breath.

Drago. She pressed a hand to her forehead. *What have I done?*

"You will be on your best behavior. You will not speak a word unless I allow it, and you will be meek, kind, and appreciative of Babs no matter what she says. We're lucky she'll tolerate you at her house."

"Yes, Mam."

Mam studied her. "We have one shot at redemption, Isadora," she whispered. "One shot to make this right, or you'll live a life of utter rejection. You'll be lower than Lucey, with birds as her only companions, on the edge of Anguis. Coming and going without anyone to care. Gone for long snatches of time—probably to find *some* purpose. I didn't almost die in childbirth and lose my ability to have more children for you to be lonely for the rest of your life."

Like a will-o'-the-wisp, Isadora's freedom darted away the moment she'd thought she'd caught it. She wasn't free at all. The dragons still held her in their hot claws.

Or was it Mam?

"Do you see what I must save you from, Isadora?" Mam stood up. "Yourself. I must save you from yourself. You may have failed to impress the dragons, but you will *not* fail to serve them. I'm changing. Be ready to leave for Babs's in an hour."

She withdrew from the room, slamming her bedroom door behind her. Isadora stood up, set her napkin on the table, and stepped outside.

Isadora's headache danced into a violent storm.

Leaves whipped her face as she hurried down the old gnome trail, one thing on her mind as she shoved branches out of her way. She ignored her fears. Mam's reaction. The pain in Daid's eyes. She ignored all of it, her mind fixed on one thing: sharp green eyes.

What felt like hours later, she skidded to a stop and leaned on a tree, panting. A minute passed. Then two.

She straightened.

"Maximillion!" she yelled, head tilted back. Birds fluttered by. Sweat trickled down her cheeks. She winced as the headache grew from the base of her skull.

"Maximillion!"

She focused as hard as her buzzing mind would allow, trying to recall his face. His strangely perfect hair. Bright eyes. Could she bring him here by sheer desperation? Her vision blurred with pain. The empty trail stared back at her.

Unable to bear the silence, she kicked the tree next her.

"Stupid dragons!"

A skein of moss fell from the trunk, landing on a bright

mushroom. She reached out, tangled her fingers into the remaining moss along the bark, and ripped a patch off. It tore free from itself, little hairs swaying in a strangely satisfying way.

"Stupid dragons!"

She tore another skein.

"Stupid wall!"

Another.

"Stupid Babs!"

She pushed all her frustration into her hands, tearing at the tree like a wild thing. Her hair loosened around her shoulders. Sweat saturated her collar. A metallic scent hovered in the wake of the shredded mess. Her chest heaved as she stared at the bald patch, realizing that an immense pressure had evaporated off her chest.

That felt *good*.

"The good gods."

Isadora whipped around, heart in her throat. Maximillion stood on the trail, eyebrows halfway up his forehead in bored disdain. The cool green of his eyes cut right through her again.

"Should I be disgusted or terrified?" he asked.

"You came."

"Not willingly. The paths can be quite persistent."

"Did you know that I wanted to talk to you?"

He frowned. "I had an inkling. Or so the paths indicated, anyway. You're as snotty as a two-year-old. What happened?"

"It's ... been a bad day."

"Clearly."

"When can you teach me more magic?"

His expression didn't waver, although she saw a flicker of surprise in his eyes. "You seem very much in earnest."

"Yes."

He wore a pristine, white shirt with an open neck and starched collar. His hair seemed a bit askew, as if he'd driven his hands through it. He wore no cufflinks nor a gold chain this time. In comparison to their first meeting, he appeared downright lax, though she doubted he could ever be anything so casual. He'd have a heart attack if he ever met Sanna.

When he didn't say anything, she broke the overwhelming silence. "Why aren't you wearing cufflinks this time?" She tucked her hair behind her ear.

He blinked, as if coming out of deep thoughts. "One doesn't wear cufflinks while doing paperwork."

"One? Who is *one*?"

"You must know basic grammar."

"Of course."

"Then why are you asking that question?"

"Is *one* a person? I know it's a number but—"

He rolled his eyes. "The good gods."

"Who?"

"Never mind. You wanted to talk to me to see if I could teach you magic? That's why you wanted me here so badly that the paths perceived you?"

"Er ... yes?"

"I could."

Her eyes widened. "Now?"

"No. Not *now*. But I could teach you. It's at least a good sign that you're thinking about it, though I've never mentored a heathen like you."

His staunch, implacable expression remained on his face as they stared at each other.

Isadora let out a long breath. "That's wonderful. Shall we begin here?"

"Ah, but there is much you don't understand. The magic I teach has nothing to do with incantations, spells, or curses. It's far more powerful and selective than that. One has to really want it before they dive in."

"How?"

"If you have to ask, it's not time for you to know."

"If it's selective, how do you know I can do it?"

"I wouldn't be here if you couldn't."

Something in his expression made her stomach catch. He was still annoyingly cryptic, leaving her more confused than ever. Paths? Selective magic? It made no sense.

He advanced a step, seeming to cross the distance with one stride. Questions rose in her throat like a flock of ravens, fluttering and wild and blocking out the light.

"That's why you came last time?" she asked. "Because I've been selected by whatever magic you're referring to?"

"Yes. I came to see if, indeed, you were."

"And?"

"You are."

"Then why haven't we started?"

He rolled his eyes. "I told you. It's not time."

"Listen, whatever it requires, I'll do it. I just ... I want to know more about the world. About magic. You're the only witch I've ever met that could teach it."

He scoffed. "You don't understand what you really want. Not yet, anyway. It's ugly out there. Rumors of war and incompetent leaders who play with witches' lives like a game of *Networks*."

"Networks?"

"Oh, forget it."

When he turned to leave, she threw out a hand.

"Wait!"

He stopped with his back to her, his jaw clenched. "What?"

If he left, she feared he'd never return. She'd be doomed to a life of intricate wordplay with the other wives and the damning memories of what she *hadn't* done.

"I need your help."

"I just told you—"

"No, for something else. I think there's something wrong with me."

He hesitated, then glanced back. A deep curiosity glittered in his narrowed eyes. His voice dropped. "Why?"

"My headaches." She pressed a hand to her head. "They're getting worse. Nothing Lucey gives me helps. I—"

He whipped around, gaze as sharp as talons. "What name did you say?"

She stepped back. "L-Lucey."

"The bird witch?"

"Yes."

He made a sound deep in his throat. "How interesting."

"You know her?"

"I know everyone. Keep talking."

"I-I think my headaches are something else."

"They are. Keep going."

"M-maybe something ... broken. You fixed it last time for a little while. You must know. What is it? What's wrong with me? Why am I so ... different?"

"A few hours reprieve is hardly a fix."

"It's more than I've ever had before. Please," she whispered. "It's ... terrifying."

He stared hard at her. His expression returned to the strange, distant quality she remembered from last time. His lips parted slightly, showing the edges of his straight, white teeth. He blinked, coming back to himself.

"More paths," he muttered, driving a hand through his hair. "The gods. There's no time for this."

"Paths?"

"Quiet."

"I'm just supposed to stop asking?" she hissed, fists clenched.

"Yes! Glad we can agree on something. Let me know when something changes with your headaches or your vision. We can talk more then. Any attempt now will just yield more confusion."

He turned to leave again, but Isadora reached out and grabbed his sleeve. He jerked it away with a hiss, his eyes flashing.

"Never touch me."

"Maybe you're right." She swallowed. "I have no idea what's waiting out there. I have no idea what questions to ask or where to even start ... but at least I understand what I don't want. And it's everything that I am and everything that is my future right now. If you can't help me, I may never escape. I'll suffocate here until I die."

The last words fell off her lips in a stark whisper. His gaze flickered as if, for a moment, he found reason to believe her. Isadora held her breath, her knuckles aching.

"And what in the name of the good gods *don't* you want?" he asked silkily.

"To be a slave."

A haunted, pained expression glimmered in his eyes. "You're too late for that. You're already a slave. You don't even see your own chains yet." He sighed. "The headaches won't last forever. There's nothing that will help them but enduring through. At that time, I can help you. I don't know a time frame, either. It's different for each witch. Suffice it to say, you'll know."

"Really?"

"Yes."

"Why not now?"

"To attempt learning it before you've transitioned … you have no idea what you're asking. Try not to think of me in the meantime. I have wars to prevent." He glanced at the naked spot on the tree. "And mine aren't with the flora and fauna."

She started after him. "But how will I—"

He disappeared into thin air.

Isadora stared at the spot where he'd vanished, a terrible loneliness filling her chest. Maximillion might be the coldest witch she'd ever met, but at least he wasn't lying to her, even if he wanted nothing to do with her. He seemed to know something about her that she didn't know about herself yet.

Which may be my only hope.

THE SHELTER WAS an aged wooden structure near the stream, on the witches' side, halfway down the meadow. It had been built just after the Great Massacre over a century before. Knives, animal traps, leather bags made from lion skins, and an untold number of rusty nails filled the interior.

"The decline of the current generation is unaccountable," Finn Chandler drawled the next morning, shooting Sanna a passing glare when she stepped inside. "They don't care about anyone but themselves. Certainly not the dragons."

Finn, a Servant and second to Daid, sprawled out on a creaky wooden chair, his stump of a leg dangling off the edge. A bad encounter with a livid dragon, now dead, had cost him his leg from the knee down. He inspected a knife that cast prisms of light on the ceiling, where rusty traps hung from hooks. A bucket of rags sat in one corner, near a kettle of grease and a bottled cleaning potion.

"That's enough, Finn." Daid strode past.

Finn grinned at her, his thin, yellowed teeth gleaming.

Sanna hissed.

Fog obscured the view of the meadow from the window, blocking the wild dragon's prison on the far right. Sanna checked anyway, wishing it would clear. If she could just *see* him again, feel an inkling of the same confidence, she'd know she made the right decision. But the forest kept him from her.

That voice that had spoken to her. Where had it come from?

Daid tossed four marmot carcasses in a heap on the ground, then leaned both palms on the edge of the oak table in the middle of the room. No one seemed to mind the putrid stench of dead marmot, the foul creatures. Not even *they* could be left alone. The dragons would devour them, though they were reserved for the hatchlings.

Jesse pulled out a wooden chair, settling next to Sanna. "How is Isa?" he asked under his breath.

"Jolly."

Elliot, Jesse's father and the third Servant, stepped into the shelter behind his son. Sweat dripped down the sides of his round face, trickling into his patchy beard. "Sorry we're late," he said, wheezing. "Negris tangled himself in a curtain of stinging briars and almost blew fire. Forest would have gone up in a plume. Took us hours to get him free."

"Let's begin," Daid said.

He unrolled an oval map, weighting down the ends with two stones. It illustrated the northern section of the Central Network, where Letum Wood ran untamed. Anguis was in the upper-left corner of the sprawling forest. The rugged mountains of the Northern Network lingered above them, only a couple weeks' walk away. All of the Central Network lay to the south, but the map stopped right at the capital, Chatham City. Sanna didn't really care what lay outside the forest. Daid ran a hand over his face.

"We need new hunting ground."

"Don't bother," Finn called. "Drago is god of forest *and* dragons. He will provide food, even to the unfaithful."

"Drago provided my hog to the dragons last week," Elliot muttered.

"Our chickens," Daid said.

Finn snorted. "Sounds like you should have protected your animals better."

Sanna fumed, her fists clenched. She opened her mouth, but Jesse kicked her under the table and shook his head in a sharp back-and-forth. Elliot patted his sweaty forehead with a meaty arm, then jabbed a finger at a dot on the map. "We should move east, toward Berry. We can't go much farther west. Turns to sand out at the Borderlands, and we've already hunted the land between there and here."

"What about the Northern Network?" Jesse asked.

"Too cold," Daid said.

"Talis will never agree to move anyway." Finn picked at his nails with his knife.

"We've not been stationed *here* for all of the last two thousand years," Elliot snapped. "The Servants used to roam through the forests with the dragons. Haven't you read the Chronicles?"

"More than you, no doubt!"

"Silence, both of you," Daid said. "Bickering won't get us anywhere."

"What says Drago?" Finn asked.

Daid's lips pressed into a thin line. A flicker of something dark lingered in his eyes. "Drago remains silent on this matter."

Finn stabbed his knife into the tabletop and glanced at Sanna. "Drago will provide. Assuming he wants to save us at all, given the heathens in our midst."

Sanna's nails dug into her palms. She bit back a retort when Daid sent her a warning glare.

Daid turned back to the map with a frown. "Food is on the decline in this area; there's no denying. The forest lion attack proved that. We'll have a terrible winter if it continues. However, Drago has always provided in the past, and this *has* been our safest haven since the Great Massacre. Leaving it is no small task."

"Drago is not providing right now," Elliot said quietly. "Perhaps there is more to this than first meets the eye."

Daid shifted, the creases in his brow deepening.

"We're hunters, not leaders," Finn said. "The dragons only listen to Talis. Good luck convincing him to leave."

Elliot pointed a chubby finger at the area between Anguis and the Northern Network. "I propose we expand our trapping ground to the border of the Northern Network, and farther west. Jesse and I will scout it out and report next week."

"In the meantime, I'll speak with Talis," Daid said with a heavy frown. "If this new trapping area doesn't help, we may not have any choice."

Finn rapped on the table. "Agreed."

Elliot and Daid did the same.

It would be another week—possibly two—before they knew if it would be a sufficient step. Daid, with only Sanna for help, suffered the most. Elliot and Finn had other sons to help bear the burden of finding and trapping their share of the food. Now that Sanna had just pledged allegiance to a wild dragon?

No telling what would happen.

A glimmer of black and sunburnt orange broke through the mist, catching Sanna's eye. The dragon slept in his clear prison, tucked in a ball just inside the trees. He'd worn a track in the earth from pacing. Three fallen trees lay across the ground, covering a hole near the edge where he'd tried to dig himself out. His bright yellow eyes opened a slit, trapped hers for a heartbeat, and disappeared again.

Sanna turned away, her heart in her throat.

Did *he* hunt for himself? He must. Perhaps he would know where there was more food. Was there any way to ask him? Daid gathered the map and tucked it into a back pocket of his elaborate vest. He grabbed the carcasses and slung them over his shoulder.

Sanna moved to follow him, but he held out a hand.

"Not with me."

"But—"

He tossed her a leather satchel that had hung from the wall. "You're picking up dragon scales."

"That's a child's chore!"

"Not my punishment. If you don't like it, take it up with Talis."

She chased after him as he thudded down the three stairs leading off the shelter's porch. Her knee-high sandals slapped the wooden floor.

"Punishment for what?"

"For choosing a wild dragon."

"That's not against the rules! Not the official rules, anyway. And there aren't supposed to *be* wild dragons."

"It was an act of defiance."

"He needs to be tamed! What better way to prove that I can work with dragons than to actually tame him? I was trying to help the brood. Maybe this dragon can help us."

"I'm acting under Talis's orders. You'll pick up dragon scales until he says you can stop."

"Daid, wait. Please. I've waited for this my whole life. I had to choose him."

"Why?"

"Because I ... I just knew I was supposed to."

He snorted, striding into the trees. She had to run to keep up with him. Telling Daid she'd heard a voice telling her that the wild dragon was *hers*—whatever that meant— would only worsen an already horrible situation. Daid didn't approve of any magic that didn't come from Talis, and that voice *hadn't* been normal.

"Aren't you the least bit curious about him?" she asked. "He's been living out there all alone! He might even know where we could find food. Maybe he could hunt *for* us. He flies, after all. He—"

"Enough."

"But—"

"I said *enough*! Do you want Talis to hear you? Do you want him to think you're trying to stir up a mutiny?"

Sanna's mouth opened and closed. "I didn't mean to do that, Daid. I just ... I think he may know more than we're giving him credit for."

"Talis isn't going to trust any of your ideas right now. Certainly not as they pertain to the wild dragon."

"Maybe Thyris will listen to me."

"Did you think about what you've done to your relationship with Thyris? He chose you, Sanna; something he's never done before. You rejected him."

"But Daid!"

He whirled around. "You made a decision, and now you have to live with it."

She paused, stricken by the frustration in his eyes. Would he *ever* approve? Even if she'd chosen Thyris, he probably would have thought she should've had Talis choose her.

"Daid ... I'm sorry."

His shoulders fell. He closed his eyes for a long breath. When he opened them again, they'd hardened into discs of blue steel.

"Don't give Talis a reason to punish you. He was lenient when you crossed the stream. For some unknown reason, he's being easy on you now. You're lucky he hasn't kicked you out of Anguis for what you did. Let it go, Sanna. This is the way we do things. Change brings—"

"Disaster," she whispered.

With that, he strode onto a trail, leaving her stunned into silence.

A week later, Sanna stared at the wet, mulchy earth with a feeling of dread.

An old burlap bag hung over her shoulder, awaiting the dozens of dragon scales she'd fill it with. Her back ached from gathering the day before—and the five days before that. Black earth rimmed her fingernails permanently now, staining her skin. She didn't mind the dirt.

She hated the silence.

No hatchlings scampered her way. Sanna hadn't sought out Cara, Junis, or Rosy since the Selectis. She hadn't even gone into the trees on the dragon side, and she missed those paths in the upper canopy. Resigned, she scoured the forest floor again, head down and ears alert.

An hour later, when she overturned a fallen branch with a toe, the hair on the back of her neck rose. She stopped.

Something was watching her.

She ducked, backed into a tree, and scanned the canopy. No sign of movement, but lions rarely moved before they pounced. She stepped away, her feet cushioned by the pillow of pine needles on the forest floor. Then again, her great-uncle Trenton the Unsuspecting had died when—

Sanna gasped.

A feeling like a cold waterfall rushed down her shoulders and arms. She stumbled back, tripping over a tree root. Her arms wheeled as she fell onto the far bank of the stream, her head striking a rock. Water drenched her skirt and legs. She groaned. Pain reverberated through her skull in dull waves.

"*Mori,*" she muttered, gripping her head. "What—"

A cloud of heat hit her right in the face. Her eyes flew open. The wild dragon loomed over her, steam hissing between his teeth. She blinked. She must have—literally—stumbled into the magical prison. Could witches enter it?

Apparently.

"Ah." She winced. "Right, well ... *avay.*"

Threads of sunlight set fire to the coal-like scales on his forehead, which gave way to the diamond-shaped scales around his eyes. His chest rolled like thunder. He hadn't eaten her yet, which she took as a good sign.

She pushed herself back up to her feet. He didn't seem aggressive. At least, not in the same way he had been with Talis. Just ... curious.

The rumble in his chest moved up his throat. He snapped, stopping a breath away from her face. She stared at his pearly teeth with a wave of annoyance. If he hadn't flown into her life, everything would have been perfect. She would have worked with Thyris and been well on her way to earning her place as a respected Servant side-by-side with Daid.

"Calm down," she muttered. "I stumbled in here by accident, all right? I'm leaving. Assuming I can, anyway. I didn't even know I could come in here."

He shrieked, wings unfolding. She bared her teeth and growled back. His head tilted to the side. Water ran from her clothes in streams as she waded out of the water. He shot a plume of fire into the air above her. It crackled, consuming a small branch, charring it a thick black.

"Stop! You'll set the forest on fire."

He closed his mouth. For a long stretch of time, they studied each other. Cara and the hatchlings aside, she'd never been this close to a dragon for so long. If he wasn't actually violent, why snap at her? Why throw fire? Was he testing her? No. Dragons didn't *test* witches. They didn't even like them.

"Well," she said. "You're not so scary."

He yawned, showing rows of shining teeth. She'd expected him to be ... different. Uncontrolled, perhaps. Maybe half-crazed. But he seemed like a normal forest dragon. Indifferent expression. Sleeping in the middle of the day.

A loud gurgle from his cavernous chest startled her.

"*Mori.* Was that your stomach?"

He snarled.

"Oh. You're hungry."

The wild dragon snorted flames. She ducked.

"Stop already! If enough trees catch fire, all the deadfall in this place will burn in seconds."

She motioned to the forest with a wave of her arm, then stopped. Something behind the wild dragon caught her gaze. Her head tilted to the side.

"What the ..."

Sanna advanced a few steps into the prison, dumbstruck. Flecks of black, charred wood were scattered across the ground. The bushes were gone, yanked free and burned to ash. Three old trees had fallen—score marks circled the bottoms where he'd attacked with his talons until they fell. Only their burned husks remained.

Even the grass had been clawed, dirt churned up, old twigs burned. The meadow aside, she hadn't seen this much *dirt* anywhere else in the forest, where piles of old trees, dead bushes, and more littered the ground. In fact, she'd never seen something quite so organized.

She whipped back around. "You *burned* all this?"

He acted as if he hadn't heard her. Overhead, a squirrel chittered, hopping across a branch. He snatched it and swallowed without chewing. She ducked, narrowly avoiding pieces of falling tree. Most dragons ate every three to five days. On Talis's orders, he hadn't eaten once since they'd put him in the prison seven days before. No doubt Talis planned to starve him into giving his allegiance to the brood. Dragons were finicky when hungry.

Dismissing the strange, cleared space as a weird quirk, Sanna motioned to the creek with a tilt of her head.

"You ... ah ... want a toad?"

He snorted.

Taking it as a *yes*, Sanna stepped back, still facing him, until water lapped her ankles again. Once there, she studied the bank. The stream tinkled over rocks and mossy boulders in a lazy flow. She bent down and dangled her fingertips in the water. If toads had any brains at all—which she couldn't imagine—none would be this close to a dragon or its fire. The dragon pretended to lick one of his talons, but his eyes flickered toward her every few seconds. He slowly advanced to the edge of the stream, poised like a cat ready to pounce.

Sanna dug into the soft mud, poking around moldering logs and peering underneath stones. She found slugs the color of a summer sky and a handful of small fish. The wild dragon lay down as if he meant to sleep, but his gaze never faltered. He twitched when she stumbled over a turtle and struggled to pull a leech off her thumb. Just when she was ready to give up, a strange mound caught her gaze.

Then it blinked.

"*Avay,*" she sang under her breath, picking up a stick from the forest floor.

The wild dragon's ears perked up. Sanna whacked the slimy toad, stunning it. Its long legs dangled out of her hand when she plucked it from the dirt, exultant. Muddy water trickled down her arms in a cool stream.

"Here you are!"

The dragon leapt to his feet, wings perched. Sanna tossed the toad with a shout of glee. He caught it, swallowing it whole.

"Nothing better than toad first thing in the morning. I—"

A roar rippled through the air. Thyris.

The wild dragon whipped around, facing the meadow, and growled. His wings unfurled. His nostrils flared.

In a panic, Sanna felt for the edge of the prison and stuck her hand through it. She threw herself to the other side of the bank, slipped on a rock, and stumbled out of the water. The ground trembled as she scrambled up, reaching for her dropped satchel.

An enraged scream rose from the left.

Sanna tripped over a patch of moss, landing flat on her face, a hand's breadth from the bag. She blinked, dazed, until she saw a telltale glimmer of black in front of her. With a grunt, she grabbed a dragon scale from beneath a layer of dirt and yanked it free. When she spun around, Thyris hovered over her. She held up the scale.

"Talis's orders!"

He snorted. The wild dragon was nowhere to be seen. Thyris glanced around, sniffing. Finally, he lowered his wings. Casting one last venomous glance at her, then at the magical prison, he backed away. Sanna waited until he was gone before she dropped her head back.

"Mori."

The quiet sounds of Letum Wood returned. The gentle soughing of wind in the highest treetops. A chittering bird. The distant squeal of a screaming gnome hunting for lady-bugs. Sanna stood up and shouldered her pack.

Just before rounding the bend in the stream, she glanced back. A glint of marmalade set amidst black scales winked from the thick underbrush. The wild dragon peered at her, his nose tucked into his tail, which curled around his body. When he saw her, he narrowed his eyes to a thin line of sandy yellow.

THREE DAYS LATER, Sanna yawned and rubbed her bleary eyes. She sat on top of the shelter table, her petal skirt betraying bare knees that would have made Mam faint. She readjusted her sandal strap where it wound up her calf, digging into the skin, and fought off another yawn.

A rainy day unfurled overhead, dawning over the bruised-green meadow. Steam billowed from the wild dragon's prison as the raindrops fell on him, unabated. No doubt he was still curled on the ground, still as death. Dragons hated water—the rain was akin to torture. Ten days in captivity, a full day of deluge, and only a few toads to eat had made him surlier than ever. Until he submitted to Talis, he'd continue to go hungry. She couldn't fault his stubbornness.

He'd probably die from it.

Unfortunately, she had the feeling that Talis was waiting to see what happened before he decided what to do with her. Sanna jumped when a loud *bang* clattered next to her. An iron trap dropped on the table as Daid strode past.

"Why are you so tired?" He moved toward a half-filled bucket of water hanging from a peg on the far wall.

She curled her dirt-crusted fingers into her palms to hide them. "Ah ... didn't sleep well."

"Really?" He frowned. "You went to bed an hour early."

Sanna crossed her muddy ankles and tucked them under the table. Daid wouldn't appreciate her sneaking off every evening and morning for the past five days to hunt for toads to feed to the wild dragon. But she couldn't just let him starve, even if Talis had ordered it to *teach him his place*.

"What's wrong with the trap?" she asked.

If Daid noticed the change in subject, he gave no sign. "Broken. I think a screaming gnome did it."

Ragged teeth, as if taken from a monster, poked out of the trap, ready to snap at the first opportunity. A metallic scent filled the air. Sanna touched a dried drop of blood along the blade. One of the levers controlling the sharp jaws of the trap had split, making it unusable.

"Setting traps today?" she asked.

"Yes."

"A bit boring, isn't it?"

"Boring work is the most important kind."

"I thought Servants would have a bit more excitement," she mumbled. "Like fighting off animals or putting out fires or something."

"Good luck finding a fire in this weather."

Daid rummaged through a cupboard, his shirt hanging loosely off his shoulders, falling in folds where it once hugged his chest. Their meager meal last night—a few roasted turnips, a shared cucumber, and the last of the apple preserves, had left all of them unsatisfied. Not hungry, but not full, either.

A collection of leather bags, a pile of dirty rags, and three folding scythes lay on the table. The thick scythes were Daid's favorite hunting weapon. Sanna preferred poisonous darts. Coils of steel-braided rope hung from wooden nails in the wall. She liked those too. He grabbed one and flung it over his shoulder.

"Daid, when can I come with you? I've gathered every scale in Anguis."

"When Talis says you can."

"That could be never."

"Could."

A distant sound caught Sanna's ear. She frowned. "What was that?"

Daid's head whipped toward the door. "A dragon."

"Injured?"

"Sounds like it."

Sanna leaped off the table. An answering roar followed, louder this time.

"Pera," Daid said, grabbing a scythe. Pera, a white dragon. She'd just laid two eggs only three days before. "Stay here, Sanna."

Daid darted into the rain. Sanna hesitated, then plunged into the forest behind him. Legs pumping, she flew down the foot trails, trying to keep up with his faster pace. The shrieks strengthened.

The ground trembled. Sanna skidded to a stop at an ancient oak she knew well. It spanned broader than Talis, growing so high she'd only reached the top once. She scrambled up the trunk before Daid saw her.

From the lowest branch—which looked down at least thirty paces—she caught glimpses of a dragon fight through the thick, cluttered undergrowth. Rain had long since saturated everything, leaving the forest as limp as a dishrag.

Pera stood in front of a mossy cave, her teeth bared. Rain ran down her hot scales, steaming upward in a misty cloud. Her short, unfurled wings blocked the cave entrance. Another female dragon, Ivis, nipped at the edges of Pera's wing. Pera screamed, slashing at Ivis with a talon. Blood dribbled down Pera's foreleg in a blue river, trickling into the dirt.

Daid and Finn stood below Sanna's tree limb.

"Ivis's weak hatchlings have driven her almost mad

with desperation, I think," Finn said. "The fifth one just died last month."

"Talis warned me she might try something," Daid said. "Yet again."

"Talis is going to have to do something. This is her third attempt to steal."

Despite her small wingspan and usually gentle temperament, Pera sent Ivis reeling with a blow from her thick tail. Ivis rushed forward, throwing her meaty flank into Pera's body. Pera's left wing crashed into the cave wall with a sickening *crack*. Sanna dug her fingers into the tree to keep herself from jumping down and breaking the fight apart.

Ivis charged again, jamming her head into Pera's broken wing. While Pera screamed, Ivis angled her tail into the cave. Her back leg followed. She shoved her way in, snapping as Pera's attempts to defend herself grew weaker.

Sanna balled her hands into fists. Ivis was going to steal —or harm—those eggs. Why didn't Daid *do* something already? What good was being a Servant if they just waited for the dragons to fix everything?

Unable to bear another moment, Sanna grabbed a vine and dropped to the ground, snatching a fist-sized rock. A cold hand gripped her wrist just before she threw it.

"Stop."

Finn loomed over her, tall and spindly. He sniffed. Daid was gone.

"She's going to kill Pera!" Sanna growled, trying to wrench free. "The eggs will die."

He pointed to the forest just behind the cave.

"Look, you idiot."

Three dragons appeared in the murky air, running on all fours. Talis, Thyris, and Rubeis.

Pera collapsed when they sprinted out of the fog. Talis grabbed Ivis's neck with his teeth, and Rubeis snagged her tail. Together, they jerked her out of the cave.

Once free, Ivis attempted to bolt with a terrified shriek, but Talis grabbed one of her wings, jerked it back, and slammed her to the ground. For a long pause, they stared at each other, speaking to each other's minds.

A hot silence swelled.

Ivis's wild eyes relaxed. Talis's wings slackened, allowing the tension to ebb away. Sanna released the vine. Perhaps Talis had more mercy than she'd expected. At least—

Talis tore into Ivis's neck with a savage snap of his teeth.

Ivis screamed. Blood gushed in torrents from the wide wound in her neck. Talis snapped a second time, anchoring his teeth into her flesh.

Ivis flailed.

Sanna bit back a scream when Talis jerked hard. Bones cracked.

Ivis stilled.

"Talis takes care of the dragons," Finn whispered. "It's not your job to interfere. You'd know that if you had an ounce of sense. Servants have been killed for less."

"He killed her."

"She had plenty of warnings."

"But..."

Her words trailed off in a haze of confusion. But dragons were precious and rare. There were only twenty-seven—now twenty-*six*—in all of Alkarra. Drago cared for them personally. Did *Drago* approve so drastic a measure for a mourning mam? Ivis's desperation didn't justify stealing an egg, but neither did her behavior necessitate murder.

"Those are Rubeis's hatchlings," Finn said. "If Talis hadn't killed her, Rubeis may have."

Sanna scowled, yanked from her spiral of thoughts by his nasally tone. She forced herself to turn away, ignoring the blood dripping from Talis's mouth. Rubeis stood over Pera, licking her injured wing as Daid approached the dragons.

Talis dipped his head to Daid, then looked toward Finn and Sanna. Daid followed his gaze, frowning when he saw Sanna there.

She stiffened.

He glared, then turned away, pressing his hand into Talis's snout before dropping to a knee. Within a few seconds, Daid stood back up again.

"Sanna," he called. "Talis gives you permission to approach and learn while I set Pera's bones."

Sanna obeyed, giving a wide berth to Talis, her throat tight. Trampled saplings littered the ground as she cautiously navigated fallen vines and branches.

"Pay attention," Daid said once she stood at his side. "But don't touch her."

The ridge of bone at the top of Pera's shredded wing had shifted, broken in three spots. Blood cascaded from it in thick, rich blue rivulets. Daid's eyes narrowed as he examined the wounds, rain hammering his face.

"The skin will heal overnight, and the scales will grow after that. But I'm afraid we'll have to reset these bones right now. Do you have an open wound on your hand?"

She held them out for his inspection. "No."

"We can't take the risk of your blood mixing with Pera's and bonding the two of you."

Daid pulled a thick pair of gloves over his hands and set a gentle hand on Pera's flank. Her groans dissipated into quiet moans. Daid looked at Talis, who nodded.

"I have to climb onto her back to reach her wings," Daid said. "Don't follow. She's not as hot as the males but could still burn you."

Sanna chewed the inside of her cheek. "What about you?"

"My pants and shoes are reinforced with layers of forest-lion leather. I'll be fine."

"When do I get a pair of *those*?"

"When you've earned them. I'll reset the bones and then jump off. She'll be all right in four or five days."

"It only takes four days? *Mori.*"

"Pay attention. You'll have to reset the next broken dragon bone. And stop swearing."

Daid gently climbed up Pera's back and onto her shoulder and gripped either side of the first broken bone segment. He slid them together with a grunt.

Pera flailed.

Daid flew back, sliding down her scales, and landed in the mud at Sanna's feet. He stood up, brushed his pants off, and cracked his neck.

"Two more."

Sanna drank in every detail. Daid's confident movements. The way the dragons stared at him. Pera's trusting moans. He worked efficiently and with great skill. She'd never seen him so firmly in his element. So absolutely certain. By the time he stepped away, Pera had fallen into a shallow sleep. Rubeis stood over her, glaring into the forest. No one would steal his eggs now.

A jolt ripped through her.

"The eggs!" she cried. "Daid, can I check them?"

Talis nodded before Daid could ask permission. It would be far easier for a witch to go gently into the cave and pull the eggs out for inspection. Caves were rare in Anguis, most of them created by Talis and other dragons out of rock formations and massive boulders. There were only three here, two saved especially for mams with eggs and one for the brood leader.

Sanna crept into the steamy darkness. Daid advanced behind her. A glittering, opalescent egg lay off to the side, half in the rain.

"Pick it up. Carefully," Daid said.

Sanna bent down, scooping the warm egg into her arms. It spanned the length of her waist and weighed as heavy as a bag of apples, but she carried it with certain steps. Outside, Rubeis shuffled toward her, sniffing.

"Give it to him," Daid said.

Sanna set it at Rubeis's feet. He breathed on it. The egg flared with a swirl of colors, glowing like a rainbow coal. For a brief moment, the outline of a tiny dragon stirred inside. Rubeis tucked it under Pera's leg with an affectionate grunt.

"Sanna," Daid called from just inside the cave. "Come."

She stepped back, and a cry lodged in her throat. A mangled, cracked egg lay in the middle of the floor, near the back of the cave. Several broken, opalescent shards revealed the tiny head of a new baby dragon. Liquid dribbled down the sides, forming a puddle. Sanna dropped to her knees.

"Ivis trampled it," she whispered.

The scaly head, free of horns, was as large as her hand. A female. Tiny slits for eyes. Scales the size of her smallest fingernail. Wings barely larger than her forearm lay flaccid against a little body. The hatchling didn't move. The faintest strands of crimson ran through the scales like miniature blood veins. She would have been a beautiful dragon.

Daid gathered the hatchling with a gentle touch, extracting it from the broken egg. He stood. The gray, murky light behind him accentuated his proud chin and strong shoulders. A tiny wing fell loose across his arm, limp in death.

"Change brings disaster. Remember that next time you're bored."

Sanna trekked behind Daid to the shelter, her mind buzzing. A prickle raced up her back. She looked up to see the wild dragon staring at her through the mist. He lay near the prison wall, his head resting on the ground. Talis slipped into the forest next to her, blood still trickling down his jaw, trees *swishing* in his wake.

The wild dragon closed his eyes and turned away.

CHAPTER
FIVE

The first day of fall dawned with bright sunshine. Beams of light twinkled through the canopy, slowly warming the forest and igniting the furnace of pain in Isadora's mind. The pain that had been there since she'd last spoken with Maximillion. When she'd begged off seeing Babs because of the sheer agony and Mam had reluctantly complied, ordering her upstairs with thin lips and a frown.

The pain that hadn't left her since.

An escalating headache plagued her all night, worsening right as day broke. It ebbed enough for her to crawl out of bed mid-morning. She lurched downstairs, eyes clenched, moving one painful step at a time. Mam had already left—to who knew where. They spoke only out of necessity these days, which often meant not at all.

Isadora hadn't seen Sanna for three days now. She crept away at the strangest hours, returning late at night, filthy and wet.

Isadora sank down at the bottom of the stairs and pressed a hand to her temple. When she thought she couldn't bear another moment, a soft rap sounded at the back door.

"Isadora? Roxy?"

Isadora's stomach clenched. Lucey. Why was Lucey here?

Gritting her teeth, she stood and shuffled toward the back door. She fumbled for the doorknob, and a rush of warm air slipped over her when the door opened.

"Isadora?" Lucey asked. "The good gods! What's happened to you?"

"*Avay,*" she croaked.

"Here. You need to sit down."

Lucey grabbed Isadora's arms, directing her back to the table. Isadora sank into the chair with relief.

"A headache again?" Lucey asked.

"Y-yes."

"They're getting worse, aren't they? Much worse. The good gods, look at you."

Isadora peeled her eyes open, but fuzzy black spots filled her vision. She quickly closed them, clutching Lucey's arm for support.

"Lucey, I-I can't see."

A long pause.

"I'm going to leave for just a moment, Isadora. I'll be right back. Don't move. Just stay here on the chair. I'll only be gone a little bit."

With a gentle sigh, the room went silent. No footsteps departed. The door didn't open and close. But Isadora could *feel* that Lucey was gone. She must have used magic. Minutes later, the rustle of someone moved toward her again.

"Isadora," Lucey said. "I'm back. Maximillion is—"

"Here."

His cool voice sent a ripple of dread through Isadora. She swallowed. Not him. Not here. Not *now* of all times.

"Your headaches are worse," he said.

"Much worse," she whispered.

Two warm fingertips pressed into the sides of her head. Lines appeared in her mind like crackles of lightning. They funneled the pain toward his hand. The pressure faded slightly, taking the edge off, but the fog continued to eddy through her mind. When she opened her eyes, the black spots had disappeared. A strange halo of light surrounded Maximillion, blurring the normally sharp edges of his constant disapproval.

"The headaches should be strong," he murmured, "but not *this* strong. How long have they been like this?"

"I don't ... I can't think..."

"Stop. You'll hurt yourself. You're very close, I think."

"What is happening?"

"A baptism of pain." He was frowning in earnest now. "Although I must admit, I've not seen it this intense before."

"Make it stop?"

"It's nothing that I can control."

His voice came from a distant place. A fuzzy tunnel. The sound of a scraping broke through the haze, but Isadora was sinking into the pain. Lucey stood next to Maximillion now.

"What can I do?"

"Keep a close eye," Maximillion said. "Something's wrong. Might destroy her before it manifests. Roughest transition I've ever seen."

"It can destroy her? You never told me that!"

"Has before. We'll find out soon enough."

"If it does?"

"She'll die."

"What do I tell her parents then? Roxy already loathes me."

"Tell them that the headaches have taken a turn for the worse, and there's nothing more to do but wait it out. Tell them you've done all the potions you know, or something to that effect. Put her in bed. She'll pass out soon. I've seen it plenty of times now. Let's just hope she wakes up. She's no good to anyone dead."

Maximillion's voice died away. The raging storm turned into a silent wall of black, and Isadora faded into the oblivion with relief.

A LEAF DRIFTED from the canopy of branches above Sanna, landing in her strawberry-blonde hair. She crouched on a high tree branch near the far edge of the meadow, hidden in the leaves above the wild dragon's prison. The burble of the barely visible creek passed far beneath her. The wild dragon lay on the ground in an unmoving black ball with his wing tucked over his face.

She dropped two toads. They squished, dead, on the ground next to him. His wing lifted. A forked tongue flickered out, and his neck extended slowly before he nibbled at the morsels.

"*Mori,*" she muttered. "Talis really is going to starve him."

She'd been hoping Talis would break first. That he'd feed the wild dragon before it died, but more than two weeks had passed, and no food had been offered. Anxiety filled Sanna's chest when she recalled the dead hatchling in Daid's arms. Ivis's blood gushing out of her wounded neck. The vicious descent of Talis's wrath. Talis doled out life and death to dragons without hesitation, but she couldn't just let the wild dragon *die*.

She couldn't kill an animal big enough to save him from starvation, either. Talis would likely kill *her* for going against the brood again. Or worse—banish her. Sanna quirked her lips to one side of her face. Would Talis kill a Servant as readily as he killed a dragon?

Probably.

Above her, a branch groaned, creaking as it swayed. She tilted her head back, peering into the canopy. After so many weeks of not eating, the wild dragon would need a demmed pack of forest lions to walk into his prison.

She froze.

A pack of forest lions.

With a muted cry, she leapt back to her feet and dashed away.

LETUM WOOD HAD a fathomless depth at night. A strange sense of the surreal.

Sanna perched on a high branch and clicked her teeth in time to her heartbeat. Her thoughts buzzed in a spectacular, wild mess. Could she really pull her plan off? Would the wild dragon have enough energy to do his part?

Sanna shook her head, forcing her mind back to the task. Once Daid's candle went out in the bedroom, she dropped to the ground. She landed silently and stole over to the hunting shed, choking at the smell of rotting carcasses.

She grimaced, lifted her shirt over her nose, and threw open the door. Her eyes watered when she reached for a brace of marmots Daid had caught on the trapline earlier in the day. He'd hung them up to ferment overnight for the hatchlings, who preferred them smelly and stiff. She kept herself from gagging by sheer willpower.

Once she closed the shed behind her, she reached into her pocket and rubbed a few herbs on her chest, feet, hands, and underarms to conceal her scent. Then she tied the carcasses to her waist and silently skirted up a tree. The dead animals thumped along behind her.

She climbed as high as she could go, stepped onto a branch, and started walking. Verdant moss trailed the branches, dripping in virescent curtains. She knew every path along the high canopy by heart, having navigated their crisscrossing branches with ease for years. The wide branches, sometimes twice as wide as she was tall, provided ample room. The dead animals dragged beyond her, scattering their wretched scent.

In the folds of darkness, life appeared. A set of winking blue eyes. The low croon of an owl. A sudden flap of wing. Hisses and shuffles. The sounds were oddly comforting, for no real predators—dragons aside—usually bothered Anguis. She hoped the forest lions' previous desperation would serve her now.

When she heard the distant roar of a forest lion, she swung the brace of marmots against a tree trunk with a satisfying *thunk*.

"Come, come," she sang.

An hour passed. Then another. She covered a wide circle that slowly spiraled inside itself. By the time midnight came, her muscles dragged, and her brain felt like mush. The scent of rot permanently filled her nose.

"*Mori,*" she muttered, wiping sweat off her brow. Her dress clung to her skin, saturated. She longed for a cool drink of water as she swept aside a drape of leaves. Below, the faint sound of the stream trickled by. She picked her way across the branches, using vines to bridge the greatest gaps, anticipating the cool rush of magic at any moment. Two steps later, it swept through her limbs. She shuddered.

Finally. The wild dragon's prison.

Sanna clutched the brace as she worked her way down the tree. Every now and then, the ground peeked up at her through the boughs. Greater gaps existed in the branches here, certainly thinner than the clogged forest floor, where deadfall cluttered the ground in piles. When she was still over a hundred paces from the ground, she tied the brace to a limb, anchored the stiff marmots to the trunk, and pulled herself back to a higher branch. A thick groove in the trunk protected her as she wiggled inside.

In the strange quiet that followed, Sanna counted her heartbeats. Her eyelids grew heavy. Flecks of dried marmot blood covered the backs of her legs. She studied branches, the grooves, the ants scuttering by. But the forest was so warm, and the darkness so sweet ...

A twig snapped.

Sanna jerked awake. The hair on the back of her neck stood on end. Except for a strange, putrid scent, nothing had changed. No breeze. No hint of life. Then a rolling purr sounded above her. Sanna's head snapped up.

She stared right into the pearly teeth of a forest lion.

"*Mori!*"

She leaped out of the wedged space and off the limb just as the lion dropped, its sinewy tail wrapped around a branch above it. Her ankle twisted as she landed hard on a bough. The moss gave way beneath her, and she plummeted to another branch. Her ribs stung when she landed on her side. She scrambled for a hold, the tips of her right hand barely gripping a smaller limb at the last second. For a long moment, she dangled there, attempting to catch her breath again with deep, shocked gasps.

Her chest flared with pain.

The lion had disappeared but returned seconds later in a flash of brown fur overhead.

"Ah!"

Sanna dropped onto a lower branch, then rolled to the side just as four paws landed where she'd been. The lion roared, its trailing, shaggy mane brushing the moss. Sanna scrambled back, heading toward the end of the limb.

"Any day now, dragon," she called, glancing down. Perhaps she should have told him her plan, but there hadn't been time, nor opportunity. When she'd left at dinnertime, Talis had stood by the prison again, staring at it with his queer, intelligent gaze.

No movement shifted from the ground now, but the wild dragon couldn't have missed the forest lions' nasty smell. Saliva dripped from the lion's mouth as he stalked toward her, a low purr in his throat.

"Wake up, you stupid dragon!" she bellowed.

Her toe caught on a knot. She stumbled backward just as the lion lunged. She ducked, avoiding the pounce, and skittered back toward the trunk. While the lion spun around, strangely agile on the slick branches, she ripped a dead bough off the tree and swung. He batted it away with a paw the size of a dinner plate. It fell, clattering to the branch below, right in front of another lion, twice the size of the first, with meaty shoulders and paws the size of her face.

Another hiss sounded. And another.

Sanna looked up. Four forest lions surrounded her from above. One on her branch. At least one below.

"*Mori*," she whispered.

A damning silence prevailed; forest lions always went silent before attacking.

"No!"

With a cry, she threw her hands up and ducked. A heavy weight slammed into her back, driving her onto the branch. Pain spiraled through her chest. Claws sank into her right shoulder and tore down, through her back, like fingers of fire. She threw her head back and screamed. The lion's weight shifted, and Sanna rolled free.

She existed for a mere moment in the air, plummeting toward a hard fall, when a flare of heat stopped her. Fire wrapped around her waist, jerking her upward again.

She cracked her eyes open to find the wild dragon's talons around her waist. His sinewy body wound through the massive tree, snaking toward the lions, nearly imperceptible in the dark. Heat seeped through her clothes. She cried out when her skin started to burn. Her head spun. Blood trickled down her back, saturating her clothes. No matter how hard she tried, she couldn't get enough air. The pain.

The agonizing pain.

The dragon snatched the biggest lion and broke its neck in one shake, then dropped it. The others dodged into the canopy, but a plume of fire caught two of them. Their fur burst into flames. One stumbled, roaring, and fell off a branch. The dragon snaked his head through the limbs, catching it mid-fall. The sound of crunching bones preceded total silence.

The dragon tossed it with a growl, his eyes pinpricks. His nostrils flared as he faced the remaining lion, who backed away, hissing, ears flattened.

With a snap, the dragon silenced the beast. A heavy *thud* followed.

Sticky blood seeped through Sanna's shoulder and down the small of her back. Her chest burned like dragon fire with every breath. Something was wrong. Something was *very* wrong. No matter how hard she breathed, she couldn't get enough air. Her chest burned. The weightless sensation of flying overcame her.

Her toes, her fingers, even her face tingled. Darkness edged around the sides of her vision.

She knew, right then, she wouldn't make it.

Everything went black.

SIX

Isadora jerked awake with a gasp.

She stood in a circle of twelve sprawling, gargantuan trees. They spiraled so high she couldn't see where they ended. Two full houses could fit in their trunks —and then some. Their roots stood as tall as she, stretching into the earth with knobby, searching knuckles. The rich canopy, the subdued sunlight, and the foggy forest comforted her.

Letum Wood.

"Hello?" she called. The sound faded. Had she died?

A thick, glowing trail snaked into the distance. She started on it, then hesitated and reached out. Her fingertips ran down the surface of a nearby root, but she couldn't feel it.

She wasn't really there, wherever she was.

Pulled by an unknown power, Isadora stepped onto the trail. Fog filled the empty space between trees. She moved slowly. No birds. No animals. Not even flowers dotting the ground. Just the ancient trees.

She stopped when a bluish light appeared a few paces

to the right. It shimmered near the ground in a vague shape that coalesced into something else. Her eyes narrowed.

"Sanna?"

Sanna's face appeared from the fog, formed from the vague, blue light. In the image, she lay on the ground, her face contorted in a grimace. A thick, crimson stain seeped across her shoulder. Blood. The rest of her body faded into the strange vapor.

"Sanna!"

Isadora reached out, but her fingers combed through mist that gathered back together in a swirl. Another burst of light drew Isadora's eyes higher up the trail. Another cloudy wisp just down the path.

"Magic."

How could it not be? The feeling bathed her skin. Coated her in the strange way she'd always imagined it would.

She ran, skidding to a stop at the next image. Sanna again. The agony on her face was frozen in a strange, vaporish texture. Fog slipped through Isadora's fingers when she touched Sanna's cheek.

Movement caught her attention again. The trail split into two separate directions ahead, but each widened with every passing second. Sanna appeared on both paths.

The trail on the right hinted at something else. It blanched white as if exposed to great light. Fire?

As soon as Isadora stepped closer, another image popped up behind the first. She blinked. Daid. Only part of his face was shown, the rest faded. Something sparkled on his cheek. A tear?

Isadora spun on the trail, head tilted back.

"Where am I?" she called. "What's happening to me?"

The sound echoed, lost in the strange cavern of trees.

Not a bird. Not a gnome. Not a single call in the underbrush. She swallowed, her throat thick. Was she lost in a nightmare?

The trail split again, this time diverging into five different footpaths. Nothing filled those paths, which dissipated into mere lines in the ground. Isadora whirled around, lost amongst the grainy, strange images. She tried to pick her way back, but images arose around her until she felt lost. Isadora sprinted through them, her chest heaving, lost in the surreal wildness.

"Get me out of here!" she screamed.

Moments later, she found the scene with Sanna on the ground again. A second trail to the left beckoned her with a bright flash. A new wisp. Her heart leapt into her throat.

Sanna lay on the ground, her expression slack. No other trails sprang from this one. A thick mist of darkness overtook the path.

Isadora screamed.

Isadora jolted awake with a gasp.

The old wooden beams of the attic immediately comforted her. A cold sweat had left the sheets and pillow damp on the back of her neck. Her body trembled, rattling like she had a fever, draining her energy. She rubbed her forehead, pulling the scattered pieces of her mind back together.

Paths.

Sanna.

Darkness.

With a cry, Isadora threw the blanket off her legs and scrambled free. She stopped dead. A figure sat at the edge of Sanna's bed, cloaked in shadows.

"Now you know," Maximillion murmured.

"W-w-what's happened to me?"

"I'll explain later. You must come with me now."

"But—"

"Do you want to change the world? Do you want to be free?" He leaned toward her, his words a hot challenge. "Do you want to do magic or not?"

Isadora's breath hitched, startled by the intensity of his bright gaze. Her fear dissipated. She'd found her path, hadn't she? Or perhaps it had been given to her. There was no more life for her in Anguis that wouldn't be miserable and riddled with more failure—the quiet village would never be enough for her. Not when the tingle of magic still hummed in her veins. Not when she could conquer something else.

"Yes," she whispered.

"Good." He stood. "Then let's go."

"Wait." She lifted her chin. "Not until I find my sister."

A PINCHING sensation nipped at Sanna's ribs. It woke her before slowly rolling to her shoulder and then down her spine, prickling like a bird pecking at her skin.

After it faded, warmth flooded her body like a languid bath. So warm. So *inviting*.

No. Wait. Too warm. It was getting *too* warm. She tried to roll away but couldn't move. The heat crescendoed until it boiled against her skin. She shifted, a cry lodged in her throat.

"No." She thrashed. "Too hot!"

The sensation scalded her chest and her back, erupting in an explosive wreath of flames within. Knives stabbed her heart. Pressure constricted her lungs. The heat would consume her at any moment. Destroy her. Rip her from the tendrils of—

It stopped.

The pain collected into a point over her spine, gathering like veins, then suddenly fading. Her panic ebbed. No agony remained. Her lungs expanded in wide, delicious breaths. Her heart slowed.

She groaned and tried to roll onto her side but couldn't. While lying there, trying to surface out of the deep, murky shadows of confusion, her memory returned all at once.

Letum Wood. Lions. Wild dragon. Death.

Sanna sat up, gasping.

The wild dragon loomed over her like a blazing coal, eyes narrowed in assessment. He nudged her with the edge of his snout, blowing warm air on her. She shrank back.

"Your breath smells terrible."

The dragon snorted and moved away, allowing Sanna's focus to strengthen. Blood stained the ground. Tufts of a ragged, curly mane lay in wild curls around her. The end of a lion's tail dangled from a piece of bark, near two detached claws tossed behind a rock on the ground. She blinked, her mental faculties warming. The wild dragon had demolished three adult forest lions. Maybe unconsciousness wasn't the worst thing.

The *smell* on the other hand...

Her hand flew to her shoulder with a gasp. No pain. She could breathe freely; her lungs worked again. The forest lion had shredded her shoulder and back, but no wound remained. How could that be possible? When she pulled her hand away, a silvery blue substance filled her palm. Her stomach turned cold. She turned to the wild dragon in horror.

Dragon's blood.

"Oh, no," she whispered. "Did you—"

"Sanna!"

Daid burst through the prison wall, his breathing ragged. He looked from the dragon to her and back to the dragon. The wild dragon hissed, his lips curling up over his teeth, and slithered between Sanna and Daid.

Daid's nostrils flared when he looked at Sanna's bloody hand. He paled.

"Please," he whispered. "Don't tell me you bonded with him."

"Bonded?"

"His blood!" Daid cried, driving a hand through his hair. "Did he give you his blood?"

"I ... I don't know. Maybe. I just ... I just woke up and—"

"Is that his blood?" he demanded, stalking toward her.

The wild dragon growled, shifting to block him.

"I think so," she said. "Let Daid through!"

With a reluctant hiss, the wild dragon stepped aside.

"What happened?" Daid asked, crossing the singed grasses. "Why are you covered in blood?"

"It all happened so fast. I ... Daid, I was dying and..."

A distant shriek rippled through Letum Wood. Daid jerked up, looking into the trees in horror. A deep, reverberating bellow followed.

Daid grabbed her shoulder, shoving her toward the trees. "Go!"

The wild dragon advanced again with a snap. Daid

released her and stepped back, hands in front of him in a placating gesture. Sanna moved between them.

"Daid, what's wrong?"

"Leave!"

"Why?"

"Get out of Anguis right now. Talis is going to kill you."

"Kill me? But Daid, I..."

"You've bonded with the wild dragon! There's no changing it. When Talis finds out ... if you leave the village, there's a chance, with time, he'll..."

His panicked words faded into the background. She whipped around, staring at the wild dragon, who met her gaze without fear. Her mouth opened and closed, but no sounds came out.

Bonded with the wild dragon.

She closed her eyes, remembering Pera's attack and Daid's paranoia about her touching dragon blood with a wound of her own. But what did *bonding* even mean? Only Daid was bonded with Talis. Wasn't only a brood leader able to do it? She gathered up the courage to slug the dragon right in the face, but the panic of not being able to breathe, the moment of her probable death, played back through her mind.

It hadn't been that simple. She would have died if he hadn't used his blood to heal her. The wild dragon hadn't just bonded with her—he'd saved her. Now Talis would kill her.

Really, the wild dragon had both saved—and ended— her life.

There was too much to comprehend. Too much change. Sanna swallowed.

"A-all right, Daid. I'll go. I—"

A tearing sound rent the air, followed by a bellow that

shook the ground. The prison walls split, cascading down like gossamer petals. Sanna ducked away from a wall of fire that swept out from the trees. A flash of bruised blue flickered in the corner of her eyes.

Talis.

The wild dragon threw himself into the flames, blocking them with his body.

Daid fell. Sanna stumbled back, protected from burns by the wild dragon's extended wing.

"Talis!" Daid cried, scrambling to his feet. "Wait!"

Daid darted past the crouched wild dragon, arms held high. Talis stopped, drawing himself higher. His eyes fell on Sanna and the dragon blood dripping down her shoulder and back. He snarled. Snatches of gold and red glittered behind him.

The wild dragon growled back, his lips pulled up over his teeth.

Daid fell to his knees between the two beasts. Talis pressed his snout into Daid's outstretched hand but kept his livid glare on the wild dragon. An eternity seemed to pass.

Sanna held her breath until she grew dizzy, then let it out. When Daid pulled away, he stumbled back. He fell, groping for something to hold, as if all the energy had been sucked from him.

"Daid!"

Sanna rushed forward, but a trumpet of fire from Talis sent her scurrying back. She crouched, tucking into a ball. The flames licked at her neck, stopping only when a shadow moved over her. She glanced up through her arms to see the swirling orange of the wild dragon's underbelly.

Why did he keep protecting her?

"Sanna," Daid gasped. "Run!"

Talis snapped at Daid, who recoiled, ducking into the grasses. The high-pitched scream of another witch broke the air. Isadora sprinted into the prison, hair wild.

"Sanna!"

Isadora skidded to a stop on a carpet of old leaves, her eyes wide. Talis crouched, faced Isadora, and drew in a deep breath. Flames built up in the back of his open mouth, gathering into a glowing blue heart. Sanna sprinted out from beneath the wild dragon.

"Isadora!"

A flash of horror crossed Isadora's face just as flames raced from Talis's mouth. A blinding light cleaved the air, pushing the fire back.

Sanna fell to her knees.

Talis shrieked, wheeling away from the light. In a few moments, the light ebbed, giving way to the figure of another witch. Commanding the brilliance was a man with fierce green eyes and a powerful stance. He stood in front of Isadora, shielding her from Talis's wrath. Isadora stared at him, her lips forming a soundless word.

Both of them disappeared.

Sanna whipped around, screeching up at the wild dragon as Talis advanced. "Fly! Take us away. Now!"

The wild dragon unfurled his wings, shattering what was left of the magical prison. A few glittering crystals exploded, fading to wisps of smoke as they drifted to the ground. A confident, firm voice filled Sanna's mind.

Hold on.

A claw wrapped around her body and pulled her from the earth. Daid stared up at her as they winged away. Seconds later, Sanna was in the sky, Talis screaming and flapping wildly in their wake.

SEVEN

The bright flash of light that sprang from Maximillion's hand blinded Isadora. Talis reared back. Isadora covered her eyes with her arm. A cold wave washed over her. When she looked down, her body had disappeared.

"Run!" Maximillion cried, teeth gritted. He held his hand in front of him, casting the protective dome that had shielded them from Talis's fire.

Isadora obeyed without hesitation. The protective bubble broke as she pushed through it. Behind her, Talis roared. She stumbled over a boulder, disoriented by the invisibility of her body, like she kept missing a step she didn't know was there.

Maximillion grabbed her arm and jerked her to her feet. "Keep going!"

"I can't run like this."

"Figure it out!"

Isadora pressed on. Branches whipped at her face, slashing her cheeks and grabbing at her ankles and skirt.

With a cry, she fell to her knees. Maximillion gripped her shoulder and hauled her back up again.

"Seriously?" he cried. "Are you always this clumsy?"

"No!" she snapped. "I can't see my feet."

"You shouldn't look at your feet while you run anyway!"

She tried to jerk free, but he kept his hand clamped around her arm as they bolted through the shadows, feet flying. Her chest burned. The edges of her slippers began to appear. Then the vague outline of a dress, wispy and ethereal. She could almost see her legs. It helped. She tried to press harder, but her lungs began to fail.

"Keep ... going..." Maximillion hissed.

He released her as they spilled onto a path near the Anguis boundary. Lucey, with her unobtrusive blonde bun and pale-blue eyes, stood next to the wall with a worried frown. The piles of black and brown trees loomed over Isadora's head, covered with sheets of poisonous green ivy. If touched, the ivy would eject a hallucinogenic mist that sent most witches into madness—thus preventing them from climbing over the wall and into Anguis. Talis had planted it over a hundred years before, and it had proliferated ever since.

"You made it," Lucey said with relief in her eyes. "I've been worried."

"Not for long." Maximillion glanced back. "That disgusting lizard may still be behind us."

"Then we better hurry." Lucey murmured under her breath, and the ivy wall peeled back, tiny leaves shuddering.

No poison billowed out. No dragon leapt from the shadows. Demons from beyond didn't swoop in to kill Isadora— as she'd always been taught. All *those* dangers lurked inside,

Isadora realized. Underneath the ivy lay a thin break in the wall, just large enough to slip through.

"You first, Isa." Lucey nodded to it. "Hurry up."

Isadora hesitated.

This was it. Her final moment in Anguis for who knew how long. She reached toward Lucey with a tremulous smile. Lucey, who had always been her friend. A sort of mentor, almost.

"Tell Mam I'm sorry, Lucey. And thank y—"

"Not now!" Maximillion growled. "Go!"

A dragon roared in the distance as Maximillion shoved her through the gap. She tumbled to the earth outside with a huff. After disentangling herself from the dried roots and old branches, Isadora risked a glance over her shoulder. The slit in the wall had closed. Ivy covered the hole again. No doubt Lucey had left. Isadora swallowed, forcing herself forward. The only thing she regretted leaving in Anguis was her family. The cemetery of failures and anticipation of future regrets could stay there forever.

They ran for another fifteen minutes, picking through the dense carpet of leaves, bushes, and deadfall before Maximillion slowed, then stopped.

He eyed her, nostrils flaring as he tried to breathe. "You can't transport, can you?"

"No. Lucey has ... told me about it, but..."

"Demmet. We have to keep going on foot and make it to the carriage by dawn. I have meetings and a life to get back to, thank you very much."

"Carriage?"

"Just follow me." He gave her his back. "It's going to be a long night."

THEY WALKED until the dark shadows bled into a bruised blue, and then into the gentle, subdued light of daytime. Letum Wood thinned and thickened at odd intervals, clogging their path with tangled brambles, then clearing into a stretch of thin trees and patchy undergrowth. Isadora hardly recognized it in the shadows. When she couldn't manage another step, she stumbled. A hand shot out, catching her.

"Thanks."

Maximillion released her and pointed to a wall of pink brambles tainted with poison thorns. Beyond it lay something that gave her pause. A two-track dirt road. A large box on wheels, drawn by what must have been horses, waited on the road. She'd seen a painting of such animals before on an old scroll in school, but she hadn't imagined them to be so muscular. Or tall.

"There. Your ride."

Isadora blinked, staring. "My what?"

"Hurry! Meetings, remember? Dostar of the Western Network isn't *exactly* lenient."

Too tired to protest, she followed him around the poisonous brambles and toward the carriage. A young boy with freckles and wide ears hopped down from it.

"Sir?"

"Not a word, Marty," Maximillion snapped. He opened a small door and motioned Isadora inside the carriage with a sweep of his hand. "Climb in. Now."

She ventured forward hesitantly, eyeing the stranger. Marty. He had long limbs, a pimply face, and gangly legs. When she met his gaze, he looked away. She followed suit, wondering about the strange red cap on his head. Inside, she settled on a seat along the back part of the carriage. The window at her elbow afforded her ample view of the forest.

"Where am I going now?" she asked.

Maximillion slammed the little door shut. "To Pearl."

"Pearl? Is she a friend?"

"I don't have friends. She'll see to your filthy clothes and get you a decent pair of shoes, at least."

Isadora opened her mouth to protest but decided against it. She swayed with fatigue, so tired the world spun. Her stomach ached with hunger, and her throat begged for a cool drink of water. She nodded.

Maximillion said, "I'll stop by as soon as I can."

"Wait—"

The carriage jolted onto the dirt road. Isadora scrambled to look outside, but Maximillion had already disappeared. She sat back with a heavy sigh and ran her fingers along the worn velvet, then lay down, closed her eyes, and fell asleep.

Isadora woke in a room she didn't recognize.

No rafters soared overhead. No branches squeaked against the windowpanes. No distant roar of dragons or quiet murmur of Mam singing filtered up the attic stairs. Isadora stared at a blank wooden ceiling with an overwhelming sense of awe.

Had it been real?

She slowly sat up and scanned the room. Definitely not a dream. Light spilled from a small window next to her, barely illuminating a square room with a bed, an oak armoire, a washbasin—and no Sanna.

The smell of something soft filled the room. Roses? No, lavender.

She braced herself for the usual headache, but none came. Her shoulders relaxed. The rest of her body felt like a tightly coiled spring as she tried to remember the last thing that had happened. Her memories returned in snatches, then a flood. Maximillion. The carriage. Falling into a deep sleep. Vague recollections of a strange woman's voice and shifting light.

"Merry meet!"

The door flew open and banged against the wall. Isadora squeaked, jumping back. A squat woman bustled into the room. Her hair flew in wild salt-and-pepper curls all over her head, and her full smile and cheeks almost hid her sparkling eyes. She had a kindness about her, like a soft, candlelight glow. Pearl, surely.

"How did you sleep?" she asked Isadora. "Oh, forgive me. I'm Pearl, by the way. It's going on seven, you know."

Isadora struggled to keep up with the rapid shift in subjects. "Seven?"

"In the morning. You slept a full day yesterday. Not unexpected, of course. Transitioning is exhausting, and you had to run afterward for hours! Dunno how you did it. I have a kettle simmering in the kitchen; how do you take it?"

"Take what?"

"Your coffee."

"I've never heard of coffee."

The woman blinked, drawing herself up. "You don't know coffee?" she whispered.

Isadora scrambled to parse the strange, quick words together. The bow dangling from the woman's apron strings bounced as she waddled to the window and yanked the curtains back. More sunlight flooded the room. The windows peered out on a lush, manicured garden. Beyond lay nothing but sky.

Isadora squinted. She'd never seen so much sky. "What day is this?"

"Sorry? What? I couldn't understand you. Your accent, you know. Sound like a forester. Did you hail from the forest?"

Isadora spoke again, this time more slowly. "What day is this?"

"Oh! Yes. Sorry. Anyway, it's the first day of the third week of winter."

"Lunda?"

The woman stopped, one eyebrow raised. "Pardon?"

"The first day of the week. Lunda."

"I wouldn't know what *Lunda* means. It's just the first day."

Isadora blinked. "Ah."

"Isadora, is it?" she asked.

"Yes. *Avay.*"

"Avay?" The woman's forehead bunched. "You want me to go away?"

"No. Why would I want that?"

"Then what is *avay*?"

"It's..."

A greeting you don't know, Isadora thought with a rush of uncertainty. "I-I'm sorry. I'm not used to the dialect of this region. Where, ah, am I exactly?"

"Maximillion didn't tell you?"

"No."

She rolled her eyes. "I shouldn't be surprised. He rarely does. Hard to love sometimes, you know. Anyway, welcome to Berry. We're always happy to have newcomers. Come on out for some breakfast, and I'll explain everything about transitioning. In the meantime, I'll go ahead and put sugar and cream in it."

"In what?"

"Your coffee!"

Pearl smiled, reached over, and patted Isadora's knee. Isadora recoiled in horror. A stranger seeing her bare knee! She shoved a blanket over it, but Pearl was already pouring water into a basin on the other side of the room.

A nudge of memory stirred in the back of Isadora's mind—an image of Daid's old map. Berry was a small village nestled between farms that backed up to Letum Wood. Nothing to be frightened of, surely. A perfect place to learn more about magic.

"You said *transitioning*." Isadora discreetly pulled her nightgown over her knee. "It has something to do with the magic, doesn't it?"

Pearl reached into the armoire, riffled through it with a few murmurs, and whipped out a dress of deep burgundy. She tossed it to Isadora with a flick of her wrist. Isadora caught it, looking over the wide neckline and elbow-length sleeves with a frown. Mam would never approve.

Then again, Mam wasn't here.

"Transitioning into your powers, of course. Maximillion said it happened for you last night. Very exciting. Frightening that first time, of course, the way you stumble in the darkness with nothing around you."

"I'm not sure what you mean."

"The darkness!" Pearl cried. "I'm a Watcher, too, you know. When I transitioned, all I saw was darkness for days. It'll soon coalesce into something else." Pearl waved a vague hand as she sorted through another drawer. "Don't worry."

Isadora's brow wrinkled. "But I didn't see darkness. I saw trees and the forest. You mean the forest?"

Pearl paused, her head cocked to the side. "Forest?"

"When I saw my sister in the forest? Is that what you're talking about?"

Pearl's forehead furrowed. She shook her head, waving a hand. "Ah ... whatever you say. Maximillion will help you sort all that out. Get dressed. We have lots to do to prepare you for school tomorrow. Maximillion said he'll stop by tonight for your first lesson."

Isadora brightened. "I'm starting school?"

Pearl beamed. "Of course! Get dressed. I'll have some crumpets and coffee ready for you at the table. You said cream and sugar, right?"

"That sounds lovely."

"The books Miss Sophia requires at her school are different from the other schools. Took me a while to hunt them down. *Advanced Oil Painting* and *History of Charcoal*. Strange, don't you think?"

A tottering pile of eight books appeared next to Isadora on the bed. She fought back a gasp of surprise. Such a *normal* use of magic.

How lovely.

"They're old as sin," Pearl said, "but they'll do."

"I've never seen so many. May I open them?"

"Do whatever you like. They're yours."

Isadora's hand stopped halfway to the pile. "They can't be mine. I have nothing to give in return."

"Don't want anything."

Isadora withdrew her hand. "Then I can't accept them. Nothing I haven't earned or traded for."

Pearl stared at her with a queer expression. "Can't you?"

"No."

"But they're just books."

"Something of such great worth."

Isadora's heart crinkled with a moment of uncertainty as Pearl's stare deepened. Had she said something wrong again?

Pearl tilted her head to the side, gaze tapering. "Where are you from again?"

Isadora swallowed her momentary panic. Tell the truth and she'd betray the dragons, but she couldn't lie. This woman had taken her in, provided her *books*, even.

"Ah ... the ... ah ... forest?"

"You're a forester?"

"Yes. That."

Pearl's shoulders relaxed. She laughed, a light, airy sound that made her belly bounce. "Oh, well, that explains it! Have you never left the forest before?"

"No."

"Really?"

"I swear it by Drago."

"Drago?"

"N-nothing. Never mind. May I please work for these?"

"If it's that important to you, yes. The good gods know I hate laundry. You can deal with that this afternoon."

Relieved, Isadora smiled. "Thank you. I would love to help with your laundry."

Isadora turned her attention to the books and ran the tip of her finger down a leather spine. They only had the *Book of Chronicles* at home, which they shared with the other families in Anguis. The rest of their reading materials had been dilapidated scrolls. These leather-bound books smelled like aged paper and brittle ink. When she touched them, a light gray storm churned in her head, knotting the back of her neck. She grimaced.

"Are you all right?"

Isadora attempted a smile. "Lingering headache."

Pearl frowned. "Hmm ... you shouldn't have them after you transition. Quite strange. Well, maybe it's from all the running. Coffee, my dear. You need some coffee. See you in a minute!"

Pearl slammed the door behind her, muttering something under her breath.

School. Isadora inspected the burgundy dress again, glanced at her new room, and grinned. Her whole new world, her greatest adventure, had started.

With coffee, whatever that was.

THAT EVENING, the light-blue fingers of twilight stretched through Pearl's house, casting a dim illumination on the small, square cottage. A fire crackled in the hearth. Isadora sat in a plush chair while she looked through a *Western Network Art Today* textbook, her eye roving from page to door and back to page again. Her leg bounced, and her fingers twitched.

The moment the door opened with a groan, she gasped. Maximillion stepped into Pearl's house, and Isadora shot to her feet.

"Let's get started," she said.

His crippling gaze shot daggers into her. "Calm down," he muttered and slammed the door.

"I can't."

He tossed a jacket into the air. The nearby coat rack reached out, snatched it, and withdrew back to its corner. Pearl slipped into the room with a happy cry and threw her arms around him.

Maximillion wriggled free with a scowl. "Stop that! You *know* I hate being touched."

Pearl backed away, giggling to Isadora. "He does hate it when I do that, but I just can't help myself. I'll be back with coffee!" she called over her shoulder.

Isadora folded her arms tight against her chest, then dropped them. She set the book aside and began to pace. It felt like hot beans were jumping under her skin. Her thoughts zipped from one to another in endless circles. She strode back and forth in front of the fire, where she'd been pacing for the last hour, alternately staring at the sky and the pile of dresses Pearl had been adjusting for her to wear at school.

"What is wrong with you?" Maximillion asked.

"Where is my school? Does everyone use magic all the time? What happened to my sister?" She pressed a hand to her forehead. "Why can't I think? My body is moving fast and slow."

He eyed her warily. "Did Pearl give you coffee?"

"Yes."

"How many cups?"

"Just three. It's quite good with cream and sugar."

"Have you ever had it before?"

"No. Why? What does that have to do with anything? I don't see what that has to do with anything. Why are my knees shaking?"

"Pearl!"

Pearl peeked around the wall. "Well! She *had* a headache. I didn't think she'd act like a squirrel. And I didn't know she had three cups."

"A headache?" Maximillion murmured. He turned to Isadora, pointing to the nearest chair. "Sit down."

"I don't want to."

"Sit. Down."

A chair skidded across the floor, scooping Isadora up like a doll. She clutched the sides as it slid to the table and anchored itself there. She squirmed but couldn't move.

"You're using magic against me!"

"Your powers of observation are astounding."

"Let me go."

"Not until you listen."

"It's too hard to think when I'm sitting still. It … it takes over."

He frowned. "What takes over?"

"I don't know!" she cried. "My mind can't stop. It won't settle. I can't … I can't think!"

"That's the coffee." His frown deepened. "I think. Some of our kind are more sensitive to it, although I've never seen it this bad."

"*Our* kind?"

He sank into a chair across from her and scrubbed a hand over his face. "Watchers. You're a Watcher. That's what all this glorious mess really is. Welcome."

Watcher. Pearl had said that word earlier. Or had it been someone else? Her mind wouldn't slow enough for her to remember.

"What's a Watcher?"

"Witches who have special … *abilities.*"

"Abilities?"

"Powers. Talents born within us, so to speak. They manifest on their own when a witch is between fourteen and fifteen years of age, and the powers are different for every witch. They must be mastered. Your powers are currently like wild toddlers raised by wolves."

"On coffee," Pearl said with a titter.

Deep-seated thoughts surfaced through the chaos of Isadora's mind. Strange abilities. Magical power. Strength. Reasons to be feared. That's all she could remember, but even that seemed distant. Like vague rumors, tall tales told by other Anguis kids.

"That's what's been giving me the headaches?" she asked.

"Yes."

"How is *that* a talent?"

"It varies. Typically we can view possibilities for the future. For ourselves or one other. There are Watchers who sense other things in small quantities, such as personality traits, but I've only met one. He saw only for family members, which didn't do much good."

She frowned, taking that in. It seemed such a strange thing to have given her so much trouble. "What's the point of such a power?"

"What's the point of magic?"

He stared at her so intently she realized he wanted an answer. She paused. "I don't know. To give us an easier life?"

He hung his head.

Isadora scowled, casting about for an adequate response. What *was* the purpose of magic? She knew little enough of it. Clearly, though, Maximillion really believed this madness. That witches could be born with magical powers that made them different. That Drago would allow a Servant child to have powers that worked *outside* Anguis and the dragons.

Her mind spun. Then again ... if *Drago* were to allow it, that meant it held a very real, functional purpose.

"If I could see the future, I could..."

Words failed her. The possibilities multiplied all at once in an overwhelming mass. Maximillion frowned, as if detecting the frenzied routes of her mind.

"Yes," he said. "That is precisely the issue. There is a limitless number of things you *could* do. Of course, if you attempt to do all of them, the powers consume you. On the other hand, if you do nothing, the powers may still consume you."

"Sounds promising."

"You would die."

Her mouth dropped open. "Do some..."

"It happens."

Something lingered in his tone, both hesitant and terrible at the same time. Isadora studied the forced ease in his muscles, his expression. If Maximillion hadn't come along—albeit reluctantly—would she have ever known her powers? Likely not. Then it would have killed her. She understood that without him saying it. Perhaps she did owe the miserable cretin something.

Isadora drew her shoulders back, chin high. "All right, then. What do I do first?"

"Bring yourself out of total ignorance."

"What?"

"Learn." He tapped the side of his head with a finger. "You need to figure out how to control the power so it's not controlling you. That's why I'm putting you into school at Miss Sophie's. It's a good environment to learn, both magic *and* the powers. Chaos, and all that. Besides, it's the safest place for you right now."

She couldn't imagine what would threaten her safety

but realized she didn't want to know. Not yet. Not on top of all of this. She'd ask later.

"Great."

"Great?"

"I can do it. I'm smart and willing *and* ready. I'm here, aren't I?"

It couldn't be any harder than living in Anguis, she added silently.

"Sure you are," he murmured silkily, with a dark flicker of annoyance. The spell loosened, releasing her from the chair. The worst of the heightened buzz had faded, leaving her sliding down a slope of fatigue.

"Where do I start?" she asked through a yawn.

"By recognizing your own thoughts apart from the powers. Right now, many of your thoughts are run by your power since it's not under control. Decipher those thoughts. Pull them apart. Decide what is from your mind and what isn't."

"All I ever see is a gray blur."

"It's more than that."

"I assure you, it's not."

"Focus on what's *behind* the blur. That's what I want to know about. I'll return in a week. By then, you'll have integrated yourself into school and some semblance of a normal life. One that doesn't draw attention, preferably."

He turned to go, the edges of his coat flapping behind him. Isadora shot to her feet.

"Wait!"

He paused, one eyebrow lifted. "What?"

So many questions circled through her mind, not the least of which was the hope for a morsel of reassurance that she *could* do this. Despite his horrid attitude and frosty glares, he was her only acquaintance in this new world aside from Pearl.

"N-nothing. I forgot my question."

He held out a hand. The coat rack leaned toward him and dropped his hat into it. "Don't tell anyone at school that you're a Watcher."

"Why not?"

"Because you clearly value your life, that's why. And you're useful to no one, least of all me, if you're dead."

Maximillion disappeared in a burst of magic, leaving a hint of vetiver in his wake. Isadora drew in a deep breath.

"Pearl," she said. "I'm ready to begin."

Pearl let out a sigh. "They always are, in the beginning."

With that stolid farewell, Isadora flounced to bed, her veins buzzing in anticipation of starting over, of success, of more *magic* and witches and places.

Starting out with little old Berry.

EIGHT

The sound of silence woke Sanna.

She jumped to her feet, reached for the knife tucked into her wide belt, and nearly toppled off the side of a tree branch. Something stopped her fall. She glanced down to see a vine wrapped around her waist, anchoring her. She stared at it in confusion until her sleepy mind caught up.

Talis. Wild dragon. Flying into the darkness.

The wild dragon had flown until she couldn't stand the heat from his claw—a surprising distance—then dropped them into the canopy far from Anguis. She must have fallen asleep on this branch at some point, still half-delirious from almost dying. Twice.

Once she touched the vine around her waist, it snaked away. Faint lavender light leaked through the leaves over-head. She was near the top of the canopy, far from the ground. Dawn approached.

She struggled to make sense of the strange colors and angles that filled this part of the forest. Dead, fallen branches. Tangled vines tied into knots. By mischievous fairies, perhaps?

Curtains of ivy clogged the air like emerald fire, making it nearly impassable. It might as well have been a different forest. When she caressed the wood, no glimmer of familiarity zipped through her hand. There were no worn paths. No cleared highways for her to run. No scorch marks singed by out-of-control hatchlings. Moss and lichen grew thick as pillows beneath her feet. Sticks, twigs, dry branches, and a few nuts littered the branch where she stood.

Sanna sank to her haunches when a flicker of darkness moved behind her. She wheeled around to meet a familiar, glowing gaze. The wild dragon lay draped across the next branch, looking bored. Heat ebbed from his scales. Once she turned, he perked up, as if he'd been waiting.

He lowered his head back to the branch. She hesitated, then sat facing him, her legs folded beneath her.

"So ... what now?"

The wild dragon's tail slid over, the thin, pointed end lingering an arm's length away from her hand. She frowned and stared at it. What was *that* supposed to do? The tail paused, then slipped toward her until it stopped a hand's breadth away. Then once more forward, resting on her ankle. He bored into her with his gaze.

"What?" she asked, pulling free. "Why are you touching me?"

His nostrils flared. He sought her ankle again. When he touched her, something stirred in the back of her mind. A heavy pressure, like a pulse. She put a hand on her head.

"Ow."

The dragon growled. His tail tightened around her ankle. The force returned to her mind, like something trying to intrude. The odd, rippling sensation felt like ... like magic? She couldn't be sure, so she resisted, mentally shoving it away. Magic hurt dragons *and* witches. Magic was one of the three things responsible for the Great Massacre. When the pressure continued, she kicked his tail free and scrambled back.

"Get off me," she snarled.

He gnashed his teeth, a protest rumbling deep in his chest. A long moment passed while they stared at each other. Finally, the tail snaked forward again, hesitating just out of reach. Sanna paused.

Why would an adult male wild dragon voluntarily touch a witch? Cara and the hatchlings nudged her often enough, but females were always more affectionate. Sort of. Besides, she *knew* Cara. There had to be a reason he touched her—and he *had* saved her life. She could give him a chance, at least. She sighed and leaned forward, palm open.

"Fine," she said. "Whatever this is, just do it."

The tail slid into her hand, where it rested with a warm, pleasant burn. "Not hot," she murmured in surprise, expecting the same bright flare of heat that emanated from his body. The tail fell, wrapping around her ankle again. This time, she straightened her leg out. The pressure in her mind pulsed into a frenetic beat. He peered at her intently again, stretching his neck across the gap in the branches.

Like he wanted to say something.

Wait—*hadn't* he said something when he saved her from Talis?

Sanna relaxed the resistance in her mind. A warm tingle, like the sensation of stepping into a bath, flooded her.

You resist magic, do you? came a quiet, rolling voice.

"*Mori!*" she yelled, leaping away. The dragon tightened his hold on her ankle, jerking her back. She slipped on the pillow of moss and dropped off the branch, smacking her nose on the wood. The dragon dragged her back up, setting her gently on her knees.

"Ow!"

Perhaps not as intelligent as I expected.

Tears sprang to Sanna's smarting eyes. She pressed a hand to her nose, and the coppery taste of blood filled her mouth. Blood dripped onto her fingers. She tilted her head back, letting it run down the back of her throat instead.

"That wath your fault!"

My fault? he asked, seeming genuinely surprised. Confused, even. *Did I push you off?*

Sanna scowled, eyeing him through her lashes. "No, but you stopped me from falling."

I should have let you fall?

Logic failed her. She shoved it aside with a growl of frustration. "What are you doing in my mind, anyway?"

Not having a pleasant time, I assure you. Also, I'm not in your mind. I'm speaking to it. There's a vast difference.

Sanna backed away, putting as much space between them as she could. He didn't relinquish his hold but hissed quietly with a forked tongue. A billow of steam came with it.

"Let go of me."

We cannot speak without touch. I should have thought that would be obvious. If we cannot speak, that means we cannot depart. I don't plan to stay here any longer than I have to. I've been gone long enough. I do not enjoy when my schedule is awry.

He had a strange way of speaking—easygoing, light even, but firm, like he had more confidence than she would have expected. He couldn't be *that* old. She pegged him at fifty, at the most.

"How can we speak at all? Dragons can't talk to witches.

Unless, you know, you're the brood leader." One of her eyebrows lifted. "Are you a brood leader?"

He straightened off the branch, uncoiling from his lazy ball. He appeared far bigger than she remembered.

There are no brood leaders.

"That isn't true." She pointed at him. "Talis is a brood leader."

Talis is a fool. I gave you my blood and spared your life. That is why we can communicate.

"Oh. Right. About that." She rubbed the back of her neck, grimacing. "Uh … thanks. F-for doing that. I, uh, appreciate being alive. Even if I'm kicked out of Anguis." She glanced around. "And not sure how to make it back. And possibly doomed to being an outcast forever."

He closed his eyes and inclined his head.

You assisted me with your foolish plan to lure forest lions. Removing you served a greater purpose, anyway.

"You weren't complaining when you ate the lions. And I didn't *assist* you. I saved you. You were going to starve in there."

Was I?

He peered at her with the same unnerving intelligence she detected in Talis. The calm cadence of his voice set her oddly at ease, even though hearing him in her mind felt a little too … seamless. As if his every nuance and flicker of tone communicated perfectly, leaving no doubt as to what he meant.

Sanna squirmed. Did he perceive her the same way? She studied him up close, startled to find that tiny gray scales flecked the edges of his eyes, almost like lashes.

She blinked. "Uh…"

We shall discuss that later. Now, we must be going. My

captivity extended far longer than I had anticipated, and there is much to be done. Come, witch. We must be on.

"Hold on. You anticipated captivity? You *wanted* to be captured?"

I had to be.

"Why?"

So I could save you.

"Save me? Why would you do that?"

Because I was told to. For that purpose, I also have my own reasons.

"You aren't going to share them?"

Of course I will, which is precisely why we must leave. I cannot do that here. It's not safe.

"Are you trying to say that you could have broken free sooner? That this was all part of some great plan?"

His eyes gleamed. *I could have done much more than I did. But that was not my intent. Come, witch.*

"Wait."

What?

Could dragons get exasperated? She certainly heard a note of it in his response. "Why me? Why not Isadora?"

Because, I was sent for you, not her. Your sister wasn't listening. She has her own path.

"So, she's okay? Did Talis get her?"

I doubt it.

She frowned. "Why? He was really angry. I don't—"

Because greater forces are at work for her and for you.

"But *why?* And who sent you?"

His nostrils flared. *As I've said, I will answer your questions, but not here.*

"What's your name? Give me *something* to go on."

He paused. *What is yours?*

"Sanna."

Sanna. He seemed to ponder it. *I am Luteis.*

"Nice to, ah, meet you?"

You seem unsure.

"I am."

I am not sure how to respond.

"Me neither."

A long silence swelled between them. Luteis turned away, his tail loosening around her foot.

We must be on. My plan is still in motion.

"Wait! One more question. Did Drago send you? I'd feel a lot better about all of this if I just had his blessing. Before I throw away all chances of working with Daid and the brood. Or life with my family. Or happiness in general."

He tilted his head to the side.

Drago?

"Yes. Drago."

Who is this of whom you speak?

Sanna blinked. "You must know Drago."

Is Drago a dragon?

"No. Well ... maybe? I don't actually know what he looks like. I mean, he's the *god* of dragons. And forest. So maybe a dragon?"

His deep growl vibrated the branch. Now he was for *sure* annoyed.

I have no idea of whom you speak.

"What? How can you not know Drago? He's the god of dragons."

Do you believe this Drago is real?

"Of course he's real!"

You've seen him?

"Well, no."

You have spoken with him?

"Not directly."

Have you touched or felt his presence?

"Uh ... not really?"

Another question. Do you even know your own mind? If you haven't seen, touched, or felt him, how do you know he is real?

Sanna held up two hands. "Whoa there. You're going to get cursed for that. Trust me—it's not pretty when Drago curses."

Oh? What happens?

Sanna squirmed. Now they were broaching vague territory. "Let's just say that Drago doesn't look too favorably on witches—or dragons for that matter—who don't believe in him."

How would he curse me?

"Ah..."

Sanna wracked her brain, whirring through the thousands of passages she'd read from the *Book of Chronicles* and the curt discussions she'd had with Finn during monthly village dinners, but she recalled nothing to prove her point. She hesitated as she remembered Ivis's blood oozing from Talis's jaw. Surely Drago wielded *some* punishment if he allowed Talis to be so ruthless.

"Well, I can't exactly speak for Drago and what he would do—"

Have you seen his punishments?

"Not personally?"

Luteis's brow grew heavy. *You are uncertain yet again. How do you plan your life?*

Stubborn dragon! How could Drago have brought the two of them together? Luteis was wild, for sure. Clearly ignorant. Didn't even know his own *god*. Sanna put her hands on her hips and glared at him.

"No, but..."

She let the unfinished thought trail away, realizing she had no response. Infuriating beast.

The insult to her certainty was all the greater because he didn't seem to care that he was right—or at least a better debater.

Luteis snorted, his wings straightening. Wood shavings flaked off the branch when he dug his talons into it.

You live in a false world of certainty, Sanna of Anguis. There is no logic to reinforce what you believe. Concerning, at the least, but nothing we need deal with now. I assure you, I don't fear Drago.

"If you know so much, why don't you tell me who sent you?" she snapped.

Luteis's head snapped to the side. His pupils constricted. He sniffed the air, nostrils flaring. His sinewy body unfurled with ease.

We must be on.

"But—"

Now. Climb on my back.

Sanna froze. "I can't. You'll burn me."

We must ride to my dwelling.

"It's going to burn me!"

Then use the magic.

"What magic?"

His sharp gaze cut over to her again. *You don't know the ancient magic?*

"What are you talking about? Servants aren't allowed to do magic. It harms dragons! Do you want to bring the poachers back?"

He snorted again, his eyes burning with fury.

Talis, the fool!

"Listen, massacres happen when uncontrolled magic is—"

The tree trembled. Sanna held out her arms, stabilizing herself. Luteis hissed, wings spreading wide. Sanna gulped, glancing down. Shadows shifted in the darkness below. A screech rang through the air.

"What was that?" she whispered.

A belua.

"What's a belua?"

Blind, awkward monsters. They have exceptional hearing and smell and far more strength than you. They'll snap you in half with one hand.

"Is that all? We're in the trees." She spread her hands. "No problem. I practically own the upper canopy."

Not this one.

"How different could it be?"

He nearly cut her in half with his sharp glare. *Your arrogance will get you—or me—killed. Get on my back. Beluas live in the trees. They never touch the ground, and I assure you, they're far stronger than you.*

Sanna swallowed a nervous lump in her throat. "S-surely they won't fight a dragon."

Not alone, no.

"So, we're fine."

I smell four!

The tree shook, and then a deep, guttural bellow chilled Sanna's heart. Below them, a blue-gray creature four times Sanna's size crawled up the tree, its broad shoulders and muscular arms carrying it with alarming speed. Its wide, pointed ears spread to the sides like wings. No eyes filled its blank face. Nothing except a bulbous nose and razor-sharp teeth in a wide mouth. It screamed, emitting purple phlegm in acidic ropes that burned through leaves, sizzling into the tree bark.

"Time to go!"

Climb the tree, Luteis said. *Climb as fast as you can. I will distract it for as long as I'm able, but I make no promises.*

Sanna groped her way up a vine, hauled herself onto the branch above, ran to the trunk, and crawled up its thick seams. Behind her, Luteis bellowed, sending a spray of fire into the air.

"Stop throwing fire!" she yelled over her shoulder. "You're going to burn the whole forest down."

He made no response, and she didn't wait for one. Heat steamed past her in shimmering waves as she worked her way up. Sweat beaded on the backs of her arms. Despite her best efforts, the unintelligible belua cries followed her. The creatures moved lightning-fast despite the clogged canopy.

She dared a glance down, panting, to find two of them only twenty paces away, their sprawling ears twitching toward her and their long, veiny arms propelling them upward. In horror, she stared at their fingers, which spanned the length of her forearm.

She shrieked and flew faster up the trunk.

The canopy thinned, and she clambered toward the sunlight. The beluas pressed on, closer and closer. Something burrowed into the back of her leg, stinging hot. She reached back with a cry of pain, smacking off the slimy, purple spittle. Her fingers tingled.

"Gross!"

She wiped it on her shirt and clambered upward, kicking back when the beluas' sultry breath warmed her ankles. One of them reached for her, grabbing her knee. She yanked a dead branch free and swung, dropping it right onto its face. It flailed, bellowed, and released her.

Beneath the beluas, fire flared as Luteis roared again. Sanna's sweaty hands lost purchase when the grooves in the bark thinned and disappeared. Her shoulders burning, she broke through the canopy and into the glaring sunlight. She clung to the tree, momentarily blinded.

"*Mori,*" she whispered.

Fields of emerald treetops rolled toward every horizon in gentle, ebbing waves. A cerulean sky sparkled in the early morning light, strung with wispy, cotton-like clouds. She'd never seen the whole sky during the day, had never ventured that high. Legends of gryphons—massive, flying lions—had always kept her low. Right now, gryphons were preferable to the beluas' razor-sharp teeth and acidic spit.

A livid roar snapped her out of her trance. The second belua had crawled up the far side of the tree in swift pursuit, its teeth dripping venom. Beneath it came a smaller one. A child, perhaps, but it still dwarfed Sanna. In full daylight, they were uglier than ever. Mottled skin. Broad forehead crawling with web-like veins.

Sanna edged around the trunk, deftly moving just out of reach of the adult. Her sweaty fingers slipped just as the belua swiped at her, barely missing her with its long, yellowing fingernails.

She leaned back, lost her grip, and dropped with a scream.

Luteis's tail caught her around the waist and bore her away. The belua flailed at the top of the tree, gnashing its thick, pointed teeth at her. The young belua screamed, a high-pitched sound that made her ears ache.

Trust me, Luteis said, oddly calm, as if he faced this kind of threat every day. *It's very different out here.*

HOURS LATER, Luteis landed.

Sanna untangled herself from his tail, half-asleep from the lulling ride. She vaguely recalled seeing ragged, orchid mountains in the distance right before they dropped back into the forest. Wherever he lived, it must be close to the Northern Network and far, far from Anguis.

Luteis yawned with a belch of fire when he settled on a tree branch. His regal wings folded onto his back. He seemed perfectly at ease in the canopy. She'd never seen an adult male dragon in the branches before.

She rubbed her eyes, then stopped. The tree she sat in had a strange texture. The spindly branches were only as wide as she was tall but seemed to go on forever. They twisted into each other, driving deep into the forest like long arms. No moss. No lichen. Although the canopy still extended hundreds of paces overhead, light suffused the trees.

Sanna pushed to her feet. An oak tree. It was a massive, ancient oak. There had been one on the edge of the village boundary years ago. When it fell, Talis used it to reinforce the border that kept everyone out.

"Where are we?" she asked.

Home.

Luteis had kept the end of his tail wrapped around her ankle. The constant touch had her on edge, but she didn't kick him away—she had far too many questions.

"But it's so..."

Healthy?

"Open."

Same thing.

Grass sprouted between trees here, a vibrant carpet that gave way to occasional flowers. Several oak trees, thick as dragons at the base, extended into the canopy. At the top, their leaves grew big enough to wrap around her like a blanket.

Light spilled into her eyes. Hardly any saplings clogged the forest floor. She could climb as fast as she wanted and never have to crawl over tangled vines, fallen branches, or piles of deadfall. Black torch marks darkened the bottoms of several trees—and even the rocks—but the grass showed no sign of flame.

What a strange place.

"But how?"

It's amazing how a forest can look, he said, strolling past, *when one cares for it.*

His tail released her. She jogged along behind him, entranced by the sheer *openness* of the forest. Healthy. He was right. It did seem healthy. Far less gloomy, at any rate.

The sound of water caught her ear as they moved around the oak. Just ahead of them, a stream spilled over a rock wall, falling in lacy signatures to a pool, which eventually narrowed back into the stream. His tail caught her ankle again.

Drink. We won't be back for several hours.

It wasn't until she felt the cool liquid sliding down her throat that Sanna realized how thirsty she was. She cupped her hands and drank until her stomach ached. Only then did she stand up, wiping the water off with the back of her arm.

Her hair had fallen into the stream and clumped together in a damp mop. She shoved it out of her way. Luteis tilted his head to one side as he regarded her.

And they say dragons are the wild ones.

She let that one slide.

He continued walking, and Sanna hurried to keep up as

he slipped through the forest with ease, navigating the maze of gargantuan trunks with practiced steps.

"Where are you taking me?"

His tail whipped around her knees until she grabbed it, holding the lukewarm scales near the tip. *To the only place Talis would never return.*

"Where is that?"

The place of your ancestors.

She released his tail out of pure consternation, then scrambled to grab it again before he moved away. "My ancestors?"

Did you not hear me?

"I heard you."

Did you not understand?

"Of course I understood."

Then why did you repeat it?

"An expression of shock."

You are surprised that you have ancestors? Confusion crept into his voice.

Sanna's forehead ruffled. "What? No. Just that ... I suppose I never thought I would know much about them. Or see their, ah, *place*. You're very literal."

Or you are very vague.

As they walked, the trees grew larger. Thicker trunks. Higher branches. Luteis stopped without warning near a massive evergreen and peered through a thick curtain of leaves. He snorted flame, blasting a hole through the ivy, then stepped through. His tail wrapped around her ankle.

We are here.

Sanna pushed through the straggly curtain and found herself inside a ring of twelve soaring trees. Even the roots sticking up from the ground surpassed her own height. The entire meadow at Anguis could fit in one trunk. The soaring branches were stacked so high she saw only an endless climb of boughs.

Muted light filtered down to them on the forest floor, oddly bright despite the sheer size of the trees. Something about them felt archaic. Ancient. As if these trees had been alive forever. Within the ring—which spanned a circle hundreds of paces across—lay a small grove. Pines. Firs. Oaks. Aspens. A strange mixture growing oddly close together. Compared to the soaring circle around them, the grove looked miniature, even though it still towered over Sanna.

"What is this place?" she whispered.

The Ancients of Letum Wood.

"It feels … old."

Letum Wood began here, planted thousands of years ago. At one time, your ancestors inhabited this space.

"And you live here now?"

I call the entire forest home.

Sanna advanced into the ring. A village of wooden houses occupied the middle of the circle, not far from the scattered grove. Time didn't seem to touch the buildings. They looked as if they'd just been abandoned minutes before. Like her own home, they had two stories, with sharply sloping attics and one chimney in the back.

Scorch marks charred the tops of several roofs. A gaping hole pierced one. Claw marks stood out on another. Some of the wood appeared darker, as if stained. She counted ten houses, at least. Worn paths led from house to house in vague trails. She spotted a well between two of them. A rope swing.

Somehow, she knew exactly where she was.

"Talis won't come here because this is where the Great Massacre happened, wasn't it?"

Luteis lowered his head in affirmation.

A hallowed quiet filled the air. One hundred and fifty years ago, poachers from the Southern Network had attacked unexpectedly, leaving thirty dragons and twenty-five witches dead within an hour. Only fifteen dragons remained, all of them hatchlings except for Talis, who was just out of adolescence at thirty years old. Ten witches had survived. The poachers had drawn as much blood from the dead dragons as they could carry and then left.

Flecks of sapphire shimmered in the wooden grains of a nearby trunk. They flaked off when she touched them. She turned to Luteis.

"Dragon blood?"

From the massacre, yes.

Sanna stepped onto the porch of the nearest house and pushed through an old door that groaned when it moved. No vines ran amok inside. No chittering animals inhabited the empty room. In fact, she saw no errant signs of life at all. Belongings dotted the interior. A moldering gray dress hung over the back of a rocking chair, near a shattered cup and kettle. The hole in the ceiling allowed light to spill inside, illuminating more blue stains streaking the floor and walls. She ran her fingers along one stain. It shimmered away in a cloud of silvery dust. Sanna backed away, eyes darting over every last detail until she stepped back outside.

Shaking off a chill, she slipped into the next house. Broken dishes. Overturned furniture. A shattered oil lamp. On the outside, several arrows, as thick as her thumb, stuck out from the house. Hardened streaks of silver had drained beneath them. Wherever the murdered dragons and witches ended up during the destruction, nothing of them remained.

She kept moving.

Dolls. Dresses. Old slates with half-worked sums. Half-open books. Scrolls. Quills. A goose-feather pillow. The massacre had happened in the midst of everyday life, descending with death and fire and fury the Servants had never seen before. Sanna had always known that, but she'd never understood it until now. She slid past a table, trailing her hand along an old vest made of glittering dragon scales before she returned to Luteis.

He waited just outside.

"Why is everything so intact?" she asked as his tail flicked to her ankle.

For you.

"Me?"

Deasylva protects it.

"Who is Deasylva?"

You shall see.

"Is it a witch? A dragon?"

Luteis pulled his wings up onto his back. His neck straightened. *Neither of those things, but more information is not mine to give.*

Something lingered in his gaze, but Sanna didn't have a chance to draw it out.

Are you done exploring, Sanna of Anguis?

Sanna wondered why he changed the subject, but she let it go. Outside the ring of Ancients, the forest appeared as *healthy* as what she'd seen when they landed. Aside from the occasional scorch mark, every plant and tree seemed purposeful. Full. No disintegrating wood. No fallen trees. She'd never imagined Letum Wood could be pristine.

If you so desire, this is where you may stay. It would only be fitting, and it is yours by inheritance, anyway.

The Ancients would protect her—no belua or forest lion

would descend from those heights. She'd have shelter, at least. Water too; a creek burbled just outside the ring. Remnants of life in the knickknacks left behind.

"How long am I going to be here?"

That is not up to me.

"If it were up to me, I'd already be back home," she mumbled. If he heard her, he gave no indication. His wings drooped on his back, and he blinked several times, as if tired. He *had* flown for hours, carrying her by his tail, which couldn't have been easy.

"You need to rest," she said. "You should go sleep. I'll be fine on my own."

Will you?

His sincere curiosity staved off her initial burst of annoyance. He had a lot to learn about her abilities in Letum Wood. She might not be able to read old Dragonian texts or write out geometry proofs, but she understood the forest. The idea of solitude for a while appealed to her more than exploring a little further anyway. She needed to *think* without someone else speaking into her head. She craned her head back. She wanted to find a way up into those trees. Her stomach growled. Right. Breakfast first.

"Yes. I'll be fine."

The forest is not the same here. I feel I should warn yo—

"Trust me. Beluas aside, there's nothing Letum Wood can throw at me that I haven't seen before in Anguis. Really. I'll be fine. Go get some rest."

Luteis eyed her, then ruffled his wings. *Very well. I must hunt and then sleep through the night. If you're confident you'll be fine, I'll see you in the morning.*

Sanna started back toward the stream, waving a hand.

"Sleep well."

TEN MINUTES LATER, delicious, cool water lapped at Sanna's calves. She couldn't see her feet beneath the foamy surface of the stream. With her head tilted back, she stood and tried to orient herself.

Not dead, she thought. *That's a start.*

Living away from Anguis would certainly lengthen the time it took her to become a full Servant and work with Daid, but all hope wasn't lost. *Surely* she could return. She splashed some water on her face, shivering as it woke her. She just had to figure out a way to earn Talis's trust again.

Her mind slipped back to Luteis.

A wild dragon. Surely if she tamed a wild dragon and returned to Anguis, they would welcome her. How couldn't they? She'd restore yet another dragon to the brood and bring back information on better hunting grounds. She'd be the hero, for sure.

Not even Daid could be upset about that.

Her stomach growled. Sanna shook her head, clearing her thoughts. Food. Food would be the next priority. Once she ate, she could formulate a more detailed plan to earn Talis's trust back and work next to Daid. In the meantime, where could she find—and trap—food?

A sudden movement drew her gaze to her toes. Fish darted in and out of sight with mad, frenetic movements around her ankles. She grinned.

"*Avay!* I didn't even think about you."

With a trained eye, Sanna crouched. The edges of her knee-length skirt skimmed the top of the water, sending the fish darting away. She froze, hands hovering just over the surface. A minute passed. Three minutes. Then five.

Her legs and back burned. Her patience ran short until a fish cautiously approached her leg, undulating against the lazy current. Its mauve body glimmered in the clear water, bright against the mossy ground. She'd never seen a fish quite like it. Whatever it was, it would probably taste delicious.

With a *thwack*, she chopped the water, plunging her hand in at an angle. Her fingers closed around the slippery creature, then jerked it out of the water. The plum-colored fish wriggled in her fingers, bulbous boils blossoming all over its body.

"Ha! Stupid git. I got you!"

Just as she turned to wade out of the stream, pain ripped through her hand. She shrieked, wheeling back. The fish had clamped its teeth onto her fingers, breaking the skin. Bright orange pus bubbled up around its jaws. The pain turned to fire.

"Off! Get off!"

Sanna flung it toward the bank. The hideous creature plopped onto the grass with a meaty *squish*, glassy eyes wide, bulbous lips stilled. Blood dribbled down Sanna's palm, flowing over her wrist, mixed with the strange foam. Her hand prickled like a thousand needles had plunged into her palm at the same time.

"*Demmet.*"

Nausea rose in her belly. She fell to her knees with a cry when the trees pitched to the side, nearly taking her with them. Water lapped around her, bitter cold. Her stomach spasmed. She crawled through the stream, collapsing half onto the bank, and dry heaved.

Bright spots broke across her vision when she closed

her eyes and moaned. Perhaps fishing *hadn't* been the best idea. Fire raced through her veins, wrapping her body in flashes of heat and ice. She retched again and again, moving in and out of a hazy fog.

She rolled onto her back, gasping when the shaggy mane of a forest lion loomed over her. The lion sniffed at her face.

She opened her mouth to scream, but her throat had swollen, restricting her air intake to a mere whistle. The lion disappeared. A tree branch hovered over her cheeks with a gentle caress now, stroking her face with a bright pink leaf. The leaves turned into birds that wheeled away with frantic chitters and swollen bellies. Screaming gnomes chanted somewhere near her right ear. Flashes of light spiraled overhead. The prickles expanded from her hand and sprinted through her limbs. Mam's voice rang through her ears, as if through water. "Sanna. Sanna?"

Mam, she mouthed. A pair of hazel eyes appeared. Something tugged at her shoulders. A strange scraping raked down her back like long fingers. The cool water disappeared from her legs. She felt the grass on her back. Heard a whistle in her ears. Was it wind?

For what felt like an eternity she lay there, slipping in and out of delirium. Talis walked around her in a circle, then turned into a belua, then a column of flowers that exploded into fluff and blew away. Sanna lay rigidly still, too frightened to move, drawing air in through her swollen, ragged throat one breath at a time. Slowly, the hallucinations faded. Her throat eased. She blinked, barely comprehending the endless canopy overhead.

Lightheaded and tipsy, she slowly sat up. The world spun, then righted. Next to her lay the purple fish, dead, its color seeping into a strange gray. It sank into the ground, as if consumed by the grasses. Enough time had passed that her legs had dried. Only then did she see that she lay several paces away from the stream, in the grass. But how had she gotten *out* of the water?

She blinked, peering overhead. A tangle of vines swung in a gentle breeze. Perhaps she hadn't imagined *all* of it. She thought of the vine that had fallen when she'd fought the lions, the yellow smoke. The sensation of being pulled from the water.

Was all of it magic? If so, from where?

Sanna shook her head. She pulled her knees into her chest and set her chin on top.

It was going to be a long day.

NINE

Beams of sunshine broke through the clouds the next morning, illuminating everything in Berry. Isadora closed her eyes and felt it dance on her face.

No murky shadows. No blunted light. The full power of the sun drifted across her face like a fairy dance. For a moment, her mind was blessedly silent, as if her rampant powers wanted to soak up all that sky.

She tore her gaze away and hurried down the cobblestone street after Pearl. The number of witches in Berry captivated her even more than the sky did. Every other minute, a new one appeared. Full skirts. Squalling babes. Men with fabric tied around their necks.

Pearl hummed under her breath, a mug of coffee in hand as they walked away from her cottage. She took a sip every few steps, eyes closing with a low murmur and sigh. The cup never emptied despite her constant sipping. She motioned ahead with a wave of her hand.

"Here we are!"

An aging house made of faded brick loomed on the other side of a rickety fence. An out-of-control garden lay off to the right, cluttered by a towering oak tree and wild shrubs that spread onto the grass. A crooked sign hung off the fence.

Miss Sophia's School for Girls.

Rampant, half-dead ivy clung to the middle of the house and wound around grubby windows across the front. Four on the first floor, five on the second and third floors. Steps led up to a door with peeling black paint and a dull handle. Smoke belched from one chimney, though two stood on either side of the sloping roof. In front of those were two statues of misshapen creatures with bent backs and bared teeth. Delightful, ugly things. Sanna would have loved them.

"Gargoyles," Pearl said, following her gaze. "They could do with a good cup of coffee themselves, don't you think?"

"What are they for?"

"Decoration. Protection, too, perhaps. Might be enchanted."

Isadora followed Pearl up the gravel path in silence. The school wasn't *exactly* what she'd envisioned. Perhaps the inside was less ... forgotten. A trunk floated in the air next to her, packed with new dresses, undergarments, an apron, pins for her hair, and freshly starched tunics. Isadora fidgeted beneath a calico dress of sprigged bluebonnets set in a deep wine. She'd never worn such a rich color and felt oddly disobedient in an open neckline.

Once they arrived at the top of the stairs, Isadora stood at the door for a full minute.

"Nervous?" Pearl asked.

Every thud of her heart shook Isadora's chest. The misty cloud in her mind gave way to heavy foam. She remembered again Maximillion's admonition to separate her thoughts from the powers, but it didn't make any more sense now than it had last night. *What* thoughts did the powers give her? Nothing existed behind the blur. The blur was simply there. She cast it aside to deal with later. For now, she had school to start and a new life to dive into headfirst.

She pulled her shoulders back. "Not nervous. Just … excited. All right, maybe a little nervous."

"Lay low. Listen more than you speak and … don't talk about anything controversial."

Isadora eyed her. *Lay low?* What was that supposed to mean? "What's controversial?" she asked instead.

"Greta."

"Greta?"

"The High Priestess. The one … maybe causing all these wars? Just … don't bring up the war. And don't let anyone know that you don't know much magic."

Isadora's jaw dropped. "There's a war?"

Pearl sighed. "No. There's three of them. Never mind. Don't bring it up, all right? I've tucked a newsscroll in your trunk. Read it every chance you get, and it'll eventually make sense."

When Pearl rapped on the door, Isadora swallowed. She forced her arms to hang at her side instead of fidgeting with her sleeves. Seconds later, the door blew open, revealing ten sets of wide, curious eyes. A chorus of screeches followed.

"The new girl!"

"The forester!"

"She's here. Oy, Catie. The new girl's here!"

"Merry meet!"

"Oy! Her eyes are two colors."

"Just look a' that braid! Your hair must be longer than a Letum Wood tree."

Girls spilled onto the porch amid gobs of old fabric and

unbound hair. The *tap tap tap* of feet descending wooden stairs followed, bringing another surge of skirts and boots. Isadora stumbled, borne backward by the wave of bodies surrounding her.

"What's your name?" one called.

"Can you do sums? I need help."

"Did you live in the forest?"

"I've read that book you're holding. It's very boring."

"She hasn't brought an easel."

"Pearl?" Isadora cried as the swarm of hands nearly choked her. "Ah, some help?"

"Oh, dear," Pearl said, laughing. Her coffee cup hovered high above the chaos, carried to safety on a spell. "It seems you're quite welcome after all! I best be going. Merry part, Isadora! I'll check on you later."

Pearl disappeared down the path.

The barrage of questions continued. Isadora managed to answer one, only to be interrupted halfway through that answer by another question. The girls shouted in a terrific cacophony that sent her into another spinning headache. By Drago, she'd never heard such *noise* in all her life.

"Silence!"

All sound ceased.

Isadora spun to see a girl with wild, kinky red hair standing in the doorway. Her bright emerald eyes flashed. She couldn't be much older than Isadora, but she carried an air of authority and power in her pert little nose, heart-shaped face, and pointed chin. Unlike the rest of the girls, she wore no shoes.

"Everyone stand back," the girl commanded. "Don't be total heathens."

"Baylee's here," one girl whispered.

"Quiet."

"She'll eat the new girl alive."

They scuttled like bugs in the light, retreating until a pathway formed, leading Baylee straight to Isadora. Baylee studied Isadora with a crisp, narrowed gaze, closing the gap one step at a time.

Isadora held her breath, refusing to look away by sheer willpower. Baylee stopped a few paces away, just within arm's length. She wore the same blue frock and knee-length dress as the other girls, except hers seemed a bit older than the rest. A faded apron with fresh flour stains and what appeared to be tomato juice covered her frame. Dirt rimmed her fingernails.

"Yer it?" Baylee finally asked.

"Er ... *av*—merry meet?"

Baylee rolled her eyes. Heat flooded Isadora's face when the girls tittered. Baylee put her hands on her hips and stepped forward. The girls lurched back, throwing themselves out of her way. She didn't seem to notice as she circled Isadora.

"Where ya from? Ya sound a bit hoity-toity if ya ask me. Ya not from Ashleigh, are ya?"

The thick drawl and slow cadence of Baylee's words didn't give *her* any credit where accents were concerned, but Isadora pushed that thought away.

"Letum Wood."

"Oy!" Baylee said, laughing. "Another forester! Remember what happened to the last one?"

The girls giggled in unison again, a wild pitch to their hysteria. Isadora tightened her grip on her books. Where was Miss Sophia?

Baylee stopped a breath away. The sour, fetid smell of vinegar washed over Isadora when she spoke. "The other forester left here crying in the middle of the night. Couldn't handle the new life, ya know. Poor lass. Never returned. What's ya name, new girl?"

Isadora pressed her lips together. "Are you the Head Witch of the school?" she asked.

"Do I look like I adore birds' nests?"

The girls tittered again. Isadora lost herself in the comment. *Birds' nests?*

"No," Baylee continued. "I'm *not* Miss Sophia, but I'm in charge when she's gone. And she's gone a lot. This isn't so much a school as it is ... a redistribution establishment."

The girls giggled again. Did Isadora imagine their thin faces? Gaunt eyes? The air of desperation that permeated their expressions? Surely this wasn't the school that Maximillion intended.

"A what?" she murmured, feeling as if the girls were closing in on her again.

Baylee folded her arms across her chest. "Can ya cook?"

"N-not really. I mean, a *few* things. My mam—"

"Clean?"

"Yes?"

"What are you doing here?"

"Getting an education, of course."

Baylee's gaze narrowed. "No one comes to Miss Sophia's to learn. We're certainly not going to pamper ya just because ya parents were stupid enough to send ya to a place like this."

"They didn't," Isadora said.

"Oh?"

"I ... I'm banished from home."

Baylee snorted. "Well, that's something, at least. What jobs can ya do?"

"I can paint."

"Paint? Yer kidding. How is that going to make dinner? Can ya peel potatoes?"

"Yes! I can do that."

"*And* mop a floor at the same time?"

"Of course not. Who can do both?"

Baylee nodded to all the girls. "Every one of us, thank ya very much."

"Why not do them separately?"

"Because there's no time."

What in the name of Drago were they doing that required so much *time*? Isadora opened her mouth to ask, then decided against it. Whatever a *redistribution establishment* meant, she didn't want to know the details. All she wanted was to throttle Maximillion. What was he *thinking*?

"I'll learn to do both," Isadora said. "I'm a fast learner."

"I'll believe that when I see it," Baylee muttered.

Isadora cast about for something else to say. What could be said? Baylee had already made up her mind against Isadora, and the girls clearly followed her. There wasn't much left *to* do but prove herself.

"Put ya stuff inside," Baylee said. "Ya can clean the breakfast dishes. I'll see ya in the kitchen in an hour. I'm busy rolling cigars."

Baylee whipped around, her bouncy red hair flying with her. The girls ignored Isadora as they followed Baylee inside. Before the last one left Isadora standing on the porch, alone, a meaty girl with fists like hams slapped the books out of Isadora's hand. They scattered to the ground. The girl sniggered.

Isadora picked the books up, waited for the girls to disappear, and followed quietly behind.

Isadora found her room by accident.

After perusing every floor, seeking an empty room, she stumbled onto one on the third floor. The door rattled, a small, high window was cracked, and there was no clear source of heat. Lines fractured the walls, giving way to peeling sheets of *something* that littered the ground with white ash. A bucket filled with rags sat in the corner. She ignored it.

Outside, belligerent shrieks and muffled screams echoed in the hallway. The girls banged on the door with their fists as they ran past.

"Tell us about the forest!"

"Can we wear your clothes?"

"Do you like math?"

"Braid my hair!"

Isadora sank to a dingy wooden bed with a musty mattress. Bits of straw poked out of it. Despite the warm fall day, a chill permeated the air. She wrapped her arms around herself with a shudder. At least she had her own room. Something she'd never had before. The enthusiasm she'd hoped to muster didn't come. In fact, nothing sat in her stomach except a hard rock. What had she done? How far had she gone from home?

She already missed Sanna.

She was studying a drifting cobweb when a burning pain sprouted in her wrist, climbing up her arm. She yelped. A thin, black circle blossomed on the pale skin of her inner wrist. The slight curls and strange edges almost looked like letters but not in a language she knew, and too small to really tell.

"Lovely," she muttered. The school had already branded her.

Isadora opened her trunk and started to unpack her dresses. She hung two of them on nails sticking out of the wall, then left the rest inside. She had a feeling these girls wouldn't take kindly to her having more clothes than them. The books she placed inside the trunk. For a moment, she listened to the call of a girl from outside and felt a shot of fear.

With resolve, she banished the morose thoughts, brushed her hands on her dress, and steeled herself. At least she was out of Anguis and far from the dragons. She had *that* much. As soon as she finished breakfast, she was going to find the library. She *would* learn more magic. This was nothing but a momentary ruffle in her plans. A weakening.

Not a single one of them would stop her.

Sanna struggled around Letum Wood for the rest of the day.

After the fish incident, she didn't dare go far. She stayed near the circle of trees, listening to the forest and sorting through houses. No food remained, of course. She scrounged up a few mushrooms but, not trusting their violet dots, threw them away. Broken nut shells taunted her, no doubt thrown from the treetops by squirrels. She found nothing amongst them.

When evening fell—much, *much* sooner than anticipated—she found a blanket in one of the houses, shivered at the thought of ghosts, and curled up in a corner, eventually falling into a restless slumber.

The warmth of Luteis's tail hugging her ankle the next morning stirred her from her shallow sleep littered with dreams of the attic, Isadora, and Cara.

You survived.

She opened one eye and stifled a yawn. Despite herself, she was glad to see him. At least he was something familiar. She wouldn't be alone in the dark anymore.

"Are you surprised?"

A little. Did you manage to find nourishment?

"Food, you mean?"

Yes.

"I *found* some. I just ... couldn't eat it."

Her injured fingers still smarted, occasionally falling numb. Bright crimson teeth marks slashed across her bulging hand, swelling her fingers like sausages. No signs of infection so far. She thought of asking him for another drop or two of his blood but dismissed it. It didn't seem like the kind of thing to ask for.

Luteis glanced at her hand. *Ah. You attempted to fish.*

Her gaze dropped. Was this where she admitted he'd been right all along? "Ah ... something like that."

He snorted, turning away. *Come, Sanna of Anguis. We have a meeting, then I will find you breakfast.*

She leapt to her feet. "A meeting?"

You shall see.

"Where are we going?" She jogged behind him across the circle. He headed toward the biggest tree.

Up.

"For our meeting?"

Precisely. Would you like help climbing to the meeting point?

"I can *definitely* climb on my own."

He eyed her. *Those are extremely tall trees. No vines extend this far down.*

She hesitated, rubbing her still-swollen fingers, a painful reminder of her hubris. The words stuck in her throat at first. She choked them out.

"A-all right," she said with a heavy sigh. "I ... could probably use some help."

As you say.

Luteis climbed the tree with all four legs, sinking his talons into the bark, and held her by the waist with his tail. The humiliation of being carted up the tree burned, but she swallowed it back. The farther they moved, the uglier the truth became; she *wouldn't* have been able to scale it. She'd never met a witch that could climb faster than her, even though Jesse had tried to beat her several times. Luteis, however, left her in the dust. He sped up the trunk and then wound around branches with enviable ease.

By the time the ground disappeared, a new world emerged around her. Crossed branches, carpets of moss, and a familiar, thick closeness. Chains of bright white lilies draped the trunks, shifting in the gentle breeze. Honeysuckle thickened the air. She knew the canopy of Letum Wood, but as they ascended, she realized this was something else. Vines, glowing an iridescent green, hung in the space between branches. Ivory flowers were strung amongst them, dripping with petals that curled into low-hanging ringlets. A gentle whisper of wind made them dance.

"*Mori,*" she murmured.

It's because of Deasylva, Luteis said as he leaned into the breeze, eyes closed. *Her presence creates such beauty.*

"Deasylva?"

In answer, silver, sloping letters, scripted one at a time, glowed from the tree trunk next to Sanna. She froze.

Sanna Spence, daughter of Rian Spence of the royal Dragonmaster line of Gregorus, the High Dragonmaster of the Ancient Days.

"What?"

Welcome.

Sanna blinked, stunned into disbelief. Sure, she'd always believed trees were *alive*, but this was something new. She reached out to feel the empty air next to the trunk. No one was hiding under a spell, scripting the words. She saw nothing around them. But still ... writing on a tree? Impossible.

Or not. It *was* there.

Goosebumps covered her skin. Around her, branches waved with soft sighs, and the birds fell silent. Sanna trailed her fingers along the shimmering letters etched in the umber trunk. Magic, it had to be. From where? And why? And what was a Dragonmaster?

The words faded one letter at a time, making room for more.

You have come as I desired.

"Who are you?" she asked. Was she mad now? Had the break from Anguis and her family caused a mental collapse? Being at home in the trees was an entirely different matter than *talking* to them. Perhaps the poison from the fish was still in her veins, concocting an impressive hallucination.

I am she whom your ancestors knew, but you do not.

A voice drifted by on the wind. Low. Melodic. Distinctly feminine. *Sanna,* it whispered. Sanna whipped around. No one stood there except Luteis, who peered into the distance, seeming perfectly at ease. The written words disappeared. She pressed her palm to the trunk and scowled.

"You have to give me more explanation than that!"

A bright flash of silver preceded another word. Sanna read each letter as it appeared. *You are here to learn the truth.*

"I'm here because Luteis carried me. But if we're going back a bit further, I'm here because I kind of *maybe* made a mistake and—" Her frown deepened. "Wait. The truth about what?"

Yourself.

She gazed past the trunk to the tree behind it. The branches swayed, whispering. *Sanna.*

Were the trees talking to her? All of them? Her fingertips burrowed into the rough bark. She flattened her palm. Something buzzed there. A current of life. A feeling of ... *breath.* As if the tree had a pulse, a heart buried within the layers of bark. Another whisper of wind ruffled her skirts and hair.

Sanna.

A terrible thought prickled all the way to her heart. She fell to her knees and bowed her head, prostrating. Her question burst from within the cave she made with her arms.

"Drago? Is this ... are you Drago?"

No. It couldn't be Drago. Drago was male. This was ... *whatever* she was ... female. But who else could it be? She peeked back to the trunk to find new words.

Drago is the work of a deceiver.

Sanna opened her mouth to respond, but words failed her. She straightened, sitting back on her haunches. Drago couldn't be a lie. He was the god of forest and dragons. He was ... everything.

"Talis?"

As you say.

Sanna stared at the words for a long time. "Talis," she murmured. "You mean that ... that Talis is a deceiver? With all due respect to ... well ... whatever or whoever you are, that's impossible. If Talis is a deceiver, then ... you're trying to say that Drago isn't real."

The tree warmed beneath her legs.

You understand.

"I don't believe you. Drago is god of forest and dragons."

Prove him to me.

"Sure. That's ... yes. I will."

Sanna's nostrils flared. She remembered too late that Luteis had asked the same thing of her, and she'd failed then. She wracked her brain, plunging into thoughts the depths of which she could hardly fathom. Prove her god? She had no authority. No power to sway him to show himself to her. No scales to burn on the pyre. She didn't even have her prayer book. Daid, Drago's Servant, couldn't even ask such a thing. Only Talis.

Only Talis.

A deceiver, the sculpted words came again, as if knowing her thoughts. *A liar.*

Sanna's mouth felt like a field of cotton when she whispered, "It ... it can't be."

A swirl of leaves blasted past her, whipping her hair into her eyes. She ducked, reached out, and clung to the tree until it passed, as if the wind—or whatever spoke to her— was angry with her. She shoved away, glaring into the bark.

"Then who are *you*?" she snapped.

I am the magic in the forest, the power of the dragons, the instincts of the Dragonmasters, and the force that brings and maintains life in all the forests in Alkarra. Letum Wood is my home.

Sanna's forehead ruffled.

"You're ... Letum Wood?"

A flare of heat warmed her feet, spreading into her calves. A bubble of light rippled out from where she stood, crawling across the tree. New branches curled out of the trunk and elongated in budding green arms. Lilies tainted with a soft blush of pink appeared, one at a time, in a chain. The chain reached out, circling Sanna's shoulders, pulling her closer to the trunk. The words flared.

I am the goddess of all forests and all that lies within. They obey me.

The words shone so brightly on the trunk that Sanna shielded her eyes with a hand. "Does Talis know you?"

Very well.

"Then ... he made up everything? Drago. The pyres. The prayer books. Ev-everything we did was just ... a lie?"

True sincerity is never a lie.

"I don't ... I don't understand."

A knot formed in Sanna's chest as she recalled her diligence to her prayer book. The ache in her back from foraging for dragon scales for days so they could sacrifice them on the pyres every month and plead for Drago's approval. The thick, bitter smoke that curled up from their offerings seemed to clog her lungs even now. All of it had been a ruse.

Peace, daughter of Gregorus. Rage will only harm you.

The warmth of the tree spiraled into Sanna's body, curled through her chest, and eased into her heart. The livid knot unwound, soothing into coiling strands of light that took her breath away. Her muscles relaxed. Sanna drifted in the feeling for a moment, letting the thoughts of revenge pass her by. The words appeared again, shimmering.

You are here to restore my home and my dragons to their former glory.

The words faded back into the bark. Sanna blinked. "Restore Letum Wood? Has it fallen?"

Very far…

The glittering words faded, giving way to a patch of mossy olive and rich brown against the bark. An image appeared, shimmering over the trunk. Dead trees strewn haphazardly on the forest floor. Billowing clouds of overgrown bushes clogging the ground and preventing new growth. Fields of wilting saplings. Beluas everywhere.

"Oh."

The dragons and Dragonmasters were my caretakers, but they have not fulfilled their duties for many years. The forest is out of balance.

"One hundred and fifty years, I'm guessing," Sanna murmured as the image faded away.

Yes.

Sanna swallowed a rising lump in her throat. So Talis had gathered the dragons into a safe spot for one hundred and fifty years, preventing them from caring for the wild wood. What was *she* supposed to do about that?

"You said the Dragonmasters. Who are they?"

You.

"I may be many things, but I'm no master. I'm a Servant. You have your facts confused."

Your family. Your twin sister. All those in Anguis. All of you are Dragonmasters by birthright. Serving slothful dragons is not your destiny, nor is wasting away theirs. Talis has allowed fear to control his vision.

"You know Isadora?"

I know all creatures in my forest.

Of course she knew Isadora. If she were a true goddess, she knew all of them. But seeing it in front of her allowed her to understand. Talis's insistence on his own authority, that only he had access to Drago. Constant pyres. So many unanswered questions that all seemed to shuffle into one big, fat lie. Why had he killed Ivis so quickly?

Why hadn't she wondered all along? Or had she, deep inside?

Sanna pulled herself from the thoughts.

"Now? You couldn't have restored the truth at any other time in the past one hundred and fifty years?"

No.

"Why not?"

Only you have listened to my call.

The words came slowly now, as if each letter was carved with a painstaking hand. Sanna's heart thudded dully in her chest. "You can't do it yourself," she murmured.

There are limits, even for goddesses. Fire is a necessary part of my life cycle, yet it still gives my trees much fear. The forest knows me; fire and water do not. I cannot control fire. Talis knows this. The descent of his wrath could be unstoppable in an uncared-for forest. He knows this as well and uses it to control me.

Another image appeared in the bark. Talis loomed over another dragon, his teeth bared. The dragon lay sprawled across the ground, bleeding underneath Talis's sharp talons. Behind him, Letum Wood burned, licking with greedy tongues of fire.

"Talis?" she whispered.

I have spoken to many dragons. Some have tried to leave Anguis. But without a witch to fight with them, there is no hope. Many times I tried. When Talis found them, he destroyed them, then burned everything he could reach. A message to me.

Sanna swallowed. The scene faded into another and another. More fire. Burned, scorched earth. Branches plummeting, consumed by sapphire flames.

Sanna's stomach roiled. Panic streaked through her. "But ... Daid! Mam! What about my family? They're still with him. He could kill them next. H-he tried to kill Isadora."

They are alive.

"Isadora too?"

Yes.

"But Talis could ... what if he..."

This is why you are here.

"You're a goddess!" Sanna cried. "*Do* something!"

The scene changed. Sanna gazed at the track in the upper canopy back at home. She reached out, her fingertips hovering over the shimmering image. A hint of a dragon wing lingered in the background. The scene shifted—Sanna sleeping on a branch, one braid hanging near her face. Then to her climbing into the heights, chased by Rosy and Junis. Her heart ached like a bruised thing. She missed *home*.

The images sank back into the bark, giving way to the shimmering words again. *You have always listened to my call.*

"I didn't know. I just ... I'm just happy there."

Exactly.

Drago. Talis. Daid. Mam. Isadora. The truth moved deep into her mind, all the way to her bones, as if taking root. Erasing her god made null years—generations—of devotion. False devotion in the face of a violent liar. For years, she'd been lied to. Discarding Drago felt like extracting a slice of herself, and her heart throbbed.

Another quiet sigh shifted through the branch and into her, calming her agitated thoughts. The touch of magic caused her blood to whirl through her veins, singeing like fire. She *wouldn't* let Talis get away with it. He would lie and harm no more.

Certainly not her family.

"How can I defeat him?"

Restore my dragons and the Dragonmasters to their former glory. They can save my home, and themselves, once they remember who they are.

Another scene sprang to life on the trunk. A female witch sat astride a dragon's shoulders. They soared through an open meadow carrying a wounded bird. Then it faded, revealing a dragon slinking along the forest floor, stalking a belua, a witch at his side. The images sank back into the tree.

The sheer number of questions numbed Sanna's mind. "I see."

The responding letters appeared one at a time. The writing thinned; it seemed to be withdrawing.

The dragons do not know what they are anymore. Dragonmasters have lost all dignity. Defeat Talis, and restore who you really are. You are not alone. Luteis will be with you—I have promised him.

Sanna curled her fingers into her palm. Her nails cut into the skin, sinking in so sharply her bones ached.

"I don't know anything about Dragonmasters. And I understand that you're a goddess, but I don't see *how* we can defeat Talis."

You shall soon see.

"What if I don't want to? What if I just want to save my family and get my life back to what it—"

She sputtered to a stop. Another scene arose on the bark, displaying a twisted dragon wing. The blue shimmer of dragons' blood steamed on the ground, mixing with the earth. She took it all in. Scales hacked at odd angles. Limp, cold dragon bodies. Broken eggs. Crying hatchlings, alone on the burning earth. Sanna whirled away.

"Stop!"

Another massacre will come. Soon. There is more at stake than honor or home. Violent days come.

Sanna closed her eyes. If loss of balance meant a massacre, then *yes*, she did want to restore balance. She just didn't want to fight *Talis* to do so.

"Why *didn't* you save them from the massacre?"

The lettering paused. *Another time, I shall explain.*

Sanna scowled. "Fine. I'll ... figure out how to defeat Talis and restore the Ser—Dragonmasters."

I must leave and visit the other forests. I will return.

The brightness of the remaining words flared, then faded one letter at a time. Sanna reached out, pressing her fingertips into the light as if she could pull it out and into herself. She cursed Talis under her breath with a fresh burst of wrath.

The sweet air withdrew. The quiet chirp of a bird sounded in the distance. Rustling leaves drew Sanna's gaze higher. Overhead, a cluster of globular red fruits, speckled with buttery dots, dipped toward her on a vine. She grabbed them.

"Thanks."

Luteis's tail wrapped around her ankle.

You understand why I said nothing?

Sanna could only nod.

TEN

After devouring all the fruit Deasylva had given her, Sanna wiped her face with her sleeve—earning a tilted head from Luteis—and stood back up. To her surprise, the sweet, slightly mushy fruit had restored her good humor. Perhaps it had goddess-juice in it, giving her an extra bump of tolerance.

"Well?" she asked. "What now?"

You learn how to ride so we can eventually return to Anguis.

"Even though—"

With precautions, a flying dragon is not a dead dragon.

Her mouth clamped shut for a moment, annoyed that he'd read her mind. "I disagree, but if you insist, it's your life."

He cut her a sharp glance but dismissed her comment as he sidled next to a stump in the middle of the circle. She followed. He motioned with a bob of his neck to the stump, which was as wide as Daid's shed, and clasped her ankle again.

Do you see?

The stump's strangely smooth surface held rings within

rings. They stretched almost as tall as she. Compared to the rest of the forest, however, this had been a young tree when it died. She reached out, running her fingers over it.

Light bloomed beneath her touch.

She sucked in a sharp breath and pulled away. The light faded. When she touched it again, it formed a circle. Words appeared in its wake, glimmering a bright silver, much like Deasylva's writing. Sanna leaned forward.

Sarasam the Lovely, Dragonmaster, fourteen years.

"Who is that?"

Your ancestor.

Sanna touched the ring beneath it. Another circle illuminated, this one thinner. It swept around the tree, finally coming back around with words so thin and slanted Sanna could barely make them out.

Loxly the Mighty, Dragonmaster, three years.

"What is this?" She pressed her entire palm against it. The light rippled out, activating all the rings. Words popped up in bright shots of light, shining from the darkness of the trunk. When she pulled away, the words faded, ebbing into a soft butter yellow.

A tree that was planted by your ancestors over three hundred years ago. It fell during the massacre. Deasylva allowed it to die.

"Why?"

So you could see. The trees chronicle the world around them, if your eyes are open.

She swallowed a lump in her throat. "Sarasam is a woman's name."

Yes. And?

"I-It's just good to see that there was a female Dragonmaster."

There were many.

A silence stretched between them while Sanna watched

the final slivers of light fade back into the bark. The temptation to touch it again, to memorize their names, feel some tangible connection to the witches that were part of her, flared. She pushed it back.

Later.

Simple Dragonian magic has two purposes. Luteis's voice purred through her mind with a new, strange intensity, bringing her out of her thoughts. *The magic will protect you from my heat and from falling off my back.*

"Is that all?"

Yes.

"I don't have to do a spell or something?"

The magic comes from within me.

Her tense shoulders relaxed slightly. "Well, that's not so bad."

He nudged her toward the stump with a not-so-graceful shove from his nose. *Climb.*

"Oh," she murmured, glancing from him to the stump as she ascended it. The distance was perfect; she could climb onto his wing and up to his shoulders without flailing. "Nice."

A perfect mounting stump, consequently.

Waves of heat simmered off his back and dissipated into the air. Sweat already trickled down her spine just from standing near him. He was so much hotter than the brood dragons. "So," she drawled. "How am I supposed to ride you if you're so hot? A saddle?"

A burst of fire issued from his mouth.

She recoiled.

A saddle? Don't be absurd.

"How am I supposed to know?"

When we connect, the magic will protect you.

"You're sure?"

He hesitated just long enough to shatter her confidence.

One never knows until one tries, of course.

"Or is scalded to death! Haven't you done this before?"

I confess, I have not.

"Look, I'm the one taking the risk! You at least owe it to me to be certain."

You are the first witch I've met.

"And you're asking me to take the risk?"

I didn't imagine you'd be frightened of anything.

Sanna's jaw dropped. *Frightened?* Had he just insulted her? She pulled her shoulders back. "I'm not afraid. I never said I was afraid! Why would you say that I'm afraid?"

He sniffed, turning away.

Clearly.

Livid, Sanna stepped back, dashed across the trunk, and threw herself onto his back. She caught hold of the juncture of his wings with her palms and pulled herself up in a quick movement. His neck smoothed into his shoulders where the wings met, leaving a small crook of space that fit her body. She could straddle him with a leg on either side of his neck.

If it weren't for the scalding heat.

"It's hot!"

She hopped on her feet. Balancing on his slippery scales proved almost impossible with her sandals on, as the heat seeped through even those. She slid down his back, arms wheeling. He caught her with a wing and bounced her into the air. He didn't hold her ankle, but she heard his voice when his wing held her back.

Calm yourself.

"Burning alive here!"

Allow me in.

Pressure thudded at the base of her brain again. It was

restless and powerful, wanting to get in, just like the first time he'd attempted to speak with her. Reluctantly, Sanna released her mind and braced herself for a sweep of magic. Instead, all the heat seemed to drain away, evaporating like mist. The burn faded to a light tingle and then disappeared. She stared at her legs and checked the bottoms of her feet for blisters.

She saw only clear, uninjured skin.

"Mori."

See?

"I mean ... it's kind of cool that you can do magic."

She could have sworn he rolled his eyes.

Sanna carefully crouched on his back, the bottoms of her feet pressed to his scales as she tested the space out. Details she'd missed while scrambling to save her skin became more apparent. The scales at the back of his neck were wider, with a rounded point, which made it less likely they'd jab her. They glittered with greater intensity, flushed a bright, burnished orange. She crouched, then stood, arms held out until she balanced on his back without fear of fall-ing. She pirouetted, then staggered to the side but didn't fall.

"Am I heavy?"

You are no burden.

"Can you feel me?"

A light pressure.

"Can I touch your wings?"

Can you?

Sanna rolled her eyes. "*May* I?"

Yes.

She reached out and gently caressed his leathery skin. It stretched tight from the base of his spine all the way to the bone that narrowed to a point. Tiny scales lined the ridge of bone, glittering like flames. Standing so close made it apparent just how powerful his wings were.

Luteis glanced back. *How do you feel?*

She looked down at her fingertips. "The same. Maybe..." A buzz, like the hum of a curious bee, filled the back of her mind. "Something."

A good sign. We won't go into the intricacies of Dragonian magic now. Much is possible. Another time, perhaps, but Deasylva says there is much power in a merging. Although she warns me that it can be dangerous.

Sanna advanced a step, her hands held out to her sides, and let his voice fade into the background. Straddling either side of his spine and walking between his powerful wings came easily without the heat. Luteis said nothing, but she thought she heard a low hum of pleasure.

"This isn't so bad. It didn't require any magic from me, which is just the kind of magic I like."

I can imagine.

Her mind swirled with questions. Could she stand up in flight? Was she supposed to feel such anticipation even though flying was dangerous?

"Do dragons ... er ... bond with more than one witch?" she asked instead as she settled onto his back, her legs folded beneath her. Even sitting felt almost natural, as if dragons were made to bear witches. He stepped away from the stump. Her body shifted with the movement. Everything up here felt big. Larger than life. She wanted to hold something, but there was nothing to grab. She slipped each leg on either side of his neck and squeezed with her knees. Better.

I don't know.

"Really?"

Merging is new for me as well.

"That's not very reassuring."

Neither is the smell of your feet.

She held up her leg and wiggled her toes. Dirt rimmed the leather straps that crossed her feet and wound up her ankles, all the way to her knees. Fair enough.

"Think we're stuck for life?"

He hesitated. *Perhaps.*

Sanna bit back all her questions. Did he communicate regularly with Deasylva? Was he truly tied to the goddess of the forest in a visceral way, or did she just provide extra guidance for the last of the wild forest dragons? None of the questions mattered right then.

It's a tentative merge in which my magic allows you safety while riding. This is not a full merge.

"Oh."

In a full merge, you and I will be one. If something happens to one of us...

"It happens to the other?"

As you say.

"What about when we're talking?"

No. Communication is based only on touch, not on the merge.

Sanna leaned back on her palms, tilting her head to see the first joint of his wings. Right now she felt stable and sure, but his wings weren't in motion. She wondered how it would feel in the air, the wind buffeting them, his muscles flexing.

"So, if you're shot down, I'll die also is what you're trying to say."

Yes.

"That rots."

It is the merging.

"Well ... all right. Then let's merge already."

He craned his head back to see her better. *You're not upset about that fate?*

"I can't change it, right?"

He paused. *Pragmatic. Unexpectedly so. I didn't expect logic from a wild witch like you.*

She frowned. What exactly did he mean by *a wild witch like you?* Like *he* had so much room to talk about being wild. He clearly had a lot to learn about witches.

"I'm full of surprises, apparently, so I'll let that one pass. I'd rather figure out a way to have light that isn't a full fire. It was so blasted dark last night."

Ah, yes. The depth of this forest casts an early shadow, and a late light in the morning. It's glorious for sleeping.

She rolled her eyes. Dragons.

"Can we get going now?"

He hesitated. *Not until we fully merge. Based on how well you've tolerated this one, I believe we'll be safe to proceed, but Deasylva cautioned me that the first full merging is very powerful.*

"I'll handle it."

Shall we plan how?

She blinked. Plan?

"Uh, no?"

Foolish. You must have a plan.

"Must not, actually. I don't know how I'll react until I feel the merging, right? So, let's just do it and see what happens. We'll go from there."

I don't like this. It may be too much. It—

"Do it."

I am not comfortable proceeding without a plan.

"Then figure out a plan where we fully merge."

That still does not include your response.

"That's something you're going to have to get used to."

He scowled, steam issuing from the sides of his mouth. *As you say. A warning: my expertise stops here. I don't know what you should anticipate from here out.*

"Fine."

Sanna waited, breath held for a long pause. A bird twittered overhead. The buzz of a dragonfly streaked past her ear. Nothing happened.

"Uh, Luteis? Today please."

Do you not sense me?

"Nope."

I am here.

"Where?"

In the place you must go. Do you not see it?

She glanced around. "No."

It's in your mind. Can you feel my magic?

"No."

That's because one cannot merge with an agitated mind. As I said earlier, about a plan—

"If you want my mind to be calm, we're never going to merge."

He snorted.

"Fine. I'll try to ... calm down, or something."

Sanna shoved a lock of hair out of her eyes, forced to introspection. *Was* she agitated? Yes. Leaving the brood. Feeling magic. No Isadora. Dragons flying. Drago *supposedly* dead—no, he couldn't die. According to Deasylva, he never existed. If that were even true. Sanna pulled in a deep breath through her nose. No helping it—they had to see this through. She'd never be able to find out the truth about Drago if they couldn't get back home.

Quieting her teeming frustration didn't come easy. Minutes passed while she sat on Luteis's back, fists clenched, jaw tight, Talis spinning through her mind.

Then she thought of Isadora. Of lazy summer nights in the attic with the window thrown open, the breeze twining through the room. Of running through the canopy, skidding along the moss, using her toes to direct her body. The gentle play of light and the scent of juniper in the forest eased her mind. She sank into Luteis's back, her muscles relaxing. The tension in her neck softened. She sensed something. A place—no, a thing. Something muted and vague, like a will-o'-the-wisp. She chased it, plucking at the moving light. It flared, illuminating, then raced over her in a rush of heat.

Light flooded her mind. Power swept through her with stunning force, robbing her of breath. Her fingers tingled. Her skin burned. She gasped and tumbled backward. Luteis slipped away right before the magic overcame her entire body.

She plunged into darkness.

Isadora woke up with rain in her eyes and ground pepper coating her pillow.

She sneezed for ten minutes, spraying her already-wet mattress with snot. Pepper wasn't the worst of the pranks the girls had successfully attempted in the last week. Glue in her shoes. Wrong directions through the whole school. A worm in her cold pudding. Flakes of dried potato in the soap box.

Baylee put her on dish duty on the first day, and Isadora's fingers had turned almost permanently pruney. Although she couldn't confirm it, she had a hunch that the girls cooking the meals used every possible dish just so she had to wash them.

Miss Sophie still hadn't made a full appearance. Glimpses of her showed here and there. Streaks of blonde hair. A slender body. A gentle hum. The only tangible sign of her was a pervasive, earthy smell that flowed from her office on a cloud of bluish-gray smoke—when she wasn't in the garden smoking a cigar. The girls giggled every time they passed her bedroom, which had shrooms growing underneath the door.

Isadora hadn't yet braved eating in the dining room—the chaos sent her into an immediate headache. Not to mention the brawls over food that often turned violent. Maximillion didn't send a word, although Pearl transported a fresh cup of coffee over every morning.

Just to get you through, her notes said.

Isadora turned the coffee into tea and tried to pretend she wasn't homesick.

Despite the sheer number of dishes, the mold growing in the rafters, and the pervasive scent of dust, Isadora didn't mind the school itself. She could carve out three separate hours a day for studying magic and improving her use of it. What she couldn't get used to was the sheer amount of *talking*.

A gaggle of girls ran by her room, tittering despite the early hour.

"They're like chattering gnomes," she muttered to herself, rubbing her eyes. Rain leaked through the roof, gathering in puddles on the floor.

"What are chattering gnomes?"

The question came from the doorway.

Isadora jumped. "Get out of my room!"

Baylee advanced inside, a candle hovering next to her.

Her hair shone a bright red in the soft glow. Only a dim light filtered into the room from the small window. The storm clouds must be thick outside, Isadora decided.

The door closed behind Baylee with a *slam*.

"Ya didn't come to breakfast today, so I came to see if ya left." Baylee dodged a stream of water from the ceiling. "This is the old storage closet, by the way. Not a girl's room. Ya can have a different one if ya want it."

Isadora's nostrils flared. Of *course* no one had mentioned that. "No, I haven't left yet."

Although she couldn't *exactly* say why she was staying, either. Of all schools, why had Maximillion sent her here? Why did he want her in the chaos? There was little time to focus on her thoughts and not a single bout of silence in the whole day.

Isadora moved to stand, then let out a cry. The grimoire on basic household spells she'd gotten from the library lay on the floor, coated in water. She snatched it off the ground and dried it with her pillow, but even that was wet.

"Demmet!"

Her cheeks warmed in shame. She'd never cursed before, even though Sanna did every other minute. What did it matter? Mam wasn't here to disapprove. Still, she didn't like the feeling it gave her. Like everything was out of control.

Baylee leaned back against the wall, arms folded loosely against her chest. She didn't seem to have noticed the swear word. She yawned. "Just dry it with a spell."

Tears clogged Isadora's throat, making her voice thick. "I don't know one."

The pages of the book flipped open, landing with a squishy *plop*. Isadora blinked, staring at a paragraph with instructions on a drying incantation. Had Baylee done that?

Isadora turned to the side, her back to Baylee, and attempted it. A two-second, limp breeze stirred her hair and then died.

"Ya pronunciation isn't right."

"Like you have room to talk about correct pronunciation," Isadora mumbled. She could *feel* Baylee roll her eyes. Isadora couldn't blame her. She didn't even like her own attitude.

"Fine," Isadora said and softened her tone. "I'll try again."

Five attempts later, and pockets of the water had started to slowly dry. The pages were wrinkled, but the ink stopped swirling.

"Faster than placing it near the fire," Baylee said. "The girls would probably use it for scrap paper anyway if they found it down there."

"Uh ... thanks."

"It's crummy here," Baylee said. She shoved away from the wall and flopped onto Isadora's bed. Which, Isadora realized a moment later, was now completely dry and pepper free. Another incantation from Baylee, no doubt. Who was this girl, anyway? "Sometimes painfully boring, ya know. Unless we can get the jig up on Sophie. Then it's a bunch of laughs."

Baylee's coppery hair swung in bright, voluptuous curls around her shoulders when she landed. The careless way she flopped onto the mattress, her skirt drifting up to expose her knees and her wild hair lying unbound on the flat pillow, reminded Isadora of Sanna.

"I see," Isadora murmured. She had no idea what *jig* meant, or whether she even wanted to meet Miss Sophie.

"But it's better here than any forest could give ya, that's for sure. Better than the streets too. Better than a cabin in the woods, I bet. If ya want it, ya can get civilized here. But no one really wants that."

"The girls are horrible."

The words rushed out of Isadora before she knew they were there. She snapped her mouth shut, horrified when Baylee started to laugh, a great, deep belly laugh that rolled through the room.

"You'll never make it in the Network if ya think it's bad here."

Isadora's stomach churned. Surely that couldn't be true. A bubbling frustration welled up within her. At Maximillion for putting her here. At the girls for being so nasty. At Baylee for not caring. At the magic in her head for being totally uncooperative. It wasn't *supposed* to be this way.

"A few pranks?" Isadora rose to her feet, towering over Baylee. She clenched her fists. "They tried to cut my hair! My clothes were tinted purp—"

A rhythmic *bang, bang, bang* sounded against the door. Isadora sucked in a sharp breath. None of the younger girls had the strength to knock that loudly.

"Who is it?" Isadora snapped.

"Open immediately."

A bolt of fear shivered through her. Maximillion. She hadn't once managed to separate her thoughts from the magic in the last week—although she *had* tried. Sort of. His instructions made no sense whatsoever. Admittedly, however, she hadn't tried very hard, lost in the mess of her new life. She strode across the room and pulled the door open.

Maximillion stood outside with a burning scowl.

"Move aside. I haven't all day for this."

Isadora planted her feet. "No. You're late."

"I was busy."

She held up two fingers.

"Two days. You were supposed to be here two days ago."

"I don't answer to you."

"This place is *utter* madness! Not a single thing can be accomplished here except survival. I won't stay. I can't. Not if I'm to ever control—"

"We'll talk about this like civilized witches inside your hovel. I don't have time for childish games. Move aside, or I will move you."

"This is my room. You cannot invade my privacy simply because you think you're important."

Behind her, Baylee rose to her feet, eyes wide. Maximillion only gave her a cursory glance, then looked at the ceiling, which still actively leaked.

"It's a closet."

She gritted her teeth. "Not anymore."

"Let me in," Maximillion snapped. "We have a lot to do and not a lot of time to do it. And I *am* important."

"Not nearly as important as you think. If you wish to speak with me, we can discuss your concerns downstairs after you kindly inquire whether I'm available. I'm quite busy. As, apparently, are you."

He growled. "Have you separated your thoughts from the magic?"

Her pause deepened his scowl.

"You *haven't?*"

"I've been surviving!"

He clenched his teeth, his fingers curling over a watch. His eyes darted into the hall, then back to her. "Of course not. We shall talk right now or not at all."

Fury engulfed her, buoying and hot as dragon fire.

"Fine."

Isadora slammed the door shut.

"Wait!" Baylee cried. "Let him in! Are ya mad? You can't slam the door on *him*."

Isadora brushed past her. She definitely *felt* better. She only wished she could see his shocked expression. "He deserved it."

"But ... that was Maximillion Sinclair."

"So?"

"He's the Ambassador of the Central Network, ya dolt! He can have ya hung."

"Cannot."

Baylee scratched the top of her head. "Well, *rumors* say—"

Isadora commanded her trunk to the wall beneath the small window and stepped up onto it. "I've read articles about him in the *Chatterer* and learned about the governing laws of the Network thanks to a book from our rather dismal library. The only thing you have to fear is how he feels about himself." Isadora reached for the lock on the window and pried it open. The glass panes groaned when she shoved it free. She stood just tall enough to see a familiar cloud of bluish smoke rising from the garden. As she'd suspected, Miss Sophie sat below, cigar at her lips.

In a downpour.

The door rattled on its hinges under Maximillion's fist. "Isadora!" he called. "Open this door, or I'll do it by force!"

"Miss Sophie!" Isadora called, hands cupped around her mouth. "Oh, Miss Sophie? We have a visitor here at the school. Ambassador Sinclair would like to talk to you about a personal matter."

The banging on the door grew louder. "*Isadora!*"

Miss Sophie's head popped out from behind a mulberry bush. A bird's nest made entirely of spare pieces of string drooped from a blonde side braid, revealing an enchanted bird that flew in circles around her left ear. A sopping cigar sat in her hand.

"Really?" She leapt to her feet.

"He's in a frightful hurry!"

Baylee jerked her back by the elbow. "Isadora! He's livid. He's going to murder both of us in our sleep."

"Will not."

"He killed an entire hoard of chewing locusts with a spell. He spoke face-to-face with the High Priest of the West, Dostar, when they tried to poison our cattle. When Dostar shoved a sword against his throat, Maximillion acted *bored*. This man works with Greta every day," she hissed, lowering her voice. "He's not afraid of anything!"

The racket at the door had stopped. Isadora held up a hand, hushing Baylee.

"You've not heard the last from me," Maximillion muttered, laying one final *thud* on the door. Seconds later, the shadow of his feet disappeared. Miss Sophie pattered down the hallway, calling his name as she passed the room. No doubt she'd transported in.

Isadora frowned. That didn't seem entirely safe. Too exhausted to think about it, Isadora sank back on her bed.

Baylee stared at her in horror. "Isadora, you *are* mad. Forester mad, you raving lunatic!"

"No. I'm ... tired."

"He's been a savior to many, ya know."

Isadora blinked, straightening. "What?"

"High Priestess Greta is a mess. The Southern Network was about to declare open war last year, but Maximillion talked them down at the last minute. He donated his mansion to injured Guardians." Baylee's brow furrowed. "He visited the orphanage in Chatham City where I grew up once. Can't remember why. After that, the Network rebuilt it."

Isadora blinked. "Really?"

"Swear it."

"I'm shocked."

"Maybe. If I were Ambassador, dealing with Greta and Charles all day, I'd probably be irritable as a bat too."

"He can go stuff a bat, for all I care." Isadora folded her arms across her chest. "I'm tired of him treating me so rudely."

Baylee frowned. "I'm not sure if yer brave or insane."

"Hopefully a little bit of both."

"Watch yaself," Baylee said, drawing herself taller. "Enemies aren't worth it. Especially politicians."

"He's not my enemy or my politician," Isadora muttered. "He's my mentor."

A blank slate, Isadora thought three days later. *That's all I see. Nothing but gray. Smooth, endless gray, like the edge of the pearls Mam used to wear. No, those were ivory. Like the papierlily flowers in the spring. Oh, so many flowers! Sanna always did hate them. I wonder if she—*

Isadora's eyes flew open, and she growled. Failed again. Keeping her thoughts straight and focusing on the magic wasn't as easy as it sounded.

The sooty spires of Berry stared back at her. Stone chimneys. Feathers and dirt and discarded food littered the roads. Fog lingered in the lane, swirling around witches as they passed.

Certainly nothing of worth to look at. Not like she'd imagined there would be in the Network, anyway. Witches were lazy. They rarely seemed to clean up the streets, and often pitched whatever they didn't want to carry into the lane. Talis would never have allowed that.

"Egads," she muttered, rubbing her forehead.

A passing witch, his shirt sodden with sweat and dirt, gave her a strange glance. She sat near the edge of the garden at a spot that overlooked the road. A boxy carriage pulled by horses—such gentle creatures—clattered over the cobblestones. Behind her sat the school, oddly silent. All but three of the girls had left on some obscure holiday. They met for meals and ignored her entirely. She returned the favor, grateful to not wash so many dishes for a few days. The extra solitude, she found, wasn't as nice as she'd hoped. She listened to them laughing over a game with envy.

Isadora ignored the street, closed her eyes, and attempted again. This time, she tried to stare *into* the metallic storm.

At first, nothing happened. Her head ached, the way it usually did, but then it shifted. Something seemed to be nipping at the edges, hoping to break through. Isadora tried to chase it. To find the weak spot, but nothing happened. The blur swelled again, flickered in the depths, but revealed nothing.

Annoyed, she opened her eyes.

"So much for what *he* knows."

With a sigh, she turned back to the newsscroll in her hands. Maximillion hadn't returned. With the help of another grimoire, she'd learned how to transport an envelope. She'd transported him several messages over the last few days, but all returned with her name burned off the front and the seal unbroken.

Snippets from the news caught her gaze.

New attack. Western Network Attempts to Invade South. Southern Network Wall Construction Halts.

The words faded in and out, rapidly bleeding away and returning with an even grimmer new reality. She'd read so much of the *Chatterer* that she could point out each writer by artistic style. In the endless cycle of updates, however, nothing was ever explained. *Why* was the Network at war? What was everyone angry at? From what she could tell, rumors had created reality, and most witches seemed to ignore the truth.

"The fairy wishes to leave the pack, does she?"

Isadora jumped. She whipped around to find Miss Sophie behind her, so close Isadora smelled smoke on her breath. Sophie had a lovely face and sparkling teeth despite her constant cigars. Flecks of green nestled in her hazel eyes.

"Fairy?" Isadora asked.

Sophie gestured to the world beyond the fence with a vague wave. "I see you standing here often. But you never leave."

"It's quiet out here."

"Only to those not listening to what the sprites say."

"Ah." Isadora retracted the newsscroll and tucked it under her arm. "I was just thinking about the wars, actually."

"The many battles for our lives, yes."

She'd had no one-on-one interaction with Sophie yet. Anyone who talked to the Head Witch found themselves the target of a slew of fresh pranks from undisciplined twelve-year-olds who, although Isadora suspected they didn't realize it, were jealous of the attention. Only Baylee seemed to get away with talking to Sophie. Isadora suppressed the urge to back away. She let silence fill the time instead.

"Does the young fairy enjoy this side of the world?"

"Berry, you mean?"

Sophie just closed her eyes, as if that were an acknowledgment. Despite Isadora's thirst to see more, Mam's words haunted her daily. *It's dangerous out there, Isadora. Witches harm each other for no reason. Sometimes just for enjoyment.* To her horror, she could see what Mam had meant.

Across the way, a witch with a squalling baby strapped to her chest crossed the road, drawing Isadora's attention. She wore a simple dress of sprigged muslin, but layers of fabric filled the skirt underneath. Even the poorest witches had underskirts that bloomed their dresses out in a style Isadora thought fit for the High Priestess. What a strange waste of material.

It wasn't until Sophie spoke again that Isadora realized she hadn't answered her question. Then she realized she didn't want to.

"What is it you seek here?" Sophie asked.

The sudden appearance of a scowling expression and a pair of bright eyes prevented her reply. Maximillion stood on this side of the fence, his lips puckered in steep disapproval. Isadora's stomach caught, and she let out a gasp of fear.

"The god of fireflies," Sophie whispered. "He's here!"

Maximillion strode toward them, jabbing a finger at Isadora. "Not a word," he hissed, ignoring Sophie entirely. It was only when Isadora saw Sophie standing there with her mouth bobbing open and closed that she realized he'd set a spell on her.

"That's extremely rude," Isadora snapped. "One shouldn't use magic on another witch. Take it back."

"No."

Isadora used a yelling incantation to overpower his. Sophie's throat unlocked. All the suppressed words came barreling out of her throat in a shout.

"PLEASE STAY BY MY SIDE! MY TEACUPS DESIRE THE TOUCH OF YOUR HAND. DON'T LEAVE! MY HEART BEATS FOR YOU."

Sophie grabbed her throat, eyes wide. Maximillion's glare burned through Isadora.

"Very clever."

"Better than not being able to speak at all."

"You've been learning more magic, have you? But there hasn't been time to separate your own thoughts, has there?"

She growled. "I tried what you told me to do for almost two weeks now. It doesn't work."

Maximillion grabbed her by the arm and shoved her toward the school. "Inside. Now."

Isadora jerked free. He held up another hand but lowered it when she followed. The two of them tromped into the school without another word. Maximillion entered the dining room and pointed to a chair.

"Sit."

She folded her arms in front of her. "I don't feel like sitting."

"You're being difficult on purpose."

"I have an excellent teacher."

His nostrils flared. "We have work to do and a short time to do it. Tell me more. Why didn't it work?"

His cravat, half-tied and skewed to the left, dangled from his neck. His normally perfect hair had fallen over his forehead in wild disarray. She eased herself into a chair and folded her hands while he paced near the fire.

"Nice to see you, Maximillion. How have you been?"

"Is it darkness that you see? The headaches come with noise? No. That can't be it. Too many images, perhaps?"

"Oh, I'm fine, thank you for asking."

"What *is* it?" he hissed.

"I've taken up a new life, by the way. A very dramatic one. One not particularly conducive to learning. Why in the name of Drago did you put me here?"

"That's all you've done?"

"Don't diminish it! These girls are mean and out of control. They stuffed a handful of itchy weeds in my undergarments."

"Am I supposed to feel sorry for you?"

"I'd never expect you capable of that kind of emotion."

"Your first words of sense."

"What were you thinking? This is the worst possible place to learn anything."

"I know."

"You *know*?"

"This place is chaos itself," he muttered, driving a hand through his hair. "Sophie's enough to make anyone go mad."

"Then why—"

"Because you need it."

She shot to her feet. "You don't get to tell me what I need."

"Chaos!" he cried. "You need chaos in order to learn."

"I need peace and quiet."

"There's no challenge in silence!" he bellowed. "You'll never be forced to master the powers, and you'll grow weak. You'll die. I've seen it."

Isadora's heart crinkled at the thought. "Really?"

"Working on your power in silence is easy. It's simple. But you won't ever live in a silent world without distractions. If I train you at too low of a level, the powers will slowly consume you, and you won't even know it."

The fury in his voice ebbed, returning to its usual tight crackle of annoyance. He drew his shoulders back. Isadora opened her mouth to reply but closed it again.

"Why didn't you just tell me that?"

"I didn't want to scare you so early." Maximillion studied her with his usual cool hauteur. "Perhaps I should have. Now that *that's* out of the way ... your powers," he said through gritted teeth. "What. Is. Happening?"

"I try. I promise, I really try. But nothing ever comes of it."

"You focus the entirety of your attention on what you see?"

"Yes."

"And no feeling appears?"

"No. There's nothing but gray. I've tried. There's absolutely null beyond."

He frowned and fidgeted with the button at the end of his sleeve. "Gray. Yes, you said that before. Not darkness?"

"No. There's never been darkness."

"It should be impossible. Your powers have awoken. There's no reason for the magic to be so unpredictable..."

Isadora waited while he paced across the room with long strides. "When you transitioned, did you see darkness then?"

"No. A forest."

"A forest." He shook his head. "A bloody forest."

Isadora crossed her arms as pain swelled through her

head. She pressed a hand to her temple and turned away from him.

"What's wrong?" he asked.

"Nothing."

"You have a headache."

"Yes. My headaches have returned. Every day."

He strode across the room, grabbed her chin, and jerked it up. "How long?"

Her nostrils flared. "Let go of me." But the words carried little power. His fingertips dug into her cheek as he stared hard into her eyes, as if attempting to see through them.

"You're not supposed to have them anymore. You're supposed to see darkness and feel the difference between thoughts and magic. It's how it always begins."

Isadora pulled free of his touch. "Clearly, I'm a new case."

"Yes," he murmured. "Indeed. Stop."

"Stop what?"

"Stop doing what I told you to do. We need to take a different direction."

She let out a long breath of relief. "Really?"

"Yes."

"Then what do I do?"

"Nothing. I need to explore something. Wait until I get back to you."

"What about the headaches?"

He frowned. "I won't take long. If they become unbearable again, transport me a message."

"That didn't work so well for me the past week."

"Yes, well, I didn't want to speak with you. You could do with a little rejection. Here." He reached into the inner pocket of his jacket and pulled out a small scroll bound by a length of twine. "In the meantime, I brought this for you to read. I can't find the other one, but you won't need it. I'll be in touch."

With that, he strode out the door, the dull thud of his heels reverberating behind him. Isadora held her breath until he disappeared, then let it all out. Instead of relief, a hollowness filled her belly, like something had crumbled away inside of her. What if she *couldn't* do whatever she needed to do? What if the power was too great? Isadora picked up the scroll and sank back into the chair.

The light faded from the dining room long before her whirling mind calmed.

CHAPTER

ELEVEN

You are well?

Sanna groaned, her body throbbing in a low, intermittent pulse. When her eyes cracked open, bright orange scales hovered over her like thousands of twinkling candles. Luteis blinked, his globe-like eyes disappearing for a moment.

"*Mori.*"

You cannot say I didn't warn you.

"How long have I been unconscious?"

I do not reckon time like witches. Enough for me to contemplate the stubbornness of your kind.

She paused. "You know, I never thought about it, but I suppose you don't track time."

There is much you don't think about.

She sat up. The forest spun around her for a moment, then settled. She blinked, feeling ... *different.* Her fingers and toes were the same. She certainly hadn't lost any parts of herself, like the heart-shaped freckle near her ankle, the broken nail on her third toe, or the long, jagged scar across her hand. But something *else* thrummed inside of her.

189

She spread her fingers and studied them. Nothing about her was physically different, but something inside had awoken. A feeling. A movement. It shifted underneath her skin, seeking, wandering, spinning.

"What's happened to me?"

One cannot merge with a dragon and remain the same witch. Or so I would presume, anyway.

She pushed to her feet. "See? We couldn't have planned for that."

He glared at her.

She ignored it, peering past him into the canopy. Where were they going to fly from, anyway? There wasn't much room down here.

"Can we try flying now?"

You are so eager after all that?

"If it gets me closer to getting home to work with Daid, then yes."

And defeating Talis.

She hesitated. "Right. That too."

He cast her a sidelong glance but said nothing about her pause. *I will not fly until it is fully dark. And you need to accustom yourself to the magic. And calm your mind. I fear that your strong reaction came from a lack of preparation and an unsettled mind. Our plan is to wait until the night, and until your mind is calm.*

"You flew in the daylight before."

A great risk. But we were fleeing a greater one.

"Talis would never have left the village to chase us."

Wouldn't he?

Sanna drew in a deep breath. She didn't know anymore. Deasylva had shown her the images of Talis killing other dragons, then setting fire to the forest, but what if it had been a misunderstanding? He *had* killed Ivis. But could that erase the one hundred and fifty years of safety he'd provided the dragons? She shook away the thoughts.

There is much you don't know, Sanna of Anguis. Rest. Find food. Take the next couple of days to relax your mind. You need mental space in order to safely sink into the magic.

"Oh, you know *that*?"

He ruffled his wings. *I may not know much about your kind, but I do know how difficult it is to adjust to magic. In the meantime, I will hunt and return at twilight.*

"Any chance you could grab some food for me?"

He snorted as he slipped into the trees, his massive body slithering in silence. Although she loathed the idea of taking his orders, she *was* exhausted. Several days of rest did sound nice. The residual magic had faded, and she felt like a brittle shell in its wake. She curled into a ball at the base of the trunk where her ancestors' names were inscribed, tucked her arm under her head, and fell into a fast sleep.

A WEEK LATER, as twilight swept over Letum Wood, Sanna clawed at an oak tree in the smaller grove at the base of the Ancients. Above her, a flaky, cylindrical *ratata* nest loomed like a tease. The bright orange insects, half the size of her pinky nail, had wings that glowed in the dark and four antennae sprouting from their head. They would probably bite her for stealing their thick nectar, but even if she itched all night, it'd be worth the sweet prize. Her stomach growled again. *So* worth it.

If only she could untangle her hair from this branch.

"Get. Away. From. Me."

As she tugged with her hands and head, the ensnared branch cracked in half and fell dangling down her back.

"Finally," she muttered.

She left it there and continued to climb, intent on the prize. The longer she waited, the more she risked the nocturnal ratatas waking up. Alert ratatas were violent creatures. In their drowsy daytime state, however, they'd be less precise. When a knot of vines blocked her path, she wrapped her legs around a branch, grabbed a sharp rock she'd tucked into her pocket, and sawed at the interconnected mass. Minutes later, the vines dropped with a *thud*.

"Sweet nectar, here I come."

She gripped the rock in her teeth and continued her ascent, passing a bright, luminescent patch of moss. She paused, transfixed by the shifting colors, like coals that gave off no heat. The rock dropped unheeded from her mouth

"*Avay,*" she whispered.

Underneath, the wood of the tree blanched white. Tiny hairs, like goose feathers, waved from the top of the patch. What a delightful pillow it would make.

"Hullo there," she murmured, reaching out to stroke it. "What are you?"

A heavy *thud* slammed into her chest. She dropped off the branch with a gasp. Before she smacked into the tree, a familiar tail snatched her leg and carted her away upside down.

Sanna growled. "Let me go!"

Luteis soared to the stream. He tilted sideways to fit his wings through a gap in the trees and nearly slammed her into a trunk. She curled away, missing it by a hair.

"What are you—"

He released her.

She dropped, landing hard in a pool. The water enveloped her in a chilly embrace. She surfaced with a gasp and shoved the hair out of her eyes.

"Are you trying to kill me?" she screamed.

He hovered over the water, wings beating. Leaves scattered into the air and pelted her face. Before she could draw another breath to scream, his tail shoved her back under. She surfaced on the other side of the pond, a rock in hand. Water dragged her hair into her eyes as she whipped around, ready to throw. His tail snaked toward her again. She pulled her arm back.

"Do it again, and I'll shove this right down your fiery throat."

Luteis stood at the edge of the pond, staring at her through slitted eyes. His gaze dropped from the top of her head to her shoulders, her hands, and finally her legs.

"What's the matter with you? Are you trying to drown me?"

His tail, which hovered just out of reach, relaxed. She eyed it, then, seeing him ease off, wiped the water out of her eyes. A tug cranked her neck to the side; the stick still swung from her hair. With a growl, she yanked it free and tossed it at him.

"Not funny. I—"

His tail slammed into her again, shoving her under. She rose to the surface with a livid sputter, ready to draw blood. His words filled her head before she could strike the first blow.

It's called strickenine moss.

The calm cadence of his voice stopped her. His tail pressed into her shoulders. Sanna's heaving chest slowed.

"What?"

The moss you were reaching for.

"Strickenine moss?"

It releases deadly spores when touched. I've seen creatures with blood spurting out their nose, ears, and mouth within moments of standing over it.

Her rage dissipated.

"Oh."

The water will ensure you have no spores on you to breathe in.

"Couldn't you have said something when you grabbed me?"

He gazed off into the distance with a little twitch of his tail. Could dragons smile?

Perhaps.

Sanna scowled and slipped back under the water. She used her fingernails to scrub her hair, scalp, and skin for good measure. The water muffled the sounds of the forest, so she remained there, enjoying the strange silence until her lungs burned. Once finished, she climbed back onto the bank, her fingers numb. Luteis touched her shoulder again.

Headache?

"No."

A good sign.

She tilted her head to clear the water from her ears. "I've never heard of strickenine moss."

Talis would have destroyed it years ago.

"*Can* it be destroyed?"

With fire. Lots of fire. There are sections of Letum Wood overcome by it. I cannot breathe enough fire to beat it, so I had to burn all the trees and bushes around it so it could not go further. Still, it continues to ravage other areas. It travels on the wind.

With a sigh, Sanna stood up. "Well ... thanks, I guess. But next time, a little warning?"

Certainly.

She eyed him. He definitely wouldn't, but she couldn't really blame him.

"Turn around, please."

He obeyed. She peeled her clothes off and wrung them out. With no direct sunlight, the fabric would mold if they didn't dry soon.

"I'm done," she said several minutes later. The damp clothes still clung to her skin. Goosebumps rose along her arms, although the impromptu bath *had* felt nice. Luteis blew a warm, gentle breath on her. The heat, just right, warmed her. Her clothes flapped as they dried out.

"Thanks," she said, leaning into it. "I hadn't thought of that. Find your hog?"

Luteis reached for her ankle with his tail again. *Several.*

"Do you always eat so much?"

Yes.

"Our dragons never ate as much as you."

Lazy prisoners rarely do.

Prisoners? Is that what they were?

Are you ready to fly? Twilight will be here in an hour.

"It's time?"

Over a week had passed since their first attempt to merge. Sanna had been grateful for the break, though she hadn't admitted it. Food had been scarce. She still felt uneasy in the old house, but she didn't have so much confusion now. Thanks to careful exploring, she felt a bit more grounded. She missed the branches, though.

It's time. Do you not want to go?

He tilted his head to the side.

Sanna shifted, unable to break the cycle of her thoughts. *A flying dragon is a dead dragon.* Even *if* Talis had banished flight to control dragons, there was some truth to the saying. They were vulnerable in the open sky. Although she'd enjoyed flight when he'd carried her in his talon. The passage of the treetops. The wind on her face. Freedom. But it wasn't worth losing a dragon over.

She hugged herself to stave off a shiver.

"Fine. I'll go. I-I just don't like the idea of it."

His eyes gleamed. *Perhaps I can change your mind.*

Twenty minutes later, the muscular expanse of Luteis's back undulated with every *thud* of his wings. Sanna felt every up and down of his even, gentle strokes.

At first, the bobbing motion made her sick. Eventually, she settled into it, uncertain whether she was nauseated from hunger or the motion.

Riding on his shoulders was vastly different than in his talon. For one, she wasn't burning hot. For another, she could see far better. There was no sound this high in the air, either, and she relished the chance to study the stars that peppered the sky with glitter.

The dragonian magic, if active, gave little indication of its presence. If she drifted across his scales, *something* shifted her body back to center with a subtle nudge. Compared to the first, the second merging had been anticlimactic—even weak. A few flickers of something had buzzed through her mind, bringing a sense of being somewhere new without having left.

Magic hovered somewhere in her, but she couldn't find it. She just felt *something*. For now, that was more than enough.

Are you still awake?

"Yes."

How do you feel?

"Not that different."

Luteis made a sound deep in his throat, then blew smoke forward and soared through it. The smooth darkness of Letum Wood passed underneath them. Sanna's mind wandered as she studied the murky woodland below. If Deasylva truly encompassed the depth and breadth of every forest—if she was connected to everything in them— she had to be a goddess of *some* power. A small part of Sanna still flared with rage at the accusation against Drago and Talis.

They *wouldn't* lie.

But then, maybe he would. Talis had always been controlling, even terrifying. Sanna crossed her arms to keep out the cold and burrowed back into her thoughts, grateful Luteis couldn't read them.

Are you interested in a little excitement? I have planned what you could call an experimental ride.

She perked up. "Oh?"

Hold on.

A shriek leapt into her throat when Luteis dove. Air roared past her ears, whipping tears from her eyes. Her stomach climbed into her chest. Just when she thought they'd hurtle into the forest and break her neck, he evened out. The tops of several trees barely brushed his underbelly.

Sanna held her breath.

Were they stable?

Are you well? he asked.

She blinked. Her stomach resettled. The air was calm as before, only this time they skimmed the tops of the trees. A branch grazed her left foot.

"Whoa."

I do not understand this meaning.

"That was ... amazing."

You were not afraid?

"Don't insult me."

Would you like to do more?

"What do you think?"

I think it unlikely you would take such a risk. Then again, you have surprised me before.

"Of course I want to go again!"

Then let us fly into my second planned maneuver.

Luteis turned, climbing higher, forcing Sanna to lean into him. She clutched the ridge along the back of his neck. Despite their vertical angle, her body remained firmly in place, locked by an invisible power.

Trust the magic. You will not fall.

"You're sure?"

Of this one thing, yes.

Sanna swallowed, then, one finger at a time, peeled her grip away. Her hands rested on his scales. She didn't budge, which gave her the courage to spread her arms and tilt her head back. She laughed.

With his chest bellowing from exertion, Luteis soared in a wide circle, gliding over the tops of the clouds. The moon illuminated his giddy expression when he glanced back at her.

Are you ready?

She grinned. "You know it."

He dove.

Blood skipped through her veins as they plummeted in a straight drop, gaining speed like an arrow. The wind tore at her hair and clothes. They accelerated until Luteis pulled up into another smooth sail. Sanna shrieked when he spun in a narrow circle, inverting around and around and around until the stars blurred together in a velvety tunnel. She folded forward and leaned her forehead against his neck with a breathless laugh.

You enjoyed that?

"Definitely."

I am pleased—and surprised—to hear a witch say so. I expected more ... restraint.

"If you'd tried that with anyone else, you would have gotten it."

He flew with steady wing beats now. Sanna kept a hand on his back, watching the gleam of his scales flash in the moonlight. Luteis, though she suspected he wouldn't accept the praise, was a magnificent creature. The elegant lines of his neck. His muscular, certain wings.

She bent over, glancing at the ebony treetops. For a long stretch of time, they said nothing. She observed burned circles in the forest, enclosing trees bleached white beneath the sucking power of strickenine moss. Charred sections, reduced to black nothingness. Desolate, shriveled patches without water. Dried stream beds cutting through the parched trees. At some points, the forest seemed almost deserted. Ten beluas stood around a single trunk, tearing it apart. Luteis shot fire at them as he soared past.

They screamed.

Her heart ached. "It really has fallen," she murmured. She thought she heard a distant keen, a cry in the night. It faded like a wisp.

Now that we know you tolerate flying, the next step is to figure out how to defeat Talis. Letum Wood need not remain this way. With more dragons to work, we can restore it.

"Do you work for Deasylva or for Letum Wood?"

He paused. *They are one and the same.*

"Are they?"

He didn't respond. Sanna straightened up, looking at the horizon instead of the pockets of devastation below. Regardless of whether Talis was a liar or simply misunderstood, Letum Wood *did* need help.

"How long have you been by yourself, Luteis?" she asked, breaking another span of silence.

Always.

"You have no siblings?"

No.

"Parents?"

No.

"You must have had family at some point. How did you—"

That is not a discussion for now.

The clipped edge to his voice made Sanna hesitate. Should she press him? Before she could say another word, his nostrils flared, and he angled his body down.

Hold on.

They slipped into the forest, darting between the trees. The close press of branches sent Sanna's stomach into a whirl. She clung to Luteis again. Diving into Letum Wood— instead of through open air—brought an entirely different set of challenges. Vines. Branches. Animals. Luteis navigated the complicated tangle with practiced ease. He landed on a branch, reached around a trunk with his willowy neck, and snapped at something. A stifled roar cut off mid-snarl. Luteis's head reappeared clutching a limp, mangy forest lion.

Dinner for both of us.

"Ah."

I formally request the organs.

Sanna's upper lip curled over her teeth. The taste of

forest lion reminded her of dry leather, but she was so hungry she probably would have eaten that too. Living in the wild hadn't been conducive to eating three meals a day like at home.

"You can have whatever you want."

Much appreciated.

Sanna's stomach grumbled as Luteis used his talons to climb up the tree trunk. At the top, he leapt free and rose back into the night sky. She leaned forward, pressed her face against his warm neck, tucked her arms beneath her, and fell into a light sleep, lulled by the rhythm of his wings.

Isadora stared at the shifting shadows on the ceiling until the school fell silent. The second month of fall had begun, bringing with it the crisp scent of drying leaves and pumpkin pie. She closed her eyes and drew in deep breaths, relishing it.

After walking headfirst into a string that dumped a bowl of slimy green water on her head, she'd spent the day scrubbing off the sludge by practicing cleaning incantations. Tired of the close space of her closet, she crept out of bed, stuffed the scroll Maximillion had given her into her sleeve, pulled a robe around her body, and slipped into the hall.

Gloom bathed the corridor. Not even a lone giggle broke the silence. Isadora moved through the bruised darkness, grateful to have the place to herself. She yanked an apple out of a basket, grabbed a crusty loaf end, and headed to the far side of the school. The library door groaned when she cracked it open. The tiny box of a room had at least fifty books—an exorbitant number but nothing like other libraries that the *Chatterer* spoke of.

At a murmured incantation, several candles sprang to life, their warm flames bouncing in the dim room. A fire crackled in the grate, sending out tentative tongues of heat. No tinderboxes like they'd used at home. No fighting back the smoke as it filled the room instead of going up the flue. No gathering firewood. Just an immediate, friendly fire.

Oh, how she loved magic.

She fell into an overstuffed chair. A slit in the upholstery belched stuffing in white clouds. She batted it away and unrolled the scroll. Maximillion had given it to her only two days before. Old writing filled the page. It appeared ancient, with blocky letters and thin lines in burgundy ink. It seemed to be a collection of snippets taken from other books and transcribed into one place. She beckoned for a candle with a spell.

***Excerpts from the book* Observations of Ronan the Traveler.**

3rd day, 4th week, 1st month of spring

Durston, Northern Network

They burned my brother on a stake.

My grief and questions have driven me to study his "mental condition," starting in the Northern Network. I feel I must scour Alkarra from top to bottom in my search to understand his decisions. My questions cannot be ignored—I feel restless in my heart and soul. He died from this strange ailment—or rather because of it. His confinement was wrong. He was not crazy. Something was different, yes. But not harmful. Not dangerous.

Something gave him sight. I will figure it out in his name. This seems the best place to start.

. . .

2ND DAY, 1st week, 2nd month of spring

Durston, Northern Network

... the locals are kind. They seem unafraid of my questions. When I ask about witches with special abilities, they are unbothered, unlike those at home. They simply shrug and say little. Perhaps they have not seen many...

2ND DAY, 4th week, 3rd month of spring

Flux, Northern Network

It has been two months now, and they continue to say little, although I believe out of indifference rather than fear. I'm not sure which is more frustrating. The mountain peaks are, I admit, stunning. Perhaps everything seems inconsequential compared to these soaring rocks. I'm beginning to wonder if I should move on. I have found that I enjoy their simple life amongst the goats.

The greatest information I have is still only what I know from my brother: these special witches have the power to foretell events. Perhaps their own kind of magic, as preposterous as it sounds.

We know so little about the origins of the "normal" magic that burns within us...

4TH DAY, 2nd week, 3rd month of summer

Soltana, northern tip of the Eastern Network

The lack of engagement from the North forced me to press on.

As expected, there is terror here in the Eastern Network—they burned my brother, after all ...

... speaking to witches here has proven unsafe. I only gleaned

information when a witch heard me asking an inn owner about it. She pulled me aside later, invited me to her home. Once there, she spoke reluctantly about the ability. Said her mother had been mad and claimed she saw things before they happened. About one in five times she had been correct.

A few others came forward after assurance of absolute secrecy and my desire to understand, not harm. Three were able to see events, like my brother. One was the wife of a witch who died unexpectedly after an enormous headache. I can't help but feel it's related to this strange power.

From what I've observed speaking to them—and a few in the North—the power seems to be unpredictable in origin. Found in every sort of family throughout the Networks with no real common tie that I can ascertain.

6TH DAY, *1st week, 1st month of fall*

Purva, southern edge of the Eastern Network

Continue having a hard time discussing it here. Was driven out of a village for asking about witches with the power to see future events. There have been threats on my life. Some witches are sending notes ahead of me so that entire towns have blocked my access, though I don't bear this ability myself.

Still, some come out of hiding when I'm alone. These witches living in fear spur me to greater action. May they not burn the way my brother did.

May they one day not live in fear.

5TH DAY, *3rd week, 3rd month of fall*

Eastern border of the Southern Network

... I gratefully left the East behind and am eagerly looking forward to the South. Everything is colder here, including the

natives, if that's possible.

In my recent studies, I've noted the occurrence of these abilities to be almost exactly half in males and half in females. Such a strange finding. Sometimes the power reoccurs in families but not with regularity and always with at least one generational gap between them. There is much not understood.

More to find.

3RD DAY, *4th week, 3rd month of fall*

Location uncertain, Southern Network

Winter sets in early here. It seems my fingers are always cold, sometimes too cold to write.

... Recently, I have taken to calling them 'Watchers.' It seems most appropriate. Local natives here in the Southern Network have called them Gespara. Translation amounts to something like evildoer or bad spirit. When I asked them more, they crossed two fingers in front of them before speaking about the Gespara. Supposedly to ward off the evil gods that enter a conversation at the use of the word.

According to the tribe with whom I reside for the month, the ability to foresee the future is reserved only for their loving god, Hulu. Any witch with foresight must discern through their selfish god, Chthu.

My brother was a gentle witch. Those who have admitted their ability are prone to headaches and paranoia but not violence.

Under the circumstances, both seem fitting.

2ND DAY, *1st week, 1st month of winter*

Taize, Southern Network

Finally, a breakthrough.

Led by vague rumors from the tribes, I found a city of wealthy witches in the Southern Network willing to speak openly about Watchers. They've long revered them, even pushed them into political positions, and keep them happily within their city walls. Although I can't speak with certainty, they seem to revere Watchers only because the poor tribes despise them. There's a strange dynamic in the South.

I'm quite overwhelmed with information, and it will take me time to sort through my many interviews (and I've only just arrived). Inasmuch as I can tell, the powers have a twofold nature.

1. They allow the prediction of possible future events— although these do not always come to pass.

2. They allow for the understanding of the nature of a witch.

The second variation is new to me. I feel that many Watchers may not have cultivated their powers and may not know this second one. Perhaps it is the lesser of the two. At any rate, I'm eager to learn more.

My plan to stay here in the Southern Network will extend through the winter. They're eager for my company, and I require their knowledge.

3RD DAY, 3rd week, 2nd month of winter

Taize, Southern Network

My research continues.

Variations on the two Watcher skills are clearly enormous— I've spoken extensively with ten Watchers so far here in Taize, and there are more. One Watcher can foresee the future of her bird, but that is all. Another can foresee possibilities for his twin sister but not himself. While yet another could discern, with exactness, what kind of strengths any witch had simply by meeting them. He saw no future events. He predicted my strengths accurately. He is the only one I have met that does not see something. What to make of this? Some fractionated part of the magic? I wish I could know if it was intentional.

I'm in awe of these variations. The overwhelming majority of Watchers see future possibilities for themselves only. Those are most often in the immediate time frame, within days. Occasionally they can see for a family member or close friend, or for weeks at a time. These seem to be rare cases. I've asked if a single Watcher has ever had the ability to see for themselves and others, and this is emphatically denied.

I can't help but think of my brother. What his life would have been like had he lived here...

5TH DAY, 4th week, 3rd month of winter.

Taize, Southern Network

I prepare to leave soon for the Central Network. I believe their High Priest may have an interesting viewpoint, and I tire of the constant snow. They have the Great Library of Burke in the Letum Wood Covens. I plan to study the historical scrolls and see if I can learn more before returning home to the West. I imagine that more Watchers have been in power than we know about...

Before departing the South, I wish to record my final thoughts after living in close proximity with many active Watchers.

... I've recently been quite struck by the Watchers of political power whom I've met. In retrospect, it seems clear that with their powers of understanding and observation, Watchers would naturally rise into positions of social power. It's difficult to say whether this power is a gift or a curse. I believe that entire Networks could fall on the whim of one evil Watcher. Then again, the power can have a positive effect. In fact, an over-

whelmingly large one, if used correctly. The structure of Taize is exemplary—aside from their clear disdain for outsiders. Crime is minimal. Despite desperate winters, they are able to store appropriately beforehand thanks to Watchers who foresee what the seasons bring. In this, they work together.

I believe that the rest of my answers lie in the Central Network, where I shall continue my studies ...

The scroll ended.

Isadora stared at the final words with a terrible sinking feeling in her chest. Her mind crawled so many places at once she had a hard time knowing *what* she thought. Burned at the stake in the Eastern Network. Revered in the Southern. All because of an arbitrary power. Perhaps witches still feared Watchers. Her fingers chilled at the thought.

Isadora's hands fell to her lap, limp. She closed her eyes, leaned back against the chair, and let out a long breath. She needed Sanna. Sanna was stable in moments of great stress. She was oddly calming—her occasional snide comments and the way she acted without thought or plan or fear for the next moment.

Isadora curled the scroll in her hand, extinguished the candles, and sat in the darkness until the moonlight wore away and a crack of sunshine split the night open. When dawn crossed the sky in a bright spill of color, she rushed back to her bedroom.

She had to talk to Maximillion.

TWELVE

Isadora drew in a deep breath, clenched her hands into fists, and opened her eyes. "I won't get lost in Berry. I won't get lost in Berry."

The cool morning woke her from a tangled haze of sleep as she stumbled out the front door. Hints of fall lingered in the air. Sunburnt colors peeked through the leaves in ribbons of orange and butter yellow. Her breath billowed out in front of her. A change of clothes, the scroll Maximillion had loaned her, and the *Chatterer* lay inside a bag that rested on her hip.

"I can do this."

Two painful, frightening days had passed since she read the scroll. She'd sent at least ten messages to Maximillion, with no response. Going to Chatham City was the next logical step, if also the most terrifying one. She felt as if she hadn't slept since reading the scroll and knew it would only get worse. The sheer number of questions ...

A scream from inside the school broke her out of her trance. No doubt little Naomi had found a mouse under her pillow again. Isadora hastily stepped off the porch and forced herself down the path. She passed through the gate alone without dying. When she turned right, no girls followed her or pointed her out as a deserter. Would Sophie even care if she knew Isadora was leaving?

Isadora scurried down the lane as fast as she dared, just in case. Her repeated refrain gave her some comfort.

"I won't get lost. I won't get lost."

Thatched roofs and stone cottages lined most of the streets. Isadora pulled out a scroll tucked into her sleeve and consulted her poorly sketched map. In the school library, she'd found a patchy scroll, dated ten years earlier, that had laid out a basic structure of Berry. Not much could have changed in the intervening time. The spaced houses gave way to taller, stacked homes as she moved toward the middle of town. A market appeared on the right with wooden tables and a red-bearded man calling out, "Get your milk here!"

Isadora hurried past, heart hammering. She passed a milliner—whatever that was—and a barber. In the heart of Berry flowed a bright, looming fountain. Ice rimmed the edges, although water still tumbled over itself.

Isadora stopped. Now what?

Her plan had taken her to the heart of Berry, where she could most likely speak with another witch—who wasn't one of the girls—about how to get to Chatham City. She couldn't trust the students to tell the truth. Three witches fanned through the square already, walking here and there with their heads tucked down, hands in their pockets. She hesitated.

Could she just ... *talk* to them?

There were no strangers in Anguis. She'd never approached anyone, except Maximillion, without knowing them. Even then, *he* had been the one to speak first. Isadora bit her bottom lip. What would her reception be in a place like this? After several moments' observation—not a single witch spoke to another—she realized she'd just have to do it.

"Ah, excuse me?"

A tall witch who passed within an arm's length didn't seem to hear. He continued to stride away, his long legs bearing him at an impressive speed. Isadora drew in another breath to gather her courage. A woman with two small children approached, a red scarf bouncing around her elbows.

"Excuse me?" Isadora called.

The woman turned toward her just as the younger of the two, a little boy about the age of four, began to wail. His older brother snapped at him to stop, and the mam whirled around to shout at him. They scuttled past, the mam jerking the oldest along by the ear.

Isadora sighed.

A creaky voice called out behind her. "Lookin' for something?"

Isadora whirled around. An old female witch stood behind her, clutching a cane as knobby as her knuckles. She had a milky left eye that didn't move and a threadbare shawl draped around her shoulders. A pathetic shield against such deep, bone-chilling cold.

"Oh. Yes," Isadora said. "I just need to find a way to Chatham Castle. Do you know how I can do that?"

"Isn't one."

"Ah ... what?"

The old witch shrugged and lowered herself to sit on the edge of the fountain. She breathed fast and a bit shallow, then coughed into her hand.

Isadora suppressed the urge to step back.

"The transports to the city stopped in the spring. Horses had to be reserved for guarding the Borderlands. The Network sends workers here to take the food instead of us sending it out. Most just transport it to the front lines, especially near the southern border."

A stirring of familiarity moved in the back of Isadora's mind. She'd read something about the ugly battles in the Southern Covens in the *Chatterer*.

"Then how do witches get to Chatham City?"

"Transport, of course. No one has the currency these days to pay for a ride. Can't get any freer than magic. The few fools who don't know how just walk, but that's at least a week, if not more."

Isadora blinked. Of course. Lucey had told her about transporting often in their hasty, hidden lessons, but never anything extensive. A few of the girls did it here and there at the school. It seemed easy enough. It must be since everyone seemed to know it.

Besides, it would solve *many* problems. Getting to Chatham City. Back. Exploring more of the Network—if she ever worked up the nerve again after this trip. In fact, learning transportation could change *everything*. She could visit home more often. Whenever she liked, actually. A little thrill zipped through her at the thought of seeing home again.

"Right," she murmured, settling onto the edge of the fountain next to the witch. "Transportation. That I can do. Is learning it difficult?"

The old witch waved a hand. "Pah! No. Easiest incantation in the book."

"Is it safe?"

"Of course! No one would do it if it wasn't."

"Oh. Well ... that's wonderful. Can't imagine why I

hadn't learned it before now. Could I ... could I beg you to teach it to me? I urgently need to go to Chatham City and speak with Maxi—a friend. It would be very helpful."

Her wrinkled brow furrowed. "Teach you? Well ... I suppose I could."

"Wonderful!"

"It'll cost you."

She looked at her small bag. "Yes, of course. Something for something. I haven't any gems or things to trade. I could help wi—"

"Some food?"

"None. I suppose I should have—"

"Pentacles? Sacrans?"

"What's that?"

The old woman frowned. "Then your cloak, at least."

Isadora hesitated. It was the only warm garment she owned, and the chilly days of fall had arrived with a vengeance. Or perhaps it was normal weather, and without the thick clog of trees she felt the full weight of the cold. Deciding there was no way around it, she reluctantly undid the clasp at her neck.

"All right."

The witch stood on shaky legs, whipped the cloak out of Isadora's hand, and wrapped it around herself. Cold air settled on Isadora's shoulders and neck in a gentle caress.

"Oh ... lovely fabric," the old lady murmured. "Velvet, I think? And still warm. All right, the incantation is simple. It has four words. Say them out loud while picturing where you want to go."

"What if I don't know where that is?"

The witch paused, and Isadora tilted her head to the side. Had the old witch been moving backward? Isadora opened her mouth to ask, but the witch quickly said,

"That's fine. Just say the name of it over and over in your head. Really focus on it, that's the key. The magic is smart. It'll know where to take you."

"I've never been to Chatham City. Is that—"

"Fine."

"Wait! What are the four words for the incantation?"

In her haste to get away, the witch collided into a bench with the back of her knees and nearly toppled it. She called out with a hand cupped around her mouth and shouted a thick tangle of words.

"Wait!" Isadora cried. "Where are you going?"

"You'll be fine. Just concentrate really hard." The witch held up a fist with her pinky finger straight up. "I've given you all the information you need. Merry part!"

Isadora swallowed a sudden wave of nervousness. Had the woman said *volo* or *bolo*? Did she say the words and *then* think of the place, or try to think of the place and the words at the same time? Before Isadora could take off after her, the witch disappeared into thin air. Isadora sighed. Well … it certainly couldn't be that hard, then, could it?

"*Volo celere?* No, no. *Pray* something?" She shook her head. "*Prametare?*"

A tingle bloomed in her chest once the words escaped her—something that had happened occasionally before she did a spell. So, they must work, at least. Isadora cast her gaze around, seeing only one other witch asleep on a bench nearby. She closed her eyes. If it didn't work, she'd simply ask someone else to clarify the words. Not knowing what Chatham City looked like, she tried to picture the words she'd seen in the *Chatterer*. She imagined the words taking root in her mind.

"Chatham City. I want to go to Chatham City."

She repeated the words of the incantation.

Her legs flew out from underneath her.

Berry disappeared. Her *body* disappeared. Darkness overcame her. She whirled around, feeling as if she were toppling head over heels in a dark miasma. When she opened her mouth to scream, no sound came out. Pressure bore down on her face. Her eyes. Her hands. She thought her teeth would shatter from the pressure. The fast-moving, in-between world stole away her breath. She tried to gasp, but there *was* no air.

Chatham City, she thought frantically. *Take me to Chatham City!*

Just when her thoughts began to blur, her very awareness fading from fear to sheer panic, her mad tumble in the darkness stopped. She landed, face down, on something hard. Her lungs, nearly paralyzed, spasmed. Coughing and sputtering, she flipped onto her back. The dark spots in her eyes began to clear. She blinked.

Sunshine burned hot above her. Hot, like an oven. *Very* hot. Too hot. Like a fire.

A nearby scream broke the air. Isadora leapt to her feet, but the ground shifted and she fell onto her back, one hand reached out to cushion her fall. Sand. It spilled between her fingers. Another scream issued from not far away, this time deep and guttural. Isadora looked up at total devastation.

Witch fought witch against a sandy backdrop. A blood-red sun glimmered on the horizon, illuminating bodies on the ground. Some of the witches wore tattered crimson uniforms. Central Network Guardians? She'd seen them in the streets of Berry before. Others had no clothes on at all except for loose pants. Broad shoulders, bare skin. Above them all, the sun burned bright, blazing with radiant heat. Just behind her, someone gurgled. A wet weight fell onto her shoulder—a bloody hand.

Isadora whirled around, a scream in her throat. A Guardian lay on the ground.

"Help..." he whispered. Blood stained his teeth. Coated his face. A weapon, something Isadora had never seen before, stuck out of his back. With a gasp and a shudder, he collapsed. His face dropped into the ground, burying his nose in sand.

Drago.

She'd transported into a battle. She screamed the words to the transportation spell.

This time, she sucked in a sharp breath beforehand, but the pressure was just as painful, the whirling as disorienting, the darkness as encompassing. It was as if, for that space of time, *she* didn't exist. Her body was gone. Elsewhere. Twirling in the madness of an in-between.

Chatham City! she screamed. *Chatham City!*

The pressure disappeared. She landed in a blanket of snow and struggled to her feet. A vista of snowfields spread around her, undulating in smooth ripples. The wind whipped past, tearing at her bare skin as if it wanted to rip her clothes off. The sweat from the Western Network froze almost instantly on her skin. Her teeth chattered. She wrapped her arms around herself and yelled.

"Stupid old lady!"

The witch had duped her. Her greedy, bent hands, her desire to escape—it all made sense now. She may have given her words to *an* incantation, but who knew if it was even the right one? Sure, she was traveling the Networks, but she wasn't going anywhere! Would it kill her? Would she survive? Why hadn't she seen it all along? This wasn't easy magic at all. This was downright dangerous.

But she couldn't stay here.

No *one* could stay in this barren, frozen wasteland and

survive. She had to try again and risk being torn apart by the pressure and darkness, lest the wild, frozen winds overcome her. With chattering teeth, she shouted the words again.

This time, the darkness embraced her in a cold vise and robbed her breath. The pressure bore down until she imagined her bones shattering. Did her body exist? Could anyone see her on that frozen plateau? Or was she just a collection of dust in some dark space? She could still form thoughts. Surely that meant something.

No matter how many times she repeated the words "Chatham City," no reprieve came. The edges of her thoughts began to blur. Darkness wrapped around her—or was it *in* her? Had it become her? Her breath failed. Her mind went blank. In one last, desperate plea, she cast out a memory. Trees. Vines. Leaves all around her. A protective ring of trees.

A flash of light overcame the darkness. It reached for her and wrapped her in a long tendril before pulling her back.

She dropped.

Isadora drew in a ragged breath.

Dirt clogged her nostrils, filling her mouth with a mineral taste. Birds twittered overhead. Cold crept along her stomach and her arms. She sucked in breaths until her ribs stopped aching. When her fingers dug into the cool soil and the tingling receded from her face, she opened her eyes.

Letum Wood surrounded her.

She straightened up slowly. Her head pounded in a way it never had, fast and thready. Isadora reached out to hold onto a tree. She was alive. She pressed a muddy hand to her face and forced herself to recall those last moments. The shreds of life. The piercing, encompassing darkness.

In the present, something whispered by. A breath of wind. A warm caress. Isadora followed it and turned around, knees shaking, to see Chatham Castle rising through the drapery of trees to her left.

With a cry of relief, she collapsed into sobs.

An enraged roar ripped through the air, jerking Sanna from a deep sleep. She dropped off the porch of the abandoned Dragonmaster home where she slept and landed on a stone.

"Mori!"

Her body rebelled as she straightened, spine and legs stiff. Her shoulder throbbed where it had landed on the pointy rock. Late daylight diffused the air with a gentle glow. The canopy had burgeoned into the flaming colors of fall.

Sanna shook her head and rubbed her eyes. A third flight over Letum Wood the previous night hadn't helped her sore muscles. Another livid bellow rippled through the air, drawing her attention to the left.

Luteis.

She stumbled into the forest, heart thumping.

"Luteis!"

Another scream followed. She shoved vines and bushes

out of her way. They snagged her clothes as if to draw her back.

"Luteis! Where are you?"

At a burst of fire in the bracken, she veered to the left again, hurtled over a boulder, grabbed a vine, and swung over a tangled patch of undergrowth. She dropped, ducking just as his tail whipped through the air where her head had been.

"Calm down!" She dodged another whip of his tail. "Stop!"

His thrashing fury calmed. Sanna's eyes widened.

"*Mori.* What have you done?"

The thick vines of a black *cohereo* tree clung to his neck and upper body. Mucus-like sap and long, winding tendrils hid his face from view. He shot fire, attempting to burn off the sludge, but the tentacles only tightened around him, blunting the flames.

"Luteis, calm down! The more you fight it, the stronger it gets. It's fire repellent."

He froze. Sanna scrambled up his back, the scales hot at her feet. Moments later, her mind shifted. The sizzle faded. Luteis snorted one last burst of flame at the vines, which tensed around him.

"Stop using fire!" she snapped. "You're only making it worse."

What has ensnared me? What is happening?

"It's a cohereo tree."

I have not heard of this. I cannot see. Has it blinded me?

She stopped at the base of his shoulders, unable to move any farther. The thick vines knotted his entire neck and face, engulfing him. One vine reached for her, but she snatched the end and pinched it between her thumb and forefinger. It hissed, retreating to the trunk in an ebony coil.

"You aren't blind. It puts mucus on your eyes. Just … hold on. Let me see how bad it is."

How do you kill it?

"With troll urine."

A pause. *Of a truth?*

"Unfortunately. But there's a way to get the vines to retract. I just … I have to grab the bottom of each vine."

As she suspected, the vines twisted around his neck, sending a waterfall of thick mucus bubbling down his hot scales. It melted away and dripped to the forest floor, releasing a bitter smell. She untangled a superficial vine attempting to wrap around the base of his wing, then pinched the end. The vine hissed, slithering back into the tree, forming a knot at the trunk. She tilted her head back, peering into the mess.

"This is bad, Luteis. I'll have to do this one at a time," she said. "It may take a while."

A foul plant.

She grunted, wrapped both hands around a particularly meaty vine, and pulled. It flapped, attempting to whack her with its thick body. She scrambled, grabbed the end, and searched for the squishy spot. Once she pinched, it retreated, leaving a goopy filth coating her hands. She grimaced and wiped her hand on Luteis's scales, where it bubbled, gave off a foul stench, and slid to the ground.

How many have you done?

"Two."

How many left?

"A thousand?"

Neither of us may survive this. Allow me to burn it.

"Nope." She grunted, peeling another one from his wing. "Just makes it stronger. Our only hope is to extract you before they recover. I'm pinching a tender spot that paralyzes it for three hours or so."

Is that enough time?

She eyed his lumpy, goopy torso. "Let's hope. I can't believe you haven't been tangled in one before."

Never.

"How did this happen?"

That doesn't matter.

She grinned, pinching three small feelers that branched off another vine. They disappeared with tinny shrieks, leaving a lash of mucus behind. "Sleepwalking?"

I don't know what that is.

"Chasing a butterfly?"

A pause. He ruffled his wings.

A wild hog if you must know.

She laughed. "Ah, yes. Same thing happened to Rubeis once, before Talis figured out how to kill the tree. The hogs make their homes underneath the base of cohereo trees for protection."

Hogs have more intelligence than I originally credited them with.

"So many things do."

I shall not chase them again.

"A wise choice."

Why are the vines not attacking you?

She whacked away a vine before it grabbed her knee. The sludge already caked her legs. She slid toward the wing on the thick coating and scrambled back toward Luteis's spine, using her palm to clear a new spot to sit. "Because I'm stopping them as they come. You ran into the bush, so it ensnared you all at once."

What would it have done with me?

"Devoured you."

I shouldn't have asked. How is it that you know this tree, and I do not?

"Rubeis ran into one once, near the Anguis border. Daid and Elliot had to go hunt a troll to kill the tree before one of the hatchlings was caught. Got pretty ugly, I guess. I can't imagine it's easy to get troll urine."

Who taught you how to defeat this monstrosity without the urine?

"Talis. Said he was stuck in one as a hatchling. Almost killed him."

Luteis fell silent.

One at a time, Sanna pinched the tentacles free. The residual sludge caked her hair and arms. An hour passed before she freed enough of his neck to climb toward his face. Another half hour while she freed his face, raking blood from the tiny scales around his eyes. She rubbed his eyes clean with the underpart of her skirt before he opened them, blinking rapidly.

Not quite so suffocating this way.

Sanna unwound a particularly tenacious vine from his snout. It attempted to roll back together, preventing her from releasing it, but she pried it back with a grunt. The moment she pinched it, it snaked away.

This is one of the most miserable experiences of my life.

"There are others comparatively miserable?"

She leaned back, holding herself against his neck with her knees as she wiped more mucus from her face. It smelled bitter, like the ink Daid used for the ledgers. The small bones and muscles in her hands ached, but vines still wrapped his foreleg and lower neck. She sank back on her haunches, surveying the thick, tangled knot ahead of her.

Your patience is unexpected and exemplary.

"Thanks." She dodged a vine as it whipped away. "I think."

Your daid would be proud.

"Ah ... maybe. He's hard to please."

Her mind wandered as she continued the painstaking work. What would have happened if she hadn't been there? Would Luteis have died? Floundering in a slow, frightening end, blind to his last moments? The question hovering at the back of her mind slipped free before she could stop it.

"Would Deasylva have let you die?"

His response was immediate. *If she were here, then no.*

"If she wasn't?"

His silence spoke for him. Sanna swallowed hard. Perhaps there was wisdom in pairing witches and dragons as partners.

"Is she back yet?"

Intermittently. For a very short time, she is here. She says she will have to leave again soon to visit another forest.

"Then why didn't she just save you?"

What do you think the answer is?

Sanna scowled. "*I* have no idea." She smacked a particularly strong vine with the back of her hand, then pummeled it with a fist. It finally retreated. She pinched the end with a surge of vengeance, feeling a little better for it.

The moment she pinched the last vine, her forearms cramping from fatigue, Luteis extricated himself with a roar and a snap. He shot a pillar of fire into the trees. The cohereo rustled, hundreds of black knots hunkered against the branches and trunk of the gargantuan tree.

Sanna thought she heard a snort and shuffle, like a hog settling in.

Together, they trudged back to the creek. Sanna jumped in, luxuriating in the fresh, cold water. The ropes of sludge tore away from her hair as she ran her fingers through it underwater, surfacing slowly. One piece at a time, she pulled her clothing off. Luteis stood back, breathing fire on every part of his body, burning the mucus free. Once finished, he slunk into the forest with a snort.

Grateful for the distance and the space to think, Sanna floated naked in the pond, staring at the intricate canopy unfurling above. Her thoughts continued to roam. How could she know Deasylva was any more honest than Talis? Luteis seemed to have total allegiance to the goddess, but perhaps *he* was brainwashed too.

She rubbed her fingers together to find them sludge-free and pruney. With a sigh, she ran a hand over her body and through her hair and climbed out of the water. The strange stillness meant Luteis hadn't returned.

She crossed the space naked, clothes dripping in her arms. A fire, built with sticks stacked in a disorganized fashion, crackled in a stone circle near the stream. Next to it lay three newly-dead pigeons and a small marmot.

CHAPTER

THIRTEEN

We dig a pit, then lure Talis into it with dead beluas.

"Talis is the most intelligent creature I've ever met." Sanna hacked at a tenacious bush with a hatchet she'd found in an old shed. "It will take more than a couple of nasty beluas to draw him in."

It's hard to find them outside family packs, anyway. No dragon would be foolish enough to attempt that alone.

Bushes filled with thorns lined the creek, making it impossible to access for hundreds of paces. On the other side, obnoxious purple flowers bobbed up and down. Their seeds were poisonous. Once they dropped into the water, they released toxins that had been killing entire families of screaming gnomes downstream. *Once we have their roots, we burn these plants and prevent their return,* Luteis had said. When she made a face, he followed it up with, *Fire is not our enemy. Under control, it is our friend.*

Fire-happy, this dragon.

Not far away, several uprooted bushes burned in a pile, the flames licking through their oily leaves with greedy tongues. Four small grouse eggs roasted at the edge of the fire pit. Sanna turned them every few minutes.

What if I challenged him? he asked, using his teeth to rip up yet another bush. She scowled. He removed ten for each one she did, and the thorns didn't prick *his* flesh. Still, she hacked at another bush because the physical work felt good. She cursed under her breath when a thorn tore her sleeve.

"Challenge Talis to what?"

A Dragellen.

"What is *that?*"

A fight between dragons. It's ancient, I've heard. Deasylva tells stories of Dragellens in the early days.

"But you've never actually seen one."

No.

"So, it could be made up."

He cocked his head to the side. *Why would Deasylva make such a thing up?*

Sanna brushed the question aside, deciding it would lead to too many others she didn't feel like answering. "Would Talis even know what it is?"

Doubtful.

"What if you died? We'd be no closer to fixing things."

He snorted.

Perhaps. How about poison?

"What poisons a dragon?"

Only silver.

Sanna tilted her head back with a sigh. There were still at least fifty more bushes to clear before they could cross this portion of the stream and uproot the noxious weeds. Luteis's focus on destroying Talis meant he wasn't tearing them up as quickly anymore.

"Silver isn't easy to come by."

I suppose starvation isn't working?

"Only putting a greater strain on the Servants, I think."

Risha berries? Deasylva has spoken of these before.

"They're sedatives. I doubt we could ever harvest enough to sedate a dragon, if they even *affect* dragons."

Luteis snorted. *What does Talis fear?*

The question caused Sanna to pause. What *did* Talis fear? Only one word crossed her mind, and just thinking it felt traitorous. She stepped away and rolled the grouse eggs free of the embers, tucking them into the crook of a root to cool. Smoke drifted off the sooty shells in lacy wisps.

"Poachers."

The first sign of lucidity from him. Alas, we cannot—indeed, should not—bring poachers. Strickenine moss wouldn't work, as we might perish ourselves attempting to take it over.

"Yes, let's not try that one."

Luteis's tail slumped. He stared into the forest, eyes slitted.

Trolls wouldn't kill only Talis. They're too feral for our purposes, and I want no other dragons harmed. Even then, Talis could defeat a single troll, and I've never heard of two trolls together. The risk isn't worth betraying our intent. Our justice has to be swift and successful the first time.

An awful feeling rose in Sanna's stomach. One option existed. One that gave her the chance to possibly save Talis's life *and* learn the truth, but it felt like a betrayal of Luteis and Deasylva. Although wouldn't it be a betrayal of Daid and Anguis to believe rumors without proof?

She swallowed.

"There, is ... ah ... one way to find out what he fears."

Luteis perked up, ears high. *Oh?*

"Daid. He knows everything about Talis."

But he is in Anguis.

"Yes, but we'll have to go there anyway, right? If we have to win on the first try, we must know exactly how to fight Talis. We don't. We're just wasting precious time here. I think we should sneak into Anguis, talk to Daid, and find out."

That sounds like you made a plan.

"Sort of. I'd rather just go and see what happens as we venture in."

She tugged at a root instead of meeting his gaze. If she could find a way to get to Daid without Luteis, she could find out the truth. Was Drago real? Had Talis lied all these years? How could she stop a wild dragon and supposed goddess from killing everything she knew and loved? The thought of asking Daid for help sent a cool sweep of relief through her.

See what happens? Act without a plan? I cannot even fathom. Although ... time is short.

"Very short."

I'm not comfortable with this, as it detours from my plan.

"Which was what?"

To make a plan here, and then execute.

"You planned to plan?"

Always.

Sanna rolled her eyes. "Look, this is our best bet. If you want to be effective right away, we have to have more information—information that only Daid has. Besides, it's sort of a plan, right? We go to Anguis, get in, talk to Daid, and come back. It's been three weeks. Maybe things will have changed, anyway."

So much time passed without a response that Sanna glanced up. Luteis blinked and nodded once, as if resigning himself to something.

I see this is so. Very well, Sanna of Anguis. I will plan a route for us to take this evening. Prepare yourself for a very long ride. We launch at twilight.

Anguis lay in quiet repose.

Any minute now, it would stir. The roosters—if any were left—would crow. Daid would likely already be at the shelter, getting ready for the day's hunt or dragon rounds. Isadora would still be asleep—probably for hours more—if she was still here.

Was she here? What happened to her after Sanna fled? Nothing that brought Sanna any comfort. Mam would be warming a pot of tea and toasting bread over the fire. Sanna's stomach grumbled at the thought. She missed tea.

Luteis circled overhead, following her scent as she ran through the high canopy. The distant horizon lightened into a robin's egg blue, seeming to push back the darkness. The long flight had been more tiring than she'd expected. The up-and-down motion, the constant wind, and sitting upright all night. Just as she prepared to swing to another tree and head toward the shelter, a flicker of blue caught her gaze. She skidded to a stop on some moss, arrested by the sulfurous stench of burning dragon scales.

Who was at the pyre in the morning?

Curiosity overcame her. Sanna descended slowly, crawling down the trunk from branch to branch until a shock of sapphire flame came into view. She straddled a small bough and peered down. A gasp caught in her throat.

Daid.

He lay in a pile on the ground, next to a feeble fire,

which billowed gray plumes of smoke. She grabbed a vine and dropped, crashing hard. Her ankle twisted, but she ignored it and hobbled toward the pyre.

"Daid!"

Chains wrapped his ankles and wrists, scarred with dried, crusted blood. Undergrowth and bracken had been swept aside to make room for him next to the pyre, but dead wood and rampant growth clogged the rest of the floor. A tattered copy of the *Chronicles* lay next to him. Dragon scales continued to smolder on the stone pyre, lit by the strange cobalt flames. The scales crumbled to a gray ash, then scuttled away on a gentle breeze.

"Daid!"

His eyes fluttered open when she touched his shoulder. For a second, he peered at her in confusion. Then under-standing seemed to wash through him.

"Sanna."

The word came out a breathy whisper. He pushed off the ground but collapsed with a grunt. "What are you—"

"I-I need to speak with you. It's about Talis, a-and ... what's happened?"

His lips formed a word, but he made no sound. Sanna cast about for a drink of water or some food, but she found nothing except stacks of old scales and mounds of ash. She grabbed the chains and tugged. The thick ovals of metal barely shifted.

"Mistakes," he croaked. "So ... many m-mistakes."

"Daid, listen. Let's get you home. We can figure out from there. I—"

Something snatched her ankle. Pain spiraled through her leg, jerking her away from Daid. She let out a cry, whip-ping around. A massive dragon loomed overhead, his belly glittering with a soft sapphire design.

Talis.

You have returned, as I hoped. Perhaps you can help your father in ways that I cannot.

Sanna scrambled back. Talis released her.

"Don't kill me!"

His tail returned, tentative at first, then with a gentle wrap around her ankle.

Kill you?

The genuine curiosity in his tone arrested her flash of panic. Sanna lowered her arms, which she'd thrown high to cover her face. Talis stooped to peer into her eyes. Another shock of pain rippled through her. She grimaced. Was the pain because he was touching her or because he was actually talking to her? His tail wasn't hot. Like Luteis, it had a light warmth. His voice was gentle. Soft, even. Like a caress.

Why would I kill you, little one?

Sanna swallowed hard. Was Talis actually speaking to her? It seemed almost impossible. "Because you banished me. Y-you tried to kill me."

Did I banish you? Or did you run before I could speak directly with you?

Sanna paused. Had he technically banished her? There had been so much fire and confusion. It was possible he'd been reacting to Luteis. But no. Isadora had been there. He had almost shot fire ...

Confusion clogged her thoughts. "Uh, I'm not sure now..."

Never would I banish you. Servants are precious to dragons. I was attempting to protect you and the brood from the wild dragon that flies. That threatens all we have done here to ensure safety.

"But you roared. You—"

Wanted to kill the wild dragon.

Talis stepped back, and the intensity of his heat faded. Sweat dotted her forehead. She wiped it free, shifting closer to Daid. Daid's eyes had closed again as if he were exhausted. The *Chronicles* lay underneath him now, pressed against his heart.

Was she remembering that horrid night wrong? Bursts of fire. Remnants of pain from her fight with the forest lion. Of course, Talis would have been protecting the brood. Why couldn't she see that before?

"What happened to Daid? W-why is he here?"

He asked to be prevented from making another mistake.

"Mistake?"

He believed your departure the result of a personal flaw. Your sister is gone as well. He feels he has failed as a Servant and a father.

A feeling of horror welled up in her. Isadora gone? Daid, a *failure*? Impossible. Had she pushed him to such a state because of her decision? And where had Isadora gone? Was she with that stranger? She'd suspected such a thing, but the confirmation sent a chill through her. Everything had fallen apart. Were the rest of the Servants struggling to eat? Where was Mam?

"He hasn't failed!"

I agree. He feared that he had made great mistakes. Talis turned to Daid, his voice dropping to a low tone in her head. Another shot of pain jolted through her, but it seemed to fade more quickly. *He wants to make no further ones. He has been imploring Drago for help. He chained himself here.*

Sanna gazed at the manacles, the sturdy clasps on the outside. Rust had already started to form. Had he been out here so long?

"And Mam?"

With the other Servants. She is fine. Distraught, but surviving.

"But what about Daid? I—"

You and I know that he did nothing wrong, of course. But he expects perfection. Your return may remedy this. I am relieved you are here.

"Yes," she whispered. "He does expect perfection."

You seem well? Letum Wood can be an unforgiving place.

"I-I came back because I have questions."

Of course.

Perhaps she'd really come back to see Talis. Maybe it hadn't really been about Daid, after all, but her burning need to just *see* if Talis was a monster. To decide whether he really was capable of such treachery. She opened her mouth to ask, but stopped.

I'm willing to assume that you have questions about Deasylva and Drago, he said, with another shock through her legs. She winced, even though relief washed through her at the same time.

"H-how did you know?"

Deasylva and I have been longtime acquaintances.

"So, you know her?"

Yes. Her lies have circulated for many years.

Sanna swallowed. "Lies?"

Her war against Drago has waged for almost as long as I can remember.

"She's at war with Drago?"

A vicious battle.

Her mind spun back to the flight with Luteis over the Northern Network, when he'd mentioned Deasylva taking part in some kind of war.

"Oh."

She's not very subtle, is she? Don't you find it odd that she's willing to harm a dragon for her own selfish interests? She told you, among other things no doubt, that dragons were her caretakers.

"Yes."

Talis snorted, but no flames emerged. Only a roll of hot air swept past her.

Slaves, really. Isn't it odd that a goddess cannot care for her own forests?

"I thought so."

Because of her, we have been chained to caring for a forest that wouldn't even protect us when we needed it most.

"The Great Massacre, you mean?"

He shifted, his sapphire scales shimmering in the waxing daylight. He stood across from her, not far from Daid, who groaned and attempted to sit up. His strength failed him. He curled his fingers around the *Chronicles* and moved his lips.

Sanna peered closer. Reddish purple rimmed his mouth, like a berry stain.

Yes, the massacre. If Deasylva is so powerful, where was she when the world almost ended? When poachers descended with strange fire and magic and silver?

Sanna swallowed against another shot of pain, this time twice as powerful as the others. Heat expanded between them, rolling through the air in great waves. She turned away, arm thrown high to protect her face. Talis calmed, though pain lingered in his voice.

She did nothing, he whispered. *Nothing to save us as we died. What kind of goddess is that?*

His muted pain, the strength of his bitterness, forced her into silence.

Thyris will be glad you are back, he said, this time with more control. *He has mourned the lost opportunity to work with a witch of your discernment. You have shown more promise than anyone.*

Sanna blinked, as if coming out of a reverie. The trees stirred behind Talis, revealing a glint of color amongst the shadows. "Thyris still wants to work with me?"

Of course. Why wouldn't he?

"I-I chose Luteis. I left."

Struck temporarily insane by Deasylva, no doubt, he said. *She has ways of speaking that can be very convincing. If you return to the brood, all will be forgiven. Your daid will then forgive himself, I'm sure. You can work together, the way you have always dreamed. This is Drago's desire for you, if you want it.*

She stared at him, dumbstruck. He was offering her a chance to return. To work with Daid. To be a respected Servant. Everything she had ever wanted. Talis was *willing* to give her everything she'd ever wanted. Or was it Drago? Her gaze fell to Daid. His lips continued to move, repeating the same thing over and over, but her mind spun too quickly to decipher it.

If she came back, what of Luteis? Deasylva was *real.* Was Drago?

Could Talis prove him?

"I can't believe you'd give me another chance."

Sanna, he said gently, *have I not always protected you? Have I not always cared for Anguis, the dragons, and the Servants? My concern is for you. Not the forest.*

"Ivis," she asked. "Why did you kill her?"

Ah, Ivis. There was much there you didn't understand. His wings lowered onto his back. *I could not sacrifice more hatchlings because of her lust for one. Shall I risk the safety of many for the safety of one?*

Another burst of color in the trees behind Talis caught her gaze. Not Luteis. Not Thyris, either.

Cara.

She stood on a thick branch only thirty paces from the ground, barely visible, as if she didn't want to be seen. Her talons dug into the trunk, and her nostrils flared wide, smoke trailing from them. Her ears were flat against her head. Something brimmed in her eyes. Terror. Daid struggled to roll to the side. Sanna glanced at him.

There were berry stains on his lips.

The hair on the back of Sanna's neck rose. She stepped back. The shackles he wore were sealed on the outside; he couldn't have put himself into them. He wasn't struggling from fatigue, but delirium. Talis—or one of the Servants at his command—had given Daid risha berries to sedate him. A chill swept through her when she recognized the word Daid was repeating soundlessly over and over.

Run.

Sanna bolted.

Talis's tail slipped from her ankle as she plunged into the forest. Leaves whipped her face as she sprinted away. Talis screamed behind her. Heat licked at her ankles, spurring her faster. The ground trembled. She leapt over a fallen branch, dodged around a network of roots, and skidded to a stop at a familiar tree. On the far side from Talis, she climbed as fast as she could.

"Luteis!"

She'd barely made it to the first branch when Talis slid to a stop on the ground, snapping after her. He sank his talons into the tree and began to climb. She scrambled onto a branch twice as wide as she was tall. Within seconds, Talis joined her with a sultry bellow. Sanna grabbed a vine and threw herself off the tree.

Instead of soaring toward the next branch, the vine caught on something above, swinging her in an arc back toward Talis.

"Luteis!" she shrieked.

Talis snapped for her legs. She shrieked and lifted them out of his way. With a kick, she shoved his snout, hitting him with her heel. He reared back, clawing at her.

"You're a liar!" she screamed. "You sedated my daid. You've put him there as punishment for disobeying you. You don't care about me or the Servants or the forest! You're just as selfish as Deasylva, wanting to stay locked up in Anguis when the forest is dying. There won't *be* a forest if it stays like this!"

He snarled as she circled back around again. Sanna dropped down the vine, crashing to the forest floor. Talis leapt to the earth, wings spread. The ground rippled when he landed only a few paces away. His tail whipped around, slapping the backs of her legs. She grunted as she fell onto her back, the air fleeing her lungs.

Talis loomed over her. She struggled to her hands and knees. He slammed his tail into her chest and pressed her down.

You have chosen the wrong god to obey! I will have my revenge. I don't need you or Deasylva to protect the brood.

The pain of speaking with him shocked her body. Her chest unlocked, flooding with air. She coughed, sputtering through the black spots at the edge of her vision, but he kept her anchored to the floor.

"You?" she shouted. "Don't you mean Drago?"

A screech overhead broke through the trees. Sanna grabbed Talis's tail and bent it back. A thunderous *crack* followed—the sound of breaking scales.

Talis screamed, releasing her. She darted for the nearest

tree and began to climb. Talis lunged, but another dragon slammed into his side.

Cara.

Sanna made it to the first branch and whirled around just as Talis threw Cara off himself. She slammed into a tree.

"Cara!"

A glitter of orange swept through Sanna's peripheral vision. Luteis soared by, snatched her off the branch with his back legs, and tossed her onto his back.

"No!" she screamed. "Cara!"

Luteis clawed his way up the trees, burst through the canopy, and winged away.

Isadora lay on the rich soil of Letum Wood and breathed in the steady forest air for at least an hour. Once her anxiety ebbed away, she straightened, brushed the dirt away, and forced her feet to walk. When Chatham Castle in all its stony splendor filled her view, she stared at it for five minutes.

Then she kept going.

After thirty minutes of observation and attempting to count the sheer number of witches, she picked her way through a crowd and entered the lower bailey in front of its soaring turrets. As she stared into the rheumy eyes of the Guardian on duty, a gutted feeling filled her chest.

"What do ya mean ya want ta talk ta Ambassador Sinclair?" he cried. "Ya can't just waltz in here, ya know."

"It's really quite simple—"

"It's not."

His surly interjection caught her by surprise. Why should he care?

Behind her, the sounds of a market bounced off the stone walls of the castle bailey, creating a cacophony. A man selling wagon wheels shouted when a chicken scuttled under his feet. Silk dresses fluttered in and out of the aisles. Isadora longed to wander the tables, but the pressure of the scroll tucked safely in her sleeve kept her on course. Not to mention the witches staring right at her and her hair, which she hadn't taken the time to pin up. No one *else* had such long locks.

What had she been thinking? Coming to Chatham City had been deadly—foolish. Attempting to see Maximillion was *insane*. For many reasons. Still, she had come. She'd see it through.

"I just want to—"

"Ya have to have a letter with his seal on it. Ya dress is too plain, anyway. Greta would have ya kicked out if she saw ya."

She ground her teeth and thought to beg Drago for patience, but dismissed it. Drago couldn't help her here.

"Can you tell him I'm here?"

"Right. Ya want me to go into Ambassador Sinclair's office? Have ya ever met him?"

"Unfortunately."

"Then ya should know better. Be gone with ya."

He stomped a foot toward her. Isadora scuttled away with a growl and pretended to go back to the market.

The air lay heavy with soot, refuse, and Drago-knew-what else. A metallic taste filled her mouth. Sharp, sooty spires poked the sky in front of Chatham City, which sat a little way south of the castle bailey, connected by one long dirt road. At least she didn't have to navigate all the high-ways *and* Chatham City.

The *Chatterer* had reported an upcoming meeting between Maximillion and the Eastern Network Ambassador Cecelia Liam at Chatham Castle later this week. Cecelia's arrival would break a three-year silence from the East. If one counted constant political bickering and threats of bloodshed along the border as *silence*.

Isadora spun on her heels, studying the wide, sprawling stones of the castle. She'd never imagined such a massive building in her life, and she fell into thought studying the stonework. A back entrance, perhaps? No. The castle had its own protective magic—or so the history book had said. But there *had* to be a way inside.

A scuffle off to the right caught Isadora's gaze. A congregation of witches teemed around a rounded wooden door built into the stone wall. They wore identical black-and-white dresses. One of them shouted, "On the day shift, eh?" to another across the way before he disappeared inside, leaving an old, world-worn Guardian to patrol the exterior.

Servants. They had to be. The market blocked the Guardian she'd just spoken with from seeing that entrance, which meant she could sneak over to it.

With a deep breath for courage, Isadora squared her shoulders and trained her eye on the far door. Now *there* was an entrance she could slip into.

Isadora meandered along as she observed the market. Egads, but she'd never seen so much *stuff* in her life. Pelts of fur stained outlandish colors that witches draped around their necks. Bottled potions meant to cure arthritis that smelled like rotten eggs. Witches murmured that it was a quiet market, but Isadora had already seen four times the number of witches she'd ever known. She walked out the other side, her heart hammering.

The Guardian at the servants' entrance looked like he could use a cup of Pearl's beloved coffee. A paunchy belly and drooping eyelids proved him a much older witch than most Guardians. No doubt he'd been stuffed here, stuck on a duty no one else wanted when war threatened the Network on all sides.

She paused again, pretending to survey the market.

A servant stepped in or out once or twice a minute. They wore black linen dresses and white aprons as stiff as a wooden board. Could she slide by and say she left her uniform inside? Surely he didn't know *all* the servants. The Guardian flicked his gaze toward her, scanned the bailey, and returned to the stone floor. His jaw tensed, as if he were fighting off a yawn.

"I can do this," she murmured, drawing courage from her own voice. "I can do this."

An aged witch with a shock of white hair and arthritic hands stepped out of the servants' door, nodding to the Guardian as she passed. Once the door closed behind her, Isadora advanced. The entrance waited only thirty paces away. She clenched her hands into fists at her side.

"Murderer!"

"Failure!"

"Ya know nothing about diplomacy."

The *squish* of a tomato falling on the cobblestone in

front of her forced Isadora to pause. Juice splayed around the rotten fruit in goopy, translucent streams. Seeds dotted her pointy shoe. She stared at it, her head tilted. Who would waste a tomato?

Behind her, the portcullis leading into the bailey from Chatham City groaned as it retracted farther up, having only been opened enough to admit witches walking through. Trumpets blared from the top of the Wall, a sprawling structure that enclosed the bailey. A shock rippled through her bones at the bugle. Her blood ran cold. No. It couldn't be.

Cecelia had come early.

Beyond the portcullis waited a garish carriage lined with gold. Creamy white horses pranced, releasing the high-pitched tinkle of several small bells. Witches from outside teemed around the carriage in a livid throng. The spooked horses reared and darted into the bailey with wild eyes.

Isadora stumbled back as they whipped by, cords of muscle sticking out of the driver's neck as he attempted to control the reins. She caught a quick glimpse of a female witch inside, wearing a dress buttoned all the way up her neck, with clouds of silver-blonde hair piled on top of her head. She gazed out the window down a long, perfect nose, seeming indifferent to the raging screams.

Witches in the market streamed away in rivers, headed for the safety of Chatham City. Moments before the carriage would have crashed into a cart of radishes, the horses clattered to a stop on the cobblestones.

"Drago," Isadora murmured. "That was close."

The malingering crowd of witches surged forward to surround the carriage—and Isadora. As quickly as the protestors came, the Guardians followed. Curses, spells, and magical balls streaked through the bailey. Isadora tried to push through the madness, but the crowd bore her toward the carriage with their fury. Their shouts at Cecelia echoed off the bailey walls.

"Ya don't want peace!"

"Yer here for power!"

"No witch from the East can be trusted!"

"Burn the East ta the ground!"

Isadora's throat tightened as she struggled against the inevitable flow, terrified by their livid eyes. The driver attempted to back the horses away from the market, but the crowd stood too thick. Isadora ducked when something black, the size of a marble, whizzed by her head. Witches attempted to climb the carriage and wrench open the door. Every grubby hand that clutched the door handle lost its grip. A protection spell, no doubt.

"They're casting curses!" a voice called.

"The Guardians are throwing blighters, the traitors. You're supposed to be on our side!"

"Get back!"

Next to Isadora, a man doubled over and vomited slugs. Another screeched as boils popped out over his skin in livid welts. She stared in horror. Guardians using magic against their own witches?

Despite her renewed efforts to get away, the press of bodies kept her locked in the middle of the wild hysteria. How could they behave so ravenously against someone they didn't know? Three witches managed to get ahold of the driver and push him off. They claimed the reins with victorious shouts. The furious chants calling for Cecelia's head rang in Isadora's ears in a terrifying melody. A cry of alarm came from the crowd.

"Oy. Look there."

"On the stairs."

"Shut your mouths. Look on the stairs!"

A telltale darkness crept in from the edges of Isadora's vision just as her ears started to ring. Pain tore through her mind, forcing her to grab the carriage wheel to stop herself from falling.

A voice bellowed through the crowd. "Silence, you idiots!"

The ruckus calmed like a settling sigh. Standing on the stairs, descending one precise step at a time, was Maximillion. His eyes flashed with fury as he took in the crowd, staring down each witch until they turned away with a sheepish mumble. No one moved, not even a Guardian. One of the horses nickered, breaking the reign of silence.

Maximillion turned toward a Guardian. "Release the carriage."

Two Guardians leapt into action and grabbed the reins from the stunned witches. Witches parted to allow the animals through. Maximillion descended the rest of the way, the crisp, even staccato of his shoes clacking against the stone. "Back away," he commanded.

The witches blocking the stairs faded like wraiths. The pressure from the crowd on Isadora's ribs lessened. She ducked to draw in a deep breath of air and calm her wild heart.

Peace, she spoke into her mind. *Calm.* But the whirling gray headache continued, spinning at a reckless speed. Why *now?*

The carriage door groaned open and then shut again. Isadora lifted her head, catching a glimpse of exquisite black lace and a pair of slender shoulders. The back of Cecelia's right earlobe caught Isadora's attention. There was a tattoo there. Something like a bird? No. Something else.

Cecelia moved away, staring straight ahead as she crossed the short distance to the stairs, her profile impassive. Maximillion offered a hand. Together, they turned around, the very picture of decorum. Isadora couldn't tear her gaze away from their equally beautiful forms.

At the top of the stairs, Maximillion spun around. His gaze met Isadora's with daggers of ice. "Take the instigators to the dungeons for the night. Give them a full meal and release them in the morning."

Her throat thickened into a lump. He'd seen her in this massive, riotous crowd. Lovely.

Maximillion spun on his heel and disappeared inside Chatham Castle with Cecelia's elegant hair and billowing silver dress rustling at his side.

It seemed Isadora would get inside the castle after all.

CHAPTER

FOURTEEN

Isadora paced her dungeon cell like a ravenous wolf.

Her headaches had been more relentless than ever the past day. Banging. Pulsing. Pounding. As if cutting her off from sunshine had crushed her whole being. Movement helped—or perhaps just distracted her. She drew in a deep breath, let it out, and pushed through the pain to pace again.

Down the dingy dungeon hall, at least four cells away, two sets of curious eyes peered at her like globes in the darkness. When she tried to speak with the other prisoners, they disappeared. Untrusting lot, these city witches.

She turned at the edge of the cell to pace again. In the distance, a slamming door rang through the fetid air. She glanced up, then scowled. Two Guardians opened the cells to the other prisoners and let them free. Over the past day —or had it been two?—the other rioters had been released. It had been two days, at least, she was sure. Time passed in a strange way without sunlight. She'd never realized how much light *did* permeate Letum's thick canopy until now.

She alone remained as the last witch.

246

Of course.

Exhausted, she dropped onto the musty straw mattress but jumped back to her feet when something translucent slithered out from a hole at the mattress's end. With a shudder, she crossed to the other side of the cell and shrank back against the chilly stone wall. The air, barely stained by the distant torchlight, sank into her cold bones. No warmth permeated the dank walls, which dripped with moisture.

Maximillion, all hard lines and cutting glances, flashed through her mind again.

"Odious witch," she muttered.

It's not like she'd done anything wrong, anyway. She'd simply been standing there. She wasn't even upset about being put in prison with the rest of them. She was livid about being *kept* there.

Admittedly, her timing in the bailey hadn't been the greatest. And perhaps from his point of view, it *had* seemed as if she were part of the riot. She thought of Sanna with a wry sliver of amusement. Sanna'd be bellowing in a fit of rage by now. It would be entertaining, at least.

Another door slammed, reverberating through the floor and into the metal bars to which she clung. The *clank* of a Guardian striding toward her lifted her spirits. She stood, then pressed her face to the bars.

"Am I to be released?"

The Guardian, a kind man with bright blue eyes, had been around once every hour. Sometimes he spoke with her. He'd also discreetly slipped her a red-and-white striped candy. This time, he frowned.

"No, miss. Just dinner."

He slid a plate to her. A limp, sliced onion, a splat of soft white cheese, and a mug with what she suspected was tepid tea that had likely been his own—none of the other prisoners had received mugs. She wrapped her hand around it. Still slightly warm. Enough to permeate her frozen fingertips. Perhaps it would help a little with the headache.

"Thank you very much. This was kind."

Color rose to his cheeks. "Sure enough, miss."

"Any word from—"

"Your duties are complete here," said a cold voice. "You may go."

Isadora's eyes flickered behind the Guardian.

Maximillion.

She stepped away from the bars as if they'd shocked her. The Guardian sent her one last, apologetic look before fading away, the plate in his hand.

"I have a hard time believing you'd step into a place this dirty," she said.

Maximillion sneered at the stagnant water on the floor. "You have a nasty habit of forcing me into undesirable situations. Are you prepared to behave yourself for the next hour? Or should we have this conversation here?"

"What's my other option?" She airily waved at her cot. "I don't really mind this so much."

"There's a worm in your hair."

A niggling movement squirmed at the top of her head that instant. She reached up, clutched something squishy, and flicked it carelessly against the wall. Far worse had fallen into her hair at home.

"You seem to really enjoy this place," he said. "A favored vacation spot, perhaps?"

"I do. Thank you."

"An investment in acting lessons would serve you well. If you can avoid being a total shrew—or criminal, for that matter—you may come to my office."

"I'll try to control my womanly impulses."

"See that you do."

With that, he spun on his heel and strode to the end of the row. He spoke with the Guardian for a few seconds, then disappeared. Moments later, the Guardian returned, wreathed in a smile.

"You're free, miss."

She cast a wry glance at the empty cell, catching a glimpse of a wiggling worm inching its way across the floor, and set the cup off to the side.

"I suppose I won't need to gather my things."

"Naw. Just follow me. We're taking some back staircases, so don't get scared. Spiders, 'n all that."

Isadora suppressed the urge to roll her eyes. Admittedly, she didn't enjoy bugs, but spiders the size of her fist had once invaded the attic while she was sleeping. The creatures of this castle held no candle to those that lurked in Letum Wood.

"Yes," she drawled. "I'll try my best to keep courage."

"Good to hear."

He crossed the floor, forcing her to jog to catch up as they passed by several cells. At the far wall, a metallic ring the size of her hand protruded from the stone. He grasped it, whispered a spell, and yanked. Dust billowed from a crack that appeared, brushing her face with musty air. She held up a hand to push aside a drape of cobwebs as he led her through the doorway.

"Secret passage?" she asked, pulling the door closed behind her. Darkness spiraled ahead, dimly illuminated by the feeble torchlight.

"Not so secret to the right people."

The torchlight spread shadows before them. A rat screeched. Something rattled far above her head. She swallowed, appreciating his warning with fresh respect. Perhaps it was a *bit* jarring in such a narrow space. If a rat darted by, it would have to touch her, the walls were so close.

She followed the Guardian through an eternity of converging staircases, damp walls, and uneven steps. Finally, he stopped on a wider landing and rapped three times on a wall. Seconds later, the wall itself opened. He stepped back and motioned her forward.

"Good luck," he whispered as she passed. "Ya'll need it."

The moment she stepped through the doorway, Isadora recoiled.

Light accosted her sensitive eyes, sending a blinding spear of pain through her head. Several long seconds passed before she could open them again. No doubt he invited her to his office at the brightest part of the day just to torture her. She held up an arm and stumbled into a bookshelf, knocking over a vase. It shattered on the floor. The wall slid closed behind her, locking her firmly in Maximillion's office.

"As eloquent an entrance as I expected," he said. The vase gathered back together, shuddered, and returned to the shelf in perfect condition.

Isadora blinked through her haze. Maximillion stood behind a sprawling desk. The edges of his furniture filled a surprisingly small space. She'd expected a wide suite with servants and liveried footmen and *slaves* for Drago's sake, but all she saw was an office littered with ...

Not much.

She rubbed her eyes, advancing a tentative step. A bank of long windows cast streams of light on a mahogany desk covered with scrolls, a quill, and an inkwell. A slightly cracked windowpane admitted crisp fall air, offering a view of the top of Letum Wood. She breathed deeply while admiring the thick cushions on the chair behind her. All in all, the office felt downright ... bland.

"This is your office?"

"Try not to sound so impressed."

"It's so ... normal."

"I don't eat small children."

"Shocking."

"Let's get this over with, shall we?" He leaned over his desk onto his fists, fixing her with his terrifying, arctic stare. "What in the name of the good gods were you thinking?"

He'd removed his jacket. Like usual, his hair was tossed, as if disheveled from sheer frustration. Something about the tension in his jaw—shadowed with a hint of stubble— made her apprehensive. He looked a bit leaner, as if he'd lost weight. For the briefest moment, she swore she saw a flicker of uncertainty in his gaze. Isadora swallowed a heavy lump in her throat.

"It was an accident."

"You've turned to rioting in the short time since I've seen you?"

"Sophie's is quite boring."

He snorted.

"You left me in that dungeon on purpose, didn't you?"

His eyes flashed. He picked up a glass filled with amber liquid and sipped from it. "Yes. But two days is hardly torture."

"Is that ipsum?" she asked.

"Yes."

Her nose wrinkled. "I've read a lot about it. Isn't it poison?"

"In great quantities, perhaps. In small quantities, it's a

serum that saves many lives. Namely the people I have to work with. Don't change the subject."

"We were talking about your eagerness to see me again. And the reasons you kept me locked up in that horrid dungeon."

"I certainly didn't rush to release you."

"It was an accident that I was there in the first place. I had nothing to do with the rioters. They happened to be there at the same time I arrived."

"A likely story from a guilty party." He slammed the glass on his desk. Liquid sloshed over its sides. "How did you get here?"

Sheer luck, she thought. "I transported."

His frown deepened.

"What? Who taught you?"

She hesitated, the words frozen on her tongue. Deciding he'd probably know if she lied, she finally said, "An old lady in the square at Berry."

"How long was your lesson?"

"She told me the words."

"And you tried it?"

"I didn't know *not* to."

"The good gods! How did you make it out alive?"

Her heart twisted at the memory. "I don't know. I ... I think she lied to me or something. I actually ended up several places. Something pulled me back just before I think I was about to be lost. Can you die while transporting?"

"Of course you can!" he cried. "What incantation did she give you?"

Isadora repeated it. He calmed slightly.

"It's the right one, but your pronunciation is wrong. And you can't transport somewhere you've never been. Not without a lot of experience and more skill with magic than you have. It's too dangerous. You need to be able to *know* where you're going."

"She also held up a fist with a pinky extended. What does that mean?"

He waved that off. "A sign of farewell."

Maximillion repeated the correct pronunciation of the incantation and forced Isadora to say it twenty times before he was satisfied. "And now I've saved your bloody life in more ways than one. Don't be an idiot again," he muttered into his ipsum. "You can transport back to Berry, I'm sure. But practice with well-known spots before attempting something that idiotic again."

Isadora's brow scrunched. "How else have you saved my life?"

"From yourself, for starters. And from a far more powerful witch than you could ever hope to be, for another. I had to leave you in the dungeons until Cecelia left."

"What? Why is Cecelia a threat to me?"

"For many reasons."

"Is she a Watcher?"

He hesitated. "Not really. But yes … of a sort."

Isadora lifted one eyebrow, grateful to switch conversation topics. "How can a witch be a Watcher but not be one?"

"It means she's not like me or Pearl or Grey or you or any of the others. Have you read the scroll?"

"Yes. I sent you several letters. It's why I came."

"I didn't receive them. I've been out of the Network."

She pulled it from her sleeve and extended it to him with a spell. It lowered onto the desk with only a slight wobble, she noticed with some satisfaction. Her execution of simple spells certainly had improved since she'd left Anguis.

"What I read frightened me."

Saying the words cost her some pride. She tilted her chin up. He turned around, his back to her. "Good."

"I wanted to speak with you about it."

"Later."

"But—"

"I know you're concerned. You have reason to be until we figure out how to bloody manage your wild powers. When that happens, I'll address your fears. In the meantime, I have more information for you." Five books soared off the top shelf of a floor-to-ceiling bookcase against the far wall. She held out her hands and gathered them as they descended, stuffing aside her questions for later.

"What are these?"

"Introductory reading." He rummaged through a drawer in his desk and replaced the scroll she'd returned. "You have a bit of catching up to do. I've done some research and interviews and have a few ideas on how to work with your odd powers. I'll return to Sophie's tomorrow morning for your next lesson, and we'll begin with the new strategy. Have all of this read."

"All of it?"

"I could have all of those read twice in that amount of time."

A rap on the door quieted her. Maximillion held up a hand to his lips in warning, then strode over and peered through a round peephole in the wood. He motioned her back with a jerk of his hand. She retreated against the wall.

"What is it?" he called through the door. "I'm busy."

"Of course, Ambassador. I'll return."

The sound of footsteps faded away.

"Who was that?" Isadora asked.

He cut her a quelling look. "My Assistant, if you must

know. Now leave and start reading. You have a lot of work to do."

He returned to his desk, picked up several folded messages, and tore into one. Isadora hesitated, then floated the books next to her with a spell. She paused halfway to the door.

"Should I be afraid of Cecelia?" she asked over her shoulder.

"Immensely."

"Am I in danger?"

"Not immediately, if you leave."

"Do you have a carriage I could take?"

"I don't."

"Really?"

"Yes. Even if I did, I wouldn't loan it to you."

"But you're the Ambassador. Don't you have a carriage that's so protected by incantations it's almost impervious or something like that?"

He glanced at her with scathing annoyance. "I gave my carriage to the Guardians in the spring so they could evacuate their wounded. Tomorrow morning." He glanced at the books. "Don't be late."

He motioned her out with a flick of his wrist, his eyes already lost in a letter. Isadora slipped out of his office with the books floating at her side. Her headache had abated. Attributing the relief to the fresh air, she continued down the hall, determined not to get lost in the castle. Despite a feeling of utter, wretched fatigue, she'd still transport from the forest.

Where everything seemed far safer.

WHEN ISADORA SLIPPED into the library the next day, her headache had returned with full force. Maximillion waited by the fire. He eyed her with something close to amusement. If that were even possible for a witch like him.

"You made it."

"I did."

"You look terrible."

"The result of a little trip to a dungeon, I would imagine." She brushed her second-best dress off even though there wasn't a speck of dirt on it. When a gaggle of girls ran down the hallway, she tensed. They continued on.

His gaze narrowed. "No," he murmured. "It's something more. You're not well."

"The headaches were relentless in the dungeon. They got better for a bit in your office but returned last night. I didn't sleep much. Can we do anything about it?"

"You need an Apothecary."

"I need to use my powers, right?"

"No. I think it's more than that."

The urge to yawn tugged at her jaw, but she suppressed it. Her nostrils flared with the effort. "I don't want to see an Apothecary here, anyway. I'd rather have Lucey."

"Follow me."

He strode past her into the hall. Isadora blinked, then scrambled to catch up with him.

"Maximillion, wait!"

He didn't. Once outside, he squinted in the sunshine, saw Sophie standing near the garden with a tremulous smile on her face and two uprooted daisies in her hand, and dodged closer to the road.

"Where are we going?" Isadora asked.

"To fix your headaches."

She snapped her mouth shut and followed, curious despite herself. If any witch could rid her of the pain, she'd meet them. He continued down the dirt road, heading for the center of town.

"Maximillion, I'm really not comfortable with a new Apoth—"

He gritted his teeth. "I *know*."

She waited for an acerbic response. A scathing condemnation of her fear of crowds, perhaps—especially after the terror of Chatham City. Some sharp retort about her inability to cope with life in the outside world. None came.

How odd.

Farmers' stands lined the main road, leading toward the distant backdrop of Letum Wood, which surrounded the village like a high wall. The cry of witches haggling back and forth filled the air. The smell of fresh lye soap, the sharp tang of lamp cleaner, and the musty scent of fresh leather mixed in a strange cacophony. Isadora's gaze combed through the tables in fascination. Knitted shawls. Soap shaped like roses with petals that peeled back. They offered everything out here. More than she could have ever imagined wanting.

Maximillion strode through the chaos, ignoring witches who started at the sight of him. Isadora half-jogged beside him and grimaced at the up-and-down motion that caused such pain. They barreled toward Letum Wood.

As they neared the forest, something stirred in her blood. She straightened, drawing in a lungful of heavy, familiar air. Soon, she caught up with Maximillion and matched his stride—her whole body infused with the texture and taste of *home*.

"We're going to my home?"

"Depends on how you define it."

"Letum Wood."

"Then, yes."

Her stride lengthened. New energy infused her veins. He matched her pace with a flicker of annoyance. They sped through decayed rows of drooping corn, past old wooden houses, and into the cool shadows. Trees towered over them. Isadora rushed ahead onto a footpath. Skeins of moss danced along tree trunks as she sped by. Vines dangled from the canopy, reminding her of Sanna. A figure stepped out of the trees ahead of them. Isadora slowed, her heart pounding in her throat. The coiffed, dirty-blonde hair. Kind blue eyes.

Lucey!

Rustles of color fluttered around Lucey's shoulders. She'd even brought some of her birds.

"Lucey!"

Lucey opened her arms with a warm smile. "Isadora. How wonderful to see you."

Isadora darted into Lucey's embrace with half a sob, cherishing the warm crush of someone familiar. Lucey patted her gently on the head—just the way all mams did. Tears dribbled out of Isadora's eyes when Lucey pulled her away, studying her with a critical gaze.

"You didn't exaggerate, Maximillion. She looks terrible."

He lifted one eyebrow.

"Why?" Isadora asked, pressing a hand to her cheek. "The headaches—"

"Getting worse?"

"Yes."

Lucey sat on a mossy rock and patted the spot next to

her. Maximillion wrinkled his nose, refusing to join with a flick of his hand. He eyed a latticed design in the moss of a nearby tree instead. Lucey pressed two fingers to the pulse at Isadora's wrist.

"My studies have shown that Dragonmasters, more than other witches, seem to be ... dependent on Letum Wood."

"Dragonmasters?"

"Oh, forgive me. You don't know yet. Ah..." She trailed away for a moment, chewing her bottom lip. "Let's just say Servants."

"But—"

"I don't yet understand why Servants have this problem," she continued, as if Isadora hadn't asked. "We can't be away from the forest for long. I've studied foresters who have grown up in Letum Wood. I've studied vagabonds and wanderers who eventually make their home here. None of them seem to have the physical dependence on the forest that we do."

"Dependence?"

"How are you feeling right now?"

Isadora paused. The heady air and close press of the forest had already given her an undeniable rush of ... *something*. New life zipped through her blood, like she'd awoken after a long sleep. She'd felt it momentarily near Chatham City when she'd transported into the forest, but she hadn't remained there long. It *had* allowed her to recover, though.

"I feel better."

"Good." Lucey gave one punctuated nod. "At the very least, you should be feeling something."

"How do we deal with this?" Maximillion asked. "She can't live in Letum Wood by herself."

"Give her regular access."

"Define regular," Maximillion said.

Isadora pressed a hand to her head and closed her eyes. Energy bubbled up inside her like a swelling wave, but with it came a fresh pulse at her temples.

"She'll have to tell you. I don't know what she needs. On some level, I doubt *she* knows what she needs."

"She can't come alone. You know that!"

"Then you must come with her."

"I haven't the time."

"Hold your lessons here."

"Will that be enough?"

Their voices began to fade into the expanding, pewter cloud. Isadora frowned. A headache ... but *not*. So swift? Like a wave, but a soft one. Nothing painful. Just ... expanding.

" ... Isadora?"

Lucey's voice rippled. A tunnel of darkness cocooned Isadora in shadows.

"The good gods ... *do* something, Lucey!"

"Isadora!"

A slippery, black slope afforded Isadora no chance to fight back. She gave in to the plunging chasm, expecting to fade away, back into unconsciousness. She jerked to a stop instead, standing on her feet in the middle of a vast circle of twelve trees—the ones she had seen before she transitioned.

She tilted her head back. The branches soared overhead like buttresses, intersecting in a tapestry of leaves. Every lush detail appeared as crisp as a prism. The curl of a leaf. Tiny veins snaking through their emerald skin. Flowers that blushed pink. Rich earth, as loamy and black as foam.

When she touched the tree, a slow *thud thud thud* of a heart pulsed beneath her fingers. Magic hummed, making the air crackle. She saw no sign of Maximillion or Lucey or the trail where they once stood. Just sun streaks and a lush, emerald world. Not a remnant of pain loomed in her mind. She wore the same clothes. The same shoes.

Instead of one trail, three started at her feet and snaked into the distance. On the right, a wispy shape bubbled up near the trail in shades of black and white. It formed into a freckled face and two familiar braids.

Sanna.

In the strange, ethereal vapor, Sanna stared straight ahead. Her eyes were focused, brow furrowed. The path continued until another Sanna appeared behind the first. The second wisp lay on its back, snarling. Typical Sanna.

The middle path stretched farther ahead. In another smoky shape, Isadora recognized the cut of Maximillion's shoulders despite a vague, unfashioned face. The mist extended no farther than his chest. Why such a piecemeal vision?

Drawn by curiosity, she advanced to the next wisp on that trail. Maximillion again. Or so she thought. She could only see his profile as he spoke to a woman with an elegant pile of hair and a high-necked dress studded with pearls. Cecelia? From there, his path branched into a dozen trails, all empty. Several other mounds of vapor-like foam lay along the trail, as if attempting to form into witches.

When Isadora returned back to the top of the paths in the middle of the circle, Sanna's first wisp had shifted. She crouched on her haunches now, holding a bundle of twigs. Her path split into four. A dragon wing hovered in one, but the others lay empty. Isadora reached out to touch Sanna's face again.

A ripple of movement caught her gaze. Isadora whipped around. Maximillion's paths had shifted. A wild-haired, terrified man had replaced Cecelia. Next to him, another wisp bubbled up. Lucey? No. Isadora. Or both? An endless number of trails began to sprawl out behind them. Whatever this world was, it was transient.

The third and final trail showed Lucey bent over someone ill, Lucey's own face haggard. Her path split into two. One stopped a short way away; the other wound into the forest, but no wisps awaited along it. What did it mean when the trail stopped? When the wisps weren't there?

The leaves began to blur, and the mist of magic in the air faded. Isadora hastened back to the middle of the circle just as darkness overtook her. Blackness covered her eyes like a velvety cloth. A breath later, she opened her eyes to a murky forest and two blurry faces overhead.

"There you are," Lucey said with a sigh of relief.

"Troublemaker," Maximillion muttered.

"Passing out can hardly be categorized as rebellion," Lucey said.

"She did it on purpose."

"Who doesn't love a good blackout and whack on the head now and then?" Lucey rolled her eyes. "Honestly, Maximillion. You set the bar for being the most implacable witch I've ever met."

"A compliment."

Isadora blinked. The last remnants of the picture cleared, giving way to Maximillion's intense frown. He straightened, turning away as soon as their gazes met. Lucey pushed a lock of hair off Isadora's forehead.

"Are you all right, Isadora?" she asked gently.

"Sanna!" Isadora gasped. "I-I saw Sanna!"

Lucey's eyebrows rose. "Really? Oh, I'd love to know what's become of her. There have been rumors in Anguis ... anyway, what did you see? Was there an orange dragon?"

Maximillion spun on his heel to face Isadora, eyes tapered. "What are you talking about?"

Isadora shot upright. She sat on the ground now, the feel of damp leaves at her fingertips. "I saw Sanna on a path! And you, too, Lucey, although one of them stopped and ... and I don't know what that means. Maximillion, you were with Cecelia and then a terrified witch and..." She frowned and pressed a hand to the side of her head. "But then everything changed, and I'm not really sure *what* caused it."

Maximillion tilted his head to one side. "You saw *me* in there?"

"Yes."

"On your path."

"No, on *your* path. I wasn't in there at all. Not that I saw, anyway. There were three trails. Sanna, you, and Lucey."

He exchanged a mysterious glance with Lucey, then strode over, dropped to a knee, and grabbed Isadora's arms. "Say it again very carefully. You saw a trail for me?"

"Yes."

"And me?" Lucey asked.

Isadora's mind jumped around like a drop of fat in a hot pan. "Well, yes. Yours was short, Lucey, like I said. Sanna's was the easiest. Or at least the clearest. Most of them were quite vague. But Maximillion, you had a complicated mess. I couldn't really see much. Just ... hazy blobs, really. Some of them never formed. Is this the power? Is this what it is to be a Watcher? There were trails. Or, what do you call them? Oh! Paths. There were definitely paths and—"

A burning intensity consumed his gaze. "Slow down. Come at it again, but explain yourself as thoroughly as you can. Start from the very beginning. I need every single detail."

"Have I said something wrong?"

His nostrils flared. He clenched his fists, sucked in a deep breath, and let it back out. "Nothing. Just ... start again from the beginning."

Lucey shot him a warning glance.

He glowered at her, then added, "*Please.*"

"All right," Isadora said.

She relayed everything she could remember, right down to the three trails waiting for her and the constant shift of the wisps. Maximillion's expression never wavered. Lucey blinked rapidly, her gaze shifting from Isadora to Maximillion and back again. By the time Isadora finished, Maximillion straightened.

He stared into the forest, one hand in a pocket.

"Well, damn. Now Cecelia's going to kill her after all."

CHAPTER

FIFTEEN

The smoldering coals glowed a queer red when Luteis dropped next to Sanna on the ground. After the confrontation with Talis, they'd landed only a few hours' ride from Anguis. Sanna couldn't bear to go farther from Cara or Daid. Every moment of her visit haunted her. The sluggishness in Daid's gaze. The fear in Cara's wide eyes.

Luteis curled around the fire ring and studied the dancing flames with wide, luminous eyes. His tail shot out and wrapped around her ankle.

It fascinates me that witches have fire.

Sanna grabbed two logs and nestled them into the flames. A shiver passed through the branches overhead when the fire flared, shaking the leaves like tiny coins. She thought she heard something—a distant cry—but it faded.

"We can *make* fire. I don't think that's the same as having it."

It's strange that you don't feed it from your throat.

"Not that strange."

You claim to hate magic, yet you start flames from nothing?

"Uh, sort of? Two rocks, but it takes forever. Dried moss usually catches flame pretty fast. Daid and Mam use a tinderbox at home. I saw Isadora attempt it by magic once, but she failed."

Fascinating.

"Cara could be dead."

The words flooded out of her in a rush. Luteis shifted closer to the flames and closed his eyes.

She knew what she was doing.

"That doesn't make it acceptable! She has hatchlings. And Talis might have killed her for helping me."

He won't. He needs every dragon he can spare right now, especially mams. Her life may not be as easy as it was before, but your dragons could use a little bit of strife.

Despite the awful truth behind it, his words did reassure her. Maybe Cara—and by extension the hatchlings—would be spared. She could hardly bear to think of the alternative.

Sanna swallowed, but nothing had soothed the hot acid in her throat since they'd left Anguis. Daid in chains. Mam living with another family, likely. Isadora gone who-knew-where. The ugly arithmetic of her life sent a dark chill through her. How had things changed so rapidly? She should never have stayed away for so long.

"When I spoke with Talis, it hurt." She rubbed her leg. "Almost every time he spoke, I felt sharp pain where he touched me. Some times were worse than others."

Dragons are not supposed to speak with witches they are not bonded to. The pain the witch experiences makes it unacceptable because the dragon feels no pain. Only the strongest dragons can do it.

"Oh."

You lied to me.

Agony laced his tone. It rang through her mind with more strength than normal. Her shoulders slumped. She hadn't *lied*, but she hadn't been fully honest, either. Perhaps that was worse.

"I did."

You were going to warn Talis, weren't you?

"Not necessarily. I ... I just wanted to know the truth. Seemed like he deserved a chance to defend himself. I mean ... he's not *wholly* bad. He did save all the dragons from extinction and keep us safe."

He slid away from her, tucking his tail into his body. When he looked away, his lips angled down, like an injured little boy. She shrank back, startled by the discomfort his withdrawal provoked in her. She didn't want him to be angry. She reached out to touch him, but stopped.

"I'm sorry, Luteis. I really am. I should have been more honest with you, but I just didn't know who to trust. I ... I've known Talis all my life. He *has* protected and provided for us. To just let that go..."

She trailed away, lost in the swamp of her thoughts again. A long silence passed. When she thought she couldn't bear it another moment, his tail slid back over.

Perhaps I underestimated the power of your beliefs and the depth of Talis's control over you. I should have given you more understanding.

She looked over, meeting his gaze.

"Do you forgive me?"

You were almost killed.

"I know."

All hope would have died with you. Sanna of Anguis, you are Letum Wood's only chance to recover.

She drew in a deep breath. "You're sure Deasylva isn't

using us the same way Talis did? To make her home comfortable again? That's what it seems like. I know some of that belief comes from Talis, but maybe there's truth in it."

His eyes tapered into their usual thin slits for another breath, then opened again.

I do not believe Deasylva is selfish.

"I do."

He paused again. *Forgiveness granted. We will talk no more of Deasylva tonight.*

"Thanks."

He lowered his head, eyes closed. His forked tongue flickered out, gently tickling her arm. Sanna straightened.

"Luteis, I want to go back."

What?

"I only mean to Anguis, not to Talis. I want to check on Cara, but I also want to take food to the Servants. Without Daid, there will be less food available for the dragons, which means even less for the Servants. Cara looked so thin. Even Talis seemed gaunt. They need food. And maybe Jesse can help us, since Daid can't."

You are concerned for your family?

"Yes."

A flicker of something moved through his luminous eyes. Was it pain? Envy? Or something else she couldn't possibly fathom? Perhaps dragons experienced emotions differently than witches.

Then we shall.

Sanna smiled, reaching out to rest her hand against his face. He leaned into it.

"Thank you."

In the meantime, we need to plan—again—how to bring Talis down.

She withdrew her hand with a bright blush. Such an intimate gesture. Luteis tucked his head back into his tail and closed his eyes, not seeming to notice her discomfort.

"All right, then. Let's save Letum Wood."

THREE DAYS LATER, Sanna stumbled into a familiar clearing.

Luteis dropped to the ground behind her, silent except for a rustle of leaves. Ten dead *mortega* carcasses fell off his back, their spindly legs and antlers and meaty flanks dropping hard. He'd hunted all night and appeared weary himself. She couldn't blame him. She felt exhausted from just riding.

"There," she murmured and pointed to the left.

Dusk, the usual bedtime of most of the brood, settled in the distance. Ribbons of pale blue light laced through the tree branches. Just ahead sat a tall, angular house three stories high. A smattering of hog pens and empty chicken houses ringed the outside. Dim candlelight flickered within, near the kitchen area. On the top floor, she thought she saw a shadow shift in the farthest window. They wouldn't waste candles in the bedrooms, so she'd have to take a chance that it was Jesse.

Sanna crouched, plucked a few pebbles from the ground, and hurled them at the window. They all missed except the final one, which *plinked* against the glass pane. A head popped into view. Sanna waved one arm.

Moments later, Jesse appeared at the front door, yanking a jacket onto his arms. His cheeks had thinned, hollowing his face. Jesse wasn't really handsome, Sanna thought, but he wasn't bad, either. He would—maybe still could?—make an impressive husband for Isa. She squirmed at the thought.

"Sanna?" he hissed.

She held a finger to her lips and then motioned to the trees with a jerk of her head. He followed, glancing behind him, and slipped into the forest at her heels. She stopped not far away.

"What are you doing?" he asked. "Talis will kill you the moment he sees you!"

She gestured behind her with a sweep of her arm.

"I brought food."

He leaned to the side, blinking frantically as his gaze swept the pile of dead animals. "Egads," he murmured. "Are those..."

"Mortegas. Haven't seen them in a while, have you?"

"How did you—"

Luteis snorted behind her, drawing Jesse's gaze. Jesse paled and stumbled back. He lifted a hand. "Stay away!"

"Calm down," she muttered, rolling her eyes. "He's not going to eat you. He just spent all night hunting on your behalf, so I suggest you show some gratitude."

Jesse's face relaxed. He slowly lowered his arm.

"Oh. Uh ... thanks."

"How are things? I mean ... you know."

"Not good."

"Hungry?"

"More like starving. My daid and I are out on the trap lines constantly, but we just can't get anything. It's like all the food has fled."

"It's the forest," she said. "Everything is out of whack. Too many predators in this area, I think. Now that we've been flying, I've seen beluas everywhere close to Anguis.

Once you get farther away, especially south of here, there's more meat."

"Beluas?"

"Oh. Uh ... they're really ugly creatures."

His forehead wrinkled. "Uh, all right. Listen, Sanna, your daid. He's ... he's gone."

Sanna's stomach dropped. "What do you mean?"

"After the night you, ah, *left*, Talis said Drago was disappointed and cursed your entire family. He said your father had to repent. Your mam is staying with us, but she's ... it's like she's not there anymore."

The warm reassurance of Luteis's tail wrapped around her ankle. The feeling calmed her.

"I've seen Daid," she said. "Talis has him chained up by the pyre."

"Chained?"

She nodded.

"*Mori,*" he muttered.

"Mam?" she asked. "Is she ... I mean..."

"She's here, at our house. Couldn't do it on her own, so Mam took her in."

She let out a long, relieved breath. "Good. Thanks. That means a lot."

"Losing all three of you almost destroyed her, you know. No one has heard from Isadora, either. For a while, we thought you'd died. At least, that's what your mam thinks. She doesn't even speak anymore."

"*Talis* destroyed her."

Jesse leaned back, one eyebrow lifted. "Talis, uh ... he said you'd say that if you ever came back."

"What else did he say?"

"That you were half-mad. Without Drago's blessing, Talis said that your whole family would go crazy, especially you. That if you came back, we should tell him immediately."

"Are you going to?"

"Of course not."

"Do you think I'm crazy?"

"C'mon, Sanna. You've always been a *little* crazy."

She grinned.

A hint of a smile appeared on his face, then faded. "Listen." He cleared his throat. "Things have been … bad. Really bad. Finn has taken over as Drago's servant. There's no food. Talis tells him we're not working hard enough and that it's our fault. Daid and I aren't really sure what to do. Something feels wrong." He motioned to the fresh carcasses, still warm on the ground. "This though? This will save us."

"There's a lot to explain," she said, "but I can't go into it now. I need to know everything you know about Talis."

"Talis?"

"Anything." She stepped toward him. "You've worked as an apprentice for almost a year, and I don't know anyone else I can trust."

"I-I don't know."

"Does he have a weakness?"

He drove a hand through his hair. "Probably?"

She fell silent, waiting. Luteis whipped around when a twig snapped close by. Sanna held her breath, then turned back to Jesse with a muted voice.

"Luteis and I are going to defeat Talis, but I need to know everything I can about him. Weak spots or fears or something."

"He's huge."

"I know that!"

"Really powerful? Hates fire? Water, too."

"They all hate water!"

"Well … yes. I suppose you're right. I mean, what do you want me to say, Sanna? You're the one who knows the dragons best. If you don't know, how would I?"

"In the time that you've been an apprentice, has he ever wanted something really badly?"

"Control?"

"I know that too!"

"Sanna, I can't help you. I-I don't know that much about him. I've never interacted with him, or anything. I mean, it's not like they can talk to anyone outside of Drago's Servant."

The warmth of Luteis's tail returned on her ankle.

We must leave. Now. I smell several dragons.

"Luteis said dragons are coming, so I have to go."

Jesse frowned. "He *said* that?"

"Thank you for taking care of my mam. I'll be back soon. And then I'll explain everything."

She scrambled back, clutching Luteis's wing. He flicked her back, tossing her onto his spine. The heat faded from his scales as he crouched, then pounced onto the tree and began to climb.

"Sanna!"

Luteis paused ten paces up the tree. Jesse stood at the base of the trunk, head craned back.

"What?" she called down.

"Thanks."

She grinned. "Promise me you'll feed Cara and the hatchlings."

"How am I supposed to do that?"

"You'll figure out something."

Luteis crawled up the tree, burst into the sky, and flew away.

Sanna paced outside one of the houses in the ruins, her jaw tight. Luteis's tail reached for her, then faded back when it tangled in her frenetic steps. When she almost collided with a porch pillar, she spun on her heel and started back. She stopped halfway and glanced at him.

"Drowning?" she asked.

Luteis gestured to the stream with his tail.

Her shoulders slumped. "Right. Too shallow. Talis would never drown in something that bare. We'd need an entire lake for a dragon of his size. And a way to get him into it. How about feeding him bad mushrooms?"

Luteis growled.

"Right," she muttered. "Not enough mushrooms in Letum Wood to actually poison him, probably. At least, not that would be worth harvesting."

With a burdened sigh, she collapsed in the doorway to the house and stared through a massive hole in the roof. She'd hoped for inspiration to defeat Talis but felt more stuck than ever. Deasylva, it seemed, had left again.

Luteis's tail snaked over, wrapping her ankle again.

I feel our ideas are becoming more desperate. We must be methodical.

"We've already tried to figure out a plan, Luteis! Why are we going to have one now?"

Desperation is an excellent motivator, I have found. Not a good source of a plan. We cannot give up. Your friend knew nothing of Talis's weaknesses?

"Nothing that would help us win a fight against him. It was all stuff that I already knew."

He said water.

"Don't *all* of you hate water?"

Luteis lowered his head back to the ground with a snort that stirred the trees thirty paces away. *Vile stuff. Must it rain so often?*

She brushed that off and rubbed her eyes. The past week they'd been hunting all night for the Servants and themselves. Sleep had been hard to come by. She'd tossed and turned for two nights, wrapped in half-dreams and horrifying nightmares. The distant growl of beluas, who were most active at night, in the background hadn't helped.

"Water won't work," she said. "Short of a lake, anyway. Or a really big waterfall to hold him under, but we can't conjure that. Throwing water on him wouldn't even do anything."

True.

Sanna sat up. "Jesse said something else, didn't he? What was it?"

I did not hear.

"Water, but … fire. He said that Talis fears fire, right?"

An odd thing for a dragon to fear.

"Yes," Sanna murmured. "But maybe it's true. Talis never uses fire and has always forbidden it. *Why* would he fear something that he holds within himself? And something he used to get revenge against Deasylva when he killed those other dragons?"

Perhaps something to do with the massacre. Or maybe he fears himself.

"Maybe."

Was there fire during the massacre?

"Yes, but it was a magical fire from the South. Not the

same as what you throw. Can we kill another dragon with fire?"

We cannot kill him with my fire alone. It would require at least two dragons to kill another dragon with flames, and even then, using our secundum for that long would be exhausting. We might not be able to hold it long enough to kill. Three would be ideal. Four would be easy.

"Secundum?"

Second fire. Every dragon has a second, more powerful fire they can use. It's very tiring, but tenacious. Whatever it touches, it clings to. Or so my experiments suggest. I've never used it against another creature except a belua, once, when I was a hatchling. It almost killed me.

A bead of fire issued from his mouth and attached to a piece of bark with a flare. There it sat, a citrus-colored ball gleaming on the wood. Seconds after landing, the ball disappeared. It flared one last time in a burst of energy, then faded with a puff of white smoke. She tilted her head to the side. It had burned a hole *through* the wood.

Egads.

"Whoa."

A powerful weapon.

"You say it won't work with just you alone?"

Our scales can withstand a great amount of heat. To kill another dragon would require more than one secundum. How about setting a trap?

"What kind of trap?"

I haven't gotten that far yet.

"This would really be easier if either of us knew what we were doing."

I'm inclined to agree.

Sanna opened her mouth to ask why Deasylva didn't give them some help but changed her mind. She didn't want to involve the goddess. Talis's thoughts about Deasylva's selfishness—as if *he* had space to crow—still bothered her. Deasylva certainly seemed kinder than Talis, but was she? Sanna lay back down in the doorway, legs sticking halfway out, with a violent sigh. She folded her arms behind her head. None of their plans would work against a dragon as fearless and powerful as Talis.

What were they supposed to do *now*?

A glint of something shiny caught her eye. She stared at it for a long minute, trying to make it out. She straightened up. Whatever it was lay embedded near the roof of the house, along one of the eaves.

"Luteis?"

Yes?

She pointed. "What is that?"

He lifted his head toward it with several sniffs, then recoiled as if burned. *Silver!*

A dozen thoughts ran through her head at once. Silver. Of course. The poachers from the Southern Network had used arrows filled with silver to paralyze the dragons before they slaughtered them. Once it entered the bloodstream, the silver caused paralysis. She stood up and climbed up his tail and along his back. Luteis shifted over, putting her within reach of the object, but he didn't move his head any closer.

Do not remove it.

She leaned forward, peering at it. "Is it what I think it is?"

An arrow filled with silver?

"Yes."

The stench is faint, likely because it's been there so long, which must be why I haven't smelled it before.

"Or it's just so tightly sealed. It's ... kind of brilliant, actually. How did they obtain and smelt silver into a liquid, then encase it in glass *and* an arrow shaft that could fly? Must have used magic for it. One more case against magic, eh?"

A deadly brilliance.

She touched the edge of the arrow with the tips of her fingers. Speckled feathers, a strange white and purple, decorated the bottom of it. They were soft, as if time had never touched them. The shaft of the arrow was as thick as her thumb and contained the silvery liquid within a glass vial. It was only half full, if that. The glass still appeared to be mostly intact, but the head of the arrow was buried in the eaves. Flashes of a bright metallic color had soaked through the splintered wood.

Sanna reached out, tracing a dried trickle of metal. Perhaps the top of the glass had a crack that the silver had dribbled through and then sealed back over.

"Do you think it would still work?" she asked, breathless.

Don't tell me—

"Yes. I'm thinking of using it against Talis."

That would be very dangerous. You'd have to get it directly into his body. An arrow can be shot from a distance, but this...

"I know."

What if it broke while we were fighting? If the silver touched me, I could be paralyzed.

"Doesn't it have to enter the blood?"

I do not know. I do not care to find out.

"I don't either," she murmured. "But it's our best plan so far."

Our worst. How are you going to get it directly into his blood if that's what it requires? Our scales are strong. You'd have to be on top of him and very lucky to even—

His voice blended into the background as Sanna glanced at the vines overhead, the distance between her and the ground, and the silver arrow again.

She stepped back.

"I don't know yet, but Luteis, you should leave. I have an arrow to extract."

SIXTEEN

"Kill me?"

The words slipped out of Isadora's mouth in a breath. The headache had ceased once she'd ventured into the magic.

Lucey stood. Maximillion frowned, falling into a far-off gaze again. Did Maximillion go to a similar place when he fell into thought? Perhaps all the *paths* he'd always spoken about were just what she'd seen. Lucey put a hand on Isadora's shoulder and gave it a comforting squeeze. The touch calmed Isadora's whirling thoughts.

"Why would Cecelia want to kill me?" she asked.

"Wait," Lucey murmured. "Let him see what he can. His sight has a limited time frame but not as limited as everyone else. He can explain it better than I can."

An interminable time passed while the blank stare remained on Maximillion's face. When he returned, his grim expression sent Isadora's stomach into a tumble.

"What did you see?" Lucey asked.

"Nothing specific. Not in my paths, anyway, of which there are too many to see well." His eyes flickered to

Isadora. "There's room enough for Cecelia's wrath in all the in-betweens, of course."

"In-betweens?"

"The countless spaces that I can't see. I'd need a good chunk of time to work through all my paths to learn the details, but I can't here. And there's no bloody time to just sit and sort through paths."

Isadora stood up. "Why is she going to kill me? What have I done to her?"

"Nothing yet."

"What *could* I do?"

His eyes darkened with a strange new shadow. "That's the question, isn't it? How many paths have you seen before? Is this the first time you've seen three?"

"Y-yes. I just saw Sanna the first time."

"Multiplying." He clicked his teeth together and drove a hand through his hair. "The good gods."

"Will someone tell me what's happening?"

Lucey put an arm around Isadora's shoulder. A magical blessing of calm slowed her wild, frantic heart.

"I'm not Watcher, Isa, but I know enough of them to be a trusted part of the community," Lucey said. "Up until recently, Maximillion was the most powerful Watcher I knew. And he only sees for himself."

Isadora swallowed a growing lump in her throat. The observations from Ronan the Traveler's scroll drifted back through her mind. *The overwhelming majority of Watchers see future possibilities for themselves only.*

"How do you quantify something like that?" she asked. "Power is power, isn't it?"

Maximillion sighed. "If only it were that easy. I see my own paths and, occasionally, where other paths inter-sect with mine, for at least a year into the future. Sometimes it's been more, but that's on strange and rare occasions."

"Like me? That's how you saw me in the forest."

"Yes. You standing in the forest on a bloody trail that I couldn't find," he snapped, scowling. "I know every single Watcher in the Central Network, most in the Eastern Network, and some in the South and West. Not a single one of them can see for more than one person. Or cat. Pearl sees for that bloody cat. James sees for his daughter. Marcia sees for herself but only a week ahead. Cathleen sees for whoever she's married to at the time."

A cold feeling spread through Isadora's body. She lowered back to the tree trunk, thinking of the run of paths that awaited her. Would there be more? How could she ever manage so much?

"Oh."

"And now *you* are seeing for up to three witches, if what you said is to be trusted. It's only a matter of time before we figure out how far ahead you can see. Or if you can see for more than just three. You saw your sister, and she's not present."

"Possibly more witches," Lucey said. "If this is only her second entrance into the magic."

He paced across the trail with long strides and shook his head in jerking, spasmodic mutterings. "No wonder. Headaches! Pah. She should be dead ... Pearl's not safe ... no. Not Sophie. Cecelia will..." He stopped short, shoulders drawing back, and let out a punctuated breath. "We've been going about this all wrong."

"What?"

"How many times have you seen the paths?"

"Twice."

"Here and where else?"

"Home. The night that you showed up, when Talis was going to kill me."

He threw his hands up. "It's the bloody forest."

"What?"

He crouched in front of her and grabbed her shoulders. His breath caressed her cheek, warm with the scent of mint. "The forest. That's the key to your powers. Have you been able to access them without being here?"

"N-no."

"Have you tried?"

"Endlessly."

"Yet you just did it here. Within moments. If I'm not wrong, your headache started, then *took* you to the paths. You didn't even initiate it, did you?"

Isadora sucked in a sharp breath. "No, I didn't."

"No doubt the power is restless now that you've transitioned but not used it. I'll wager your headaches disappear so long as you use your magic." He released her with an exultant cry. "Ha! Figured the bloody mess out finally. Letum Wood is the missing piece."

"Not just for your overall health," Lucey said, tapping a finger to her chin, "but for your powers as well. Very interesting. I've never seen something like this in the Dragonmast—Servants before."

"So, I have to be in the forest to access it?" Isadora asked.

Maximillion nodded once. "For now, at least, that's the theory. That may change. If you're seeing paths for more than yourself—and for who knows what stretch of time— you're wrestling a mighty amount of power. Explains so much now that I see it. All those headaches. Well, you know what they say about hindsight."

He straightened with a little hop, speaking rapidly, like

a little boy with a brand-new trinket. Light shone in his eyes, altering their bright color entirely as he rattled from one thought to the next.

"We'll have to train you differently. I've never worked with a witch with this much power, so it'll be exploratory for all of us. Just *imagine* what we could do with this! Daily lessons, I think. Even if I can't make it. You'll have to come to the forest and ... that won't work. We'll tell Sophie—"

Lucey cleared her throat, eyebrows high. "And what of Cecelia?"

He paused. All the elation drained from his features in a flash. His expression dropped into a frown.

"Demmet."

"Yes," Isadora said. "What about her?"

"She *is* a bother, isn't she?"

"Can someone please explain why she'll want to kill me?"

"Fear, for one," Lucey said. "Power, for another. Let's just say that Cecelia doesn't like to be challenged."

"No Defender does," he muttered.

"Defender?"

"Otherwise known as Anti-Watchers," Lucey said. "In magic, everything has a counter. Everything. For good, there is evil. For evil, there is good. For Watchers, there are Defenders."

"If you aren't a Watcher, how do you know so much?" Isadora asked.

Lucey and Maximillion exchanged a brief, discreet glance Isadora pretended not to see. Lucey brushed a lock of hair out of her face and tucked it behind her ear. Her face remained impassive.

"For now, let's just say it's complicated."

"Magic is a thing of balance, right?" Maximillion asked

with renewed energy. "Even our magic, which is poorly understood and less defined, has rules. That means there are opposites. Black, white. Good, bad. Cecelia is a *sort* of a Watcher. We believe the magic is the same, but the purpose different. She *sees* but only other Watchers. Nothing more. She's part of the power that prevents Watchers from becoming too strong. Unfortunately, she's also a power-hungry dog who's willing to kill to keep her superiors happy."

"She works for the East," Lucey said. "The High Priest and High Priestess employ her as the Ambassador."

"Of course," Isadora murmured, recalling the scroll's story about the fear in the Eastern Network when Ronan the Traveler passed through. "Do they still fear Watchers?"

"They always will."

"Imprison most." Lucey cast a long glance at Maximillion. "Cecelia is able to detect them through her own power, however it works. She's never explained how she knows what she knows or how the magic reveals Watchers."

Isadora felt dizzy, but she forced herself to remain standing. "How long are they imprisoned?"

"Until they're liberated by sheer luck or found dead," Maximillion muttered.

"Even if they've done nothing wrong?"

"In her eyes, they've committed a sin simply by living," Maximillion said. "The High Priest and High Priestess look to her as a savior for the East. They'd do anything for her, the High Priest in particular."

A chill brushed over Isadora. "She can't take me, right? I'm not in her Network."

"There is a growing war at hand," Maximillion said, "with a very unknown ending thanks to our strong-willed

High Priestess. Should the Eastern Network take over, your fate would immediately be sealed. A Watcher of your potential power is a sweet prize for a rat like Cecelia."

"Then why hasn't she taken *you*?"

Maximillion snorted. "Let's say I have my means. Enough of Cecelia. As long as you stay away from Chatham City and don't act like a fool, you'll be safe enough. For now. If you find opportunity to be anywhere near the East without me or Lucey, you sign your own death certificate. Now, come. Enough for today. I need to think more on how to teach you to manage your powers, and you need to get some rest. We'll start fresh tomorrow."

Gossamer leaves shimmered around Isadora.

They felt like silk on her fingertips. Overhead, sprawling branches spread out to braid into other branches from different trees. She drew in a deep breath, recalling Maximillion's explicit instructions not five minutes before.

You need to get used to … wherever you are. Most Watchers, such as me, just see darkness with paths in it. In order for you to control the power, you have to spend time there. Get to know it. Become comfortable. Talk to it. The magic is fickle. It wants to be known, but only on its own terms. It will never misrepresent itself.

After three days of exhaustive work, the paths had intensified. More wisps. More details. Already it was clearer, with specifics in sharp focus. The wisps themselves were bigger, broader, encompassing entire persons instead of part of their bodies. She tried to keep it all straight, but it felt like rainwater, all jumbled together and impossible to disentangle.

Three paths split before her this time—one featured her, lying on the ground, her eyes closed, which was the position she'd taken before entering the magic. Her path continued until it disappeared around a bend.

Maximillion's path snaked right down the middle, branching into such a multitude of paths that it made her dizzy. The images were fuzzy, their number too great to make out the details.

She moved to the right. Slipping out of sight was an ethereal wisp of Sanna. She was crouched, her hands cupped in front of her, her legs bare and skirt pulled back. Water glistened in striations of shadow and light around her legs. No visible breaking of her path veered away.

Try to speak, Maximillion had said. *See if you hear a response.*

Isadora hesitated. She tilted her head back to study the overwhelming canopy that crisscrossed so far above her. Speak to this strange shade of the forest? Could forests—or the magic—speak back? A movement off to the left caught her eye. The image of herself on the paths had changed—this time, her fists were tight balls. Isadora blinked, looked down to find her hands clenched, then cleared her throat.

"Ah ... hullo?"

Her voice dropped away, whisked off her lips. A gentle ripple moved through the world, undulating the images. Maximillion's had already shifted multiple times; somehow she'd missed it. Or was the magic so subtle that it could change drastically without her knowing? Did it mean something about her and Sanna that their paths were so blatant, while Maximillion's was so complicated?

"Can you, ah ... show me something else?" she asked.

The wisps dissipated into a shimmering fog. The mist swirled with long fingers around the trees, then faded. The trails sank into the earth, leaving a carpet of fallen leaves in the empty spots. She gasped.

"No! Wait. Don't disappear!"

She stepped forward, then halted. A wash of light spiraled in front of her, zipping in a circle until it reached a peak and stopped. Out of the pillar of light appeared a familiar face.

"Sanna!"

Her sister stood before her, a fusion of glowing particles of magic. She half-crouched, teeth bared, eyes focused, a knife in one hand, the other thrown out in warning. Her braids dangled on either side of her neck. Her freckles stood out in individual array. Isadora rushed to Sanna's side and reached out to touch her face, but the magic held no substance. It swirled, settling back into Sanna's feral form.

A prickle crawled up Isadora's back. With it came a gentle breath of wind, stirring through the trees as it brushed by Isadora's cheeks.

Fierce.

Warmth settled in her chest, affirming the word. She understood it immediately—the power was showing her that Sanna was fierce. It made sense. Fit every description she knew of her sister.

Sanna faded. This had to be another effect of the magic —another facet she hadn't known of. Hadn't Roland spoken of Watchers who could detect personality traits? Was it possible that she could do—and see—so much? It had already seemed so overwhelming the past several days. She peered back into the misty forest, her voice firm with command.

"Show me another."

The light blossomed again, as if eager to please. It climbed in a fountain of glowing specks that tumbled over each other. A pair of annoyed eyes and broad shoulders appeared from the depths, forming an exact replica of a familiar, scowling face.

Maximillion—exactly as she pictured him in her mind—his lips canted, forehead creased, expression twisted in a half-frown of concern. His hair glistened in its usual disorderly array. Although the picture was only black and white with shades of gray, the magic pulled a detailed clarity out of him that had gone unnoticed in real life. Flecks in his eyes. Stubble on his chin. A crisp, deliberate smoothness to his shirt. Isadora reached for him. Her hand drifted through his arm.

A burst of light cut through his chest, moving through her in a ray. She ducked, but he remained stoic as ever. Only now, something pulsed in his chest. A heart that glimmered with light. It beat, up and down, back and forth. The whisper returned.

Merciful.

She blinked. *The magic will never misrepresent itself,* Maximillion had said. She could have sworn his glare, though not real, deepened. As if he knew her betrayal, that she was seeing him. She turned away.

"Stop."

Maximillion disappeared. The magic settled like dust and returned her to the same quiet field of gigantic tree trunks and gentle undergrowth. Isadora sank back to her haunches, trembling. She forced her tired body to straighten.

"Show me the paths." With a gentle voice, she added, "Please."

One at a time, the three paths returned. Sanna clung to

the side of a tree. Her path separated into two different possibilities—in one, she lay on her back on the ground with a scowl; in the other, she stood, her bare feet wrapped around a branch, a hand held over her eyes.

Maximillion's branched only three times, but Isadora couldn't bring herself to look at it. He hadn't been scowling, had he? No. Not scowling. He'd been worried. Concerned about something.

Merciful.

She glanced at her own path, running a straight line back to Sophie's, where it split into three. It showed her bedroom, the library, and the dining hall. Darkness overcame her, and she gave into it willingly. Seconds later, she opened her eyes to find Maximillion hovering over her.

"The good gods," he snapped. "Did you enjoy that hour-long nap?"

Isadora straightened, groggy. The magic slipped away from her mind one tendril at a time. Looking at Maximillion only reminded her of the pulsing heart made of light. She shoved herself off the forest floor.

"If working myself into total exhaustion counts as enjoyment, yes."

"I thought you'd died."

She shoved past him, heading down the trail. "You're not that lucky."

"That's the longest length you've gone so far. What did you see? Tell me everything."

Isadora opened her mouth, then closed it again. The idea of revealing her other gift made her sick. If it even *was* a gift. What would he say? Until she had the power under greater control or some semblance of understanding it, it seemed best to keep it to herself.

"Ah ... I saw three paths."

"You're lying. You saw more than that."

"Would you like to read my mind and see the proof? There were three paths again."

"Mine, yours, your sister's?"

"Yes."

Isadora pushed past him, headed for Berry. Fatigue filled her body. Or was it dread? Fear? She couldn't tell anymore. He grabbed her arm and whipped her around. "Calm down! I've been waiting here an hour to discuss this. Why are you in such a hurry?"

"Fine," she muttered, gritting her teeth. "I'm ... I'm just tired."

He studied her. "What's gotten into you?"

"Nothing."

"Yes. You're always this happy."

"I have things to do at Sophie's."

"Dishes?"

She hesitated. *Yes, actually.*

But she didn't want to admit that she felt a driving force to prove to those girls that she wasn't a quitter, even if it meant doing dishes after every meal. *Without* magic.

"As I suspected," he said. "We'll return to our analysis. You saw three paths. Only three?"

"Yes. It appears to be the highest number I am capable of."

"Right now, anyway. Still a ridiculous number. You're present with me, so you see my path. You're tied to your sister, so you always see hers. Not surprising. The third was your own, I assume? Good. Was anything different?"

"More detail. A bit clearer. Some of the images are so strange I can't make out what they mean." She recalled the weird cacophony of all Maximillion's paths. The unfamiliar faces. Twisted expressions. Even strange spots of utter darkness.

"It's usual. When you have no context, a mere image can be almost impossible to discern. We'll go into the details of reading the paths later. The smallest observation can make the most significant difference in how you interpret it. And the farther you go from your current path, the easier it is to study. Can't really study something happening in two minutes, can you? Anyway, did you speak with the magic?"

"Yes."

"And?"

She blinked, recalling the beings of light that had appeared. "And ... ah..."

"It obeyed?" He stepped toward her, closing the distance between them. The smell of juniper drifted from his clothes. "Did it do what you told it to?"

"For the most part it obeyed me, yes."

"Did it speak back to you?"

"No! Should it be able to?"

"I have no idea. Fascinating, though, that it listened. What were your commands?"

"Er ... show me something else?"

He blinked, leaning closer. She wanted to shove him back, demand he give her more space, but her throat had nearly closed up.

"And? What happened?"

"The paths changed."

And entirely disappeared.

He eyed her. "Anything else? You seem quite pale."

"No! I mean ... no. That was all."

He yanked a watch from his pocket and frowned. "That will have to be good enough for now. We're seeing progress.

Next time, we'll work on controlling your entrance into the paths. For now, you need to get as much time there as you can. You literally cannot spend enough time in your own head. Come. We must go. I have meetings."

Maximillion's voice faded as he strode down the path, muttering to himself about the narrowing of paths and future possibilities. Isadora cast one glance into the murky forest and followed him. The voice drifted through her mind again.

Merciful.

Isadora stared at the pile of spiders teeming on top of her bed in a writhing black mass. They swarmed, one on top of another, in a giant ball.

Her nose twitched.

It wasn't that the girls constantly pulled pranks and wreaked havoc on the school. It was that she didn't know when they'd *stop*. It was probably sheer luck that Isadora hadn't been asleep when they'd attempted this trick. If she had been, she'd have removed all their hair with a spell.

The spiders disappeared with a *poof* when she used a cleaning incantation. She leaned her shoulder against the wall and stared at the now-clean bed, deep in thought. A distant roll of thunder sounded in the background just as a blast of wind rattled through the cracks in the window. Being busy with Maximillion had given her plenty of reason to disappear from the school. No one even noticed except when the dishes waited for too long. But she couldn't deny the constant twinge of annoyance at having to return.

"They'd stop, ya know, if you'd give them a reason."

Isadora spun around to find Baylee in the doorway. Her crimson hair spilled onto her shoulders in bright waves. A smudge of dirt marred her right cheek. As usual, she wore no shoes. Her dress was as tattered and threadbare as the rest of the girls' clothes. Isadora's brow furrowed. Had she not noticed how mangy all the girls were? *A redistribution establishment,* Baylee had once called the school. It seemed more like a forgotten orphanage than a school.

"What would make them stop?" Isadora asked.

Baylee cocked one eyebrow. "If ya don't know that already, ya'll never figure it out."

With that, she turned and disappeared down the hall. Isadora watched her go, her mind whirling.

This time without pain.

THAT AFTERNOON, Isadora stepped into Berry Cigars and Candy Shop and thought she'd died.

Confections littered every shelf that wasn't packed with pipes, bricks of magnesium, and boxes of carefully wrapped cigars. The heady scent of tobacco and the sweet perfume of sugar blended into a dizzying smell.

Farther into the shop, mounds of peppermint drops lay in a barrel. Gleaming black ropes twisted into a heart filled a wall, hanging above glass jars of colorful square chunks. Round lollipops hung from the ceiling on pieces of twine, bobbing in the air above barrels of salt water taffy. Isadora's mouth watered at the rows of squishy gummies the girls always stole and then snuck into the school to use as bargaining chips.

A wizened old man stood behind the counter with a snowy mustache that drooped down either side of his face. When she reached out to touch what looked like an apple covered in a shell of hardened caramel, he grunted.

"No freebies! No currency: no samples, no touching. The whole lot of you girls from the school aren't trustworthy."

"Oh. Right. Sorry. I came to see how much it cost."

"What?"

She blinked, glancing back over the vast array of candy. A fair question. When she set out, she'd never imagined there'd be so *many* choices. How was she supposed to pick something for the whole school? She didn't even know if her plan would work, but it was the only idea she had.

"Ah ... your candy."

His hairy eyebrows scrunched. "*What* piece of candy? There are at least fifty different kinds."

"Yes. So I see."

He motioned to a barrel on the other side of the room. "There are paper sacks in there. One sacran per bag."

The witches in Berry had only a mild accent, with crisp vowels and erratic emphases on different words. Far easier to understand than the thick brogue Baylee spoke with. But even Isadora wondered right then if she'd misunderstood him.

"Sacran?"

"You don't know what a sacran is?"

"No, I'm sorry. I don't."

He rubbed his thumb and pointer finger together. "Currency. You can't just take whatever candy you want. You have to buy it."

"Of course I wouldn't just *take* it. I just ... could I work for you in exchange?"

"Nope."

"But I don't have any currency."

"Then you won't have candy. Simplest math you'll ever do."

Isadora bit the inside of her cheek. Honestly. Even after several weeks, she still couldn't get used to how difficult witches were. She thought of Finn's surly personality and wondered if some behaviors were the same everywhere. Her eyes trailed around the store. Sure, the girls would love her for buying candy—at least for the moment. They were fickle little creatures. She'd probably have to keep buying them candy to make them stop.

"How can I get currency?" she asked, thinking of her dresses back at the school. "Would someone buy clothes?"

"Not for much. Maude runs a sort of secondhand clothing shop just down the road, but you won't get much for them."

"Books?"

He shook his head. "Nah."

A little curl of relief unfurled in her. Parting with her books would be a nightmare. The old man eyed Isadora's hair, which she'd braided and coiled into a shining bun at the nape of her neck.

"How long is that hair?" he asked.

She put a protective hand on it. "I can sit on most of it. Why?"

"Well," he drawled, "I know *one* way for you to make some currency."

Two hours later, Isadora sauntered up the path leading to Miss Sophie's, threw open the door, and swept inside.

Three girls playing with sulfur sticks near the door jumped, accidentally extinguishing a growing flame. One of them growled in dismay. The sound of feet running rampant upstairs rang with a dull *thud thud thud* across the floor.

Isadora brushed past the girls with a congenial nod.

"Follow me, please," she called over her shoulder. "This way."

Two young men tromped in behind her, carrying wooden crates. The three girls leapt to their feet with muted cries and followed. Whispers gathered behind Isadora as she swept through the school.

"Baylee!" Isadora called. "Where are you?"

Her blonde hair barely danced across the tops of her shoulders as she scouted the chaotic halls. Her head felt strangely light, as if a great burden had been released. Two remaining sacrans, the lesser of the two coins that the Network used, clinked in her pocket. They were all that remained of the original six pentacles—each pentacle worth six sacrans—that the candy store owner had given her for her hair.

Finally, she burst into the dining room and pointed to the two long tables. "Set them there, please. Thank you."

The young men heaved the great crates onto the tables, cracked them open with pry bars, and left. Girls spilled into the room amid frantic chatter, then skidded to a stop. Isadora reached for the first crate just as a shout came from down the hall.

"Oy!" Baylee yelled. "What's going on here?"

She spilled into the dining room moments later in a burst of wild hair and flashing eyes. She stopped to stare at the tables, then Isadora, then back at the tables. Her shoulders relaxed.

"The good gods," Baylee said. "What have ya done to ya hair?"

Isadora turned to face the crowd, hands on her hips. Nearly all the girls had gathered. They stared at her with open astonishment, mouths agape, eyes wide as a screaming gnome baby's.

"I thought it was about time for a change." She ran a hand through her tapered strands. "I cut my hair and sold it."

The ripple of excitement only intensified, hot as lightning as it ripped through the room. Their agape stares and shocked stammers felt immensely satisfying, although she didn't know why. Already, such a bold move felt entirely worth it.

"The currency was more than I expected, so I went to Maude's." Her eyes caught Baylee's suspicious gaze. "There's a new dress, pair of shoes, and brand-new undergarments for each one of you. So, take your pick, girls. And don't try anything funny." She pointed at each of them. "I'm watching every single one of you."

A long silence prevailed until Janie, a small girl in the back with a tear halfway up her skirt, shuffled forward. She had spindly limbs and knobby elbows, and her streaks of brown hair fell around her face.

"Is there something small enough for me?"

"You are not forgotten, Janie. There's a dress in there for you."

Girls surged into the room and swarmed the crates.

Isadora stood on a bench and directed the chaos. The girls didn't need candy—they stole that on their own well enough. They needed a leader. They needed a friend. They *needed* someone to care. Isadora didn't know if her plan would work, but sharing her profits couldn't make anything worse.

Besides, it felt good to do something for them.

At the back of the room, Baylee folded her arms across her chest and grinned.

CHAPTER

SEVENTEEN

Sanna woke to Luteis's voice in her head.

Be silent.

She opened her eyes to the dark underside of Letum Wood, the soil next to her warm from Luteis's body. They'd delivered a third load of carcasses—it was their second week of killing for the Servants—to Jesse before settling in a random spot in the woods that Deasylva had led Luteis to.

Although Sanna couldn't be certain, she wondered if they were close to Anguis. The upper canopy, the density of the moss. It all *seemed* familiar, and they hadn't flown far.

Sanna straightened with a yawn, brushing the leaves and dew off her arms and legs. Despite the chilly night, Luteis kept her toasty warm. She put a hand on his foreleg.

I smell another dragon, he said.

Sanna stiffened.

Climb onto my back. Quickly.

She obeyed. Luteis leapt into the tree branches. Once there, Sanna slid free and crouched on a branch to peer through the foliage.

"Where?" she whispered.

He pointed with his snout to the left. *There.*

"Are we close to Anguis?"

I'm not sure.

"Is it—"

It is not Talis.

A surge of hope caught her by surprise. "Then it's one of the other dragons! Maybe they've come looking for me."

It could be that fool Thyris. The scent was familiar but not distinct. Perhaps he's scouting for us.

"They can't be happy that we dropped off food."

They heard snorting, then a strangled cry. And then another. Luteis growled, crouching to pounce. A flicker of movement passed over the ground beneath them, giving way to a bright, familiar color.

"No, Luteis, wait," Sanna whispered. "I know that cry. That color. It's Cara."

Cara?

Visions of Cara crashing into a tree after distracting Talis rippled back through her mind. "The dragon that helped me escape Talis! She has two hatchlings. She might be hurt."

She might be bait.

"The hatchlings aren't with her, right?"

Wait!

Sanna leapt off the branch, pounced onto a vine, wrapped her feet around it, and hurtled toward the ground. In the darkness, she could just make out the gentle glimmering of mauve scales. She released the vine just before slamming into the forest floor with her butt, landing several paces away from a gigantic, black body. Bright yellow eyes appeared with a snarl.

Sanna held out a hand. "Cara! It's me."

The snarling faded to a whimper. Cara's eyes widened. With a mournful wail, she lowered her head and pressed it to the ground, collapsing. She keened in her throat, low and deep. A stump of glistening scales on her back caught Sanna's gaze.

"Cara," she whispered, rushing forward. "Your wings!"

Cara burrowed her head into the dirt. The thick bones of her wings had been snapped at the very back, near her spine. Blood bubbled from the broken skin, spilling in rivers. The wings folded over her sides, inert. Luteis slipped up behind Sanna with a growl. Cara wheeled back, her ears pressed down. Arms spread, Sanna threw herself in front of Cara before Luteis could advance.

"Cara is my friend," Sanna snapped. "She's hurt."

Luteis hesitated, his eyes darting from Cara back to Sanna. The warm wrap of his tail curled around her ankle. *You trust her now? Even though this could be a trap?*

"Yes."

He hesitated. *Then I will as well.*

A moment of silence passed while Cara and Luteis locked gazes. Luteis lowered his head. For a moment, the two dragons were strangely silent, peering intently at one another. Sanna whipped around, searching the underbrush.

"Where are the hatchlings?"

She says that Talis has taken them. He broke her wings and sent her off to die in the forest. He said that her affection for you meant she would lead her hatchlings astray. He plans to raise them instead.

"What?"

Cara has been wandering for a full day, hoping to find you, believing you to be her last hope. Talis is requiring all dragons to remove their wings, to show Drago their unwillingness to become wild, as before. Cara fears he may have already cut the hatchlings' wings. Thyris has volunteered to have it done.

"Has Talis removed his own wings?"

She says no. The pain is great for her. She's tiring and won't be able to speak much longer.

Sanna clenched her fists. "He's out of control."

He's trying to draw us in. This is certainly a trap. He wants us to come back and take the hatchlings.

"And we will!"

Sanna turned back to Cara, running a quick hand down her sultry scales, unable to touch her for very long. The blood from her broken wings had staunched hours earlier, congealing into a thick, dried plug. "Can I heal her?" she whispered, tears heavy in her throat. "Didn't you say something about magic once? C-can we use that?"

There is Dragonian magic given to witches, but not unless you're bonded. Even with that, I have not been educated. I would not know how to do it.

"Can I *talk* to her and hear her? The way you and I do?"

No. She hasn't the power Talis has. Not unless you were the High Dragonmaster.

"High Dragonmaster," Sanna murmured. "Deasylva said that. What is it?"

I do not know exactly what the High Dragonmaster does, but Deasylva has alluded that they may speak with all dragons without being bonded.

"Then what *can* we do? I can't just sit here and see her in such pain. Can I reset her wings? Daid showed me how! I-I think I could do it."

Luteis's gaze darted over Cara's injured wings, lying useless along her spine. His tongue slipped between his lips in a hiss.

Deasylva says the wings cannot be saved.

Sanna folded her arms across her chest with a scowl. "Oh, she's back now, is she?"

It has been too long. Infection will set in soon, and Cara will die.

"I refuse to believe there's nothing we can do."

Whether you believe it or not, it will be so. Unless...

Sanna lifted an eyebrow. "Unless *what?*

Deasylva says we may remove her wings and stop the infection.

"Remove them?"

With fire. My secundum.

"Can you do it?"

With Cara's permission, Deasylva's guidance, and caution, I believe I can.

Sanna crouched next to Cara. She ran her fingers along the fine scales on her face. Rage clouded her mind, boiling through her veins in streaks hot as dragon fire. Remove her wings? Talis had tortured her, maimed her, and taken her hatchlings. What further pain would sweet Cara have to endure?

Sanna's throat tightened. A dragon without wings. Would Cara be the same magnificent beast with her wings stripped from her so recklessly? Yes, she would. Cara would always be magnificent.

"Cara," she whispered. "I'm so sorry." Cara moaned, leaning toward her. She didn't burn as hot as Luteis, but her heat warmed Sanna's skin all the same. Sanna blinked tears away. "I promise you that Luteis and I will defeat him. We'll get your hatchlings back. Rosy and Junis are strong. They won't let him hurt them."

Cara made a sound deep in her throat, glancing at Luteis.

She gives us permission to remove her wings. Step back.

"But what about the pain?"

Allow Deasylva to care for her.

"Will she?" Sanna snapped.

Has she not already by bringing us here, into Cara's path?

Sanna ignored that, pressed a hand to Cara's warm snout, murmured the Dragonian expression for love, "*Amo*," and stepped back.

Luteis positioned himself behind Cara. Leaves stirred in a sudden whirlwind on the ground, swirling in a fine, glittering mist around Cara's face. She closed her eyes, drew in a deep breath, and fell into an exhausted stupor. Sanna pressed her hand to Luteis's back leg. It felt strange standing behind his face instead of right next to it.

"What was that?"

A gift from Deasylva. Now, Cara will sleep through it.

Questions whirled through Sanna's mind, but a bright, orange flame exploded from Luteis's mouth, preventing her from asking. Repelled by the intense heat, she moved behind a nearby tree and peered around its trunk. Luteis carefully controlled his fire into a single flame and touched it gently to the juncture of Cara's wings against her back. Bit by bit, the fire ate at the bone, melting the scales, destroying her beautiful, broken body.

When the first wing slumped away, falling to the forest floor, a tear dribbled down Sanna's face. Once both fell to the ground, Luteis pulled them away with his teeth and set fire to them. The heat crawled over the wing, nearly singeing Sanna even from far away. She swiped the tears with the back of her hand, her fists curled until her nails dug into her skin. The wings turned to ash. Two seedling plants, barely visible in the earthy loam, sprouted from the ground. They twined around Cara's body, swirled across her back, and settled along the sealed stumps with a gentle sigh. Cara slept on.

"Talis," Sanna murmured, nostrils flaring. "For this, I will kill you myself."

We can't walk into this blindly, Luteis said an hour later, once Cara had settled into a steadier sleep. *This is not our plan. We still have days before we're physically ready, and even then—*

"We don't have a choice. The hatchlings need us tonight."

We still have no plan for getting the silver into Talis!

Sanna pressed a gentle hand to Cara's snout one last time, then stood up. "I'll figure it out. And we aren't walking into it blindly. We know he'll be there. We have a good plan."

A semblance of one.

"It's good!"

It lacks detail.

"I'll get the hatchlings. You distract Talis if he comes. We guide the hatchlings somewhere safe. Once the hatchlings are with Cara, we go back together and fight him as one."

It has simplicity but nothing more. There is too much room for error.

"Simple is best."

You still believe that Talis will keep the hatchlings near his home? You don't think he expects us and is hiding them?

"No. The dragons tend to sleep and live far from the

boundary. He'll keep the hatchlings in his cave by the stream. I doubt he'd leave Anguis with them for fear they'd get away. He'll want the advantage of knowing the space better than us. Maybe we'll get lucky. Maybe he expected us yesterday when he first set Cara free."

He will not be the only dragon expecting us.

"Good."

Is it?

"Luteis, if you're too frightened to do this, tell me now."

I am not frightened. Fire billowed from between his teeth. *Changing plans makes me nervous, but as long as we have a plan, a good one, I will be fine.*

She lifted one side of her lips in a rueful grin. "I didn't imagine you'd be frightened of anything."

He grunted. Was that a laugh? No, assuredly not. He glared at her with all the power of his secundum.

Only of a witch like you.

She sobered. "We have to do this tonight. If Talis is maiming the dragons, there's no telling what he's done to my family. I could lose everything if we don't. He has to be stopped."

I see that you're determined. Since that's the case, then tonight, I ask only two things of you.

"Yes?"

Don't take foolish risks. We are of no use to your family, Deasylva, Letum Wood, or the other dragons if either of us is dead.

"Fine. I promise. What's the second thing?"

Give me the pleasure of retribution against Talis.

His eyes gleamed. A vein of animosity ran through his voice, reminding her of how little they really knew each other, despite having lived together for months.

"What has he done to you?"

Suffice it to say, he has much to answer for.

"Then retribution is yours. Do you think Cara will be all right without us?"

Deasylva will watch over her.

Cara hid at the base of a deep, hollowed-out tree that Luteis had found—apparently by Deasylva's direction. If the hatchlings didn't return with them, Sanna feared for Cara's life.

I'm ready. Are you?

"Born ready."

LETUM WOOD's canopy hid Sanna.

She snaked down a tree, using vines to drop from branch to branch. The moss buffered sound, helping her move with ease. An occasional, annoyed squirrel chattered at her as she passed. Everything else lay in silence.

Below, high boulders stood in sharp relief against a carpet of golden leaves. Sanna paused, cocking an ear. No typical hatchling noises. A rustle came from just behind her. A pair of yellow eyes and a subtle glint of orange followed. Luteis. Relaxing, she started back down the tree. Talis's cave came into full view moments later.

She rode down a vine, landing thirty paces away from the mouth of the cave. Darkness haunted the interior. She paused to study it. Sensing nothing, she started forward, then stopped when a shuffle came from inside. She crouched back against a tree and grabbed a knife from her belt. A figure emerged from the shadows. Two sets of eyes appeared first, then another. She leaned forward.

"Junis? Rosy?"

A muffled cry answered.

She darted into the cave. The hatchlings lay on the ground. They released weak, piteous cries as they attempted to stand. Sanna rushed to their side.

"It's all right. I'm here."

Junis pressed his muzzle into her side. She reached out for Rosy, who struggled to scoot closer.

"Your wings." She groped carefully in the dark. "Has he gotten your wings?"

She felt the bones, finding them still intact, though scales along their necks and forelegs glistened with dried blood. The wings hadn't been cut or broken. Not yet. The blood that sprayed the walls meant they'd likely put up some sort of fight against Talis, but she couldn't find any cuts. Perhaps they had already healed. That was hopeful, at any rate.

Junis nudged her with a piteous mewl. Rosy breathed a gasp of fire toward the mouth of the cave. Sanna put a hand on her snout, surprised to find it cooler than normal. A cool dragon wasn't far from death. They were still warm enough, but it wasn't a good sign.

"I'm here to take you to safety," she said. "Let's get you to your mam."

Heavy iron manacles locked them to the cave wall. She yanked, finding the anchor along the bottom. A round link of metal hooked the chains through a natural hole in the rock. Finn must have had his oldest son Patric, an apprenticed blacksmith, put it in.

She fumed. How could he watch the hatchlings get chained up? The rock loop was too thick to break. If enough pressure and heat were applied to the anchor, she could bend the metal ring and pull it free. Then Luteis would have to carry them to safety. Sanna straightened, glancing around. She just needed a little leverage. Junis nudged her leg, looking as skinny and ragged as his mam.

"I know, little one." She ran her palm over his face. He burned low as well, hardly hot at all. "I'll get you out of here."

A mighty roar ripped through the trees outside. An answering call came, this one from Luteis. A third bellow followed. Then a fourth. A fifth.

A sixth.

Sanna's blood turned cold.

She scrambled out of the cave and bolted to the nearest tree. Fire rippled through the branches overhead, revealing glints of sapphire, orange, crimson, and deep emerald. Talis had called an entire army to attack Luteis where he couldn't fly, in a cowardly canopy ambush.

"Luteis!" she screamed.

She'd never dreamed so many of the brood would be waiting—or willing—to fight. The piteous cries of the hatchlings sounded behind her, jolting her back to the present. She hesitated. She might not have another chance to save them. With another few days in these conditions, the hatchlings could die.

But so could Luteis.

Without him, all would be lost for Letum Wood. For her family. For the future of the dragons. With a growl, she shoved away from the tree, grabbed a rock from the ground, and darted back into the cave.

"Junis," she said, briefly touching his scales. "I need your help."

The hatchlings managed to pull themselves to their feet and struggle toward the anchor. She motioned to it.

"Fire. Breathe as much fire as you can."

At first, Junis managed a tepid flame that licked the metal clasp with a halfhearted curl. Rosy sparked twice before collapsing back to the ground, all four legs sprawled. Sanna signaled for Junis to stop, then rammed the rock into the link as hard as she could. The chains jangled. Dragon screams rippled from above, and branches crashed to the ground outside the cave.

"Again, Junis!"

Mustering strength, the hatchling attempted a second time. A hotter breath surged from his lips, heating the loop of metal to a soft glow. After ten seconds, he sputtered to a stop. Sanna rammed the rock into the ring again and again. The circle became an oval, flattening a minuscule amount with each *whack*.

"Keep going!" she cried. "Keep going!"

Junis breathed again. The eager flames consumed the rock this time, turning the metal ring bright orange. Heat filled the air. Sweat dribbled down Sanna's back, running along her spine. Junis stopped with a gasp. She banged the rock into the clasp again, throwing all her weight into each strike. Her knuckles scraped the wall and bled. The skin around her hand blistered from the heat of the ring.

"Break!" she screamed. "Break, you stupid—"

A tremendous *crash* sounded outside, followed by a shriek of pain. Sanna's heart dropped into her stomach. She looked up to see Luteis lying on the ground outside the cave. Blood dripped from his neck in sapphire rivers. He screamed fire.

Another dragon crashed next to him with a heavy *thud*.

Talis.

He stood on top of Luteis, crushing one of his wings. Luteis blew a plume of bright sapphire fire. His secundum.

"Mori!"

Sanna ran from the cave and skidded to a stop just outside.

"Talis!" she screamed. "This is between you and me! You've almost killed my father, you banished my sister, and you tried to fool me. You think you've destroyed my family, but you haven't. We're stronger than you!"

Talis lowered his head, glaring at her through slitted eyes. He glowed with violent energy, his chest expansive and heaving. She grabbed a rock and lobbed it at him.

"You're a demmed liar! And you'll burn in the watery, icy fires of dragon hell before I let you take anything from me again. Including Luteis! You think you've won? Just you wait."

Malice rolled off Talis in waves as he hissed, advancing toward her. Behind him, Luteis struggled to stand. He pushed himself to his feet again, but his back leg didn't touch the ground. His wing drooped, flowing with blood.

Sanna bared her teeth. Talis snorted.

The short distraction had given Luteis all he needed. He swung his tail around, slamming it into Talis's flank. Talis stumbled, one leg collapsing. Luteis advanced, sinking his teeth into Talis's haunches. Talis reared back in a howl, and his tail whipped around. Sanna rushed back just before the tail landed where she'd been standing.

With a breath of fear, she turned back to the hatchlings. Junis breathed on the ring frantically when she returned. His flames shrank into pathetic lines, eventually disappearing as he coughed. Sanna slammed the rock into the chain. Pieces of wall chipped away, flying into her braids and eyes.

"Break, you stupid chain!"

Junis's flames died into smoke. Rosy struggled to her

feet but collapsed. Sanna yanked at the chain with her fingers, burning her skin on the hot metal.

"Break! *Mori!*"

A shadow filled the cave, casting them in darkness. A dragon stood at the mouth, blocking the feeble light from outside.

"Get behind me," Sanna cried, throwing herself in front of the hatchlings. "If you want the hatchlings, Talis, you'll have to kill me first."

A gentle breath replied. Sanna stilled. Her arms dropped. Junis gave a cry.

"Cara?"

Cara slipped inside with a weak shuffle, nudging Rosy with her snout. She looked at Sanna in question. Without her wings, she seemed small, even fragile, but something bright burned within her. The stumps of her wings had healed—not a trace of blood remained. She seemed … whole. How was it possible?

"Cara, you look…"

Two bursts of blue flame issued outside; both Thyris and Talis worked to overwhelm Luteis now. A third dragon dropped to the ground. A fourth. The rest were coming. Cara growled at her.

"Right. Later. We need fire," Sanna said, pointing at the ring. "As hot as you can."

Cara drew in a deep breath and threw fire so strong that Sanna backed away and covered her face with her arms. Within moments, the metal turned white hot. Sanna's skin prickled.

Once Cara stopped, Sanna slammed the rock into the ring again. The piece bent. A second slam. It broke near the bottom. Sanna grabbed Junis's chains near his body and yanked. The ring pried up, pulling away. Junis stumbled back, free from the wall.

Outside, Luteis screamed.

"Luteis!"

Cara shoved Sanna toward the door and gathered Rosy by the neck. Junis struggled to his feet, crying at his mam's side.

Sanna hurried outside to find Talis and Thyris backing Luteis against a tree with their crackling flames. His right wing bled from a partial rent down the middle. One eye was shut, spilling blood.

She skidded to a stop, rearing away from the heat. Luteis responded with his own fire, but it sputtered and died. He limped back when Thyris swung his meaty tail, nearly cracking Luteis in the face. The rest of the dragons remained tucked in the forest, watching from the dark depths.

"Stupid lizard," Sanna yelled, throwing a rock at Thyris. "I can't believe I ever looked up to you!"

Thyris shot a fireball at her, but she dodged it by ducking behind a tree. Silence followed as Talis and Luteis sized each other up, no doubt speaking.

Thyris backed away, slithering into the undergrowth. Sanna sprinted into the forest, even as the shadows of Cara and the hatchlings slipped away from the cave and into the night.

Sanna shoved aside bushes until she came up behind Luteis. His tail bled as she pressed a hand to it. They merged immediately. His heat faded as Sanna crawled up his back. Voices immediately filled her mind.

Only a fool would think they could win just because they have a witch, Talis said.

I have more than a capable Dragonmaster on my side,

Luteis said, but the words were wobbly. Slurred. As if he only barely held onto consciousness.

And you think Deasylva will actually help you? Talis barked, as if laughing. *Where was she during the Great Massacre? Where was she when every dragon was dying? Yes, what a helpful army you have. An incompetent, selfish goddess and a hatchling of a witch who can't control her own temper.*

You don't know Deasylva.

You're right. I thought I did at one point, but she failed us. How spectacularly she failed us. I had to win for the dragons.

It's gone to your head.

No. You've fallen into Deasylva's madness. It's you that doesn't see clearly.

Am I the one who created a false god?

Order, Talis snapped. *I created order when there was none. I created safety when Deasylva abandoned us. Without me, all the dragons would have been lost.*

Luteis shivered as if his legs were about to buckle beneath him. Blood pooled on the ground. "I'm here," Sanna murmured into his shoulder, where she lay flat on her stomach. The magic kept her pressed into his scales even though she wasn't holding on. Luteis twitched his left, uninjured wing in a subtle acknowledgment.

You were a fool to come, Luteis. Just like your mam. Both you and the witch will die tonight.

Luteis snarled.

I will never submit to you.

Still, Talis replied silkily, *you will die.*

Never.

I don't have to kill you, do I? Talis's gaze dropped to Luteis's shoulder, where Sanna perched. *I just have to kill her.*

Talis spewed a burst of fire that consumed them both.

Luteis stood up, bearing the brunt of it on his chest, but the flames whipped back toward Sanna. She dropped down his spine, holding onto the ridge. The heat crackled. Blisters popped up along her arms and neck. The air warped, so hot it scalded her lungs.

"Luteis!" she screamed. "Go!"

I cannot. My leg is broken. My wing...

"W-we're going to d-die!"

She doubled over, coughing. Blood welled up in her throat. The heat stopped, followed by the rhythmic *thud thud thud* of a charging dragon. She barely had time to read-just her grip before Talis barreled into Luteis. Sanna and Luteis fell, toppling to their sides. Luteis screamed as he rolled onto his right flank, protecting his injured wing by folding it back. Sanna scrambled onto his neck just before he crushed her.

Thyris attacked from the right, Talis from the left. Luteis regained his feet and absorbed their blows, then collapsed. His breaths came out in desperate wheezes.

"Luteis! *Go!*"

I cannot.

"You have to!"

He tensed beneath her, coiled his leg, and sprang into the air, wings furled. Thyris appeared from the forest and snapped, but Luteis whacked him with a desperate swing of his tail. He hovered a few paces off the ground for a moment, his wings beating desperately. The tear in his right wing lengthened with a sickening *rip*.

Talis bit Luteis's broken leg, wrenching a chunk of scales free. Luteis screamed, clawing for a nearby tree. Talis shot another burst of fire at his back, scorching Sanna's leg. She shrieked in pain.

Finally, with a livid bellow, Luteis sank his claws into a

tree and scrambled with three legs into the canopy. The other dragons didn't follow. Sanna stifled another scream. She couldn't move—could barely breathe—without utter agony.

When Luteis burst out through the tops of the trees, she drew in a deep gasp of air. He unfurled his wings. A powerful draft of wind caught them, whisking them backward.

Too much, Luteis said. *The pain is ... too much...*

"You can do it, Luteis. Just get us far enough away. That's it. We just have to go where they won't follow."

The steady wind, violent as a gale, pressed them back and back. His wings trembled in great shudders as he strained to hold them open and stay in the thick current.

I ... cannot.

"You have to! *Mori,* Luteis. This is all my fault! I..."

My vision blurs. I cannot feel...

A terrible ripping sound broke the still air. A gaping, bloody hole appeared all the way through his injured wing. The wind increased in power, nearly ripping Sanna from his back.

"Luteis, no!"

His voice faded from her mind. His wings folded onto his back as his body slackened. Sanna screamed as they plummeted into the forest in a free fall.

EIGHTEEN

After Isadora's peace offering, the girls at Miss Sophie's swarmed her with relentless zeal. Instead of pranks, they hounded her with pleas for help, attention, stories, and paintings. They followed her around the school until late at night. She set an incantation to do the dishes after every meal, then spent the rest of the time answering questions, braiding hair, and checking the spelling in letters home.

Baylee watched through slitted eyes, bright with what appeared to be a mixture of relief and annoyance, but she didn't interfere. Escaping to Letum Wood in the early morning became Isadora's only reprieve.

Except, the girls didn't seem that bad now. Misguided. Thirsty for love. But certainly not vicious at the core.

A rainy fall day stretched around Isadora when she pressed her head against the cool bark of a tree. Magic rippled overhead in a bubble, protecting her from the torrent of hissing rain. The cold fall storm froze her bones thanks to the fog that crept along the ground, obscuring the thick bracken. Mud clumped to her shoes and stained her hem.

"Try again," Maximillion said. "I want it to be instinct."

She groaned. "Again?"

"Yes."

He stood behind her, hands folded behind his back. With a frown, he flicked a leech off one finger, then brushed at a single stray feather.

Isadora met his fierce gaze with deep fatigue. "Maximillion, I can't do another moment of this."

"You must. Again."

She growled. *So much for merciful.*

With a sigh, she closed her eyes, sought out the magic, and slipped into it when she felt a familiar darkness. When she opened her eyes, the forest surrounded her like mossy sentinels. Her own path split off to the left, branching in two spots. One—which appeared a little brighter— reflected where her body was now with Maximillion. In the other, she lay on her side, her eyes closed in what appeared to be a deep sleep, but it wavered on a weak footpath. Greater practice had taught Isadora that the brighter the wisp, the more likely the outcome.

Resigning herself, she closed her eyes, seeking out the magic again. It hummed in her mind, a bright, vibrant chord, just like when Maximillion removed her headaches. She grasped it, closing it off. The sensation of moving light lingered, like the warm aftertaste of Mam's apple pastries. Before she opened her eyes, she smelled the familiar scent of juniper. Maximillion. She'd returned to Letum Wood.

"And?" Maximillion asked.

Isadora opened her eyes. "Successful, just like last time. I slipped into the magic and closed it on my own. Just like the time before. And the time before that."

"Always reassuring, isn't it?"

"Exhausting. Maximillion, please, may I be done? I spent three hours in the paths this morning before you came, and two hours now. Clearly, I can access and close the magic at will."

His eyebrow rose. "Really? Three hours?"

"Yes."

"And what did you see?"

"Nothing important. At least, I can't tell if it is." She rubbed a hand across her eyes. "The paths are still confusing. They branch into things that make no sense at all. It's like trying to read a book in a language I can't speak. And now the wisps are becoming more detailed and ... I don't know."

"Any discernible stop in the paths?"

"Sometimes."

He paused with sharp surprise in his cutting gaze. "Explain."

"I can't, really. There are too many to remember with detail."

"Did they all stop at once?"

"No. Only certain paths stopped at random times. I couldn't make sense of it."

"What did the stop look like?"

She hesitated, recalling the strange area of pure darkness that she saw every now and then—mostly amongst Maximillion's paths. Only once or twice in Sanna's.

"Like a curtain of black, I suppose."

"A stop such as that usually means death, although it could simply mean unconsciousness."

Egads, but she'd never thought of that. Could she predict someone's death? Perhaps. But the paths shifted so often ... she thought of the few dark spots she saw on

Sanna's paths with a heavy gulp. Perhaps this wasn't a power she wanted. *Knowing* that she or someone else could die would completely alter her decisions, which would change the paths again. A terrible burden.

"Then what is this magic worth if there's no guarantee?" she asked.

"More than you think. Every second of our lives impacts our decisions in different ways, so it's unlikely that a particular path will unfurl as it's shown. But if the paths nearest you show an immediate end? Well…"

His voice trailed away. Isadora sighed.

"Well," she murmured. "At least that makes some sense. Still, it seems like madness to me. Trying to discern something that's always shifting."

"Which is why one should have a particular respect for magic such as this."

"I thought it would be more rewarding. Maybe even a little easier."

"You hardly know it."

"I know."

He paced across the trail, his coattails fluttering behind him. Although Maximillion never seemed at ease, today he acted more cagey than usual—glancing at his watch, staring at the sky. Every time a bird fluttered by, he tracked it with his piercing gaze until it twittered away. His scowl deepened with every moment.

"Can we be done *now*?" she asked.

"Increase to four hours starting tomorrow."

She groaned. "Four? But that's insane. I—"

"So is Greta, but you don't see anyone removing her from power."

"The sanity of our High Priestess has nothing to do with your demands on me."

"You'd be surprised," he quipped. "Four hours, Isadora. I mean it. If you want to control the powers and make a difference in this world, you'll do it."

"Fine," she muttered. "I'll do four tomorrow."

"And six by the end of the week."

"That's practically the whole day!"

"Don't be absurd. There are twenty-four hours in a day. That's only a quarter of them."

"My *waking* day."

"What other pressing matters do you have to attend to?"

She closed her mouth with a scowl. *Pressing?* Not many. But now that the girls weren't tormenting her with snails and bees in her porridge, she was less inclined to stay away all day. Besides, working with magic exhausted her. And it was quite boring after a while.

"Fine. I'll try to get to six hours."

"One last thing."

"Finally, yes. Anything."

"Enter the magic again."

"You're wretched, you know that?"

He pointed down the trail. "This time, do it outside Letum Wood. You've shown remarkable progress this last week. Let's make it accessible now. It's hardly useful if you have to run to the forest every time you want to access your magic. This way, we can make use of your powers elsewhere."

A prickle of intuition crawled up her back. "This is about something else, isn't it? You haven't told me everything."

"Yes." He whirled around, expression implacable. "And I won't. But it's mostly about your knowing how to access and use an extraordinary amount of power."

"I'm exhausted."

His nostrils flared. He clenched his jaw, paused, and finally said, "Then consider it a personal favor to me."

She drew in a deep breath. Maximillion had never asked for a personal anything. "Only if you do a personal favor to me first."

He rolled his eyes. "What?"

"Tell me one thing about yourself that I don't already know."

For a moment, she thought he'd transport away—the question had even taken her by surprise. The world seemed to pause in a chilled silence. An icy rage filled his gaze, then passed, leaving him as contemptuous as ever.

"Why do you care?"

She paused. Why *did* she care? "I don't know," she whispered.

Another long stretch of silence followed.

"I don't like to be touched."

"I already knew that."

"Witches annoy me."

"I also knew that."

"That's all there is."

"You're lying."

He shifted, face dark with a scowl. "Then what *don't* you know?"

"Why are you helping me?"

Maximillion blinked, drawing in a deep breath. He let it out. "Because it's the right thing to do. There, your question is answered."

"But—"

"The road to Berry. We'll access the magic there. It won't be very far away. I want to see if it's difficult for you to tap into Letum Wood from that distance."

"That answer shouldn't count!"

"Now you know something about me you didn't know before. That was the deal. Trust me," he added in a hard tone. "There's nothing in my past you want to know more of. Transport. I want you to practice that."

He disappeared. Isadora closed her eyes, tilted her head back, and took a moment to pause in the silence. Odious witch.

With an annoyed sigh, she closed her eyes, pictured the exact spot she wanted to go to, and said the spell. An instant later, she arrived. Maximillion already stood on the road, peering at a pocket watch with a frown.

"Proceed," he said.

Isadora closed her eyes and sought the magic. The warmth returned to the back of her mind in tendrils, slippery and glimmering. She clutched for it, finally grabbing hold. When she slid into the magic, she opened her eyes.

The ring of trees stood before her, but in vague lines. Patchy, uncertain darkness, revealing no paths, extended over the ground. She groped her way forward, feeling rough bark and an occasional sapling under her palm. The tree disappeared moments later, encasing her in black again. She trembled as she extricated herself from the magic.

"Success?" Maximillion asked.

"I suppose. It was mostly darkness, but I saw a few details."

"Interesting," he murmured. "Practice four hours tomorrow, and I want at least two of them to be outside Letum Wood. I'll be out of town for the next three days, and I'll check in when I return. By that time, I expect you to use the power in the middle of Berry."

He disappeared. Isadora stuck her tongue out after him,

collapsed onto a fallen log, closed her eyes, and tried to gather the energy to transport back to school.

"PLEASE TELL me ya know what Samhain is."

Baylee cast another bushel of tied twigs on the library mantel, then nestled a small pumpkin on top of them. Banners of black cloth hung from the middle of the fireplace, swooping to either side.

"Of course I know what Samhain is." Isadora turned another page of the *Basic Spells and Alchemy for Artists* book. "At home, we had a feast to celebrate the end of the harvest. Mam made apple pie almost every year. It was always one of our biggest celebrations."

Or we used to celebrate when we had food, she added silently, wondering if the village was faring any better. On Samhain, the Servants gathered for a big feast near the shelter. They wrote their plans for the next year on paper, then burned them before Drago.

Baylee stepped back, surveying her work. "Good. Now, go find something appropriate to wear."

Isadora lifted her eyebrow. Baylee had been strangely chummy ever since she'd brought the new outfits, although she still didn't wear her new shoes.

"A bit bossy today?" Isadora asked.

"Ya. But we can head down to the festival together. Without me, ya would probably get lost and wander into Letum Wood." She shuddered. "No one wants to be in Letum Wood on Samhain."

Isadora shut the book—which contained a smaller

book on Watchers that Baylee couldn't see—and decided not to elaborate on her familiarity with the forest. The pamphlet was a journal from previous Watchers recounting their visions and abilities. The glimpse into their process had given her insights on interpreting the strange wisps, but she still felt lost in her own head.

Only two of the sixty Watchers in the book had been able to detect personality traits. Both described it differently than she did. None of them seemed to see the person in their entirety. Perhaps she could do something new.

"What do you mean by *appropriate to wear?*" Isadora stood.

Baylee eyed Isadora's simple linen dress—so different from Berry's fashion with miles of fabric layered underneath—and shook her head.

"Something black, preferably. Anything that glitters and appears expensive is good. The dead don't want to be welcomed back to Alkarra if there's nothing pretty to see. If ya can manage it, find a mask to wear. But don't if ya want ya dead family members to recognize ya. Also, I have extras."

Isadora paused, deciding not to question why Baylee would have extra black masks lying around. "You must know that no one really comes back, right?"

Baylee tacked another pinecone onto the mantel, shifted it to the left, and muttered, "Shows how much ya know."

Berry was transformed.

Isadora slipped into a teeming congregation of people as the last of the sun's rays stretched above Letum Wood in buttery slants. An early darkness fell on the crowd. Lanterns, torches, and fires dotted the forest town, casting rings of light on the children scampering through the streets. Everyone wore black crepe armbands and dark clothes. Most of the women had a band around their eyes, making every grin seem coy.

"It's so busy," she murmured.

"Everyone comes." Baylee flounced past an old, black-clad man sitting on a porch. Small candles dotted his chair. "Who doesn't want a chance to glimpse those they've lost in death?"

Three men strode toward Isadora and Baylee, crepe banners fluttering off their arms and wide-brimmed, black hats shielding their eyes. One of them locked eyes with Isadora, then disappeared in the shuffle of the crowd.

She touched the band around her eyes, fascinated by the sense of security it lent her. Thanks to Baylee's glimmering red hair, everyone knew her and her heart-shaped face at once, but Isadora could slide into the cracks and be invisible. She could do or say almost anything, really, and not bear the full consequences. Wasn't that what life out here was already? Mam and Daid would never know what she did here.

The thought gave her a delicious thrill of power.

"Look!" Baylee pointed across the busiest street, packed with witches juggling apples and haggling over bags of black currant tea. "There's Maude. How lovely. She's wearing her black silk gown. Do ya see how it flows? I'm going to have one just like it one day."

Maude stood on a bale of hay, a pitcher of foaming

ipsum in her hand. She called out to those passing, "Blessings on the harvest. Cast your old habits to the good gods and become a better witch for it." A barrel burned behind her. Witches wrote on slips of silk with mulberry ink, then cast them into the flames and watched them sizzle into ash.

"Later," Baylee said, grabbing Isadora's wrist. "Candy first."

Isadora followed, weaving through the crowds. She allowed Baylee to lead her, using the opportunity to shift her attention to the magic. The teeming mass of witches sent ropes of magic whipping through her mind. She concentrated, pulled the slivers back in, and imagined the silvery strands wriggling in her hand as she closed her fingers around them.

I am in charge, she told it, the way Maximillion had taught her. *You are not needed right now. I am safe.*

The magic quelled. Her headache faded. Isadora laughed under her breath.

"C'mon!" Baylee shrieked as they rounded a corner, bringing Berry Cigars and Candy Shop into full view. "There are a few left. Some with toffee on the outside!"

Ten minutes later, they each held a paper sack and cradled an apple dipped in caramel and skewered on a stick. They slid past the Samhain celebrations, and Isadora stared at a sultry dancer beckoning the dead to return. Witches tossed horseshoes to win a steaming meat pie. The scent of roasting chicken lay thick in the air.

Isadora drank the delicious celebrations in, passing total strangers in their dark garb as the sun sank entirely. Shadows crept over them from Letum Wood, highlighting the fires that flared on every street corner. An apothecary tossed a handful of herbs into a blaze, conjuring bright blue flames.

"Wait." Baylee halted. Her hair spilled onto her shoulders in voluminous red waves. "Wait right here."

She disappeared. Isadora planted her feet near a barrel of ipsum, pulled by a tug of magic in her mind. Despite her hold on it, it wriggled, as if bothered. She tucked it aside with a frown. It had never been this persistent.

I am safe. You are not needed.

Pumpkins sat piled on top of the barrel, decorated with dry stalks of corn. In the background, a woman cackled. Two men collided, already bleary with ipsum, and a shout of laughter spilled from the nearby tavern.

Letum Wood lingered not far away. She closed her eyes, feeling the forest's power beckon. For just a moment, she released the magic, allowing it to scatter. She slipped into it, finding herself at the base of the forest, the mask still adorning her face. She gasped.

Hundreds of paths clogged the forest floor.

Witches popped up in every available space, as if they would clutter the entire world. There were so many ghostly images she couldn't make out a trail. They blurred, still nondescript—she hadn't entirely built up her power outside Letum Wood. She sucked in a deep breath, recognizing herself in the one closest to her feet. It branched into unknown places, lost amidst the chaos of all the others.

Too much, she thought, pressing a hand to her forehead. *This is too much.*

"Show me something else," she gasped. "Please!"

The paths disappeared, taking the images with them. Isadora breathed easier until a pillar of light formed in front of her. A familiar figure appeared. Dark, dressed as the night, eyes covered. He snarled, baring teeth, a sword clenched in his hands. Blood dripped from his fingers to the ground.

Isadora stumbled back, recognizing him. The masked witch, one of three men, who had locked eyes with her. Under the magic's power, she saw details, though blurry, she hadn't recognized before. A shock of blonde hair. Deeply tanned skin. Something foreign in his eyes.

Something tugged at her. She reigned the magic back in and opened her eyes to see Baylee staring at her.

"Isa?"

"Sorry."

"What happened?" Baylee's eyes narrowed. "Did ya fall asleep standing?"

"Ah, yes. Must be more tired than I thought."

Baylee held up a husk of corn with black marks on the exterior leaves. "Roasted corn. Thought ya might like it. I had them put on extra butter and salt as a favor."

"Oh. Thank you."

"C'mon. Let's go somewhere less busy to eat it."

Something niggled in Isadora's mind as she followed Baylee toward the edges of the festival, away from the dancers and callers and toward the booths where witches haggled over black veils to wear the moment the night turned to the Samhain day. They slipped past carts selling slices of pumpkin pie and spiced cider and hurried onto the main street of downtown Berry.

Isadora's mind raced. So many paths—she hadn't seen anything truly definitive. Or had she? Had there been *something* there that …

"Baylee. Stop."

She jerked back on Baylee's hand, pulling them into an alley.

"What?"

"Stay here. Just … wait."

Isadora slipped back into the paths in an instant, as if

she'd been half in each world. She stepped onto the closest path she could find, studying it frantically. While she knew nothing of the witch there, she found a sliver of trail and followed it. It led to another stranger. Then another.

She ran, sprinting through the ghostly images in a panic. *All* of the paths intersected. Isadora pushed through them, searching frantically until she found herself. She crouched with Baylee. The next trail led to an unknown witch, with mask half-ripped off and teeth bared. Terror filled the air. She could already feel it.

Isadora pushed the magic away, opening her eyes to find Baylee staring at her.

"What are ya *doing*?" Baylee asked.

"Baylee, we have to go! We have to find the girls and take them back to the school."

"What? Why?"

Isadora grabbed her arm and yanked her into the road. A shout in the distance gave them pause. Silence rippled through the witches in the street. Their eyes locked on a figure running, his arms waving. Using a spell, he called over the crowd.

"Attack on Chatham City!"

A cold heaviness settled in Isadora's chest, pulsating through her arms and legs. The magic beckoned, nearly pulling her under. She fought it, trying to mentally wrestle it back under her control. The struggle took all of her concentration until Baylee gasped.

"What?" Isadora murmured, grabbing her arm. "What happened?"

The caller's voice rang over the crowd again, drowning shocked murmurs.

"The High Priestess Greta is dead! Attacks have been

reported in nearly all the Covens. Everyone, return to your homes! Go home! Lock yourselves someplace safe."

The cries of other messengers emanated from different parts of the festival, but the crowd fell into a tense, strange quiet.

"The High Priestess is dead!" the messenger said again as he climbed on top of a barrel. "She was poisoned. The Western Network is attacking. Everyone, back to your homes and—"

An arrow hit him in the middle of the chest with a sickening *thud*. He crumbled, falling off the barrel, his body slack.

Someone screamed. Witches clothed in black surged into the festival. They fell from rooftops, teemed out of the forest, and swooped in on transportation spells.

Baylee paled. Isadora grabbed her arm and pulled them out of the street. They cowered deeper in the alley, crouched next to each other.

"What's happening?"

"The West," Isadora whispered. "They're attacking Berry."

CHAOS SWEPT the streets of Berry. The Western Network filled every road, advancing into buildings with bright torches and killing with thirsty blades.

Witches scattered. Barrels fell. Pots crashed. Tables overturned. The sound of death shrieked through the air. Within minutes, a choking smoke crawled through the streets and clogged the once-jovial air.

Isadora pressed Baylee further into the alley as two street urchins darted past them, eyes wide with fright.

"What are we going to do?" Baylee whispered. "We can't stay here!"

The pull of her powers beckoned to her again, but Isadora resisted. "We go back to the school."

"They're setting everything on fire. Maybe they've already decimated the rest of the town and moved in."

Isadora licked her lips, glancing at the mouth of the narrow alley. Witches still clogged the streets in their rush to get away. She hesitated, annoyed by the insistent tug of the powers.

"Baylee, just … wait for one minute. One minute, that's it. If I'm not coherent by then, just run and leave me behind."

Before Baylee had a chance to respond, Isadora entered the magic.

"Sixty," Isadora murmured. "Fifty-nine. Fifty-eight."

The base of the ring of trees had coiled into an unimaginable tangle even more complicated than before. She swallowed. Being closer to Letum Wood lent some strength to what she saw, but many of the distant images were mere blurs.

"Show only my path."

The images disappeared.

A single path snaked from her feet into the forest, splitting into smaller threads along the way. Isadora hurried from one to the next. The possibilities seemed endless. Most of them led back to the school, but they were weak, ending in flickers of darkness or fire or girls sleeping on the floor. Two of the paths ended in black fog. By the time she returned to the top of the trail, they'd all shifted again. One of them showed her alone, in the forest.

In another, she was with Sophie. In still another, with Sanna.

She growled. How was she supposed to know what to do?

In a panic, she realized she'd forgotten to count. With one last glance back at the paths, Isadora spotted one that revealed the end of the alley, then what appeared to be the basement of a store. It gave way to a tower clock with a bright yellow bird on top standing against a wall. To the left sat a bright teal door.

The path split into four from there, but the brightest image showed Isadora running through Letum Wood just before it twisted into the trees.

"Alley, basement, bird, trees," Isadora murmured. "Got it."

She exited the magic and faced Baylee.

"What are you *doing*?" Baylee cried. "It's been four minutes!"

"Nothing. We need to go." Isadora grabbed Baylee's arm and shoved her down the alley. "Just go."

"West Guards are everywhere!"

A scream from the mouth of the alley silenced them both. A West Guard shoved his sword into the side of a male witch, who fell to his knees, limp. His ankle twitched. The color drained from Baylee's face, leaving her ghostly pale.

"Go!" Isadora hissed. "Now!"

They sprinted off together. Halfway down the alley, a window glinted from a dark hole in the ground. Isadora skidded to a stop, grabbed a window pane, and used a spell to break the glass.

"Get in!"

Baylee crawled in first, dropping down a waist-high wall and turning to hold the window. Isadora slipped inside the half-basement and yanked the window shut behind them. Barrels lined the walls, marked with chalk and unintelligible scribblings. The air smelled thick with wine and yeast.

"I know this shop," Baylee murmured. "We might be safe down here for a while."

"No. We're just using it to move to the other side of the block, then back to the school."

"What?"

"We can't stay in Berry," Isadora said. "We need to get to the forest."

"It's not safe in Letum Wood! Besides, we can't leave the girls."

"Safer than being stuck here when the West Guards move through torching everything!" Isadora whispered. "I may not be as wise as you in the ways of Network life, but even *I* know what male witches do when they find unprotected young women."

The freckles on Baylee's face stuck out in sharp relief against her pale skin. "Oh," she murmured. "I hadn't thought of that."

"We must keep going. It's the only way we'll be able to help the girls."

They crept up a pair of short staircases and into the dim, empty shop of Berry's vintage ipsum dealer. Bottles of wine lined the walls. Light from a torch outside echoed through the mirrors in the room, illuminating every dark corner. Isadora moved first, but Baylee pulled her back.

"No. Marty's enchanted it. See that massive front window? Cost him six months' worth of pentacles. I could've eaten for years with that kind of currency. Look."

A shimmering haze hung over the room, crowding the floorboards. The subtle sheen appeared thin, almost translucent, so subtle that she wouldn't have noticed it if Baylee hadn't pointed it out.

"What'll happen?"

"Dunno. But I've heard of it before. Something about boils on ya skin and inside yer throat? Not worth the—"

The front window shattered.

Isadora and Baylee spun away as the mist expanded into a billowing purple cloud. It rolled past them, leaving a sticky layer of grit on their skin and hair, then imploded and collected on top of a West Guard lying on the floor.

He groaned, glass shards sticking out of his back. Within moments, he began to scream and scratch at his skin. The sound of voices shouting from outside followed as another West Guard was thrown into the room. He skidded on his shoulder in the glass shards, a bright green torch in his hand. Isadora shoved Baylee toward the front door.

"Go!"

"Not that way!" Baylee cried. "They're out there."

But a flicker of something familiar caught Isadora's attention. A tower clock standing against the wall with a stuffed yellow bird and a bright teal door.

"This is the way," she cried. "Trust me! I've seen it."

Baylee hesitated but nodded and followed as Isadora grabbed the door handle and yanked it open. She fell back with a gasp, heart in her throat. Three West Guards filled the doorway, blocking their path. Isadora scrambled back, but one reached out and grabbed her by the throat.

"Well, well," he drawled, eyes gleaming. "Look what we have here."

NINETEEN

Sanna and Luteis fell into Letum Wood.

Leaves whipped past them as they dropped, and branches cracked beneath his heavy, limp body. She remained stuck to him, still merged, alive because he bore the brunt of the fall.

Finally, a nest of vines snagged them, slowing their rapid descent and taking her breath away. Luteis sprang up and down in their thick grasp. One at a time, the vines encircled his body, cradling him. Slowly, they lowered Luteis and Sanna to the ground. Branches moved out of the path on their own, and leaves shifted to make way.

Sanna stared from Luteis's shoulder as they passed through the trees, descending past branches and fresh growth. The ride down seemed to take forever, the vines lengthening until Sanna feared they would snap.

Finally, they eased onto the ground. She leapt free.

"Luteis!"

His face lay slack and inert on the black soil. She touched his snout, his neck, his ears.

"Wake up! Demmet, Luteis. Wake *up!*"

He didn't stir. No amount of pressing, shoving, or yelling made his eyes flutter. Sanna ran to his chest and pressed her ear to it. A faint sound. The distant, final throes of a mighty, booming heart protesting like a weak kitten. She closed her eyes, panting as she searched. Luteis said they shared magic. Perhaps she could use it. Revive him. Bring him ...

The merging was *gone*.

"No!" she screamed, shoving away.

Several startled birds flapped out of a nearby bush, squawking. Sanna caught a sob halfway out of her throat.

"Luteis, no."

Beneath her hands, his heartbeat had slowed. Blood pooled around his tail, spilling from his half-mangled back leg. The gaping hole had torn his mighty wing in half. Blood trickled from a wound in his neck, cascading in rivulets of deepest cobalt.

"Luteis!" She slammed a fist into his meaty shoulder. "Come on. Fight! Fight to live. We still have to kill Talis. Egads. You're the only friend I have!"

A flicker of life stirred, then faded. For a moment, she thought she heard a whisper in her mind, a parting word. It faded like a wraith. Darkness broke out across her vision. She fell to her knees with a cry. Her breath vanished. Her heart thrummed like a hummingbird, threatening to pull her into a great chasm of darkness. At the last moment, Sanna pulled away, breaking the final threads of the merge with whatever life ebbed away from Luteis.

"No!"

Sobs filled her scorched throat. She slapped a blistered hand onto his flank. His chest had fallen silent. In desperation, she climbed on top of him and put her hands over the blood leaking from his neck. The pulses had slowed to a trickle.

The blood hissed when she touched it. The heat tore through her arm, but she locked her hand in place with a shout of pain.

"Heal! *Mori,* Luteis. Whatever magic it takes, I give. I-I don't know how ... maybe ... come on!"

Sanna plunged deep into her thoughts, seeking the small puddle of power she'd felt on their initial merge. She searched the darkness, rummaged through every possible thought, every source of hidden power, but it wasn't there. Nothing. Her body slowed. Her energy flagged.

She fell, leaning back against his scales. Without the merge, his body burned hot. Blisters broke out along the bottoms of her feet, and pain seared through her hand. A sob slipped out of her throat as she dropped to the ground.

A deep, mourning silence settled on Letum Wood.

Sanna's tear sizzled on his scales as she pulled away. She dropped to her knees next to him and gave in to the sobs, pressing her forehead to the ground. The cries tore from her raw throat in giant, wrenching gasps. She'd lost her whole family. Isadora. Mam. Daid. Now Luteis. There would be no defeating Talis. There would be nowhere to go. No place for safety. For love. For family. No dragon to scoff at her. No canopy. No more Letum Wood.

Her fingers curled into the steaming blood as it mixed with the earth, soaking deep into the loam. A tiny plant unfurled, springing to life with a budding leaf. She stared at it with teary eyes.

"Luteis," she whispered. "Please don't go."

A spark of light moved at the edge of Sanna's vision. A stray fairy, come to see the ruckus, no doubt. She ignored it until it fluttered past again. Then again.

With a snarl, she straightened.

"Get aw—"

She fell against Luteis with a gasp.

The trees glimmered.

Iridescent light spread through the branches and trunks, teeming like a bright, wild thing. It ran through the roots until the ground beneath her pulsed with rays that broke through the rich soil like tiny capillaries. Roots snaked through the earth and paused near her hand. A whole army of them stopped, as if staring at her.

As if *waiting*.

She swallowed. She'd seen this light before. What felt like an eternity ago, in Letum Wood, while staring at a tree.

Deasylva.

Sanna hesitated, then reached out and touched the inquisitive root closest to her. Power shot into her body like a bolt of lightning. She fell back with a cry, but the root had wrapped around her wrist. Her entire body turned to flame. She screwed her eyes shut as energy sang through her blood. It filled her with light and vision and extraordinary power. Her body trembled with the force of holding it back.

She opened her eyes and held out a quaking hand. The veins appeared like dark, bruised rivers against the backdrop of light in her flesh. Any moment now, the glittering magic would burst through her skin. Twinkling from the inside out, Sanna planted a hand on Luteis's flank. Without being told, she knew what to do.

"Heal," she cried. "Heal, Luteis."

She pictured the sinews of his body knitting back together. The blood multiplying and filling his veins again. His heart beating a steady tempo. His lungs filling with sweet forest air. The muscles of his wing rejoining in a scarless marriage.

The power rippled through her in streams of light, flowing from the roots and into his broken body. She gritted her teeth and channeled the storm into Luteis with a guttural yell. The weight threatened to crush her. The magic bound itself to her body, burrowing deep into her bones until she didn't know herself without it.

"Heal!"

Luteis absorbed the light. It swirled through his body in eddies of power, restoring scales, muscle, and tissue. His neck drew back together. Light sprinted along the edge of his wing and down the middle, pulling it into a seamless membrane. The pain in Sanna's leg faded. Her lungs stopped burning. The magic whisked away every ache.

All around them, Letum Wood burned with white-hot power. Luminescence glimmered from every surface, coating the leaves, the earth, the trees with its radiance.

The torrent slowed. One of the roots released her. Then another. They slithered back into the ground like retracting vines. Her body jarred, set free.

Sanna collapsed.

Luteis's chest expanded in a deep breath just as the last vestiges of magic whipped through him. Sanna blinked slowly once, twice, and finally pushed off the ground with the last of her strength.

"Luteis?"

His left wing twitched, then his right. They rose like giant specters, completely whole. His legs stretched, as though waking from a long, lazy sleep. He growled deep in his chest, a thick, cavernous sound that rumbled through the forest. A bright, yellow-moon eye shot open.

He leapt to his feet.

Strength radiated from him, as though Deasylva's magic infused his very bones. He was more than Luteis now. He was sheer strength and might and determined ability. Fire illuminated his eyes as surely as it blasted from his mouth. His tail, without blemish, whipped over, wrapping gently around her ankle. He leaned close, then pressed his face to her chest, right over her pounding heart. He closed his eyes.

I have returned.

She reached out for him. His scales felt cool to the touch. Sanna pressed her forehead against his. They remained there for a long, breathless moment.

"I'm sorry, Luteis. I—"

It is already forgiven.

"You were right, though. You suffered all of that because of me. I shouldn't have—"

Stop, Sanna of Anguis. The fault is not entirely yours. He pulled back, studying the trees. They still glimmered like stardust. *How much time has passed?*

"It's hard to tell. An hour? Two? Less?"

You have saved me.

"Not really."

You could not have been a conduit if not worthy of Deasylva's power.

New strength filled her with every passing moment. She suspected there were injuries she'd known nothing about that were now banished forever. She glanced down at her body, still glowing. No blisters. No scratch marks. Breathing didn't cause her pain.

"What happened, Luteis? You died. I mean ... maybe I should have died too."

He bowed his head.

Deasylva has healed both of us.

"But why?"

For her own purposes, no doubt. She does not often justify herself to me. She does not have to.

"But—"

Suffice it to say, we are alive. We have one more chance to defeat Talis.

"Luteis, it was horrible. I couldn't do anything. Talis and Thyris were destroying you, and I had to just sit there. I … we can't win if that's all we have. You said there was magic, but I don't know it! And maybe I could have—"

He lowered his head. *It is time for me to be honest, for I have not been entirely open with you. Neither of us is blameless.*

"You've lied?"

In that I have not told you all.

"All right," she whispered. "I'm listening now."

Close your eyes.

She obeyed. Her thoughts shifted into a gossamer, dark world. An expanseless void filled with an occasional whisper, a flicker of shadow. Muted light suffused the world outside, interrupted by vein-like ribbons of blue.

Me, he said. *Within my egg. My first memory. I heard and still remember things from my time growing within. My mam's voice. Talis. Other dragons who I believe are dead now.*

The strange backdrop faded, replaced by a burgundy dragon. Beautiful, lithe, with scales infused with deep, glimmering purple. No horns—a female. Her eyes were intelligent, sharp as flint and quick as time. Something familiar lived in the angular pitch of her nose, the ridge along her back. She crouched over a copper-tinted egg.

Luna, Luteis said. *My mam.*

"Oh," Sanna breathed.

I do not remember her. Deasylva has given me this image. Luna heard Deasylva's call and escaped from Talis's grasp. She lay me while in the forest, learning more about Deasylva. Talis found her and attempted to convince her to return and be his mate. That is when I heard his voice for the first time. It was far away, but I still remember it.

"He wanted Luna to be his mate?"

A most powerful position.

Especially considering that dragons didn't typically mate for any length of time. The picture of Luna faded into another. Talis stood over her, looming and furious. She didn't cower.

"She said no, didn't she?"

She refused to return. He killed her.

"What happened to you?"

Deasylva protected me.

In her mind, Sanna saw a vine descend to the egg, rolling it gently into the notch of a tree root. Leaves and mud rose up, covering the egg in a protective layer. Branches moved aside, allowing a ribbon of sun to fall on it, warming the moist earth. Days and nights passed. Eventually, a tiny nose broke through the shell. A dragon the size of Sanna's arm climbed free one limb at a time. He blinked against the light, tipping his head back. Searching, no doubt, for a mam who wasn't there.

Her heart cracked. Such a sweet hatchling. Alone from the very beginning.

A feeling of soul-deep loneliness swept through her, nearly consuming her in its strength. Bringing with it the realization that she wasn't in some void—she was in Luteis's mind. The depths of his soul. Accessing the most hidden, treasured parts of his heart. Somehow, he could share this with her. Was this the magic of the merging? Or only a glimpse of it?

Sanna opened her eyes, meeting his intense gaze. Hints

of Luna lurked in his eyes, in his bright, teeming intelligence.

"Luteis, I'm sor—"

I know your heart. Now you know mine as well. This is what I should have shared with you from the beginning. Because I held back, we could not truly merge. Deasylva says we have now completed our merging.

"But I still don't know the magic."

Not yet, no. We must defeat Talis without it.

"Then what's changed?"

You are the only witch in all of Alkarra who has earned Deasyvla's trust and fully merged with a dragon.

She shrugged. "So?"

You, Sanna of Anguis, are now the High Dragonmaster.

The ball spiraled into the West Guard's chest and threw him back. His hand released her. Baylee and Isadora scrambled back as the two other West Guards advanced, creating a v-formation. The cursed West Guard lying in the bits of broken glass groaned, welts the size of Isadora's hand ballooning across his arms.

"Isadora," Baylee whispered. "What now?"

"Leave us alone," Isadora shouted, but her voice trembled. The Guards laughed, deep, rolling chuckles that rippled with menace. Isadora backed into the post of a staircase, halting. Baylee grabbed her arm.

"On three, we run," Isadora whispered.

Baylee nodded once.

The West Guard reached out, touching Isadora's hair. He spoke to the others in a different language. They laughed again.

"Three!" Isadora cried. She spun and sprinted back the way they'd come. Just as they closed in on the cellar door, a hand grabbed her wrist, wrenching her back. She fell with a cry.

"Run!" she screeched.

Baylee paused over the cellar door, eyes wide. The West Guard shoved Isadora down, stomping on her back with a heavy boot. Her spine popped. He pushed his weight down until all the air left her lungs in a long rush. Her vision swam.

"Don't worry," he murmured. "You won't feel a thing."

A scream gathered in her throat. She tried to push up with her hands, but he increased the pressure on her back.

"I was just about to say the same thing, you wretched swine."

Maximillion's voice came from just behind the West Guard. A resounding *crack* tore through the room. The Guardian toppled, head smacking the corner of the wall before he slid to the ground. His chin hit the floorboard with a sickening sound.

Baylee rushed to Isadora and yanked her up. Isadora sputtered, gasping. Her right side burned. The splotches of black in her vision cleared, revealing Maximillion a few paces away, a heavy bottle of wine in his hand and his hair askew. The other West Guards lay writhing on the floor under a spell, their hands bound by thick lengths of rope.

"Hurry," he said, tossing the wine aside. It shattered in a mauve spray, coating the floor like blood. "We need to get out of here."

Her chest still aching and breath shallow, Isadora

obeyed, leaning on Baylee for help when her head began to swim again. Maximillion led them to the back of the store, then out a slim door that led into a side alley.

"The school," she panted. "We have to ... check on the other girls. I-I think something is going to happen. But..."

"You *think*?" he snapped. "The same way you *thought* it would be a good idea to go out the front door?"

"I saw it!"

"You don't know what you saw! I haven't trained you in interpreting the paths yet. What were you thinking?"

Isadora scowled, but her reply trailed away, lost in her own doubts. She'd been so certain that the paths had been right—that she'd seen the way out. It had been so strong. But it had been wrong. If not for Maximillion ... she shook her head.

"All the same, we need to go back to the school."

Maximillion scowled and slipped into his magic but didn't disagree when he returned. His jaw tightened.

"If there's one left. Let's go."

Heat from burning buildings surged over them as they wound through the map of alleys. In a rush, they spilled out onto the road by the candy shop. Behind them, Berry smoldered. Shops flickered with sickly green and yellow flames.

A West Guard rounded the corner, but Maximillion set a curse on him. The Guard countered it, but the three of them had already faded into the shadows by the time he recovered. Isadora's smarting chest loosened, allowing her almost a full breath as they hurried down the dirt road.

When they made it back to the school, terrified girls streamed in and out, hauling their few possessions onto the lawn. Smoke billowed from the back of the building. Maximillion paused, arms held out to stop them. Seconds later, he whipped around.

"Gather the girls and go! Run into Letum Wood. Now!"

He shoved through the congregated girls on the lawn and darted into the school. Baylee split off toward the young twins, who sat on a bench, shoulders hunched with sobs. An explosion erupted at the back of the house.

The girls skittered into a panic, rushing onto the street. Sophie called for them to come to her side, her hair a ragged, tangled mess. Isadora sprinted into the school and called Maximillion's name.

Once she stepped inside, the magic tugged her back into itself under its own power. A black mist settled over the trees, filling all the paths. With a growl, she slipped back out, grabbed a young girl on the staircase, and turned toward the front door just as Maximillion rushed down the stairs, another girl in tow.

"What are you doing?" he yelled. "I told you to leave!"

"I came to help. The explosion—"

He growled and shoved past her. "Out the back," he said to the two girls. "Run into Letum Wood. Now!"

While the two girls ran off ahead, Isadora followed Maximillion. She skidded to a stop on the porch with a gasp. West Guards filled the yard, each holding a girl with an arm across her throat. Baylee's mouth opened in a livid scream as she struggled against her captor, but nothing came out.

Maximillion stepped forward with a snarl.

"You have a fight with the Central Network, Dostar, and you're holding innocent young girls hostage? A fitting tribute to the High Priest of such a vile place."

The largest West Guard, a beefy, sprawling man with arms like tree trunks, stepped out of the crowd. His beard flowed onto a bare chest in three sharp points, like half a star. Loose, white linen pants hugged his hips, billowing in waves to his ankles. His teeth gleamed. He held a curved, thick sword.

Dostar, Isadora thought frantically. *Dostar.*

An article from the *Chatterer* came back to her in an instant. The High Priest of the Western Network. Dostar.

"We have business with you and your new Highest Witch," he said in a crisp, enunciated accent.

"Take it to the castle," Maximillion snapped. "You don't bring the fight to a farming village that can't defend itself. If you're going to fight, fight with honor, you insolent cow."

"Honor?" Dostar barked with laughter. "There's no witch in Alkarra more insulting than you."

"Only to those that deserve it, you swine."

"Honor is something neither you nor your High Priestess would know anything about."

"Well," Maximillion said with a cool gaze. "Seems like you've taken care of that problem, haven't you? Meet me on fair ground, coward, or you'll discover what my wrath can bring upon you and your witches."

"You're not the Highest Witch."

"I don't have to be."

A sickly green mist sprang into the air. It snaked into the faces of the West Guards in thin funnels, avoiding all the girls. The West Guards coughed, choking, releasing the girls, who scrambled away.

"Enough!" Dostar cried.

The mist dissipated. Maximillion took two steps forward with a growl. "There's more of that if you really want to fight me right here."

Maximillion's hard gaze didn't waver, although Isadora's knees threatened to give out just looking at Dostar. After what felt like an eternity, the High Priest relaxed.

"Chatham Castle. One hour. I will meet you there with

that idiot Charles to negotiate an agreement, or the rest of my Network will descend and kill your witches in their sleep."

Maximillion nodded once.

"An hour."

Four of the West Guards moved forward, flames blossoming from their hands in glowing petals of emerald fire. They lobbed them into the air. Isadora held up an arm, protecting her eyes from the flash of light. Glass shattered, falling to the ground in shards as flames bit into the school. With one last insolent bow from the High Priest, the amassed West Guards vanished as quickly as they'd come.

The girls regained their voices as one. Terrified howls filled the air.

"Silence!" Maximillion called. Magic amplified his voice. "All of you. Gather what few possessions you can and congregate at the river. The West Guards are gone from Berry now. We'll find you shelter there."

The girls quieted. Sophie stood up on shaky legs, waving her thin fingers. "Come," she called, her voice cracking. Tears and smoke streaked her face. A limp cigar drooped from one hand. "With me, girls."

Maxmillion whipped around to face Isadora, murder in his eyes. A flash of something else lingered there. Was it fear?

"I'm leaving to speak with the blacksmith and make arrangements for the safety of the girls in the school, then I'll go save this damn Network from the West yet again. *You* will go to Pearl and stay there until I tell you it's safe. Do you understand?"

Isadora swallowed heavily. "Yes."

He cast her one last cutting glance, then whipped around, ran through the yard, and disappeared.

THE ATTACKS on the Central Network stopped an hour later, as soon as Dostar began negotiations with Charles, the Central Network High Priest and new Highest Witch.

Berry burned all the way to the soil. The flames wiped out the last of the crops and all the homes and stores—not even the farms were spared. The cows lay dead in the field, slaughtered, their guts spilled. Steam rose from their bellies, joining the haze that lay in a thick blanket over the land.

Baylee and all the girls settled in at the river, watched by Sophie, the blacksmith, and the other witches staying there. Pearl and Isadora remained locked inside Pearl's cottage in the trees. Pearl kept her curtains drawn and fires banked. Every now and then, a neighbor slipped up to the back door, murmured an update, and left. Despite the occasional news, nothing changed.

Pearl snored on the couch, clutching her empty coffee cup, while Isadora paced. Her thoughts whirled, driven by the temptation to slip back into the paths. She turned away in disgust. Her powers could have put her and Baylee in one of the worst situations imaginable. They could have died. She'd been wrong when it counted most.

Isadora felt the truth all the way to her bones—she couldn't handle the magic. It was too powerful. Too much. She'd failed at magic, just as she'd failed at being a Servant. Mam and Talis had been right all along. People were innately evil, prone to hurt, maim, and kill. Magic was used for ill. If *this* was life in the Network, no amount of candy, no happy festival, could be worth living in such terror.

She longed for home. For Mam's soothing tea. Daid's reassuring voice. Most of all, she longed for Sanna. Her wry humor. Her annoyed glances and discreet smiles. Living in the Network hadn't been fun. It had been new—but it had been hard. Magic required grueling, boring hours of work. New witches. Terrifying situations. Perhaps it wasn't worth it.

Maybe she could do more good at home.

Midnight slipped by. Then one. When the clock ticked toward two, Isadora stopped pacing and eyed Pearl, bleary-eyed but resolute.

"Forgive me, Pearl," she whispered.

CHAPTER

TWENTY

Isa,

I don't know where you are. I don't know what you're doing. There's not a lot of time to explain, so I won't. If I don't make it back from fighting Talis (I know, there's A LOT to explain), at least you'll know a little.

In short, Drago is a lie. Talis is evil. Daid is imprisoned. Mam is living with the Chandlers. Luteis (the wild dragon) and I are going to save the Dragonmasters (whom you know as the Servants). And I am now the only living leader of the dragons, as recognized by the forest goddess, Deasylva. I don't know what that means either.

(Oh, Finn is Drago's Servant now too. It's complicated.)

Amo, sister. If I don't come back, and this finds you, just stay away from Anguis. Don't try to go home.

—S

Sanna stared at the letter with a heavy heart. If she could just *see* Isadora, this would be so much easier. If the truth about their life in Anguis had been a shock for her, it would terrify Isa. She ran her fingers over the blank slate of wood, wishing it didn't have to be so impersonal. She wished for cool nights in the attic. Isadora's calming, comforting presence.

Her eyes trailed to the inheritance stump beneath the paper. The names still circled the outer edge in a broad, subtle ring. She ran the tip of her finger over the letters, barely able to make out the ancient runes.

Sanna stopped her finger and drew in a deep breath, keeping the swirl of magic on the outer edges, the closest names. Flickering remnants of Deasylva's power remained in her body. They flared, causing random parts of her to illuminate for a second or two before fading again.

She constantly stared at her arms. Touched her cheeks. She felt different. Bigger. Not so ... closed. Perhaps being the High Dragonmaster wouldn't be so bad. Even if she hadn't asked for it, didn't want it, and had no idea what it meant.

She shook her head, clearing the thoughts. A wall of heat moved behind her, ruffling her hair.

What is this?

Luteis peered over Sanna's shoulder as she re-read the letter one last time, hating it even more. With a scowl, she shoved it under a stone on top of the stump. Luteis's voice rang through her head now, almost like a shout. Whenever he spoke, his feelings spun into her, rippling like waves through her body.

"It's a letter for my sister."

Why?

She gave him a sidelong glance. "Just in case."

You are already predicting our demise?

"Just being cautious."

Hmmm.

"I'd be a fool not to be." She pushed past him to walk to the other side of the stump, ignoring the thrum of disapproval in his words. "Deasylva is gone now, exhausted after healing you. We've already fought Talis once, and *you* died. There's no way of knowing what will happen tonight."

At least we are in agreement that the attack must be tonight.

She hesitated, glancing over at him. "Yes. It's the last thing he'd expect. Surprise will be our only advantage."

Not our only one.

"What? Me being the High Dragonmaster?"

Yes.

"What does that even mean?"

I do not know.

"So, we'll just have to figure it out?"

Perhaps the rest of the meaning is not needed right now.

Her knife waited, freshly cleaned, on the ground. She slipped it into the sheath at her ankle and straightened. The ability to speak to all the dragons would help, but it wouldn't win the battle against Talis. Relying on Deasylva in any form would only lose the fight for them. They had to do this themselves—she knew that.

"Maybe."

She lifted her foot to the stump and laced her shoe to her knee. Trailing the laces that high again reassured her;

she felt like a piece of her old self had returned. Once she finished, she stepped over to Luteis's side and pressed a hand to his cool scales. They connected before they touched now.

We are ready.

"Wait. Not yet."

Sanna jumped aside, pried a rock from the ground, and reached under it. The silver arrow felt heavy in her hand, the viscous liquid moving back and forth. Somehow it had survived. No further silver had leaked out, despite their fight and their fall. Luteis tilted his head to the side. She stuffed the arrow in her vest and leaped onto his back with a wry smile.

"*Now* we're ready."

THE RUINS of Berry lay at Isadora's back, bathed in smoggy forest light.

She wore no cloak but carried a bag over her shoulder filled with food and fresh water. This time, she wouldn't transport. Her jumbled mind couldn't focus on Anguis—it returned too often to the school. To Pearl. Mostly to Maximillion.

She followed a vague, winding path. Her thoughts meandered with her feet. How would she find home? Would it find her? The paths beckoned, but she ignored them, led by the foolish hope that Letum Wood would simply guide her back. Hadn't it saved her when she failed at transportation? Wasn't *it* the source of her power and energy? She didn't know.

There was still so much she didn't know.

Darkness fell in cold drapes on her bare arms. She shivered and regretted, again, giving up her cloak for the stupid transportation spell. Animals skittered in the bracken. Glowing eyes blinked every now and then. This was a side of the forest she didn't recognize. The snap of a branch caught her attention. She froze and glanced into the canopy. Shadows hung like vines, and leaves rustled. The chitter of a squirrel fell silent. Isadora turned back around and stopped with a strangled cry.

A forest lion stood on the trail.

His hot breaths spiraled out in the icy air. The scent of rotted meat and wet fur surrounded him. Isadora leaned back, hands held up.

"Ho there, lion."

A low rumble bubbled in his throat. He lowered his head. His shaggy mane brushed the ground. Behind him, a thick tail whipped around in a maniacal frenzy, as if seeking a branch to hang from. He lifted a paw—at least the size of her chest—and shifted toward her.

She shuffled back.

"Easy, lion."

He leaned back, coiled, then sprang. She threw up her hands, calling out an incantation. The lion froze mid-leap, teeth bared. He remained there.

Isadora's breath caught. She swallowed and shifted back a step. The lion finally crashed to the trail and fell over. Saliva dripped from his pearly teeth. She cast another incantation to make him sleep. His eyes closed, and his body slackened. Isadora drew in a deep, steadying breath.

"Well, well. You *can* save your own life."

Isadora whipped around to find Maximillion blocking

the path. Glacial disapproval frosted his features. They stood face-to-face for several seconds.

"Maximillion," she whispered.

"I don't have the time to ask you what you're doing here," he snapped. "This certainly *isn't* the path back to your wretched family, for one. For another, you've made several idiotic decisions tonight, but this is decidedly the worst of them."

Isadora's nostrils flared. "I don't want to talk about this."

"This is your last opportunity to return to Berry under my tutelage."

"I want to go home."

"And I want peace for the Network. We all have to work for our rewards."

Tears filled her eyes. "I can't do it, Maximillion. I can't. You saw that tonight firsthand."

"So what?"

"I almost killed Baylee!"

"She's still alive and pickpocketing, the way she's always been."

"Only because of you!" she shouted. The words rippled through the empty, barren forest. Tears spilled onto her cheeks. "You can't follow me around forever, can you? I failed *twice*. All those girls could have died at the hands of the West Guards if you hadn't been there. Baylee and I could have been..."

"Or you might have been in a worse position if you'd acted differently."

"You can't prove that."

"Neither can you."

Isadora's bluster faded into a deep weariness. There

was no winning against Maximillion. She couldn't fathom why she even tried.

"You ask too much of me," she said. "It's too much to live out here. Everything is so much harder than it was supposed to be, and I wasn't…"

She trailed off, unable to say it.

"Another lie," he said with a frosty glare.

"It's true!"

"It's not!" he hissed, his eyes bright with fury. "It's an idea that you have in your thick head that you won't let go of. Why? *Why* do you think it's too much?"

"Because I'm not strong enough."

"Another lie."

"I can't do it. I've tried."

"Did you stop walking when you were little because you fell a few times? No. Did you stop writing letters because they were hideous? *No!* You kept going. Tell me something true, Isadora, or you're wasting our time."

"I wasn't supposed to keep failing!"

A deafening hush fell over the forest like a blanket. The words rang through the trees. She stared at him, stunned. A hand flew to her chest, protecting her heart. Maximillion let out a punctuated breath.

"Why?" He grabbed her shoulder. "Why are you failing?"

Tears filled her eyes. "I always failed at home. The dragons didn't choose me, for one. Then I didn't choose them. I couldn't go to school because of the headaches. Sewing? Hated it. Marrying Jesse? Didn't do that. I tried cooking and cleaning but failed spectacularly. I tried to *care* about the dragons, but I didn't and still don't. I failed in every single way a Servant could fail."

She turned away when a tear trailed down her cheek.

"The Network was supposed to be where I *didn't* fail. Magic, the powers, were supposed to be the thing that I did well. But I haven't. I keep failing at everything. As soon as I learn one thing, something new pops up that I don't know."

Maximillion let go of her.

"When you go into the magic, what do you see?" he asked.

"Paths."

"And what did you see the first time?"

Isadora hesitated. "S-sanna."

"Did you see whole wisps?"

"No."

"Did you see it in detail?"

"No."

"For yourself?"

"No," she whispered.

"Do you have headaches anymore?"

"No."

"Can you enter the magic on your own now?" His gaze bore deep into her.

She swallowed. "Yes."

"Do you know how to transport despite almost dying?"

"Yes."

"Do you know how to navigate life in the Network better than you did before?"

Understanding, tinged with shame, arose within her.

"Yes," she whispered.

"Then explain to me," he said, "how you have failed *everything* and should return to a place that offers nothing but further failure? Do you *really* think you can go back once you've had a taste of freedom? Do you really think you can succeed there by giving up here?"

Heat burned right over her heart, like a blanket of magma. Memories of Berry filled her mind. The Samhain festival. Cutting her hair. Doing magic as a part of her everyday life. Seeing new witches. Hadn't she just saved her own life using magic with the lion? So why didn't *that* count as progress?

The suffocating walls of Anguis waited ahead. Safe, but empty. A place to obey and fit in but forget herself and die inside. Was it really worth it? Was life in Anguis going to be better?

"No," she whispered.

Maximillion leaned closer. Juniper filled her nose. "Did you ever once think that you failed so much there because you didn't belong?" he whispered.

"No."

"Failure is the only damn way we learn. Have you failed? Yes. Will you fail more? All the time. And that's the *best* thing that can ever happen to you. When you stop failing, you stop learning. And then you're of no use to anyone."

Another tear dribbled down her cheek. She wiped it away with a sweep of her hand. She *had* accomplished great things despite imperfection. Despite adversity. Perhaps she'd expected too much. Life in a new world, alone, could hardly have been easier or less complicated than small little Anguis.

If she chose to go back to the Network now, the path would be even harder. Fraught with deeper dangers and more spectacular failures. War. Greed. Wayward magic. Hours and *hours* of boring analysis and work in the paths, not to mention separation from her family and everything she knew.

He stepped back, hesitating. For a moment, the

haughty, regal Maximillion disappeared, giving way to a flash of vulnerability. He looked like a little boy.

"If you don't go back," he said, "you can help me."

Isadora extricated herself from her thoughts. "How?"

His throat bobbed when he swallowed. "Help me save Watchers in the Eastern Network."

She sucked in a sharp breath, caught in the husky passion in his voice. All hints of vulnerability faded. Illumination brightened his eyes. He turned, pacing back and forth across the trail.

"I run an undercover operation that only a few witches know anything about. I save Watchers imprisoned by the Eastern Network and bring them to safety here in the Central Network."

Isadora's mouth dropped. "From Cecelia, you mean?"

"From Cecelia."

"But..."

The question stalled, lost amongst all the others. She cast about, stymied. Maximillion ran a mission of mercy. Of course. *Merciful,* she thought, remembering Maximillion's beating heart again.

"How long have you done this?" she asked.

He waved a hand. "Five years now? Can't be sure. Lucey was the missing link that finally brought it all together, and she appeared around then."

Isadora's eyes bugged out. "Lucey? She's part of this?"

"She does all the groundwork so I don't have to reveal my face. I use my connections to create the safety net and the escape plans. Lucey implements. We've saved over twenty Watchers so far." His expression clouded. "And lost six in the process, plus five support witches."

"Is Lucey gone now?"

"Yes. On a mission to the north boundary of the Eastern

Network. It's gone awry, unfortunately. Happened the same day as our last lesson. And yes, even Lucey fails, and she's been doing this for years."

Isadora recalled his strange, jumpy attitude with renewed clarity. Lucey had always been known for her strange habits. Gone often. Fatigued when she returned. Strangely quiet about her life and her choice to stay away from the rest of Anguis. All the details of her life had been so vague.

"Is she all right?"

"Fine. They're hiding out. As soon as they can get into Letum Wood, they'll be safe. The East won't go near the forest. I'll explain the details later. Do you see what you could do for us? You could turn the tides in our favor. You could anticipate issues for *other* witches before they happen."

"But I tried to do that with the attack. I-I was wrong."

"Because I haven't trained you, have I? I wouldn't take you onto my team until you understood your own abilities, which you don't. If you truly want a place to belong and a chance to change and see the world, this would be it."

He stared at her with such intensity that her heart quivered.

"What about Cecelia?"

"She's a problem but not an impossibility. And she doesn't know it's me. Not yet. She knows that someone has circumvented her time and time again, but we change the witches who work for us, and I stay out of sight. Lucey is a master of disguise, and she's not a Watcher, which is the key to our success. The Defenders can't detect her."

A thousand questions whirled through Isadora's mind. This was her chance. Her chance to fail on an epic scale. To see new things. To mold the magic for even greater results.

She could probably survive with all that she knew of the powers now. She *could* go back to Anguis and carve out something there. But she'd never really live.

She might fail, but at least she'd try. And sometimes succeed, the way she already had.

"I'll do it."

Maximillion lifted one eyebrow. "You mean it?"

"Yes." She smiled. "I'll come back to work with you and Lucey."

He blinked, opened his mouth, then shut it again. "Well … all right then. You realize you'll have to reckon with your powers soon enough, right? I'll never be able to work with you unless you trust the magic again. Which you clearly don't."

She nodded once. He was right. She'd have to face the distrust. She could feel it. But a deep weariness permeated her mind, and she wanted nothing more than to sleep.

"I know."

"That can be later, of course. Long day. Shall we go? I have a High Priest who's hyperventilating and a livid Council to deal with."

"Yes. I just—"

A whirl of gray flashed through her mind, followed by a familiar tug. She shook her head, disoriented by the strange shift. A feeling of dread filled her gut. No. Not now. Not when—Darkness swept over her.

The magic ripped her away.

Isadora blinked, disoriented by the forceful, unexpected shift. A flash of light burst from the ground in front of her and exploded. Paths tripled into the ring of trees, snaking through the ground amid countless gauzy images. Confusion packed the space, as teeming as the mayhem in Berry.

"No!" she called. "Not again!"

The paths shifted. Isadora covered her eyes to avoid seeing the confusion. Every attempt to close the magic met with blazing light. The powers burned too hot, too bright. She turned away.

"Let me out of here."

A wind whistled by, stirring her hair.

"What? You're going to explain it now? I didn't *ask* for this power. Are you going to tell me why you chose me?"

Wind whipped by in a fresh surge. She stumbled, barely catching herself. All the images disappeared as if whisked away. Smoke curled from the ground and evaporated. The forest remained a lone, haunted wood. Nothing more. She swallowed. Had she destroyed the magic? Forbidden it, so now it forbade her? Fear welled in her throat. She reached out.

"Wait!"

The empty darkness remained. When she pressed her hand to a trunk, she found the once-teeming life had fallen silent.

"Wait. I-I I didn't mean it. I just..."

A bright yellow leaf drifted lazily from the tops of the canopy. Her words rang back, echoing in the strange stillness.

"Stop, please. Don't leave. Come back. I-I don't know what ... I don't understand! Why me? Why did you choose me? There are so many others who..."

Her words trailed away. A fountain of light bubbled up

from the ground. The pieces climbed on each other, sliding, bouncing, sparkling until it stood as tall as she. The luminous fountain ended in a downward swirl, revealing a slender pair of shoulders, a head of hair cut at the shoulders, and bright, intelligent eyes. Her breath caught in her throat.

Herself.

A glittering version of herself stood across the way, filling the forest with quiet brilliance. She stood with her arms at her sides, her shoulders squared, her head tipped back, chin held high as if to say, *I know who I am.* The resolute tautness of her jaw, the stubborn set of her eyes. This was a girl who failed and didn't care. This was a girl who *tried.*

The wind whispered.

Powerful.

"Me?" she whispered, reaching out. Her fingers raked through the gauzy mist. "That's me?"

Powerful.

Luster pulsed from within her. Something hot raced through her body. Two trails branched out behind her. One led back to her familiar childhood home, with its sharp, sloping roof and wood darkened with mist and time. Skinny paths led away from it, stark and barren.

The other path led back to Berry. Wisps sprang up behind it, spreading into the trees. Witches. Thousands of witches stared up at her with warm expressions. Smiles. Tears. Some of them frightened, reaching for her. Others weeping. Flashes of the Network appeared in between. Mountains. Trees. Cliffs. Rivers. Stores. Houses. Farms. Factories. Foreign lands. Oceans. Things she would never see if she didn't have the magic.

"That's why you chose me," she whispered. "Because I *wasn't* a true Servant at heart."

Isadora canted her head back to peer into the canopy. Whatever intelligence or power controlled this magic, whether it was tied to Letum Wood or not, knew her. Really knew her. She could feel it deep in her bones.

"I understand."

Something inside her ripped away, like a great rending of her heart. The image of herself lifted one fist. Black sand drifted from it, released into the breeze. Through it, Isadora could make out a familiar picture. Anguis.

The light exploded again. She reared back just as the image of herself disappeared. The space was wiped clean, leaving nothing but the circle of trees. Another shimmering path appeared at her feet, leading to a bright wisp that glowed with stunning intensity.

Sanna.

Sanna stood in front of Isadora. Color infused her now. The ethereal edges had faded, leaving a solid image in their wake. Every freckle showed itself. The curve of her teeth, her lips. Her living ferocity. Sanna soared on the back of a dragon, resting at the juncture of his shoulders. Her hair trailed behind her into the night—as if they were flying. Creases drew across her brow. She frowned, biting her bottom lip. Something about her seemed ... luminescent. The wild dragon looked to the left, fire illuminating his face with a red-hot rage.

A voice whispered.

Danger.

Sanna only bit her bottom lip when afraid. "What do you fear?" Isadora murmured, longing to reach out and touch her sister. The answer came with chilling force.

Losing the dragons.

Nothing would provoke true fear in Sanna except danger to the dragons. Nothing but a life-or-death situation would motivate her to *fly* a dragon.

Had poachers returned?

Sanna changed. The light faded, then emerged into someone new. Someone familiar. Isadora's breath caught. A shocking image unfurled in front of her—one she couldn't believe. Her breath stalled. Her blood turned to slush.

"No," she breathed.

She closed the magic and transported without explaining to Maximillion, fearing she was already too late.

LUTEIS SOARED IN A BROAD, high circle over the meadow, hidden in a bank of sticky clouds. Every now and then he'd drop down, long enough to give Sanna a view of the meadow, and rise back up.

Sanna peered over his shoulder through the patchy fog. Only one lighter spot, indicating the meadow, broke the obsidian puddles below. The occasional wink of fire flickered in the branches, no doubt from the Servants. From what she could see, Talis had called a meeting of the brood in the meadow. Finn, Elliot, and Jesse would be required to attend, with Finn speaking for Talis instead of Daid.

Are you ready?

"Is it possible?"

Perhaps not. Let us finish it.

"Yes," she said quietly. "Let's save the brood."

Prepare yourself.

Luteis's chest expanded in a deep breath moments

before they plunged. He dropped, plummeting in a straight line. Her stomach climbed into her throat. Wind roared past her ears, mocking the steady *thud thud thud* of her heart. Her braids unraveled, whipping behind her in long banners, but the magic held her tight against his scaly back.

They sailed into the forest, darting past sprawling branches and tangled vines. Luteis spread his wings to slow their progress as they neared the ground. Sanna braced herself just as Luteis slammed into the meadow. Clods of dirt flew into the air, broken by the heavy crush of his body. The circle of dragons that had lined the meadow wheeled back, rushing for the trees. Sanna jumped to her feet, wielded her knife, and snarled, her hair wild around her shoulders.

"Talis! Your fight is with me."

Luteis crouched, back arched, nostrils flaring. His wings stretched out, filling the meadow with his massive presence. Yellow firelight glowed in the branches as Servants sprinted away, delving deeper into the trees. Low murmurs sang in her mind—too distant to understand. She frowned. Who was talking in her head? Before she could figure it out, a reverberating shout split the air, announcing Talis's arrival.

Ah, Luteis purred. *So comes our prey.*

Out of the depths, a pair of bright eyes flickered. A sapphire face, contorted with rage, entered the meadow. Talis slithered into the light, forked tongue flicking. Score marks crossed his neck and back, which were still healing from Luteis's deep talons.

You have returned, Talis said. *Did Deasylva heal you?*

"Maybe *I* healed him, you foul idiot," Sanna called.

Unlikely. Isn't it strange, Sanna, that Deasylva should heal the dragon who promised to be her slave and do what she cannot? Yet, she wouldn't heal or save all those who died in the massacre. Is it odd? Or is it just the way it is?

"She really doesn't like *you*, Talis. That's what this is all about."

Talis paused, regarding her through slitted eyes.

Are you her messenger then?

"Messenger?"

Yes, he hissed. *You are. The magic of the High Dragonmaster is within you. Locked up, most likely. But there. I haven't felt power like this in many, many years. Over a hundred and fifty, to be exact. How disappointing of you. Do you actually think you can defeat me and restore some inherited legacy you know nothing about? Even with Deasylva's blessing?*

"There's not a doubt in my mind."

Do you even know what it means to be the High Dragonmaster?

She hesitated, gripping her knife even tighter. She didn't—and they both knew it. Before she could respond, a fireball raced across the meadow, headed right for her. Sanna ducked on instinct. Luteis dodged to the side, narrowly missing it. It streaked by them with a blast of heat. Talis barked a grating laugh.

What a fool! You don't even know your own magic.

"Says the dragon who banished magic."

A decision born from experience. I've seen magic, Sanna. I know what's out there. Witches with magic and power and fire. Magic that can paralyze a dragon while witches hack them to death. Spells that bring blindness. Magical fire that burns and burns and burns without stopping. Yes, I know of magic. Do you?

The silver arrow rubbed against her chest, digging into her skin with its sharp, pointed edge.

"I know enough."

Her response sounded weak, like a petulant child.

Then what is that mark on your wrist?

Sanna glanced down, startled to find a black symbol there. The furled wing of a dragon. She frowned. Where had—

The sign of the Dragonmaster. But you knew that already, didn't you? Because you know your own magic so well. Or did Deasylva bestow that mark upon you without asking? Without warning?

She glanced up. Luteis snarled as Talis slipped back into the shadows, stalking them along the meadow's perimeter. The whispers in her mind surged, coalescing into a strange mix of unfamiliar voices. The other dragons, no doubt. There was nothing here that could speak so loudly or in such great numbers. What were they saying?

Luteis crouched and tracked Talis's every movement. A shadow surged out of the trees, but Talis snapped at it. It stopped.

Sanna shook her head, breaking out of her thoughts.

"This is your last chance, Talis. End your reign of tyranny, or we'll end it for you."

He laughed again. *Will you? Will you bring peace to the brood? Will you shatter one hundred and fifty years of safety simply because you're a wild thing who wants everyone to follow her way?*

"Peace without lies is what I offer. Without false gods. Without deceit!"

And you'll explain to all these dragons why violently killing me was the right thing to do? You will lead them? Provide them safety from the ills of Letum Wood? Show them how to be wild dragons? You, witch girl, who know so much?

Her confidence faltered. She hadn't exactly seen it that way when speaking to Luteis and Deasylva. From the way Luteis stilled, she wondered if he hadn't either.

"Y-yes."

Talis stopped, peering at her from the darkness. *What is it you hear, Sanna? Tell me what the voices are telling you, O Mighty High Dragonmaster.*

She paused. The low, murmuring hum had turned to whispers again. Dozens of voices drifted through her mind. This time, she understood them.

She means to kill him.

Frightening.

More violence against dragons.

The Servant revolution has begun, as he predicted.

We shall die without him.

Sanna turned, studying the backdrop of Letum Wood. No dragon had ventured out of it. Were they afraid of her? She had a mark on her wrist she knew nothing about, and all the dragons in her mind. What was happening? Could they read her thoughts? Did they know her fear? Did they understand her?

Yes, Talis drawled. *You are finally beginning to see just what Deasylva has thrust upon you. Did you agree to this new appointment? Did you agree to become the High Dragonmaster? I doubt it.*

Sanna hesitated. Yes ... but no.

Deasylva makes her own rules.

"As have you."

To restore order to the chaos she permitted, yes. Don't you see it, Sanna? Deasylva is just like me. If you kill me, will you really restore peace? Will it really be so much better with a goddess who expects blind obedience and enacts her will without explanation?

Talis advanced into the meadow again, his powerful shoulders rippling with every step. He spread his leathery wings, casting a heavy shadow.

"Luteis," she whispered. "What do I believe?"

I do not know myself.

One hundred and fifty years ago, Talis said, *poachers descended with magic and silver, paralyzing my parents and murdering them before my very eyes. I was thirty, barely out of adolescence. I gathered the hatchlings younger than me and fled. We hid until it ended. When we returned, we were the only dragons left alive.*

The poachers had tortured, murdered, and skinned our family members. From that disaster, I protected the brood. The poachers found us because they had seen us while we flew, hunting for ourselves. The remaining witches who hadn't been slaughtered were barely alive. We did the best we could with no help from Deasylva.

Luteis straightened, snarling. *And yet you have killed dragons who left your dominion, haven't you?* he snapped.

To save the brood, I would do anything.

You murdered my mam.

Talis hesitated. The surge of voices in the background escalated. Questions. Exclamations of disbelief.

Yes. For the good of the brood, Talis said. *She was a danger to our safety.*

The voices rose again, fresh with fear. Amongst the glittering scales that speckled the darkness was a familiar golden hue. Thryis. Behind him, crimson. Rubeis. Emerald, rosy pink, pewter gray. Colors ringed the meadow now. All the dragons had come forward and spoke to her mind at once.

Deasylva? Who do they speak of?

What of Drago?

Of whom does he speak?

Luna! He must be born of Luna.

Sanna's mind scrambled through the mess that

Deasylva had just plunged her into. In the midst of it swirled the ugly truth. The damning uncertainty. The realization that being aligned with Deasylva didn't sit any better with her than being aligned with Talis.

Despite Deasylva's miraculous healings, Sanna couldn't deny her own suspicions about the goddess. Why did Deasyvla act without apparent rule? Why hadn't she stopped the Great Massacre?

The truth came to her all at once, in a breathless way. Sanna didn't want to save Drago *or* Deasylva *or* Talis. Her allegiance didn't lie with them. It never had. She wanted to save the dragons. The forest. The Servants.

That was her purpose.

"I'm not aligned with anyone," she called. "Not Deasylva. Not you. Not your false god Drago. I'm here to take care of the trees, the forest, and the dragons. *That* is who I'm the messenger for. That is who I'm here to help. Your oppressive reign has consequences you aren't aware of. Because dragons are stuck in Anguis, the forest is dying. Beluas are taking over. The food shortage? That's your fault, Talis! One more decade and all of Letum Wood will be gone. Did you think of that?"

Luteis shuffled to the right, staying just out of range of Talis's swinging tail. The dragons surged in conversation again, but Sanna forced them to the back of her mind.

This is your last chance, Luteis said to Talis. *Your chance to forgo violence and step down.*

Or what?

We fight to the death.

The words sent a chill through Sanna's body.

As you say, Talis hissed. *Not even the High Dragonmaster can spare your life against mine. Certainly not one with no idea what she's doing with the magic.*

Luteis crouched with a snarl. Talis reared back and screamed before charging across the meadow. Sanna braced herself just before they threw their massive bodies against one another in a bone-shattering crash.

Luteis stumbled. Talis dug his talons into the ground as he slid back, leaving deep score marks in the ground. Once Luteis righted himself, he swung his tail and slammed it into Talis's foreleg. Talis absorbed the blow by shuffling to the side. Both roared, rattling Sanna's teeth. When Talis threw fire, the flames burned a thick, deep cobalt.

"Secundum!" she cried.

Heat expanded through the meadow, charging the air like a current of lightning. Luteis shrank back as the scorching flames crawled toward them. Sanna ducked behind his shoulders. He spun and blocked the flames with his body. His scales sizzled in the heat. Once the onslaught stopped, Luteis threw his own secundum, the edges tinged a deep, coppery orange. Talis blew through it, slinking back into the trees. Luteis stalked him. Dry grasses burned in their wake.

Deasylva doesn't fight her own battles because of fear! Talis hissed. *Fear of fire. Of flame. Of death that she can't control. I know the feeling well.*

He breathed his secundum onto a nearby tree, devouring the moss and vines that clung to it.

"No!" Sanna cried.

The feeling of being unable to stop the pain.

Wild, terrified shrieks echoed in Sanna's mind. Letum Wood. The trees? She could hear Letum Wood now? Sanna closed her eyes, grimacing. Talis stalked to another tree and set it on fire with his crackling breath. The dead undergrowth on the forest floor ignited like lamp oil.

"Stop!"

Tempting, isn't it? To exercise control? To inflict pain so your enemy knows how it feels?

The meadow caught fire. Luteis slipped away from the worst of it, protecting Sanna. For a terrifying moment, Talis was out of sight, lost in the thick darkness.

"Where is he?" she hissed.

Right behind you, Talis said.

Luteis roared when Talis raked his claws down his back legs. Sanna leapt onto Luteis's neck, just missing the tip of Talis's talon. Blood spewed into the air behind them. Luteis whipped around.

"Stop!" Sanna screamed.

You would rule this brood? Talis thundered. *You who hides behind a wild dragon who knows nothing of our heritage?*

Dragons dodged the spreading fire, their marbled scales winking in the deep night. Leaves shriveled. Smoke drifted through the meadow with an acrid scent. Moss dripped to the ground, glittering with sparks.

Talis set another tree on fire and slipped away. The flames raced up the trunk. Sanna reached for the arrow, wrapping her hand firmly around the shaft. Talis tipped his head back to call into the trees. Luteis edged closer.

How does it feel, Deasylva? he called. *Does the burning frighten your trees?*

A falling branch, billowing with flames, tumbled downward. Talis slithered back, narrowly avoiding it. With a cry, Sanna sprinted down Luteis's back and threw herself across the space between them. She landed on Talis's left wing and scrambled for purchase. He bucked, throwing her off. She slammed into a tree and fell to the ground in a ball.

Silver! he hissed, eyes narrowed on her left hand. *You attack me with an arrow filled with silver, just like the poachers of old!*

Talis dug his talons into the mulchy earth, bent his legs, and sprang into the air. With wings beating, he climbed above the meadow and flew with surprising speed. A wide shadow fell on the gathering smoke as he soared overhead.

Sanna growled. Talis broke Cara's wings and expected Thryis to remove his but flew with strength and agility that required practice. *He* hadn't stopped flying all these years! He had even faked being unable to fly!

"*Talis!*" she screamed. "You're a coward! You would maim and paralyze a dragon like Cara but give yourself free rein of the sky. Cara, who did nothing wrong!"

The dragons' voices exploded in her mind again. Their rampant confusion bogged her down, slowing her thoughts. She growled and put a hand to her head, unable to think. Luteis grabbed Sanna with a talon.

Are you well? he asked.

"Fine," she muttered with gritted teeth. "We have to go after him."

Immediately.

She vaulted onto Luteis's back and stood on the juncture of his shoulders. They climbed into the sky after Talis, dodging his glinting claw. She studied the smoky sky as they gained altitude. In her mind, she sensed shock rippling through the other dragons.

He flies.

Silver. She betrays us with silver!

We will all die.

"The air is your glory, Luteis. Take it."

With pleasure.

They rose together into the dark sky, illuminated by beams of moonlight. Beneath them, Letum Wood smoldered in great bellows of smoke. Talis circled overhead in a smooth glide. His legs hung beneath him, talons curled. Luteis threw fire, soared through it, and attacked.

Talis and Luteis collided again. Sanna dropped back to her butt. She clung to Luteis's neck and hugged him with her knees. Talis flailed mid-air before he caught his balance and righted.

Luteis whirled, ramming his tail into Talis's right flank. Talis snapped for it, narrowly missing, and dove toward Sanna. Luteis banked sharply to the left, avoiding Talis's careening wings but exposing his underbelly. Talis snatched Luteis's claws with his, dug his talons deep into the webbing, and yanked. Luteis screamed as they spun into a spiral.

Sanna ducked her chin into her chest and muffled her panic as they wheeled around again and again, talon clinging to talon. The dragons' wings unfurled in a strange, disorienting dance. Letum Wood approached as they plummeted. She shoved the arrow back into her shirt.

"Luteis!" she screamed. "Get away now!"

With belches of fire, both dragons released each other and spun into the high canopy. Branches sped by them, and leaves whipped Sanna's face.

Luteis plowed into a tree trunk with a sickening *crack*. Sanna hit next. A branch rushed up to meet her, cracking her ribs. Her shirt stuck in the tree, anchoring her as Luteis fell away.

Sanna dropped through the trees, a scream in her throat.

Sanna landed flat on her back.

A branch halfway down had caught her. Her ribs burned as she struggled for breath and fought off the blackness clouding the edges of her vision. She scrambled for a hold as her body began to fall again, and she finally grasped a half-loosened vine. Just when the world began to spin, her ribs unlocked. Her lungs expanded, banishing the onset of unconsciousness.

She hauled herself back onto the branch with a gasp of pain. Except for the distant roar of fire, a strange silence permeated the forest. Luteis was nowhere in sight. The sky remained empty, filled with glittering stars, gauzy smoke, and the promise of dawn. She pushed up, grimaced through the pain, and reached for the arrow. Still here. It had cut her skin and would leave a bruise, but no silver had escaped.

Fire glittered through the web of branches. The frenzied wails crescendoed in her mind. Whispers from the dragons played at the edges of her consciousness, too distant to understand. She dropped off the branch and scrambled down the tree.

I'll grant you one last chance, Sanna of the witches, Talis hissed. *Align yourself with me, and spare the brood.*

"You flatter yourself as the only leader."

I know what I am. It's not me they fear. It's not even Drago they fear. That's the difference between you and me. I know the secret, and you don't.

She grabbed a vine and rode it to the forest floor. Her heart gave a little hiccup when she landed on her feet again, palms burning. Luteis lay halfway into the meadow, his body limp. Blood pooled beneath him. His right wing was skewed at an odd angle again. Beyond him, colors dotted the darkness. The chorus of dragons continued in the background.

Talis loomed over Luteis now, backlit by a blaze of fire. His wild eyes were half-crazed. Blood spilled down his neck in hot rivulets. There would be no defeating him here. She'd have to pull him away, lead him somewhere else until Luteis could recover.

A fireball soared past her left ear, splattering against a tree. She ducked. The bark crackled behind her, peeling away in great pieces. She whirled around and narrowly dodged another burst of fire. Ash and embers scattered.

Talis advanced.

Sanna stumbled back. "It can be better than this, Talis! We don't have to hurt each other."

He breathed out a plume of cobalt fire. She ducked behind another tree.

It's too late for that.

Sanna darted away. Logs fell, slamming to the ground. Cinders plumed above her in blazes of crimson. She dodged to avoid a pocket of exploding sap. Talis followed, crashing behind her. His fire consumed a tree as she ran past it. She grabbed the arrow out of her inner pocket and clutched it in her fist.

You are alone, little girl. You cannot face a dragon such as me, just as you cannot replace me.

A great barrier appeared in front of her as she sprinted away. Piles of trees. Curtains of vines and moss. The edge of Anguis. She held her breath, climbed past the ivy that had shriveled in the growing flames, stood on top of the wall, and leapt to the ground.

Her ankle twisted, but she pushed through it. Her heart pounded under her ribs as she ran, searching. Behind her, Talis followed with a roar. He shoved through the border, sending logs and sticks flying through the air. Fire nipped at her heels, blistering her skin. The whispers of the dragons returned to her mind as she raced through the forest.

She cannot stand against Talis.
Talis will never allow us to die.
She is killing us with silver. She's a poacher!
He killed Luna.
Cara's wings are gone.
He can fly.

A wall of burning trees crossed the footpath ahead of her. She skidded to a stop. How had the fire spread so far so quickly? It must have spread from another part of the meadow. The flames greedily gobbled all the tired, aged undergrowth and deadfall. Everything burned.

Except for a strange, coiling tree in the middle of the inferno.

Mucus-coated vines dangled not far away, as if merely inconvenienced by the raging firestorm. She smacked one away as it reached for her. A cohereo tree. Just as she'd hoped. Talis's voice slithered through her mind.

The time of your rebellion has ended.

Sanna whipped around, breathless.

"You want me?" she screamed, arrow held in front of her. "Come and get me!"

He ran. Sanna held her ground until he was only a few paces away, grabbed a sticky vine, and threw it. It smacked into his neck. She dodged to the side. Talis continued, running straight into the tree. More vines followed. They reached out and grasped his legs. His neck. His shoulders. They tangled him in his own feet in a baptism of gooey mucus.

He flailed, threw fire, and tripped over himself until the tenacious ropes held him suspended just off the ground.

His wings crashed into a nearby tree, sending a burning branch to the forest floor.

"It doesn't have to be like this, Talis!" she shouted. Another vine wrapped around his chest to anchor him more firmly. He threw secundum but only for a few seconds. Was he tiring? "We can work together."

The time for witches' power has passed!

Crackling sapphire flames darted toward her. Sanna ducked behind a fallen tree. More of the fire consumed the forest. It would hem her in soon. Fire like this wouldn't kill Talis, but it would kill her. She tightened her hold on the arrow and straightened.

"You want safety, just like the rest of us," she called over the roar. "But I want more than that. I want equality for witches and dragons and the forest."

A tree fell behind her. Embers danced into her hair. She smacked them away. Talis struggled against the cohereo vines, spraying ropes of fire. She shrank back.

Foul witch! There is no equality. There was no one else. I saved them.

The whispers continued in the background—more dragons. More words. Talis's voice boomed above all the others. With it came his angst, his deepest emotions, as if he cracked open a jeweled heart to reveal a bruised interior. She saw the deep-rooted fear that had spawned his control. Understood the desperate space it bubbled from.

"You said that the dragons didn't fear you or Drago. You were right. They fear *everything*. They fear the world. They fear themselves. They fear chaos and disorder and having to take care of themselves. That is what you gave them. That is the legacy you want to continue."

I gave them life.

"You gave them fear! Your control went too far. You changed the natural order."

I did what I had to.

Sanna drew in a deep breath. "Yes. You did. You did something wonderful—you saved witches, dragons, and the legacy. But now it's time for something more. It's time to live without fear. To live and breathe and die and fly and hunt. To save the forest. To save the *dragons*. Not you. Not Deasylva. Not Drago. This isn't about some god or goddess. It's about the dragons, the Dragonmasters, and the forest."

She ran her thumb along the shaft of the arrow. He paused, eyeing her. Something flickered in his gaze, rooted deep in a recess of his soul that she doubted he knew was there.

Sanna pulled her arm back ...

... and threw the arrow into the ground between them.

"Work with me, Talis. I will not destroy you. Let us restore the honor of wild dragons and Dragonmasters and Letum Wood. Together. We all depend on each other. Without one, all will fall."

A long silence fell, even in her mind, as if all the dragons paused to await his response. Fire crackled, and heat surged around her.

You would spare me for this cause? he asked.

"For the brood, my home, and my family, yes."

His nostrils flared. He blinked. Blue flames built in the back of his mouth.

No. The word tore out of his throat with a deep, wrenching cry. *No, we can't. Freedom brings death. No one can protect the brood as I can—and have. Last time we had a High Dragonmaster, everything fell apart.*

Fire coiled out of his throat. He shrieked, sending the

flames in a long tongue, racing right for her chest. Sanna threw her hands over her head and ducked.

A guttural cry followed.

"Talis, no!"

Talis stopped, struck dumb as Daid stumbled between them. For the space of five seconds, he stood there, panting. His face was gaunt and thin, and his clothes threadbare and patchy. Broken chains hung from his ankles and wrists. Just behind him was Isadora, face stricken with fear and combed with dirt, sweat, and soot. Her hair drooped on her shoulders in ragged strands.

"You controlled me," Daid cried. "All my life you used me like a puppet. And now, when I did nothing wrong, you tried to say that this was my fault. It's not! All of this is your fault. You will always reign with control and fear. Always! It's not right."

What is this? Talis hissed, thrashing.

"*The Chronicles,*" Daid said. "There are mistakes. You said Drago wrote it. That it was perfection. But you made mistakes. I hadn't seen it before, but I did when you forced me to read it over and over and over. There shouldn't *be* mistakes. Don't you see? That means Drago's word isn't perfect. You claimed he was *perfect*!" A rangy, half-hysterical laugh bubbled out of Daid. "Which means Drago isn't real. For a century and a half, you've lied to us. You're the traitor. The dictator. And now you would kill my daughter when she seeks peace? No more."

Daid plucked the arrow from the ground. With a cry, he bolted across the burning embers and plunged it into Talis's heart. The arrow disappeared into Talis's massive body, shoved there by Daid's mighty arm.

Talis reared back, screaming. Blood boiled out of his chest and poured onto Daid, who collapsed to his knees.

The blood sizzled on the flames below, billowing into a thick smoke. Isadora darted forward and yanked Daid back just as Talis's body slumped forward. Sanna shot to her feet.

"Daid!"

He struggled to stand again. Isadora ducked under one of his arms. "His other arm!" she shouted to Sanna. "Grab it! We have to go."

Smoke trailed out of Talis's mouth, streaming toward the sky. Together, Sanna and Isadora pulled Daid away, setting him near an unaffected tree. Sanna hesitated, then re-approached Talis. The silver wouldn't kill him, but the arrow in his heart would.

"You began in honor," she said, pressing a hand to his snout. "You were no monster then. But fear overtook you, and you lived in fear too long. I don't want that for the rest of the dragons or the forest or the witches. I'm sorry."

His eyes closed, then opened again. He let out a long, slow breath. She sensed a fading of life. A tangible sigh of settling, expiring magic in his twitchy limbs. In the way his long breath stretched, never expanding. Always ending.

"I will honor the good things you did," Sanna whispered. Tears built in her throat.

Talis closed his eyes for the last time.

CHAPTER

TWENTY-ONE

Isadora peered into the tangled canopy.

Scorch marks marred the trunks with inky fingers. Soot lingered everywhere, even in the air. She seemed to sneeze every ten minutes. Behind her, their home—burned down like the rest of Anguis—was nothing more than a charred pile of ruins. Nothing remained of her previous life.

A fitting end.

A thin layer of frost coated the forest in a saccharine dress. The delicate winter signatures swirled like a lattice over the remaining trees. Winter wouldn't be far away now. A horrid time to lose a house.

Her thoughts ran to Maximillion. To Baylee and Pearl. To the burned ruins of Berry *and* Anguis. Only three days had passed since Talis's death and the destruction of Anguis, but it seemed as if it had been years. Her eagerness to return to Berry, even in its devastated state, had caught up with her. She itched to go back. And she would. Soon.

Mam and Daid spoke quietly behind her. In the weeks since she'd last seen him, Daid had seemed to age years.

Even Mam was different. Thick lines of stress tightened around her eyes. She was plagued by perpetual weakness and heart flutters. Still, she seemed better today than yesterday, and a determined gleam filled her hazel eyes now that Daid had returned. Alive.

The sound of crunching leaves heralded the witch Isadora wanted to speak to most. Seconds later, a familiar pair of sandals strapped all the way up to the knee dropped down from the trees in front of her.

Isadora grinned. "*Avay,* sister."

Sanna studied her with practiced ease. "*Avay,*" she finally said. "You're leaving, aren't you?"

"Yes."

"I can tell by the look on your face. Traitor." A shadow passed over Sanna's eyes.

They'd spoken long into the night, curled together near the fire, as they caught up on all that had happened. Isadora wasn't surprised Sanna felt hurt at her leaving. Isadora could see the pain there. She couldn't deny feeling it herself. Walking away from Sanna felt like losing a piece of her heart.

"It's where I can do the most good, Sanna. I belong there."

Sanna quirked one eyebrow and betrayed the first hint of a smile. "You always *were* kind of an outsider here, weren't you?"

"I was."

Sanna sobered. "Don't you belong with me?"

"Yes. And you'll always have me. But I can't grow here. I can't really help witches the way I want to while in Anguis."

"Then what now? You said the school you attended was burned down as well."

"Perhaps. There may be some of it left over. But school

isn't where I'll be staying now. Maximillion and I will be working together. I imagine I'll be with Pearl."

"And you want to do this? If there are as many wars as you say, why would you want to go back?"

Isadora pressed a hand over her heart. "Because I know I'll fail."

Sanna scrunched up her face in question, then sighed. "All right. That makes *no* sense, but I see you want it. So go. With my blessing, although I don't like it. Sister-witches shouldn't be parted. *You* shouldn't leave the forest."

"I'll never be far away. Be careful on your trip?"

Sanna peered past her into the forest with a grimace. "Probably not, but we'll try. Finding a new place to house this many witches and all our dragons won't be easy. Not with winter settling in soon. It'll be a rough few weeks. I'll be satisfied if we can at least get crude structures set up just to get through the cold months. Not to mention teaching the dragons to fly and hunt and—"

Isadora laughed. "I get it. I get it. Sounds like you have some challenges ahead of you. Let me know if I can help. Teach magic, or something."

Sanna's nose wrinkled. "We'll be fine."

"I didn't get a chance to apologize to Jesse for every-thing that happened. Could you—"

"He's fine. Don't worry about it."

Isadora threw her arms around Sanna's strong, lithe figure. She closed her eyes and sucked in a deep breath. Sanna smelled like forest and fire and everything in between. When she pulled away, tears blurred her vision.

Sanna swallowed hard. "Don't wait so long to come back to see us, all right?" she whispered, voice husky.

"Send word with Lucey of where you've gone, and I

won't. I can transport with ease now, so I can come anytime."

Sanna nodded once. "I love you, Isa."

"I love you too, Sanna."

We are not pleased with what has happened. But we accept it.

Sanna stared up at Rubeis. His warm, sparkling body loomed over her, the ruby, diamond-shaped flecks standing out on his scales. He had a wider snout than most dragons, with stubby horns and a shorter neck, but understanding glittered in his eyes. His firm decisions and outspoken opinion would make him a worthy replacement for Talis. Sanna didn't envy him his job.

"We can't take back the past."

We will move forward. For now.

She thought of the ruins. The books and scrolls that had been burned in the massacre—erasing their heritage. She thought of flying with Luteis. Feeling the merging. Understanding that, in him, she had a partner. A best friend. Would the other dragons desire such a connection with witches? Or was it too late?

Charred forest encircled the meadow as far as her eye could see. A month had passed. Everything had cooled. A layer of frost and snow covered the ash on the ground. The deadwood and saplings were gone—the ancient trees showed blackened rings, but lived. All had burned, including the houses and the shelter. Despite the rampant death, a sense of renewed life permeated the wintry forest.

Hope.

Luteis shifted behind her, his breath a warm caress on her skin. His broken wing had long since healed. Daid watched from a few paces away where he rested in the old wicker chair under Mam's watchful gaze. She was dutiful, even in her own exhaustion. Not far away, the hatchlings rolled over each other. Cara waited in the trees, standing apart.

"The dragons are free to choose whether they want to merge with a witch, of course," Sanna said. "But all dragons must learn to hunt on their own."

Rubeis huffed.

The brood is not ready for such a thing.

"As we've agreed, Luteis will be happy to teach both flight and hunting. If dragons refuse to participate, that is your issue to take care of as the temporary liaison between witch and dragon."

The bounds of our agreement begin immediately, I presume.

"Yes. There is no food left here."

Then we must leave.

"I agree."

Rubeis peered over his shoulder at the dragons waiting, shoulder to shoulder, in a half-circle behind him. They stared at Sanna with dull, distrustful gazes. Not even the great beasts of the forest were immune to feelings of shock and grief, she'd learned. Or betrayal. She still heard them in her head. Didn't know how to stop hearing them, if she could, but she allowed Rubeis, as the emissary, to comfort them.

So it begins, Rubeis drawled, his voice guttural and low. *The Servants are gone. The new age of the Dragonmaster is here.*

"No. The new age of Letum Wood, the dragons, *and* the Dragonmasters."

EPILOGUE

S anna pressed her fingertips into the trunk of the ancient tree and waited. Less than a minute passed before a white light appeared in the bark.

You have come.

"Not for you," Sanna said. "I didn't do any of that for you. You and I have a few things to work out before I'm willing to do anything else."

I am aware.

"It was you, wasn't it? That helped me save the hatchlings. You dropped the vine. Sent the sulfurous fumes from the dirt when the lions were going to overwhelm us. You had the tree pull me from the stream after the fish bit me."

Yes.

Sanna scowled. "In light of recent events, however, you haven't given me much reason to trust you. So, let's be honest now. Are you using me? Am I just another pawn in your greater game? You made me High Dragonmaster without me knowing it."

I did.

"Why?"

Greater things stir in Alkarra than you are aware of. What I do, I do out of mercy. Out of a desire for all to live.

"That doesn't make any sense."

Not now, but it will soon. I must stay powers stronger than you can imagine. Some powers that not even a goddess can prevent.

"What does that mean?"

Sanna's blood chilled as three small letters surfaced, gleaming a bright white.

War.

THE END

FLIGHT

Don't miss the next thrilling installment of the Dragonmaster Trilogy in the book *FLIGHT*. Here's an exclusive sneak peek just for you.

THE CHILLY FINGERS of winter crept into Isadora Spence's carriage through gaps in the door. She frowned at the wide cracks and pulled her cloak more tightly around her shoulders.

Winter was *so* intrusive.

The carriage wheels creaked with every jolt, both seemingly threatening to collapse and announcing their exact location. Could the traveling box be any louder? Or older? Maximillion likely chose it on purpose—just to make her more uncomfortable. Any minute now and the faded cushions beneath her would break their last string and split in half.

Still, it was safer than being out there.

A thick band of darkness stretched across the horizon, no doubt teeming with Defenders waiting to attack. The Defenders' steep hatred of Watchers seemed mandatory. As if they knew this was her first raid, her first attempt to save an innocent Watcher from their famed interrogations, as a member of Maximillion's rogue force that protected Watchers—the Advocacy.

Unable to bear the darkness anymore, she glanced at her hands. Enough gauzy moonlight slanted through the windows to highlight thick, ropy veins under her translucent skin. Her back curved into a hump. In the reflection of the window, an old woman stared back through different-colored eyes. No matter what kind of transformative magic she attempted, her eyes remained distinctively off. Like Maximillion's—only his were far subtler. Indistinguishable, really. Much like his emotions. Only now, her eyes were rheumy, red-rimmed.

Terrified.

A girl in her early teens sat across from her. Bright, wide eyes peered out of a heart-shaped face. Unassuming. Naive, even, with her perky nose and bowtie lips. No one would imagine she was a powerful witch beneath layers of meticulous transformation spells. The girl caught her eye and winked. Lucey, Isadora's mentor, hid beneath the disguise.

Next to Lucey trembled a young man—a boy, really—with olive skin and pools of umber for eyes. Alessio. His fingertips tapped an uneven rhythm on his bouncing knee. Isadora swallowed her questions for Alessio. *How did it feel when you transitioned? Is anyone else in your family a Watcher?* The strange Watcher magic operated on unknown rules. Not even Maximillion's intensive study had formed conclusions on how one became a Watcher, or where the magic originated.

Was Alessio silently saying goodbye to the Eastern Network and the only home he'd ever known? Lucey had said he was a musician once destined to work with the Eastern Network High Priest in Magnolia Castle—and that he was now headhunted by his own witches. The Defenders in the East were ruthless. Not a week ago, they'd captured a new Watcher, violently interrogated her in front of her family, then burned their house, and abducted her. Before Lucey could get to the seventeen-year-old girl, the Defenders had whisked her into Carcere, an ill-reputed prison from which there was no escape.

Isadora turned the thoughts away.

Your focus on the mission must be meticulous, Maximillion had said with a hint of irritation in his voice. *Never waver. They won't.*

She studied the unchanging landscape again.

Rolling hills, separated by stone hedges and copses of trees, passed by. Humidity lay thick in the air. Two days farther east and they would have seen the ocean. Isadora tried to picture the expanse of water in her head until an unusual flash in the distance caught her eye.

Lucey tensed.

For Isadora to ask about the strange light while maintaining their deception, she would need to use *Ilese,* the Eastern Network language. While the last six months of dedicated study since she joined the Advocacy made her speech passable, it was a halting mess. Her tongue wasn't used to the language's gentle nuance and soft edge, so she hesitated. Was it worth breaking the silence?

Lucey's young face furrowed. Her brow creased. Isadora

lifted an eyebrow in silent question, but Lucey shook her head and leaned back again.

Not yet, she mouthed.

Magic hummed bright in Isadora's chest. She let it hum through her body. The momentary reprieve of energy granted her a bit of courage. Lucey gave no indication she noticed. Eventually, Isadora calmed.

Alessio's tense shoulders remained taut. Isadora tucked the magic away again. It flared, as if impatient, then settled. Minutes passed. Alessio closed his eyes while he muttered under his breath, hands clenched.

Embrace the uncertainty of whether you'll live or die, Maximillion had said. *You'll pay more attention.*

Isadora kept her mind focused on the biggest question of all—what was the purpose of *any* of this? Why did magic have to be so beautiful and so dangerous?

"We're almost there," Lucey murmured in *Ilese.* "Just an hour to the Central Network border."

A chill swept through Isadora. Her eyes darted back to the darkness. She fought off a shudder. Lucey shifted ever-so-slightly to the left to peer out the window.

What could have been a simple extraction—requiring only Lucey's help—was complicated by Alessio's young age. At eleven, he was one of the youngest Watchers Maximillion had ever heard of. He hadn't learned to safely transport before he transitioned into his powers—and certainly not to an unknown location. He would have to be smuggled into the safety of the Central Network.

The bitter stench of rotten eggs wafted into the carriage. A metallic taste filled her mouth.

Lucey's eyes brightened, gleaming in the still night.

"Palude Marsh," she whispered in delight, still using *Ilese* for Alessio's sake. "Wonderful."

Prepare yourself. Defenders will be waiting in the marsh, Maximillion's voice said, an echo of his instructions early that morning. *If all goes according to plan, you won't even have to see them. Avoid the bog if you can help it.*

Alessio squirmed.

"Never fear." Lucey grinned, a twinkle in her eye. "Letum Wood awaits."

At that, Isadora's tension faded slightly. If nothing else, she could look forward to the protection of her forest home. A wispy blue bird with yellow-tipped wings fluttered into the carriage. It alighted on Lucey's shoulder and leaned toward her ear. No sound came from its beak—no one else could hear the message it carried. An update from Maximillion, no doubt. The bird dissipated into smoke.

Lucey squeezed Alessio's arm with a reassuring smile that seemed to ease him, no doubt in part because of her transformed, youthful face. The putrid scent intensified— the driver had taken the carriage on a road alongside the marsh. Isadora nearly gagged.

"All is so quiet," Lucey said.

The words Isadora had been waiting for. She closed her eyes and slid into the waiting magic.

At first, darkness encased her vision.

Then Letum Wood blossomed before her, filled with thick vines and a canopy that soared so far overhead she couldn't see where it ended. No sound stirred in the twelve sprawling trees that formed a circle around her, as wide as several houses put together, so tall their closest branches were barely visible in the high canopy. Light seemed to infuse their trunks, their leaves, the ground where their roots stood taller than she did. Flowers bobbed in lazy coils along the trunks, draped with vines and ivy. Not a breath stirred here.

Twelve trails appeared in front of her.

"Twelve," she murmured. When in the magic, possibilities for the future of whomever she was with showed themselves through paths. The paths populated on their own, shifting, betraying possibilities of the future. Only her twin sister Sanna's paths and her own were always present. Exploring the paths posed a legitimate danger—Defenders could sense Watcher magic at work. In nearly all cases, Watchers helping the Advocacy refrained from using their magic on a raid. Tonight, however, was different.

Isadora was different.

The Defenders already knew Watchers were there because Lucey had carefully sculpted their plan. She *wanted* the Defenders to ambush them.

They won't expect it, she had said. *And we always have to take them by surprise. Otherwise, they'll guess our next move. Their magic is the opposite of yours. You see future possibilities; they see the past. Their advantage is seeing what you've already chosen, or not chosen. Cecelia trains them to analyze our decisions to learn our weaknesses.*

Isadora turned her mind and focused on the forest. The twelve paths formed a complicated map of ethereal wisps, some of them as vague as smoke, some so articulated she felt the witch stood in front of her in the flesh. Only six of the faces were familiar to her. Lucey, Alessio, Sanna, herself, and the two drivers. That meant six Defenders awaited them.

"Show only my path," she commanded the magic. Her clear voice rang through the forest.

The others faded away. Her paths spread over the area. Almost immediately, the main trail broke into two sections; each moved opposite directions. She frowned. That had never happened before. The possibilities had always split away from the main path, which remained mostly solid.

Perhaps danger also toyed with fate.

Isadora brushed past it—there was no time to study or guess. On either side, her paths branched out five different ways. Each segmented out, spreading through the forest with wisps of light that meant . . . *something*. Isadora hesitated. If only the future were more concrete.

All the immediate paths showed her in the marsh, or in Letum Wood, except one strange one showing her on a dragon. The trail was faint—which meant it wasn't a strong likelihood. Isadora shook her head, forcing herself to focus. If not careful, she'd get lost in the paths again, which happened every time she tried to make sense of her future.

With a heavy sigh, she stepped back to the top of the trail. Already, the possibilities had shifted. Trails had moved. Some disappeared. New ones sprang up.

The temptation to stay nearly overwhelmed her. Following the paths to see endless possibilities was always interesting—the future led to amazing, wild places. Like a toddler with a paintbrush and blank canvas. Time was easily lost here. Not to mention her powers were . . . different.

She closed her connection to the magic.

Lucey and Alessio waited. A glint of something—impatience—reflected in Lucey's eyes for a moment. Isadora's breath hitched. Egads, but time passed differently in the paths. She'd likely been there too long. Her cheeks burned.

"Sorry. Six Defenders," she whispered, avoiding *Ilese* to spare Alessio the anxiety. "I recognize none of them. From what I could tell, they were all waiting in the trees."

"Near the marsh?"

Isadora shook her head. "Not that I could tell."

Lucey's brow furrowed. No doubt the Defenders had a single scout who would summon them to the ambush the moment success seemed certain. "Only six," Lucey murmured. "So few? A bit insulting, if you ask me. They sent fifteen last time, and I still managed to avoid them."

"Cecelia isn't amongst them."

"She never is."

If Cecelia, leader of the murderous Defender force and Ambassador to the Eastern Network, wasn't here, why did Lucey frown? She peered outside again. "No matter," Lucey murmured. "More may transport in as soon as we get going." Lucey looked at Alessio and asked both him and Isadora in *Ilese*. "Do you remember the plan?"

Isadora nodded. Alessio gulped, nostrils flared, and nodded.

Lucey grinned.

"Then I shall go break our axle and proceed. Good luck," she whispered.

She disappeared into a transportation spell.

Alessio straightened, eyes wide, as he studied Isadora for what seemed like the first time. He looked so much like a little boy right then. Frightened, vulnerable. His own Network would interrogate and kill him for something he had no control over—being born with powers that gave him a glimpse of future possibilities. She ignored his uncertainty and put a hand on his arm.

"I'm going to take good care of you, Alessio." Despite the terror of knowing what awaited them, certainty filled her tone. "Let's get ready."

Ready for more?

Visit www.katiecrossbooks.com to purchase your paperback copy of FLIGHT, book two in the Dragonmaster trilogy.

Merry part!

Acknowledgments

This has to be the hardest part of writing a book.

I always believed the adage that *it takes a village to raise a child*, (especially now that I have a child!) but I also imagined that true for writing and publishing a book. If I've forgotten you, I am so sorry! Write me. I'll put you in twice on the second one. ;)

First and foremost, I have to thank my amazing, dedicated, loyal fans, without whom I wouldn't have so much fun writing. Bringing you awesome stories—and getting all your emails—spurs me on everyday. To my launch team: you really are the best. Thank you for your hard work and dedication to getting this into the world and having such passion for my books.

Catherine and Stephanie, you are the two best editors a girl could ask for. Thanks for polishing and encouraging. Jenny, Kella, and Chris, you make my books lovely. Without you, I certainly wouldn't have any sanity. Tara, Stephan, Brandy, Amy, thank you for your amazing feedback when the book still wasn't that pretty—and for the occasional frantic phone call to help me work out a plot issue. Sorry those quick calls always turned into an hour!

No acknowledgment would be complete without a shout out to Husband, who pushes my buttons and always jokes about changing my stories to accommodate rainbow farting unicorns. His support is tireless.

And LM, you lovable, distracting, mountain-loving-wild-child. Without you, I wouldn't truly understand magic.

ABOUT THE AUTHOR

Katie Cross is ALL ABOUT writing epic magic and wild places. Creating new fantasy worlds is her jam.

When she's not hiking or chasing her two littles through the Montana mountains, you can find her curled up reading a book or arguing with her husband over the best kind of sushi.

Visit her at www.katiecrossbooks.com for free short stories, extra savings on all her books (and some you can't buy on the retailers), and so much more.